BEACH
BLONDES

Don't miss the second Summer:
TAN LINES

BEACH BLONDES

a SUMMER novel

KATHERINE APPLEGATE

Simon Pulse
New York London Toronto Sydney

SIMON PULSE

An imprint of Simon & Schuster Children's Publishing Division

1230 Avenue of the Americas, New York, NY 10020

June Dreams copyright © 1995 by Daniel Weiss Associates, Inc., and Katherine Applegate

July's Promise copyright © 1995 by Daniel Weiss Associates, Inc., and Katherine Applegate

August Magic copyright © 1995 by Daniel Weiss Associates, Inc., and Katherine Applegate

All rights reserved, including the right of reproduction in whole or in part in any form.

SIMON PULSE and colophon are registered trademarks of Simon & Schuster, Inc.

Designed by Ann Zeak

The text of this book was set in Bembo.

Manufactured in the United States of America

First Simon Pulse edition May 2008

10 9 8 7 6 5 4 3

Library of Congress Control Number 2008923255

ISBN-13: 978-1-4169-6133-8

ISBN-10: 1-4169-6133-X

For Michael

june

Bloomington, Minnesota. February.
Not Having a Good Time.

"I hate my life. I hate my life. And I hate Sean Valletti."

The school bus had dropped Summer Smith six blocks from her home, and now she had frozen slush in the tops of her boots. Her toes were numb. Her ears were painful. Her lips were chapped. Her face was stiff from the cold and stung by the wind whipping her blond hair. Her gloved fingers, wrapped around her eleventh-grade biology text and a three-ring binder, were weak claws. Her blue eyes streamed tears as she faced into the bitter wind that tore at her, teased her, sneaked through every opening in her clothes to slither along her goose-pimpled flesh.

As for Sean Valletti, she hated him because he was incredibly gorgeous, very mature, and did not know that she existed. Despite the fact that Summer had often stared longingly at the back of his head in the school lunchroom, despite the fact that she'd sat next to him in biology five days in a row and had even had an actual dream about him, Sean did not know she existed.

And today, as Summer was leaving school after the last bell, he had stopped in the doorway, looked out at the cold, miserable world outside, and said, "Hey, you live near me. Why don't I drive you home in my car? That way you won't have to walk from the bus stop and get cold."

Yes, he had said those very words. He had said them to Liz Block. He had not said them to Summer Smith. If he had, Summer would now be loving her life instead of hating it.

Just another two blocks to her home, Summer told herself. Two blocks she would not have had to walk if Sean Valletti had asked her to drive with him. Another five minutes of spitting out snowflakes under clouds so low you had to duck to get under them.

There was no sun. There never had been a sun. It was made up by science teachers. And there was no true love, not in the real world. True love existed only on TV. In the real world it didn't matter how young or even how perfect you were: no true love. Maybe she should have told Sean about the dream she'd had. Then he'd know she existed. He'd think she was bizarre and possibly dangerous, but he'd know she existed.

Summer had told most of it to Jennifer Crosby, her best friend, who was not known for her subtlety. Jennifer had told her she should march right up to Sean and say something like, "You're the man of my dreams. Literally." Right. Jennifer had also suggested that Summer get Sean's attention by "accidentally" bumping into him. Summer had actually tried that. The bruise had healed after a few days.

Summer smiled ruefully at the memory. Okay, so maybe it wasn't a genuine tragedy that Sean Valletti didn't know she existed. A genuine tragedy would be if he *did* know and was deliberately avoiding her.

She was carefully duckwalking up the icy driveway of her house when the wind caught her. She wobbled. She fought for balance. She lost. And Summer's already bad day suddenly got worse.

Ten minutes later she finally opened her front door. And now she really hated her life.

"Is that you, sweetheart?" Her mother's voice.

Summer closed the door behind her, shuddering with relief. She dropped the wet wad of notebook paper on the carpet. Her biology notes, all in loopy blue handwriting, were blotching and running together.

Her mother stepped out of the living room, carrying her reading glasses in one hand and a book in the other. "It *is* you," she said. "How was your day?"

"Oh . . . fine," Summer said. "Except for the part where I fell on my face, scraped my knee, banged my head against the bumper of the car, and had to chase my biology notes across the yard." Summer dug a handful of slush out of her collar.

"Your aunt Mallory called," her mother said.

"Uh-huh."

"She wants to know if you'd like to spend the summer down in Florida on Crab Claw Key. You know, she has that big house there now, practically a mansion, so there's plenty of room. And it's right on the water."

Summer stood very still. The wad of slush was melting in her hand. "You mean . . . You mean, she's asking if I want to spend the summer on the beach, in the sun, swimming and . . . and being warm and lying out in the sun and getting tan . . . and going to beach parties and getting windsurfing lessons from sensitive guys with excellent bodies? She wants to know if I'd like that?"

"Well, would you?" her mother asked.

2

Florida. June. Prophecies of Love and Guy Number One.

There it was! Summer literally bounced in her seat as she looked out the window of the plane. The clouds had broken up, and the plane had emerged into clear sunlight so bright that Summer scrunched up her eyes as she looked down below at a scene so perfect, so intensely beautiful it made her want to cry.

She noticed the guy in the seat across the aisle looking at her and grinning—the guy who looked exactly like Jake Gyllenhaal. She'd heard him tell someone his name was Seth.

Summer blushed and quickly turned sideways in her seat to press her nose against the plastic window, avoiding making eye contact with Jake/Seth.

No more bouncing, she ordered herself. Cool, sophisticated people do not bounce. And from the very first moment in Florida she was going to be the new, improved, much cooler Summer Smith. The sweet, nice, average, boring Summer Smith whose big whoop in life was hanging out at the mall with the same guys who'd known her all her life was going to be left behind.

Below her was a line of islands, green irregular shapes like mismatched jewels strung together by the wavy line of a single highway. Tiny green islands fringed by white surf. Larger islands with houses in neat rows and the white cigar shapes of boats clustered around the shore.

And in every direction the ocean, the Gulf of Mexico, blue where it was deep; green, even turquoise where it was less deep. Here and there the sun reflected off the surface, making a mirror of the ocean.

The plane sank lower. The water was so clear, Summer could see the shadows of boats on the sea bottom. So clear that in places it was as if boats were floating in air, suspended over ripply sand. Scattered on the water were bright splashes of color—crimson, purple, and buttery gold in the sails of windsurfers. And there were long white trails drawn by Jet Skis and motorboats across the blue.

They were over Crab Claw Key, and Summer laughed.

"See something funny?" the woman in the seat beside her asked.

"It's shaped just like a crab's claw," Summer said.

"What is?"

"Um, you know, Crab Claw Key. It's shaped like a . . . like a crab's claw." She formed her hand into a crab shape and opened and closed the pincers a few times.

"I think maybe that's how it got the name," the woman said.

Very good, Summer told herself. Already you're on your way to impressing the local people with your brilliance. She slid her crab hand down to her side. She was regretting the decision to wear jeans and a purple University of Minnesota sweatshirt. First of all, she was going to be too hot, judging from the blazing sun. Second, it was like wearing a sign that said "Hi, I'm a tourist from the Midwest. Feel free to mock me."

"You here for the summer, huh?" the woman asked. "Maybe you have a job here, or family?"

"An aunt," Summer said. "And a cousin. But I don't have a job, at least not yet, although I definitely have to get one. Mostly I'm just here to lie on the beach and swim and stuff."

The woman nodded seriously. She was an old woman with a face that had the stretched face-lift look, as though each eye was a little too far around the side of her head. "Here to meet boys, too, right? Find romance?"

Summer glanced at Jake/Seth, hoping he had not overheard that particular part of the conversation. "Maybe," Summer admitted in a low voice. "I mean, it would be okay if I did, but that's not why I'm here."

The woman reached inside a voluminous shoulder bag and pulled out an oblong box. "Would you like me to read your cards? No charge, so don't worry."

"Excuse me?"

"Tarot, honey. Tarot cards. That's what I do; I have a little studio just off the main wharf. Normally I'd have to charge you twenty-five dollars." She began laying brightly illustrated cards on the tray. "We'll have to make this quick; we're getting ready to land."

"I guess you know that because you're a fortune-teller, right? About landing soon, I mean."

The woman did not acknowledge the joke. She was laying out the cards.

"Ahh," the woman said.

"Ahh?"

"Hmmm."

"What?" Summer didn't believe in things like tarot cards, but this was hard to ignore.

"You will definitely meet some young men this summer," the woman said.

"Well, I always *meet* guys; I mean, there are guys at school. Half the people there are guys, so—"

"You will meet three young men, each very different, each very important in your life."

Summer glanced at Jake/Seth. Please, let him not be able to hear this. "Well, thanks, ma'am," Summer said brightly.

"Three young men," the woman repeated. "Maybe some more, too, but at least these three."

The pilot announced that they were beginning their approach. The woman sighed and began gathering up her cards.

Summer fidgeted for several seconds. She really didn't believe in superstitious things like tarot cards. But what would it hurt to find out what the woman knew? Or thought she knew. Or, at least, pretended to know.

"Three guys, huh?"

"Three." A knowing, almost smug nod. "Each very different. One will *seem* to be a mystery. One will *seem* to represent danger. One will *seem* to be the right one."

Crab Claw Key rushed up toward them suddenly, each house visible, cars and boats, and then, people lying out on the beach, tiny brown stick figures seeming to stare up at the plane. The shadow of the plane raced across them.

"Seem?" Summer said.

"The future is always shifting," the woman said. "Is your seat belt fastened?"

The wheels touched down. The plane taxied toward the little terminal, and Summer began to feel nervous. "Just act cool," Summer told herself. "Just don't act like some dork from Bloomington."

"What?" the lady asked.

"Nothing," Summer said, not convincingly.

"You watch out for the bad one."

"The bad—"

"One will represent mystery. One will be the right one. But that third boy—you'd better watch out for him."

As soon as the plane had come to a stop, Summer pried her carry-on bag from the overhead compartment and shuffled toward the door with the rest of the passengers. The flight attendants were smiling and chattering, "g'bye, havaniceday, bubbye, g'bye" like happy robots, but Summer barely heard them. She was still turning the woman's words over in her head.

She reached the door to the plane, and blazing heat jumped on her like a wild animal. It glued her University of Minnesota sweatshirt to her skin.

Hot. Very, very hot. Hot like crawling inside an oven.

A breeze like a blowtorch caught Summer's long blond hair and lifted it from the back of her neck. She pried open one eye and saw a world of blazing light. Somehow the plane had flown from the earth straight into the sun.

Jake/Seth squeezed past her on the stairs, jostling her with his bag. "Sorry," he said.

"No, it's my fault. I was just looking around," Summer said. "I should have kept moving."

"First time here?" he asked. His eyes were behind very dark shades. His smile was very nice. His smile was very, *very* nice.

"Uh-huh. Yes."

They had reached the bottom of the stairs. Jesse/Seth moved away, walking quickly across the tarmac. Then he turned, walking backward. "Hey, Minnesota, my name is Seth. I'm from Wisconsin. How long you staying and what's your name?"

"Summer!" she yelled.

"Great," he said. "I'm here for the summer too." He waved and turned away.

3

Passion! Hatred! Betrayal! And All in Just Ten Minutes.

Summer braced herself as she went in through the terminal doors, ready for the inevitable hug, the affectionate assault of "hello-how-are-you-how's-your-dad-and-mom" questions.

But they didn't come. All around her, people squealed and hugged and slapped each other's backs. But no one was waiting for her.

Summer took a hopeful look around and shifted her bag from one shoulder to the other. The crowd broke up and wandered away. Summer began looking more closely at some of the people sitting nearby. She hadn't seen her cousin Diana or her aunt Mallory in years. Not since Christmas four years ago when

Diana had been thirteen and Summer had been twelve. Maybe they had changed, maybe they looked different. A lot different.

But no. They weren't there. Maybe they'd forgotten her. Did she even have her aunt's phone number? Sure. Somewhere. Probably. But wait, was she even here on the right day? Was this the right place?

"Don't be a baby, Summer," she ordered herself. Her aunt and cousin were just a little late. She should just go ahead and pick up her luggage. They'd get here eventually.

As she walked to the baggage claim area, she noticed an obvious fact: virtually everyone was more tan than she was. More tan with less clothing. Hers was the only pair of jeans. Hers were the only pants, period, aside from a pair on a security guard.

And the pair Seth wore. He was just a little way ahead, wearing well-worn Levi's that were splotched here and there with white paint.

Summer felt odd, as if she were following him, although obviously they were just two people going in the same direction. And yet, if he suddenly turned around, he'd probably think she *was* following him. Which would be kind of embarrassing.

She came to three stainless steel carousels in a row. One was turning, and from time to time a piece of luggage would slide down the chute. Seth stood there waiting. Summer took a place a few feet away and looked nonchalant. He glanced at her with equal nonchalance.

Summer checked her watch and scanned the room. She put on a perplexed expression, doing a mime of a person waiting for someone who was late. She checked her watch again and frowned.

"You get stood up?"

Seth was suddenly directly beside her. "What? Oh, yes, I guess so. I mean, someone was supposed to pick me up. They aren't here, though." She smiled and then, idiotically, checked her watch again.

"Keep checking," he advised. "You never know when another minute will zip by. By the way, you never told me your name."

"Yes, I did. It's Summer. Summer Smith."

"Oh. Right. Excellent name," he said seriously, as though he'd really thought it over. "Nice to meet you."

He stuck out his hand. Summer took it. They shook hands solemnly. He had rough, strong hands, though he held hers gently. "Wisconsin, huh?" Summer asked.

"Eau Claire," he said. "I'm a senior. I mean, I will be."

"Me too."

"I hope my aunt gets here," Summer added, after

trying for several minutes to think of something much cooler to say.

"I'm going to call my grandfather to come pick me up as soon as I grab my bag," Seth said. "If your aunt doesn't show, maybe we can give you a ride." He took off his sunglasses and stuck them in his pocket.

Summer stole a quick sideways glance. Brown? He looked directly at her. She smiled, swallowed hard, and once again looked hard at her watch.

Yes, definitely brown. Warm, smiling brown eyes and a great smile and rough hands.

Seth leaned forward and snatched up a big canvas duffel bag. "That's mine," he said. "You need a hand with yours?"

"No, I can handle them," Summer said.

"Cool. Well, I'll go call my grandfather."

"Okay. Bye."

By the time Summer had retrieved her bags, Seth was over at a bank of phones. She left her mountain of luggage where it was, hoping no one would steal any of it, and went to the phones. She found her aunt's number in her purse, dug a quarter out of her pocket, and dialed.

Three phones away, Seth hung up his receiver and rolled his eyes. His warm, deep brown eyes.

The phone rang in Summer's ear. Four rings. Then

an answering machine. "This is Summer. I'm at the airport," she said after the beep. "Is anyone there? Um, okay. I guess you're probably on the way here. I hope. So I'll wait. Bye."

When she looked up again, Seth was gone. Then she spotted him across the hallway standing by an automatic photo booth. He seemed to be trying to feed a dollar bill into a slot. The bill kept getting rejected. It wouldn't hurt to go over, very casually, and just say hi again.

"Hi again," Summer said. "I guess my aunt is on the way to pick me up. No one answered."

"My grandfather isn't home either," Seth said. "It's not his fault, though—I caught an earlier flight. Why won't this thing take my money? It took the first dollar. Now it won't take the second one."

"You're getting a picture taken?"

He tried again to shove the bill in the slot. "Trying to. I need to get a passport while I'm down here. I'm hoping to go to the Caymans, do some scuba diving down there." He tried the dollar again.

"Here, try a new bill. Sometimes that works," Summer said. She dug a bill out of her bag and slid it easily into the slot.

"Thanks. I should have taken care of this back home but, you know, distractions . . ." He sat on the little round stool and pulled the curtain closed.

Summer saw the light flash once, twice.

"Hey, I have four more shots," Seth said. "You want them?"

"I guess so," Summer said. "I can use them for before and after pictures."

Seth slid open the curtain. Summer had been leaning against the booth, and now they were suddenly very near to each other.

"Before and after what?" Seth asked.

"Tan," Summer explained. "You know, so I can say, look how white I was when I first got there and how tan I got. I'm so pale now and . . ."

For some reason, Seth was staring at her and not saying anything. He looked perplexed, or maybe a little sick. Summer began to feel uncomfortable herself. "You look . . . uh, not pale," Seth said. "I mean, you have really pretty skin."

Summer touched her face. A blush was creeping slowly up her throat. "My face is darker than the rest of me," she said. "I mean, you should see the other parts, total whiteness."

The blush grew rapidly worse. *You should see the other parts!* What? *What?* "What I meant was—"

"Go ahead," he said quickly. "Take those other pictures—"

"I just meant my legs are like—"

"Here, just sit and then you make sure your face is—"

"I mean, they're—I didn't mean—"

He moved aside, and she tried to squeeze past him into the booth. They did a stammering little dance, him moving one way, her the other.

He took her shoulders, intending to trade places with her. She looked up at him, intending to make some joke about how uncoordinated they were.

Both of them froze. Seth's eyes seemed to glaze over. He bent down. His face was so close to hers that when she turned her head, his mouth pressed sweetly against her cheek.

They separated in shock. Then, before she knew what was happening, Summer closed her eyes and his mouth met hers in an infinitely sweet, indescribably perfect kiss.

They separated in even greater shock. Summer was too dazed to know what she felt.

"I'm sorry," Seth said quickly. "I didn't mean to—"

Now Summer was beginning to feel something. Two somethings: ridiculous and embarrassed on the one hand, and very warm and idiotically happy on the other.

Seth turned away abruptly. "I'm really sorry," he repeated. "Really. I mean, I don't . . . I'm not like some jerk who would do this."

"It's okay," Summer said. It was more than okay, but the way Seth was acting was starting to make her feel more embarrassed.

"I gotta go," Seth said. "Call my grandfather. Anyway, bye."

And to Summer's utter amazement, he took off at a fast walk across the terminal.

Diana Olan sat slumped in the passenger seat of her mother's car. She turned the volume dial on the CD player up high enough to allow Green Day's lyrics to be heard by people halfway across the island. Through the dark-tinted windshield she saw the sign for the airport and sighed. She turned the volume knob up a little further still.

Diana's mother reached across and punched the power button with her long, painted fingernail. The music stopped instantly.

"She's going to get picked up by some pervert in that airport," Mallory Olan said.

"I guess that would be bad, right?" Diana reached for the CD player.

"Maybe we'll get lucky and the flight will be late," Mallory said.

"Maybe we'll get really lucky and it will crash." Diana turned the music back on but cranked the volume only halfway up.

They turned onto the approach road. A plane roared low over their heads.

"Maybe that's her plane," Mallory said. "We'd still

get there before she could get off. I don't want her wondering if she's been abandoned, poor kid. I'll bet that's her plane."

"Oh, goody," Diana said. "Should I start jumping for joy now, or should I wait till I actually see little miss sweetness and light?"

"Diana, do we have to do this? You might try being civilized. Summer *is* your cousin, after all, and you're practically the same age."

"Then I guess everything will be perfect," Diana said. "We'll instantly become best friends. We'll bake cookies together and giggle. And slowly but surely I'll turn into Summer and be just like her. That *is* the plan, isn't it?"

Mallory gave her a sour look. Then, with an effort, she forced a pleasant smile. "I kind of like this band. What's their name?"

Diana instantly turned off the music.

Mallory parked the Mercedes in the lane where it said No Parking and checked her face in the mirror. "She'll think I look old."

"Can we just get this over with?" Diana suggested.

Mallory caught the eye of a skycap and pointed at two bags in the backseat. She checked her watch. "At least *I* won't be late," she muttered.

Diana followed her mother into the terminal. As

usual Mallory moved at top speed, like a human express train, swaggering along with the confidence of a person who expects everyone else to clear a path.

"There she is!" Mallory pointed. "Come on, hurry up, Diana. The poor thing's standing there looking like a waif."

Diana slowed down, taking the opportunity to straighten her sarong skirt, which had gotten twisted around while she'd fidgeted in the car. She wore a faded tank top that rode up, revealing a tan, flat stomach. Her feet were bare. Her long dark hair was pulled back in a French braid, accentuating large, arresting gray eyes.

Diana saw Summer weaving her way through the passing crowd: a pretty blond girl with skin from a Noxema ad, carrying electric blue nylon zipper bags and wearing something bulky and purple. Summer was smiling like Miss America and looking depressingly wholesome.

Oh, it was going to be a long, long summer. Unless Diana could get rid of her cousin.

There was no question in Diana's mind why Mallory—Diana had long ago stopped calling her "mother"—had invited Summer down for a visit. Summer was supposed to "normalize" Diana. Mallory had decided that Diana was getting depressed, not doing as well as she should in school, and becoming more private. And the solution? Fly in the happy squad. Bring on cousin Summer.

Then something else caught Diana's eye. Seth Warner, standing by a bank of phones.

Seth glanced around blankly, then did a perfect double take as his gaze met Diana's. She smiled wryly. He looked uncomfortable but gave a little wave before turning away to hide the fact that he was blushing.

Seth Warner. Well, not exactly a big surprise, given the strange phone call Diana had received that morning. His hair was a little shorter, and he'd grown a little more serious looking since the previous summer. Still, she'd recognize that face anywhere—even though it wasn't exactly his face that stuck in her mind.

Summer was still rattled from the encounter in the photo booth, still trying to get her heart to slow down enough to let her catch her breath, when she spotted two familiar faces.

"Is that them?" Summer muttered under her breath. It looked like it might be them, but the airport terminal was full of people. She didn't want to go running up to them and find out she was hugging the wrong people.

But it did look like them, and they were smiling at her. Or at least Aunt Mallory was. Diana was just looking casual and glancing off toward the baggage carousel. Casual in a totally beautiful *Glamour* magazine kind of way. She wasn't even wearing shoes. In an airport. Way cool.

"Summer!" the woman yelled, holding out her arms in a big gimme-a-hug pose.

"Aunt Mallory!" Summer dropped her bag and ran up to her. Aunt Mallory had bigger hair than Summer remembered. Big, stiff hair. Maybe it was because Mallory was famous now, a best-selling romance novelist. Over her aunt's shoulder she caught Diana's eye. Diana made the smallest smile possible and let it linger for about one second.

"I'm so sorry we're late," Aunt Mallory said, holding Summer out at arm's length, inspecting her. "I hope you weren't bored or worried."

Bored? No, definitely not bored. It had been one of the more intense fifteen-minute periods in Summer's life. She felt like a person who'd survived a small earthquake and was still shaky. "No, I wasn't worried. I knew you'd be here."

"Good girl. And how was the flight?"

"It was fine, I guess. I mean, it's not like I've been on lots of planes."

Mallory rolled her eyes very dramatically. "Unfortunately, I *have* been on lots of flights. I feel like I scarcely touch the ground anymore. In fact, I'm just on my way to another one now."

Summer took a moment to digest this. "Did you say you're on your way *now?*"

Mallory made a point of looking at her watch. "Yes, and look at the time. They'll be announcing my flight any minute now. I'm on a book tour. Albany, Syracuse, Cincinnati, and . . . and one of those other places in the Midwest I can never keep straight."

"You're leaving?" Summer asked, still not quite sure she'd understood.

"In ten minutes," her aunt confirmed. "But don't worry; Diana will take care of you and I'll be back in a week. You and Diana are going to be good friends."

Summer glanced hopefully at Diana. Diana didn't look like she was planning on being anyone's friend.

Summer was alone with Diana. Diana was politely carrying the smallest of Summer's several pieces, the video camera she'd brought along, while Summer was loaded down with the rest.

"That's the car," Diana said, pointing at the cream-colored Mercedes convertible.

"*Your* car?"

"While Mallory's away, it is," Diana said.

Summer piled her bags into the backseat. "I hope I didn't bring too much stuff."

"Hey, wait up!" someone yelled.

Seth!

Summer smiled, then decided she'd better not be too obvious and stopped smiling, then changed her mind again.

It didn't matter. Seth had pushed past her as if he'd never met her before. He dropped his bags in front of Diana.

"Well, if it isn't Seth Warner. Back for another summer?"

Seth put on a tight smile. "Diana. Hi. Yeah, I'm back, and look, I, uh, caught an earlier flight, so my grandfather can't come pick me up . . ."

"You need a ride?"

"A cab would cost me ten bucks," Seth explained.

"Pile in," Diana said. "You'll have to squeeze up front with us. This is my cousin, Summer."

"We sort of met," he said stiffly. Then he laughed, a nice, gentle laugh, still tinged with embarrassment. "Did you say 'cousin'? Summer, you can't be related to Diana—you seem so nice."

Nice. Summer gritted her teeth a little at that word. *Nice.* She'd heard that word too many times in her life. It was the kiss of death when it came to romance. Had she done something wrong when he'd kissed her? Was that why he'd run off?

Diana lowered the top of the convertible. "So," she said to Seth, "is Lianne down yet?"

Seth's gaze met Summer's and then fell away,

refocusing on his shoes. "No, I guess she's coming down next week."

Diana pulled the car into traffic. "What's it been, four years with the same girlfriend, Seth? What's the deal? You going for the faithfulness award or something?"

Seth glanced at Summer from under ridiculously long lashes. "Actually, um, Diana, I kind of . . . Lianne and I broke up."

"Oh, really?" Diana drew the word out skeptically. "You and Lianne broke up, huh? Who's next to go? Ken and Barbie?"

"It kind of just happened," Seth said. Again he looked meaningfully at Summer, as if he was trying to send her a message.

Summer looked away.

"When did it happen?" Diana asked.

"It's just been a week," Seth said. Looking again at Summer he added, "It's kind of taking me a while to get over it totally. I guess it's strange to think of being with another girl. Do you know what I mean?"

Summer swallowed hard. Was he making an excuse for walking away after he'd kissed her?

Diana laughed. "It must be even stranger for Lianne to get used to," she said, adjusting her rearview mirror.

"Why do you say that?" Seth asked.

"You said you broke up a week ago?" Diana asked.

"Yes."

"It's just that Lianne called me this morning, asked me if I'd seen you down here yet."

Summer could feel tension in Seth's arm as it rested lightly on her shoulders. He seemed to be holding his breath. "She called you?" he said.

"Lianne is under the impression that we are friends," Diana said with a sneer. "Anyway, you know how she is. She wanted to be sure I gave you a message."

"A message?"

"Yeah." Diana cut across two lanes of traffic. "She said to remind you that she'll be down on Tuesday. And, of course, the other thing."

"What other thing?" Seth asked.

Diana sent him a condescending look. "To tell you that she loves you." Diana laughed and shook her head. "Seth, Seth, Seth. It's not like you to tell lies about breaking up with people. What were you planning to do? Have a little fling with some sweet, unsuspecting tourist girl before Lianne showed up?"

4

A Most Excellent and Luxurious Mansion. But Not for Summer.

"Which pincher is your house on?" Summer asked Diana. She was trying to make conversation. Mostly because she was trying not to think about Seth's arm around her shoulders, resting on the seat back, or his leg pressed against hers. The front seat was cramped with the three of them.

Lianne! No wonder Seth had acted so strange when they kissed. *Lianne.* Boy, it was amazing how such warm, gentle brown eyes could lie. No wonder he'd run off like that. Guilty conscience. And then, Diana had caught him in his lie!

Diana stopped adjusting the rearview mirror and looked at Summer with genuine puzzlement. "Pincher? What are you talking about, Summer?"

"Crab Claw Key," Summer explained, shouting slightly as they passed beneath the highway. "You know, the two pinchers."

"You mean old side and new side," Seth said quietly.

You mean old side and new side, Summer repeated with silent sarcasm. Anything like the old girlfriend and the new girl? Toad. Faithless toad. Kissing Summer like that and making her feel . . . and then: *Lianne.*

"The smaller pincher, the one to the west, is the old side because that's where the town is and there didn't used to be much over on the new side," Diana explained, sounding weary. "Now the new side is all built up. My house is on the old side."

"Oh," Summer said. They were passing a small shopping center on their left. Straight ahead the water was coming into view, marked by a small forest of boat masts. "I saw this monster house over on the big pin—I mean, over on new side, right on the tip. I think they had a helicopter there."

Diana's condescending smile evaporated. "Yeah, that's the Merrick estate."

"Merrick?" Summer repeated. The name sounded vaguely familiar.

"As in *Senator* Merrick," Seth interjected. "As in billionaires."

"No way!"

"All the money in the world and still jerks," Diana said.

Summer could hear the anger in Diana's voice.

"You and Adam Merrick still broken up?" Seth asked Diana. "I was sure you'd be back together by now. How many eighteen-year-old billionaires are you going to run into? I thought you guys were even looking to go to the same college this fall."

"No," Diana said shortly. She bit her lip, and Summer saw her shake her head, just slightly, as if trying to clear an image out of her mind. "I don't think that plan is going to work out."

Diana turned her opaque shades toward Seth. "Although I do miss the parties we used to have over on the Merrick estate, Mr. Moon."

Now it was Seth's turn to look even more uncomfortable. Conversation in the car stopped.

They slowed as they entered the tiny town, just a few streets of white clapboard buildings decorated with sun-faded awnings and quaint hand-lettered signs. The main street was lined at irregular intervals with palm trees, looking wonderfully alien to Summer's eyes.

So what if Diana wasn't very friendly and the first guy she'd met turned out to be a jerk? There were still palm trees! Two tall, stunning, deeply tanned young women dressed in nothing but extremely small bikinis were Rollerblading right down the middle of the street. An old man wearing nothing but shorts and far too much white body hair grinned toothlessly at the car as they glided by. Summer waved and the old man waved back. A perfectly normal-looking family, two parents and two kids, all with blazingly white skin and an assortment of bright shorts and Key West T-shirts, walked along aimlessly.

Diana turned down a side street and stopped the car in front of a small, neat house surrounded by a huge blaze of red flowers.

Seth got out, more or less climbing over Summer in the process. He lifted his bags out of the back.

"See you around," Seth said to both girls. Then, to Summer, "I hope . . . I mean . . ." He sighed resignedly. "Anyway, welcome to Florida."

He still had a very nice smile, even if he was a toad.

"Later," Diana said, and took off.

Summer turned to look back. Seth was carrying his bags toward the door of the house. "Why did you call him Mr. Moon?"

Diana grinned, the first real smile Summer had seen from her. "We were all at a big party at the Merrick estate. Seth was down on their pier, looking off at the sunset. Some guys decided he was being antisocial or whatever and decided to pants him."

"What's that?"

"They yanked off his bathing suit and threw it into the water."

"Oh." Summer wasn't sure she wanted to hear the rest of the story, but it was too late now.

"I used to be into photography back then, and I was already getting ready to shoot the sunset—and Seth standing there looking at it—because I thought it would make a cool shot. Anyway, they pants poor Seth, he dives off to get his bathing suit back, and I click at just the perfect moment." Diana caught Summer's eye and gave her a devious look. "It's a really unique shot."

"Yeah, I'm sure." Summer put a hand over her heart. She tugged open the neck of her sweatshirt. It was definitely hot here. She didn't want to think about him. What had happened between them was just a mistake. She was going to forget about it, and Seth had better forget about it too. She was going to start this vacation over, beginning now.

"I still have the picture around somewhere," Diana said, obviously enjoying Summer's embarrassment. "I call it 'The Sun . . . and the Moon.'"

The town was soon behind them, and they drove faster down a road that ran right along the edge of the bay. The water could be glimpsed only in flashes between the mismatched array of houses: some new pink stucco mansions, some older, gaily painted wood homes, some simple ranch-style houses that would have been at home in the older parts of Bloomington.

Diana pulled the car into a driveway and under the shade of a portico. She turned off the engine. Summer smoothed her tangled hair back into place.

"This is it," Diana said, looking the house over critically. "All the tackiness you'd expect from a semi-rich romance writer."

"It's huge," Summer said. The house was painted yellow and turquoise and white, a complex jumble of arched windows and fantastic turrets and screened balconies.

"Oh yeah, it's definitely huge. Only . . ." Diana darted a quick look at Summer. And then she smiled. Her second smile, although it wasn't exactly pleasant. "Only not as huge as you'd think. Actually, there are only five bedrooms in the whole place. Mallory and I each have one, of course. And there's one we keep for important guests—you know, people Mallory wants to impress. So that only leaves two."

Summer smiled. "Well, I only need one."

"If only it were that easy," Diana said regretfully. "Come on, I'll show you."

Summer climbed out and began lifting her bags from the backseat. The feeling of nervousness was growing stronger. What did Diana mean, *If only it were that easy?* And wasn't Diana even going to help her carry her bags?

"Don't worry about carrying all your bags at once," Diana said breezily as Summer struggled. "You can always come back for the rest later. If you decide to stay."

If I decide to stay? It was almost as if Diana was trying to get rid of her. In fact, it was *exactly* as if Diana was trying to get rid of her.

Diana was quite proud of herself. It had come to her in a flash of inspiration. Of course! It was so simple. If she moved Summer into one of the regular bedrooms, she'd never get rid of her cousin. Face it, it was a great house. Who wouldn't want to stay in a designer-decorated bedroom overlooking the water, with a private bath and a private balcony and a housekeeper to make your bed?

Mallory had already picked out the perfect room for Summer. Way too perfect. No, Diana had a much better idea for where Summer should stay. And with Mallory out of town, well, why not? With any luck at all, Summer would be on the next plane out of town.

Diana conducted Summer through the house at a virtual run. Here's the kitchen, oh, yes, it is huge. Here's the family room. Oh, yes, it's huge, too. Here's the game room, no, I don't play pool, the pool table's only there because you need a pool table to make it a game room. Here's my room, and here's Mallory's room. . . .

"Why do you call your mother Mallory?" Summer asked.

"Because that's her name. She calls me Diana because that's *my* name. That's the way it works." Diana winced. Now she was getting *too* mean. That wasn't right. It wasn't Summer's fault she wasn't wanted here. Besides, if Diana was too cruel, Summer might get upset and start crying or something, and then what?

But Summer didn't burst into tears.

"I call my mother Mom," Summer said matter-of-factly. "So, where am I staying?"

"You know I told you there were two bedrooms left? Well, see, the problem is that one is being redecorated, so it's a mess." Technically true, Diana told herself. Her mother *was* waiting on a new dresser for that room. "And the problem with the other room is . . ." Diana paused. Was Summer going to buy this at all? Only one way to find out. "The problem with the other room is that Mallory . . . Mom . . . has to have it available for when she gets hysterical."

Summer looked wary but not completely disbelieving. "Hysterical?"

Diana nodded sagely. "Hysterical. It happens sometimes when Mallory . . . Mom . . . starts remembering

Dad—you know, the divorce and all, and the good times they had and so on. Then she gets hysterical, see, because, well, her bedroom used to be *their* bedroom, and then it's like all these memories come back and she . . . she, uh, has to sleep in the other bedroom," Diana finished lamely. "That's why there's like no room. In the house."

Right, Summer thought. Does she think I'm a complete idiot? Diana was definitely *not* making her feel welcome. Fine. So Diana hated her for some reason. Fine. So Diana wanted to get rid of her. That was fine too. Only it wasn't going to be that easy.

"So where am I supposed to stay?" Summer asked. "Am I supposed to sleep on the couch?"

"No, that wouldn't work. But there *is* a place for you." Diana showed her brief, fake smile. "There's a definite place for you. Follow me."

Summer followed Diana downstairs, down one of the twin, curving staircases that looked like something out of a movie, through the gigantic living room and out onto the porch, where the heat was waiting to pounce on her again.

They walked down across a sloping, green lawn toward the water, toward the spot where a cabin cruiser was tied up to the pier. They turned left, aiming at a stand of trees. The shade of the trees was welcome. And then Summer saw it.

It was a bungalow, squat and homely, white paint chipped and faded, looking forlorn and abandoned. It would have looked like any way-below-average house in any way-below-average neighborhood except that it was raised on wooden stilts and stood directly over the water. A shaded stairway seemed to run from the interior of the house straight down to a small platform on the water. Two Jet Skis were tied up there, knocking together haphazardly on the gentle swell.

A rickety-looking wooden walkway ran a hundred feet from the grassy, shaded shore to the house. The walkway wrapped around the house, forming a narrow deck lined with a not-exactly-reassuring railing. A pelican sat on one corner of the railing, its huge beak nestled in its brown feathers. As Summer watched, the pelican added to the crusty pile of droppings.

"It has a bedroom, a kitchen, and a bathroom," Diana announced proudly.

"And a pelican who thinks the whole thing is a bathroom," Summer said.

"You'd have a lot of privacy here," Diana said, trying unsuccessfully to keep from gloating. "Sure, there's a little mildew, some pelican droppings, and you know, the furniture isn't exactly the very best. . . ."

"This is where Aunt Mallory wants me to stay?" Summer asked dubiously.

"Oh, she's not much for details of who stays where,"

Diana said, waving a hand breezily. "You'll be thrilled to know that this is a historical house; that's why Mallory doesn't tear it down. It was used by rum smugglers back during Prohibition in the 1920s. And we were renting it out until a couple of years ago."

"Uh-huh," Summer said. So this was Diana's plan to get her to leave. She was going to stick her here in mildew manor. Diana probably thought she'd just start boohooing and run home to her mother. Well, maybe she should, if no one wanted her here.

Only, Summer didn't like to get pushed around. She was here to have an excellent summer vacation, even if it meant living with the pooping pelican.

"Do I get to use the Jet Skis?" Summer asked tersely.

Diana looked surprised. "Um, sure. I mean, if you're staying, I guess . . ." Her voice drifted away.

"Of course I'm staying," Summer said. "This place looks beautiful and perfect, and you and I are going to become best friends, just like Aunt Mallory said." *Take that, witch,* Summer added silently.

Diana swallowed. For the first time she looked unsure of herself. "We are?"

5

Video Blog

Live, from fabulous Crab Claw Key, it's . . . Summer Smith!

Okay, okay. Hello, Jennifer. I said I would keep this video blog for you, and here's the first one. I barely know how to run this stupid video camera, so if the picture's all jerky don't blame me.

What you are looking at right now is my incredibly luxurious bedroom. You will notice the way the bed sort of sags and droops in the middle—very fashionable. And now you can see the kitchen. You say it looks like it's practically in the bedroom? Funny you should mention that; it sort of *is*. That's my stove. I think someone *may* have cleaned it once, about ten years ago. Refrigerator. Hang on, let me open it. See? Someone stocked it with exactly three cans of Pepsi and a half-eaten bag of Nacho Doritos.

Here's the bathroom. Cool tub, huh? I mean, it's got some rust stains, but it's huge, and see, it's one of those old-timey claw-foot tubs.

But the tub isn't the most excellent part of this place. No, the really neat thing is where the house is. See this square door in the floor? Hang on, let me pull it open. Urrgh. That's heavy, but can you see? Water. Right downstairs, that's actual seawater because this place is right over the water.

Is that great or what?

Okay, outside. Follow me. Like you have any choice. The front door . . . and look! This little deck goes all the way around the house. And see? There's the walkway. See? It's like fifty feet or whatever to the shore.

Okay, now, there's the main house. You have to kind of look *through* those trees to see all of it. I know what you're thinking, Jen. You're thinking, whoa, that looks like a mansion and Summer's living in a shack. Okay, that may be true. However, this shack is all mine. Besides, there are Jet Skis and I'm going to learn how to—oh, jeez, oh, oh, yuck. Gross. I brushed against some pelican stuff on the railing. Great. This pelican kind of lives here. There. There he is, diving for food. Isn't that excellent the way he does that?

Okay, back inside. Here, I'm going to put this down on the table and then I'll sit right in front of it.

Okay. Now can you see me? Hi. As you can see, it's not like I have a tan yet. I just got here like an hour ago.

So far everything's fine. Except that my cousin—Diana, the one who lives here?—I think she hates me. I think it was her big idea to stick me out here in the stilt house because her mom, who is my aunt, is out of town for a week. So I'm stuck with cousin Diana, who doesn't want to be stuck with me, I guess.

Okay, I'm not getting bummed. Just because Diana thinks I'm like some hopeless case, that's just what *she* thinks.

Although she *is* totally cool; I mean, she's one of those girls you and I can't stand, you know? She looks like that model they always have in *Teen Vogue,* you know the one I mean?

Anyway. I guess it will be better when my aunt Mallory gets back. I hope so, since Mom and Dad are off on vacation themselves and my plane ticket is for three months from now. So I'm stuck, no matter how much Diana doesn't like it. I'm stuck here in mildew world.

I'm not crying.

Okay, I am crying, but just a little. It's been a

stressful day. There was this one guy I met. Okay, more than met, but it's a whole long story, so let me just give you the short version: he's a using little creep.

You see, there was this . . . this thing that happened with him. In the airport. I'll tell you later when I'm done feeling weirded out by it.

Oh, and there are supposed to be two other guys too, if you believe in that kind of stuff. But okay, later on all that. Anyway, I'm going to turn this thing off. I have to unpack and try to clean this dump up a little, and it's starting to get dark out. Let's hope this summer gets better fast.

6

First Night. Strange Dreams and Stranger Realities.

Summer lay in her bed. It definitely sagged in the middle.

Earlier she'd gone up to the main house, called her mother to let her know she'd made it to Florida alive, and gotten some sheets and a blanket from Diana, feeling like Oliver Twist begging for more gruel. Diana had seemed friendly in about the same way that a cat seems friendly to a mouse.

Maybe I should just give up and go home, Summer thought miserably. "Too bad that's impossible," she muttered into the darkness.

It was a little creepy inside the stilt house with the lights out. A silvery shaft of moonlight had appeared in her window, illuminating her desk and the video camera resting there. It made her think of her best friend, Jennifer, and that made her think of home. Home, with her familiar bedroom, and all her posters and photos on the wall, with her CDs neatly in their rack.

Summer kicked off the single blanket and pulled the sheet over her. It was hot in the house, even with all the windows open. Even the boxers and baby-tee she wore to bed felt like too much.

"Hot and depressed and lonely," she told the stifling air. "So far it's a great vacation." If she were home, she'd go get some ice cream from the freezer.

From the windows she heard the sound of the water lapping gently at the pilings that supported the house. When the Jet Skis rocked there was a hollow sound, like coconuts being knocked together softly. And the house itself creaked and groaned, but in an almost musical way.

It was sometime later that the video camera seemed to turn on and begin projecting a flickering image on the wall, like an old-fashioned home movie. Summer saw a backyard scene, the yard of her house in Bloomington. The swing set her parents had bought for her third birthday. The little play pool, filled with plastic toys. Her Oscar the Grouch! She hadn't seen Oscar in years. Whatever had happened to good old Oscar?

Summer rose from her bed and moved toward the

images. Her mother was in the picture now, gazing at her with that familiar look of concern. The look that said *Sometimes, Summer, I swear you worry me.*

"Come on out of there," her mother said, holding out her hand. Summer looked down and realized she was covered in mud. What a mess. The pelican, who was now swimming in her pool, was trying to look innocent, but obviously he was responsible.

Suddenly Summer was in her room back home, looking down at her bed, only the bed kept shrinking till it was the size of a doll bed. It made Summer angry, though she wasn't sure why. Something caught her eye. Three cards lay in a row on the covers. Two were facedown. One was turned up, and when Summer looked closer she saw it was a photograph—a photograph of a red sun and a pale, white moon. The moon made her feel very uncomfortable.

Then, all at once, Summer was back in the stilt house, hearing some new noise to add to the creaks and groans and lapping water. The flickering images of home faded out and disappeared.

Her eyes opened. A creaking sound, very clear, *very* clear and real and not a part of the dream. A creaking sound and now a tuneless, almost random humming.

Summer lay perfectly still. The sound had come from very close. But she was turned away from it and not willing to roll over to see what it might be.

It was the hatch in the floor! That's what it had to be. The hatch that led down to the water, down to where the Jet Skis were. Down to where some monster, some ax murderer, some creature had been lying, waiting for her to fall asleep so he could creep up the stairs and come in through the hatchway and kill her, hacking her up with a machete.

Summer rolled ever so slightly. Now the room didn't seem so hot. No, it had definitely gotten chillier. She wished she had her blanket back. She could pull it over her head and hope the monster/ax murderer went away.

A light!

Summer slitted her eyes and stared, barely able to breathe. A blue-white light emanated from the kitchen.

The humming stopped and was replaced by a mixture of whistling and humming.

The light in the kitchen disappeared. From the darkness came the distinctive sound of a pop-top. The whistling stopped. A satisfied sigh.

A lighter flickered, and then a candle, a brilliant yellow pinpoint of light in the dark, illuminating a startling sight.

"Aaargh!" the figure yelled.

"Aaargh!" Summer jumped back as if she'd been electrocuted, snatching her sheet around her like a shield.

"Wh-what are you—"

"Who—what are you—get out of here!"

"Chill out, don't shoot or anything!"

"Don't kill me, I'm from Minnesota!"

A silence, during which Summer listened to the panic-driven jackhammer beat of her heart. Her teeth rattled.

"Did you just say 'Don't kill me, I'm from Minnesota'?"

"Uh-uh-uh-uh, yes," Summer chattered.

"What's Minnesota got to do with anything?"

"Uh, nothing, I guess."

"Who *are* you?" he asked, coming warily closer.

Now Summer could see that he wasn't a monster. He could still be an ax murderer, but not a monster. He had long, wet, shoulder-length blond hair and wore only a madras bathing suit that clung to him damply.

"I'm Summer. Sum-sumsum-sum Summer Smith."

"Oh."

"Who are you?" Summer managed to ask. Her voice sounded strained with the tightness in her throat and the still-chattering teeth.

"I'm Diver."

"Diver?"

"Yeah." He sounded defiant. "Like *Summer* is some kind of normal name?"

"What are you doing here?" Summer demanded.

"What am *I* doing here?" Diver asked, mildly outraged. He took a sip of his Pepsi and sat the candle down on her desk, balancing it carefully. "What are *you* doing here?"

"Living here," Summer said. "And people know I'm here, so don't try anything."

"*I* live here," Diver said. "At least, I mean, I use the bathroom and the kitchen here. I don't sleep here." He pulled out the desk chair. "I usually sleep up on the roof."

"You can't live here; my aunt owns this place."

"Oh. She's that rich lady with really big hair?"

"Yes."

"Well, I don't care who owns it," Diver said. "I live here. I've been coming here for . . . for like months."

"Fine, I'm not going to call the cops or anything," Summer said. "Just go away and don't come back. Okay?" She was gaining courage from the fact that Diver hadn't done anything sudden. Yet. And, not that you could tell just by looking, but he didn't *look* dangerous. In fact, by the candle's light he looked . . . beautiful. There was no other word for it. Beautiful.

"Where am I supposed to take a shower and cook breakfast and sleep when it rains?"

Summer shrugged. "I don't know."

"Yeah, I didn't think you'd have an answer for that," Diver said triumphantly.

"You sure can't live with me, and I live here, so that's it," Summer said flatly.

"Go stay in your aunt's house," Diver said. "She must have plenty of room."

"I can't," Summer said. "I can't stay there, I can't go home to Bloomington, I have to stay here. I'm stuck."

"Me too," Diver said. "We're both stuck."

"Excuse me, but whatever you're thinking, forget it," Summer said, crossing her arms over her chest. "I don't, like, go out with guys I meet creeping into my room in the middle of the night."

"I don't go out with girls at all."

"Oh. Are you . . . not that it's any of my business. I mean, I don't have a problem if you're gay or anything like that . . ."

Diver tilted back his head and looked at her with a certain distant intensity. "I no longer involve myself with women. They disturb my *wa*."

"Wa?"

"My *wa*. My inner harmony. Haven't you ever read any eastern philosophy?" Diver smiled placidly, looking quite smug and superior. Then the smugness dropped away. "But I'm not gay," he said. "Not that I would care. I'm just saying I'm not. If I were, then women wouldn't disturb my *wa* the way they do."

"Whatever. Just get out, okay?"

Diver stood up. "It's a beautiful night. I'll sleep outside with Frank."

"Fine. Whatever you say. Just leave."

He turned away and headed for the door. He stopped with his hand on the knob. "Frank isn't a dude, by the way, so forget it if that's what you're thinking." He nodded as if he'd reached some profound decision. "Tomorrow I'll talk to Frank. Then *he* can decide which of us stays and which goes."

Summer rushed over as soon as he was gone and locked the door behind him. Then she ran back and, huffing and grunting, slid the desk over the hatchway.

"There," she muttered. "Now you and your *wa* will have a real hard time getting back in."

7

Raisin Toast, Imaginary Figments, and the Amazing Marquez

Diana took a while looking through the contents of her walk-in closet, searching for the right thing to wear. The right thing turned out to be white shorts and a white bikini top. White reflected sunlight and hence was cooler than other colors.

Also, white looked innocent. And, she decided as she descended the stairs, she needed all the help she could get in looking innocent. She didn't *feel* innocent. She felt like a selfish, rotten human being who had tricked her cousin into spending the night in a mildewy dump. Once, in the dark hours of the early morning, she'd almost gotten up and gone down to the stilt house to get Summer and bring her back.

But really, she was doing Summer a favor. Summer might think she wanted to be here, but that was only because Summer didn't understand anything.

The set of stairs led directly from just outside her room to the breakfast room. And there, sitting at the long pine table, was Summer. At least her cousin hadn't been murdered in the night. That was a relief. Diana didn't need any new reasons to hate herself.

Summer looked up from her plate and smiled. Smiled that big, happy-yet-shy smile that made you think you'd never seen anyone whose name so matched her looks.

"Hi," Summer said, chewing. "I hope it's all right. I don't have any food down at my house yet."

"Of course it's all right," Diana said quickly. She tried out her most innocent look. "You have to eat."

"Thanks."

"Did you find everything you want?" Diana asked. "I mean, here in the kitchen."

"Yeah, all I eat is raisin toast for breakfast, mostly."

"Raisin toast?" Diana narrowed her eyes suspiciously. "That's what I have in the morning too."

"No way." Summer laughed a little and looked amused.

"What?" Diana demanded.

"Nothing. It's just, I figured you had something different. Like eggs Benedict or something."

Diana went to the toaster. The bread was still out on the gray marble counter. "Why would I eat eggs Benedict?"

Summer shrugged. "I don't know. That was just the most fancy breakfast thing I could think of. You always hear about movie stars having eggs Benedict and champagne."

"No champagne," Diana said dryly. "Coffee. You drink coffee?"

Summer nodded. "Only, I couldn't figure out how to work your machine."

"I'll do it. It's kind of complicated." Diana dumped whole beans into the grinder, sent them spinning, and then measured the grounds into the coffee machine. "Coffee and raisin toast," she muttered, watching the back of Summer's head.

"Every morning almost. I'll have to buy a toaster and a coffee machine for my house."

A little stab of guilt made Diana wince. "How . . . um, how was . . . did you sleep okay?"

Summer turned around in her chair, but her blue eyes were evasive. "I slept okay, I guess. I was going to ask you, though . . ."

"Ask me what?" Diana almost snapped.

"Just that I was wondering if you knew of anyone who used the stilt house for anything."

Diana shrugged. Her toast popped up. The coffee began to dribble down, sending the aroma through the room. "No one's used it for anything in two years, at least. Not since the last renter moved out."

"Huh."

"Why?"

Summer sighed heavily and again looked evasive. "I don't know. I think I just had this dream that some guy was there. But when I got up, there was this burned candle and one of the Pepsis was gone. I guess I could have been walking in my sleep."

"You walk in your sleep?" Diana wondered.

"No. Never before, anyway. I dream a lot, though, and in my dreams I walk around."

"I try not to dream," Diana said.

Silence fell between them. The coffee machine dripped and then began its final sputtering.

"He was cute, though," Summer said.

"Who? The dream guy?" Diana poured two cups of coffee and carried them with her toast to the table.

"Yeah, he was *way* cute. Beyond cute."

"Then it *must* have been a dream," Diana pronounced. "A figment of your imagination."

"I guess so," Summer agreed. "Do you ever have dreams like that?"

"Me?" The question took Diana by surprise. "No, at least not that I remember."

"Do you have a boyfriend?"

Diana squirmed a little in the chair. "Not right at the moment."

"I've never had one," Summer admitted. "Not a real one."

Diana made a face. "Yeah, right."

"It's true. Why would I make up something like that?"

The confession, made so simply and straightfor-wardly, took Diana aback. There was nothing wrong with not having a boyfriend—in fact, in Diana's expe-rience it was probably better that way—but Summer was just so out front about it. Most girls would have tried to act cooler about it. Like, hey, the guys are after me, but they're all too immature.

"I guess you've probably had lots of boyfriends," Summer said.

"One or two," Diana admitted. This was the wrong topic. The absolutely wrong topic. It was as if Summer had some instinct guiding her to the last thing on earth that Diana wanted to talk about.

"There was a guy back home that I really liked,

only he didn't know I existed." Summer made a wry, self-deprecating face. "I have much better luck in my dreams."

Diana laughed and then quickly took a sip of her coffee. She'd have to watch herself. For a moment there she'd found herself kind of liking her cousin. "So, what are you going to do today?"

"I'm going to look around and maybe get a job," Summer said. "Would you come with me? I mean, unless you have something planned?"

"Why would you want me to come with you?" What was it with this girl? Why was she so nice? She wasn't an idiot; she *must* know Diana was trying to blow her off.

"I thought it might be fun," Summer said. "Besides, I'm new here, so if I go around with you everyone will think 'oh, okay, she must not be a total nobody if she's with Diana.'"

Diana finished her coffee and stared darkly at the bottom of her cup. Yes, she was definitely going to have to work at disliking her cousin.

In the end Diana decided not to come with her into town, and Summer was actually relieved. It was a wonderful feeling to be walking along the road, free, on her own, almost undisturbed by traffic, feeling the sun on her shoulders and arms. She turned her face to the sun, already most of the way up the sky though it wasn't yet ten in the morning.

A huge, brilliantly white bird, almost chest tall, stepped on stilt legs out onto the road before her. It tilted its serpentine neck to turn a quizzical eye on Summer.

"Hi," Summer said, standing still so as not to frighten it. But the egret wasn't frightened in the least. It tiptoed gracefully across the road.

"Reminds me of Diana," Summer said. Diana had that same grace, that same elegance.

That same disdain.

Too bad, Summer thought. She'd felt as if she were almost bonding with her cousin over raisin toast and coffee, but then Diana had pulled away again.

Summer shrugged. It was impossible to feel bad when the sun was in the sky and the air was warm. She stuck her arms straight out and tilted back her head, soaking up the light, closing her eyes to see the red suffusing her eyelids.

Something slapped into her left arm.

"Hey, watch where you're swinging those!" someone yelled.

Summer opened her eyes and saw a girl running in place, pumping her arms, sweat staining her spandex top. She had dark curly hair; huge, dark eyes; and a naturally dark complexion. An iPod was strapped to her arm, and headphones rested in her ears.

"Sorry," Summer said. "I thought I was alone."

"Can't hear you. You like the sun, huh?" the girl shouted, still running in place.

"Yes!" Summer yelled.

"Cool!" The girl ran in circles around Summer. "You're new, right?"

Summer turned slowly to keep facing her. "Yes. I just got here yesterday."

"Huh?"

"Yesterday!" Summer said in a louder voice. "I just got here yesterday."

"When?"

"YESTERDAY."

"Huh?"

"I SAID YESTERDAY!" Summer screamed.

The girl stopped running and broke up laughing. She pulled the earphones from her head. She bent over, hands on her knees, laughing and looking up at Summer with tears in her eyes. "Batteries are dead," the girl managed to gasp, pointing at the iPod.

Summer was annoyed for a moment. But then, it *was* kind of funny. She laughed at the image of herself, screaming at the top of her voice.

The girl stopped laughing and looked at her quizzically. "You laugh, huh? That's a good thing." She pointed a finger at Summer. "I can't stand people who can't laugh at themselves. People that take themselves all serious. I'm Marquez."

"You're what?"

"Marquez. That's my name. Technically it's Maria Esmeralda Marquez, but hey, every Cuban-American female on earth is named Maria, right, and there's no way I'm going to be called Esmeralda, so I go by Marquez." She extended a damp hand.

"I'm Summer Smith," Summer said, shaking her hand.

"I don't think so. *Summer?*"

"I'm afraid it's true."

"Yeah? Well, let me ask you, Summer—you think my thighs are too fat?" Marquez turned around so Summer could check all angles.

"No, not at all," Summer answered honestly.

"All right. In that case, why should I be out here running? I hate exercise. What are you doing?"

Summer shrugged. "I was going to check out the town."

Marquez laughed. "That should kill about five minutes."

"Plus I have to find a job," Summer said.

They set off toward town, walking side by side, with Marquez drying her face on her terry-cloth wristbands. "Job? What kind of job you want? What do you know how to do?"

"Nothing, really," Summer admitted.

"Oh, in that case I know where you can get a job, you poor girl."

"Really?" Summer asked eagerly.

"Yeah, the C 'n' C is looking for more victims, I mean, waitresses. The Crab 'n' Conch. Picture this—a restaurant run by the Marines. Except they're not actually Marines, because then, you know, they'd have to have *some* decency."

"I don't know how to be a waitress."

"That's okay. They don't want people who know what they're doing. They like to get them young and impressionable; you know, so they can mold you into a perfect robot. I know all this because I work there."

"You make it sound really fun," Summer said dryly.

Marquez grinned. "It's hateful, but with the tips and all it's good money. I'll take you there and introduce you to one of the managers. So, where are you staying?"

"My aunt and my cousin live here."

"Yeah? Who are they? I probably know them. I know everyone. It's a small island."

"My aunt is Mallory Olan, and my cousin's Diana."

Marquez stopped and stared, incredulous. "You're staying with Diana Olan? Wait a minute—you're *related* to Diana Olan?"

"She's my cousin, on my dad's side of the family. You know her?"

"Sure. She's in school, or at least she was, because now she's graduated. You can't be related to Diana," Marquez said. "You seem way too nice and normal."

Summer winced. There it was again—the *N* word. Nice. Nice, meaning average, meaning who cares?

"You're the second person who's said that," Summer said.

"Who was the first?"

"This guy named Seth."

"Mr. Moon! Mr. Moon is back? All right, the summer is starting to pick up," Marquez said. "He's a nice guy."

Summer nodded. Some nice guy. A nice guy who lied about having a girlfriend so he could . . . Summer shuddered a little. Why wasn't she able to just forget that stupid kiss? Why did it still seem to reverberate through her body whenever she thought about it?

"Nice *and* cute," Marquez said appreciatively. "Not my type, though. Besides, he's got this girlfriend he's been going with forever. Was she with him?"

"No. Lianne, right?"

"Yeah, Lianne." Marquez stuck her finger down her throat and made a gagging noise.

"You don't like Lianne?" Summer asked, trying not to sound hopeful.

"She's okay. She's just one of these totally dependent types. You know, hanging all over Seth and not letting him have fun. I wish I had her body, though. She shops petites. Complains because she can't find things in size two."

Summer nodded. Lianne would have to have a great body.

Forget about it, Summer, she told herself firmly. Get over it. Put it behind you. Jeez, it was just a kiss. Big deal. Actually, it was two kisses. That doesn't matter; it was just something that happened. Forget about it.

Marquez interrupted her thoughts. "So, Summer, since you're staying with Diana, tell me this—is it true she sleeps in a coffin at night? Oh, maybe I shouldn't say things like that. I mean, she is your cousin and all."

"I don't really know her that well," Summer admitted.

"Actually, she's not so bad," Marquez said. "Just strange, you know? Stays to herself, especially in the past year. I mean, she was always kind of private, right? But this last year it's like no one is even allowed to talk to her because she's become just way too cool."

"She isn't a really friendly person," Summer agreed cautiously. "But that's okay."

"Yeah, not a *real* friendly person," Marquez said, and laughed. "She used to at least hang out, and she was going out with Adam Merrick. She was going with him, and he goes everywhere so she was being more social. Then, boom. Like maybe last July she suddenly dumps Adam cold. He's totally great looking, also totally rich and nice and not stuck-up, and she dumps him."

Summer digested this information. Whatever Diana was lacking in terms of friendliness, Marquez certainly made up for. The girl talked a mile a minute and had barely paused to breathe.

"So ever since she broke up with Adam, it's been bye-bye Diana. She showed up at school, and that's it. We're all thinking it's like some R. L. Stine book or something, like she's turned into a teen vampire, you know?"

"I've seen her in the sunlight, and she hasn't burst into flames or anything," Summer said.

Marquez laughed appreciatively, an infectious sound that brought answering laughter from Summer. "You are definitely all right, girl. I like you. Come on and I'll do something really mean to you. I'll get you a job at the C 'n' C."

8

Marquez's Rules and Diana's Dolphins

Marquez waited outside the restaurant on the wharf and kicked back, leaning against a rough wood piling, legs stretched out in front of her. She looked down at them critically. They weren't pudgy, exactly, but they weren't as hard and lean and muscular as she'd have liked. And her behind, well, that didn't even bear thinking about.

"Stay off the conch fritters, Marquez," she ordered herself sternly. She wasn't going to get fat like her mother. That was fine for her mother, but Marquez had plans for the future. Finish high school, then college, then law school, then get a job as an associate at some big Washington or New York law firm and make partner. She needed to be in shape. She needed to look good in one of those boring skirt suits that lawyers wore. She needed to be able to go to the health club and play squash or racquetball with the partners.

And in the meantime, it didn't hurt to look good for guys.

The door of the restaurant opened, and the new girl, Summer, came out. She looked a little dazed, blinking like an owl in the sunlight. But she was carrying a menu, an employee manual, and a plastic-wrapped uniform. Big surprise. The C 'n' C was always looking for fresh meat. Mostly because people kept quitting. She would quit herself except that certain people still worked there. Certain people she should just forget about.

Forget it, Marquez, set it aside. He was forgotten. He was history. He was something she had scraped off the bottom of her shoes.

"Hey, you got the job, huh?" she asked.

Summer squinted and located Marquez. "Yeah, I did get it. Only . . ." She looked back over her shoulder at the restaurant door and lowered her voice. "Only, I don't know how to do anything."

Marquez laughed. "Nothing to it. I'll have the head waitress put you with me for the first couple days. I'll show you what to do."

"Thanks," Summer said. "That would be really, really nice of you. Thanks for recommending me for this job."

"Wait till you see what you look like in that uniform, *then* you can thank me, if you still want to," Marquez said. "Not to mention the fact that it's very hard work."

"The manager said it was like a big family."

"Yeah. The Manson family. Or the Menendez family. Or maybe the Addams family. So, now what?"

"What do you mean?"

"I mean, hey, it's not even noon, what have you got planned for the day?"

Summer shrugged. "I guess I thought I'd just look around."

"Yeah? You got anything on for tonight?"

"I don't think so."

"How about you go to this party with me?"

"What party?"

"Adam Merrick's having a party. He has them all the time, over on his daddy's estate."

Summer felt a rush of excitement, chased immediately by a wave of nervousness and uncertainty. Right. Like *she* should be going to parties at some billionaire's house. "I better not," she said. "I mean, he doesn't even know me or anything. I couldn't just show up."

"Where are you from, Summer?"

"Um, Bloomington, Minnesota. It's the home of the Mall of America, the biggest mall in the world." Stop saying things like that! Summer ordered herself. No one cares about the mall!

"Oh, I see. And people up in Bloomyburg are probably real polite and all, right? But see, this is Crab Claw Key. The rules are all different here. Mostly the rule is that there aren't any rules. You wear what you want. You go where you want. You say what you want. You *be* what you want. Nobody here is going to care if you're white or black or gay or straight or whatever religion you are or where you come from, all that stuff. As long as you're cool and don't hassle people and don't be all judgmental, everyone's equal."

Summer nodded. "Okay. I understand, but still—"

Marquez waved her hand dismissively. "And the only other rule is—when there's a party, *everybody* is invited."

"Okay. I get it. Okay." Summer sucked in a deep breath of hot, wet air. She was going to go for it. What good was summer vacation if you didn't take some chances? "But what should I wear?"

"Here's our old friend, Jerry. Would you like to touch him today? He's very nice, you know." Diana held the child safely in her arms, just letting the little girl's feet dangle in the water of the pool. The water came only a little higher than Diana's waist and was almost as warm as a bath.

Jerry floated patiently alongside, knowing his role, breathing softly through his blowhole.

The child, whose name was Lanessa, pointed wordlessly at the blowhole.

"Yes, that's pretty neat, isn't it?" Diana said. "That's how he breathes."

Jerry rolled partially in the water so he could see the little girl more clearly.

"He's smiling," Lanessa said.

"He sure is," Diana agreed. "Jerry likes to smile. You know why? Because Jerry is a very nice dolphin. He especially likes little girls just like you."

Lanessa nodded solemnly, still uncertain. Then she stuck out her hand, fingers splayed, not quite able to reach. But Jerry drifted closer, bringing his gray snout into contact, accepting the little girl's clumsy patting.

Lanessa patted the dolphin's head for several seconds, then pulled away again. No smile had formed on her lips, but for a few seconds there had been that light in her eyes, the light Diana had seen many times before, when child met dolphin.

"All done?" Diana asked. "You want to say bye-bye to Jerry?"

Lanessa opened and closed her hand, a silent good-bye.

"We'll come see Jerry again soon if you'd like. Do you think that would be fun?"

Lanessa had no answer. The light was gone for now.

"That's okay, Lanessa, you don't have to answer," Diana said softly. She slowly carried the child back to the side of the pool. Two other volunteers were working farther away with two other abused children like Lanessa, showing them there were still safe places in the world.

The Dolphin Interactive Therapy Institute brought children who had lost the capacity to trust together with dolphins. A silly-sounding idea that worked just the same. There was something in the basic gentleness of the big, powerful animals that seemed to calm fears and lure children out of their shells.

Diana helped the little girl get changed and brought her back to the nursery. "Lanessa and Jerry had a good time today," Diana told Dr. Lane, one of the therapists. "She patted Jerry right on his head, didn't you, Lanessa?"

"Well, Jerry is a very special dolphin," Dr. Lane agreed in the deliberately calm, soothing voice they all used for the children.

Diana gave the little girl a kiss on her forehead and said good-bye.

There was a report to be filled out, a complete report

detailing precisely how Lanessa had reacted, what she had said (not much), whether she had become agitated (no), whether she had exhibited any signs of panic (also no). Diana did this on a computer in a small cubicle of an office that was shared by all the volunteers.

Then she wrapped a sarong skirt around her barely damp bathing suit and went out to the parking lot, feeling the strange mixture of elation and weariness followed by slow, spreading melancholy she usually felt on leaving the institute.

The institute was on Cannonball Key, twenty miles up the highway from Crab Claw Key. Diana traveled south, heading home, driving her own car, a blue year-old Jetta. Somehow driving her mother's Mercedes to the institute, where even the professional counselors drove ten-year-old Volvos and minivans, would have seemed too showy.

The sun was still high in the sky, barely weakening in the long summer day. A bank of storm clouds was building up in the east, towering as high as a chain of mountains. Far-off flashes of lightning struck the water again and again.

What was she going to do about Summer? Diana asked herself. Presumably the girl would still be there when Diana got home.

Unacceptable. Diana didn't want Summer in her life. She didn't need a live-in friend. Diana preferred her privacy. There was nothing wrong with liking to be alone. Just because Mallory couldn't stand quiet, just because Mallory couldn't handle being by herself and had to rush off at every opportunity to meet her fans didn't mean Diana was some kind of freak for liking privacy.

But Mallory hadn't been willing to accept that. She'd imported friendly cousin Summer to replace all the friends Diana had blown off.

"Not that it's Summer's fault," Diana admitted to herself. Summer was all right. It wasn't that.

She got off the highway at the Crab Claw Key exit and drove to the house. Inside, the house was quiet and almost chilly from the air conditioning. The house-keeper had gone home at five, as usual.

Diana parked in the garage and took the kitchen stairs up to her room. At the top of the stairs she froze. Someone was in her room, humming abstractly and pausing occasionally to say, "Ooh, that's beautiful."

Diana took several deep breaths and entered the room. "Excuse me, but what are you doing here?"

Summer jumped and slapped a hand over her heart. "Jeez, you scared me."

"Sorry," Diana said, dripping sarcasm. "I didn't mean to scare you as you went snooping through my closet."

Summer flushed. "I wasn't snooping." She rehung

the dress she'd been admiring. "I was just wondering something."

"Like what?" Diana tossed her purse on her bed and kicked off her sandals.

"I'm supposed to go to this party tonight, and I didn't know what I should wear, so I was looking through your closet to see . . . you know . . ." Her voice petered out. "Sorry, I should have asked first."

"You wanted to *borrow* something to wear?"

"Oh, no, no," Summer said. "No way I'd just borrow something. I just wanted to see if I could figure out what people wear here." She looked embarrassed. The pink flush in her face had become a full-fledged blush.

Diana sighed. "Summer, it doesn't matter what you wear around here. Wear whatever you like."

"That's what she told me too."

"Who?"

"Marquez. Maria Marquez. She says she knows you."

"How on earth did you hook up with Marquez?"

"I met her. She kind of got me a job at the Crab 'n' Conch," Summer said.

Diana's lip curled. "The Cramp and Croak? Good luck."

Summer made a face. "Thanks."

"So what's this about a party?" Diana asked. Amazing. Summer had been here a day and she had a job, a friend, and an invitation to a party. Getting rid of her had just risen to a new level of difficulty.

"It's at the Merrick estate, this guy named Adam. Oh, wait, you used to go out with him, didn't you?"

Diana nodded slowly. Yes, she had gone out with Adam Merrick.

"Why don't you come too?" Summer said brightly. "Marquez said everyone's invited. I mean, unless you and Adam hate each other or something."

Diana smiled in a way she hoped didn't show too much bitterness. Summer had come very close to the truth. Hate—or something. "No, we don't hate each other," Diana said, working to keep her voice level. "Why would I hate Adam?"

For a brief moment Summer's intelligent, innocent eyes seemed to see past Diana's defenses, seemed to see something hidden just below the surface. Diana looked away, and Summer covered the moment with a laugh.

"I guess I thought when people broke up they couldn't stand to be around each other," Summer said.

"No. Not always," Diana said.

"I could stay home tonight if you wanted to do anything," Summer offered.

"No, no, go to the party. You'll have a good time." Diana felt agitated now, like she needed to escape the room. Get away. "You know, if you want to borrow anything, go right ahead. I have to, uh, I have to take a shower. I spent the whole day shopping."

Diana turned away, fighting the urge to run.

"Diana?"

"What?"

"Are you all right?"

"Just have to go to the bathroom. Is that okay with you?" she snapped suddenly.

"Sure."

"Good." Diana pushed past Summer into her bathroom and closed the door behind her. As an afterthought she turned the lock. Then she turned on the shower and let the water run as hot as she could stand.

She slipped out of her skirt and pulled off the bathing suit underneath and climbed under the stingingly hot spray.

The strength went out of her. She sank to the floor of the shower and sat there, knees drawn up to her chest as the water pounded on her head.

The memories appeared, as she had known they would. Memories of fear and disgust, feelings that made her squirm as if trying to crawl away from her own skin.

Just like that night, when she had come home shaken to her core and sat, just this way, in this very shower, scrubbing herself till she was raw.

9

Frank Has His Say, and Marquez Has a Very Bad Idea.

Summer left the main house and crossed the sloping lawn to the water's edge. She walked along feeling thoughtful, enjoying the lush grass under her bare feet, wondering about Diana, about the way she had seemed almost panicked.

The little stilt house didn't exactly look like home. Far from it. And yet Summer had a vague, almost affectionate feeling about the place. Not that she had forgotten the sagging bed or the pervasive smell of mildew, but already, after only one day, it felt as if it were hers somehow.

"Aren't I lucky?" she said sardonically.

She crossed the walkway and stopped to slip on

the sandals she'd been carrying, stepping over the little piles of bird poop. The pelican—the same pelican, she would have sworn—was sitting on the same corner of the railing, looking her over, its absurdly long beak tucked smugly down.

Summer opened the door and was surprised by the smell. Not the mildew, that was still there, but something new had been added. Fish? Yes, fish.

Fish that was frying in a cast iron skillet on her stove. The bathroom door opened, and out stepped Diver.

He's real! Summer realized in surprise. She'd pretty well convinced herself that Diver was a part of her strange dream the night before. But here he was, still wearing nothing but madras print trunks. Dry, this time. And his hair was dry as well, the ends just touching his broad, deeply tanned shoulders.

"Hey," he said. "You want some fish? I have plenty. He was a big one, so we'd better be eating grouper for the next couple of days."

"What are you doing here?" Summer squealed.

Diver looked nonplussed. "Cooking fish."

"Excuse me, but didn't I explain to you that *I* live here now?"

"I talked to Frank about it. He thinks we should just figure out a way to get along, you know?" Diver used a spatula to turn over first one, then another slab of fish.

"I don't care what Frank said," Summer insisted. "I don't even know any Frank. Who's Frank?"

"Frank. He's outside. This was his place before either of us ever showed up."

"Frank is outside? Where?"

"Out on the railing where he always is," Diver said calmly. "I didn't have anything to make a batter, so I'm just cooking this with some butter. I like it better batter fried, but fresh grouper's good no matter how you cook it. And this boy is fresh. I speared it like an hour ago."

Summer crossed the room to the window and looked outside. She could see most of the railing on that side of the house. The only thing out there was the pelican. Oh. No, that would be crazy, even for someone like Diver.

"Excuse me, but Frank isn't, like, a bird, is he?"

"A brown pelican," Diver confirmed.

Summer took a deep breath. "You're crazy, aren't you? I mean, no offense, I should probably say . . . sanity challenged or whatever."

Diver looked at her severely. He was holding a spatula and was, Summer had to admit, the best-looking male she'd ever seen in real life. Insane, but devastating.

"*I'm* crazy?" Diver said, as if the idiocy of that statement was self-evident. "Frank's been here since he was hatched, I've been crashing here for like six months, you just show up from Minnesota and tell me to go take a jump, and *I'm* the crazy one? How do you figure that?"

The answer was obvious, Summer knew, only she couldn't think how to express it. "Because my aunt owns this place," she said lamely.

Diver sneered derisively. "Yeah, right. Maybe you should go tell Frank that. Maybe *he'll* care."

"Frank is not the problem," Summer said tersely. "Frank is out there, not in here."

"Duh," Diver said. "He's a bird. Like he'd live in here? This is ready. If you want some, you'd better get a plate."

"Just answer me this," Summer said. "Are you the dangerous kind of insane or the harmless kind?"

Suddenly Diver smiled, a slow, almost shy smile that all by itself answered the question. "I guess I'm more the harmless kind. Only I'm not crazy."

Summer thought about that for a moment. "In Minnesota you'd be crazy."

"This isn't Minnesota," Diver said.

Summer squeezed past him. She grabbed two plates down from the cupboard and two more or less clean forks from the drawer. Then she followed Diver to the small round table.

"I don't need a plate or fork," Diver said. "I'll eat out of the pan."

"Of course," Summer said. "I should have known."

"Shouldn't use stuff you don't need," Diver explained. "Otherwise everything gets used up."

"I agree with that," Summer admitted.

She took a bite of the fish. "Whoa, this is excellent."

"Gotta be fresh, that's the important thing."

Summer watched him eat, watched him use his fingers to gingerly break pieces from the fish in the pan and pop them in his mouth. He didn't look dangerous. If he'd wanted to hurt her, he could have done it the night before. Or now.

Of course, he could still turn out to be nuts. Only . . . there was something about him. Something innocent. So innocent he made Summer feel old and sophisticated. He must have been at least her age, maybe a year or two older. But his eyes held no guile, no secret agenda. He was eating fish and happy doing just that. He believed he could communicate with a big, gray-brown, poop-producing bird.

"I guess you don't have anywhere else to live, huh?" Summer asked him.

He shook his head. "Sometimes I sleep on the beach, but the cops don't like that."

"Is your family from around here?"

He shook his head and formed that embarrassed, shy smile. "I'm the whole family."

"How can that be? You must have some kind of family somewhere."

"I don't know," he mumbled around a piece of fish.

"Okay, let me ask you this. Do you have any clothes? I mean, besides your bathing suit?"

"I have this shirt . . . somewhere." He glanced around as if it might be somewhere nearby.

Mom and Dad would kill you, Summer, if they knew what you were thinking.

Too bad. Mom and Dad were far away. Even Aunt Mallory wasn't there, so it was kind of up to her. "Okay, look, you have to swear to me that you won't get weird on me," Summer said. "I mean, any *more* weird."

His clear, simple gaze met hers. "Okay."

"Swear."

"I swear I won't weird out."

"Okay, then you can stay. We'll have to make up some rules, I guess, but I don't have time right now. I'm supposed to go to a party pretty soon. The only rule I have right now is that no one else can know about you, because if my aunt found out she'd probably ship me back to my parents, who would take turns killing me and grounding me until the middle of the next century."

"Cool. If you come home late, try not to make a lot of noise, all right? It gets Frank all upset."

"Frank."

"Yeah."

"Diver, can I ask you . . . why do you call him Frank?"

Diver shrugged. "It's his name."

Footsteps on the deck outside and a knock on the door.

Summer froze. Her first panicked thought had been that somehow, by some unknown psychic means, her parents had found out and been instantly transported down to Florida.

"Hey, you in there, Summer?"

Summer relaxed. Marquez. Then she *un*relaxed. The party. Was it that late already?

"Coming!" she yelled. "That's my friend—you have to hide," she told Diver.

"No problem, I'm outta here." In a flash he was down the hatchway.

Summer went to the door. Marquez was wearing skin-tight black shorts and a bright floral bikini top.

"Hey, girl," Marquez said, looking around curiously.

"Hi. I didn't realize it was so late," Summer said. "Pretty impressive place, huh? All the mildew you'll ever need."

"It's very unique," Marquez said, sounding sincere. "I mean, I've seen this place before, of course, but I've never been inside. Are those Jet Skis downstairs?"

"Yes. Too bad I have no idea how to ride them. By the way, you want some fish? I, uh, cooked some."

"I noticed, no offense," Marquez said. "You get to use those Jet Skis?"

"I can if I want, only, like I said, I don't know how."

"Easy to learn. I'll teach you."

"That would be excellent, someday. I just have to brush my teeth real quick and then we can go," Summer said.

"Uh-huh," Marquez said. "You know, Summer . . ."

"What?" Summer answered from the bathroom.

"Well, I don't have a car, my brother's using it, and it's kind of a long walk over to the Merrick estate; you have to go all the way around, it's like two miles unless we get lucky and someone I know comes by."

"That's okay, I can use the exercise," Summer said, trying to talk without dribbling toothpaste. Her mind was leaping back and forth from the impossible notion that she'd let a completely unknown guy practically share her house to the equally impossible concept that she was on her way to party at the Merrick estate.

"Of course, if we went by water across the bay, it would be much shorter." Marquez laughed. "Shorter and a lot more exciting."

Something about Marquez's slightly evil laugh grabbed Summer's attention. "Across the bay? How could we do that?"

"Of course I know how to ride a Jet Ski," Marquez said. "I've lived here in the Keys all my life."

Summer stood beside her on the little platform under the house. It was dark and a bit creepy, with the tar-coated pilings all around and the sense that the house, the entire house, might just decide to fall on their heads at any moment. She looked around, wondering where Diver had gone after running down here. He was nowhere to be seen.

"You don't know how to ride them, do you?" Summer asked, not at all convinced.

"I've *seen* people ride them," Marquez said. "And I know how to drive a car, right, so how different can it be?"

"Well, these go on water is one thing."

Marquez knelt and pried up the seat on the first Jet Ski. Beneath it was a little waterproof locker. "See, just stick your purse and your dress in here, no problem."

Summer pulled the other Jet Ski toward her, a move that involved leaning way out over the water, holding on to a greasy piling and hoping she didn't fall in. The Jet Ski was tied loosely by two ropes and came easily within reach. Summer put her rolled-up dress and purse in the compartment under the seat. At Marquez's insistence she had put on a bathing suit.

"Okay, now we just get on them," Marquez said.

"Marquez, are we going to get ourselves killed?"

"Summer, you need to have more faith. I've seen total morons riding these things, and we're not total morons."

"Not *total*," Summer admitted.

Marquez climbed gingerly onto her Jet Ski. She sat down and gripped the handlebars. "See?"

"Why am I letting you talk me into this?" Summer muttered.

"It will be fun. It'll be cool. You'll see."

Summer climbed on the Jet Ski, which reacted to her weight by wallowing around and spinning slowly away from the platform. Her feet were in the water, but to her amazement the water was perfectly warm, almost hot.

"Okay, see this loop thing?" Marquez called out. "It's just hanging there. You put the loop over your wrist and then you stick the pointy end in here."

"Why?"

"'Cause you need that to start it."

"Why don't they just use a key, like normal machines?"

"See, because this way if you were to fall off, the loop stays on your wrist and that pulls out the pin thing so the Jet Ski stops and doesn't go running off out into the Gulf of Mexico and end up in Haiti."

"Are you sure this is going to be fun?"

"Absolutely. Okay, now to start it, I think you push this button, this green button. And if you want it to go, you press on this red button with your thumb."

Marquez pressed the starter button. The Jet Ski engine coughed and sputtered. She pressed it again, and the engine roared to life. "Nothing to it!" Marquez yelled.

Summer was beginning to get a sick feeling in the pit of her stomach, the feeling she often got when she knew she was doing something not exactly intelligent. But Marquez was enthusiastic, gunning her engine loudly, and the enthusiasm was contagious.

Summer started her own engine, feeling the unfamiliar vibrations through the soles of her bare feet and up through her spine.

"Okay, it started!" she yelled to Marquez.

"Better go slow till we're out from under here," Marquez suggested. She pressed her throttle button and the Jet Ski moved forward. Then it stopped, straining against the rope.

"I think maybe you should untie your rope!" Summer shouted, grinning. Now she was getting caught up in it. They were going to arrive at the fabulous Merrick estate on roaring Jet Skis like a couple of modern mermaids. Much cooler than showing up on foot, all worn out from the walk.

Marquez cast off her rope, and Summer did likewise.

"Real slow, now," Marquez cautioned. She eased her Jet Ski away, carefully guiding it through the pilings.

Summer pressed her own throttle button. The Jet Ski reared and plunged like an out-of-control horse, and then, in a blur, it was roaring through the narrow pilings.

Summer took her finger off the throttle. She was several dozen yards out in the water, well clear of the house. She realized she was shaking and trying very hard not to admit to herself that her head had missed a low beam by two inches at most.

"That's what you call slow?" Marquez said, coming alongside.

"I think I pressed too hard. Now what?"

Marquez pointed across the bay. "Straight across to the other side. It's only maybe half or a third of a mile."

Summer grinned. Now that she had survived the first part, the rest felt like it would be easy. She pressed the throttle again, a bit more carefully, and aimed for the far shore. The Jet Ski roared off with Marquez close alongside.

It was the most exhilarating thing Summer had ever done. The Jet Ski seemed to fly, skimming over the surface of the water, hopping from ripple to ripple, sending up a shower of spray in all directions that soon had Summer drenched, hair flying in the hot breeze.

She glanced back and saw the stilt house silhouetted against a sky turned red by the setting sun.

This was why she had come to Crab Claw Key. This very moment. This sense of being in a new place, doing new things with new people. This overpowering, exhilarating feeling of perfect freedom in the middle of a perfect world.

Soon they were far out in the bay, and the tiny waves let the Jet Skis go airborne, taking off from the slopes of a swell, coming clear out of the water before slapping down again and surging forward.

Then the engine coughed. Speed fell away. The Jet Ski wallowed heavily, power gone. Marquez pulled alongside, idling her engine. She looked as exhilarated as Summer felt, her dark curly hair wild, her eyes lit up.

"What are you doing?"

Summer pushed the starter button. A rasping sound. "I don't know. It just stopped." She tried the starter again. More rasping, a sputter, a rasp.

"Try it again," Marquez suggested.

"Oh no. Is this the gas gauge?" Summer tapped the

glass on a small gauge. It read empty. It read less than empty.

Then Marquez's engine sputtered and died. Sudden silence, except for the lapping of water against the Jet Skis. A very ominous silence, the silence of vast, open seas.

"Yep. That's the gas gauge," Marquez said. "Mine says empty."

"Mine agrees," Summer said.

10

Lifestyles of the Rich and Sexy

"Amazing sunset," Summer said. And it was. High streaky clouds appeared in colors that looked too bright and intense to be real. The sun was a ball of brilliant orange-yellow, just peeking above the horizon, threatening to dive into the Gulf of Mexico at any moment. To the east the sky was already darkening. "Incredible," Summer said. "I'm glad I got to experience it before I get washed out to sea and end up being eaten by sharks."

"Someone is bound to see us," Marquez said. "I mean, boats pass in and out of the bay all the time."

"They do? *All* the time?"

"Well, not right now, this minute, but soon. Probably."

They had tied the two Jet Skis together by looping the armholes of Summer's dress over the two sets of handlebars. The dress was getting badly stretched in the process. Now, even if they did make it somehow, she would be arriving at a cool party at a billionaire's estate dressed as clown girl.

The water was still warm, unnaturally warm, like bathwater after it sat for ten minutes. The current was definitely drawing them slowly out of the bay, out toward the open Gulf.

"Maybe we'd better just swim for it," Marquez suggested.

"Great. And how do I explain to Diana and my aunt that on my second day here I brilliantly lost two Jet Skis?"

"Good point," Marquez allowed. "Your aunt might not be happy about that."

"Too bad I have to die this way," Summer said philosophically. "I was just starting to think I might like it here."

"You have a better way to die?" Marquez wondered, making conversation.

"Better would be about eighty years from now."

"Yes. Okay."

"My parents will be upset," Summer said. "It took a lot for them to decide to let me come down here."

"Oh. So they're the very protective type, huh? Mine too."

"I wouldn't say they're *over*protective or anything," Summer said, not sure of how much she should tell Marquez. After all, they'd known each other barely half a day, and so far what Marquez had done was help her get a job, only to turn around and lure her to a watery grave. "They lost my little brother already," Summer said at last. "I mean, I guess he'd be my big brother, but I never think of him that way."

"Oh, man, Summer. I'm sorry to hear that," Marquez said.

"It was a long time ago. I was still a fetus at the time, so naturally I don't remember anything about him. He was two years old and disappeared. I've seen pictures of him. That's all."

"What do you mean, disappeared?"

Summer shrugged. She shouldn't have brought it up. The situation they were in was depressing enough. "He was at day care, playing outside in the yard, and then, suddenly he wasn't. They never found, you know, a body or anything, but after a long, long time my parents finally gave up and accepted it. I don't mean *accepted*. You know what I mean."

"That's very major, Summer. That's horrible." Marquez whistled softly in the dark. "I wouldn't have thought you were someone with any kind of sadness in your life, you know? You seem so sweet and normal and all."

For a while they were both silent, listening to the plop of fish jumping out of the water. It had been a long time since Summer had thought much about the brother she'd never known. When she was younger, the sadness of that one event had hung over every day. It was a sadness that had been there, waiting for her as she was born into the world.

"Summer, you're not crying, are you? It's so dark I can't really see your face. I hate tears."

"No," Summer lied. "It was something that happened before I was even born. You can't be sad over things that happened before you were born."

The sun had finally plunged below the horizon, taking the last of the optimism with it. Darkness moved swiftly toward them across the water. Over on the shore a few hundred yards away they could see the lights of the party, an impression of people moving back and forth under the trees, the headlights of cars pulling up.

"Hey, there's a light," Summer said, wiping away the tears that blurred her vision. It was a green pinpoint of light moving fast.

"It's a boat," Marquez said excitedly, confirming Summer's faint hope.

"Hey!" Summer yelled. "Hey, boat! Help! Do you think he sees us?"

"Jeez, I hope so. I don't want to die out here," Marquez said.

"I thought you weren't worried," Summer accused.

"I didn't want to worry you."

"HELP!"

"HELP US! HELP, you blind—"

"He's coming. I think." Summer could hear the sound of the boat's engines, deep and powerful and reassuring. The boat was definitely coming closer. In fact, it had just begun to occur to Summer that the boat might hit them. But then it slowed, inscribing a slow circle around them. A spotlight played across the dark water and illuminated them, two insanely waving figures.

"That you, Marquez?" a mocking voice called out.

"Adam?" Marquez yelled back. "What took you so long?"

"We saw you out here, but we didn't believe it was possible for two Jet Skis to break down at the same exact time."

"We ran out of gas," Marquez said.

The boat, very long and very fast-looking with two big outboard engines, drifted alongside. There were two guys in the boat. Even in the darkness Summer could see the resemblance between them. They looked like brothers.

One dived over the side of the boat and surfaced between the two Jet Skis, spouting water and laughing. He was carrying a white nylon rope. "We'll tow you in, ladies. Let me just tie this . . ." He fell silent, looking up at Summer, who was sitting on her Jet Ski in a damp pink bikini, feeling like the biggest dork in recorded history.

"Hi," he said. He stuck a hand up to her. She shook it briefly, but he held on for an extra second, making contact. "I'm Adam Merrick. In the boat there is my brother, Ross."

"Pleased, et cetera," said a voice from the boat. A voice that sounded as if it had been affected by a few beers.

"Thanks for rescuing us," Summer said, her voice a little squeaky.

"What's a nice girl like you doing with Marquez? I'll bet you ten bucks this was all *her* idea, right?" Adam said.

"Hey," Marquez said, pushing Adam underwater with her foot. "What makes you think it was my idea?"

"I *know* you, Marquez," Adam said.

"This is Summer. She's from Idaho or Michigan or one of those places," Marquez said.

"Minnesota. Bloomington. You know, the Mall of America?" Excellent, Summer chided herself. Absolutely mention the Mall of America. That's sure to impress a billionaire who has probably been all over the world ten times.

"Guess whose cousin she is?" Marquez asked.

"Cindy Crawford's?" Adam suggested. He released Summer's hand and began looping the rope to the towing rings in the front of each Jet Ski.

"Summer is Diana's cousin," Marquez said. "Diana Olan."

Adam said nothing. From the boat came Ross's unpleasant laugh. "Let's leave her out here."

"Shut up, Ross," Adam snapped. He forced a smile for Summer. An apologetic and extraordinarily attractive smile. A movie star smile. "Come on, get in the boat."

"Okay," Summer said. Marquez made the jump easily from her Jet Ski to the boat, swinging over the side and brushing her hands together as if she'd just done a neat trick.

Summer stood up and reached for the side of the boat. But the Jet Ski slid away. She plunged into the water. It closed over her head, surprising her and frightening her a little. She wasn't a great swimmer, though she could stay afloat. But this was open sea, and it was dark, and the music from *Jaws* had already been running through the back of her mind.

With a kick she headed for a surface dappled and rippling with reflected light.

Then there were powerful arms around her, holding her firmly. They broke the surface. Her face was inches from Adam's, and the first thought that popped into her mind was that she probably didn't look great right then, water streaming off her head, spitting out seawater. Whereas Adam definitely did look great, wet or not. Her hands felt hard muscle in his neck. Her breasts were pressed against his chest, close enough that she could feel his every breath.

"You okay?" Adam asked. She could feel the rumble of his voice.

"I'm fine. I *can* swim, you know."

"That's good. Swimming is important around here."

"Yeah. You can, um, let me go now."

"Do I have to?" Adam asked.

Marquez leaned over the side, offering Summer a hand. Summer took it and pulled hard but was unable to clear the drag of the water entirely. Then there were hands firmly planted on her behind, pushing her up.

She slid over the side of the boat and gasped out her embarrassed thanks. Adam pulled himself up and over, an almost effortless move. He sat beside her and leaned across her to reach a cabinet. He found two towels and handed one to her.

"Thanks," Summer mumbled.

"My extreme pleasure," Adam said. "It's hot," he added quickly, as if he realized he'd sounded slightly sleazy. "Too hot, and a dive in the water was just what I needed."

He even seems sincere, Summer thought. But then again, he was from a political family. They probably had special genes that gave them the ability to sound sincere.

"All right, enough of playing Coast Guard, back to the party," Ross said.

The boat moved along slowly, careful not to swamp the two Jet Skis bobbing along behind. If Ross was drunk, he still seemed able to pilot the boat, berthing it neatly alongside the dock.

"I'm not exactly dressed for a party anymore," Summer pointed out, indicating her bathing suit. The dress she had planned to wear was a total loss.

"There'll be plenty of girls wearing smaller bathing suits than that," Adam assured her.

Marquez nodded, and Summer began to wonder whether this was the kind of party she wanted to attend. But Marquez gave her a reassuring wink and a little shake of the head that said, hey, don't worry about it.

"Stay," Adam said. "Please."

Again he sounded as if he really wanted her to stay.

As if she was supposed to believe that someone like Adam Merrick really cared one way or the other if some tourist from the home of the Mall of America went to his party.

"Okay, I guess. Thanks." There was no polite way to get out of it. Not now. She didn't even know the way home.

A neat, crushed-shell path led from the dock across a vast lawn toward the house. It was painful under Summer's tender feet, so she walked onto the grass, as thick and spongy as a mattress.

The house was just two stories high, but it extended in every direction, looking as large as the main building of Summer's high school. Some, if not most, of the windows were bright, revealing strangely positioned cupolas and parapets and sudden, capricious balconies.

But the party wasn't in the house. The party was in front of the house, past the looping driveway crammed with cars, past the naked, spotlit flagpole. Summer could see a mass of bodies writhing under the reddish light of Japanese lamps hung from the trees, long hair flying in time with the music, arms randomly thrust into the air, smooth, tan female legs everywhere, protruding from shorts and minis and bathing suit bottoms. Hairy guy legs as well, looking stubby in big shorts or extremely long in little European bathing suits.

Ross disappeared into the throng, but Adam stayed

close, following Summer onto the grass. As they reached the driveway he strode ahead, walking with an easy grace and absolute confidence. Nothing exaggerated or forced, no swagger, no attempt to impress anyone, just a walk that announced him as the guy in charge, at home and utterly sure of himself.

Summer was just behind him, feeling simultaneously invisible and horribly conspicuous, like a stagehand who had wandered into the star's spotlight.

The sound system was playing 50 Cent, and when Summer glanced over her shoulder, she saw that Marquez was already dancing. The beat seemed to reach across the distance and grab control of Marquez's body. She was dancing over the crushed shells, turning the gravel into her own muted rhythm section.

Around the fringes of the dancing little knots of people could be seen, here and there, faces appearing in the dim glow of a cigarette. Other groups were smaller, usually just two bodies pressed close, making out as they leaned against tree trunks or against the hoods of the nearest cars.

Summer had begun to feel increasingly nervous as she got closer to the party. The music was familiar; the dancing, too. Even the wafting smells of beer and smoke weren't much different from parties back home. But usually when she went to parties, she knew at least half the people there. Knew whom she could hang out with, which guys she could dance with, how to say no to the various offers of one kind or another. Here she was a stranger. The only person she knew at all was Marquez, and Marquez seemed to have been possessed by the music.

Ross Merrick took Marquez by the arm and led her away into the melee. "Have fun," Marquez called back to Summer.

And then Summer was alone, the instant loser, the one on the fringe with no one to talk to. Except for Adam, who was still there, close by, though he was fielding a steady stream of hellos, hey dudes, and congratulations on the excellence of the party. But the last thing she wanted was to be Adam's pity date, someone to be handed off at the earliest opportunity.

"Want to dance?" Adam asked.

The request shouldn't have surprised her—this *was* a party—and yet it did.

Dance? In a wet two-piece bathing suit? With this guy she'd barely met? This guy she'd seen on the news once, standing in a group with his famous father? But what was the alternative to dancing? Standing around gaping at people?

"Sure," Summer said, half-grateful, half-frightened. What were the chances that her bathing suit bottom would bunch up while she was dancing?

Adam took her hand and drew her to what Summer

could now see was an actual dance floor: interlocked, polished wood planks laid out on the grass. Here and there portions were raised so that some dancers were elevated above the rest.

The Kanye West song came on, and Summer began to dance, intensely conscious of what she felt must be many alien eyes on her. Although each time she glanced around she never saw anyone staring at her, it was hard to shake the feeling that the eyes were there.

"So you're Diana's cousin," Adam said, drawing close alongside her, shouting a little to be heard. He even danced well.

"Uh-huh." Summer was concentrating, trying to remember the moves she'd seen girls doing on that MTV beach show, trying to stay in time with the beat.

"Just down here for the summer. For the summer, Summer?" He grinned. "I guess you've heard that joke about a million times."

Summer smiled and shrugged. A mistake, since shrugging upset her carefully maintained rhythm, and her legs and arms and head now were each off doing different things, as if listening to three different songs.

"How do you like it so far?" Adam asked. "Crab Claw Key, I mean."

"It's beautiful," Summer said. Was the tie on her

bathing suit top coming loose? No. No, but she'd double the knot when she got the chance.

"Just beautiful?" Adam said, sounding disappointed.

"It's . . . different. I mean, it's like . . . it's like there aren't any real adults, you know? No one wears a suit or looks serious about anything."

Adam laughed. "That's exactly right. No adults. Even people seventy years old aren't adults here."

"Also I feel like people here are stranger, more out-there, you know?" Summer suggested, thinking of Diver—definitely strange. And Marquez—probably strange. And Seth, who was only strange if you thought putting a lip-lock on a total stranger in a photo booth was unusual.

"Everything is a little more extreme," Adam agreed. "Back home I'm a totally different person."

"Home? Don't you live here?"

"No, this is mostly just a summer home. We're from New Hampshire. I spend about a third of the year here between all the vacations, summer and spring and weekends."

"Oh, that's right, how stupid of me, duh. Your father is the senator from New Hampshire, obviously."

Adam looked pained. "You're not into politics, are you?"

"Not exactly," Summer admitted. "I mean, I was secretary-treasurer of my tenth-grade class, but we never had any meetings and there wasn't any money." Is it even possible for me to sound like a bigger idiot? Secretary-treasurer of the tenth grade?

"You have a boyfriend?" Adam asked, suddenly shifting course. He smiled. The music assumed a slower, more sultry beat. Couples danced closer together.

"No, I don't really have a boyfriend," Summer admitted. Sure, I have this guy I make out with in airports who has a girlfriend, and this other guy who lives with me but doesn't like girls, but no, no actual boyfriends.

They danced for a while, with Adam drawing closer, matching his rhythm to hers. He was a good dancer, graceful for a guy so large. Graceful and smooth and confident, and like some kind of a sun, so that she could feel the force of gravity drawing her toward him.

At least his bathing suit was normal, not like the little Speedos some of the guys were wearing. "Well, aren't you going to ask *me*?" he said after a while.

"Ask you what?" Summer said, alarmed.

"Ask me if I have a girlfriend."

"Um . . ."

"I don't," Adam said, grinning impishly.

"Oh," Summer gulped. What was she supposed to say now? "I can't believe you don't have a girlfriend?"

Or "Cool, can I be your girlfriend?" Or what? He seemed to think she should say *something*.

"I've never really had a boyfriend," Summer said. Instantly, even as the words were bubbling out of her mouth, she wished she could call them back. Too late. And now her brain became totally useless, because Adam was dancing *very* close, and the memory of his arms around her in the water was very clear in Summer's mind. "I mean, not a real boyfriend, not that I don't like guys because I do, it's just that the guys who . . . I mean, the wrong guys and then the right guys were, you know, and . . ." She was in full babble mode now. Words totally unconnected to any sensible thought were spewing forth, unstoppable. Full babble. Total brain lock that shut down her mind and her body so that now her dancing had deteriorated into spasms of random muscle jerks.

She was dancing in a bikini with the very attractive son of a billionaire senator and doing her best impression of a moron having a seizure.

"Oh, man," Adam said, peering over Summer's head. "The butler's calling to me."

Thank God. Just go away and leave me to my humiliation.

"I have to go see what he wants," Adam said.

He almost sounded like he was honestly regretful, Summer noted. Although clearly he was just grabbing

the first excuse to escape her. Flee, Adam, flee! Run
from the loser girl. Run before she can mention the
Mall of America again. "Okay," Summer said gratefully.

"Um, before I go, though . . ." Adam said. "There's
just one thing I wanted to clear up."

"What? Um, what would you . . . what?"

"Well, around here we have this custom. When
someone rescues someone, like I rescued you out on
the bay, well, there's this customary thing."

"Okay," Summer said cautiously.

"The rescuer gets to kiss the person he rescued."

Before Summer had a chance to object—and she
wasn't sure whether she planned to—Adam had put his
arm around her and drawn her close. There was a last
split second when she could have said no, but then the
split second was gone.

Adam's lips met hers. Only for an instant. Then
he pulled away, still keeping his hold on her. "Don't
disappear on me," he said in a low voice. "I'll be right
back."

Hot Music and Sweaty Bodies, a Long Way from Minnesota

"I saw that," Marquez said, sounding almost accusatory. "I bring you to a party and the first thing you do is throw yourself at the host? Bad girl. *Bad* girl. Shame." Then she broke up, laughing gaily at the horrified expression on Summer's face.

"I didn't throw myself at him. I hardly know him," Summer protested anxiously. Kissing people she hardly knew was getting to be a habit.

"Whatever." Marquez waved her hand. "So, how was it?"

"I didn't even know it was happening."

That really started Marquez giggling. "Well, I guess you're off to a good start, huh? Practically your first night out and Adam Merrick is all over you."

"I don't think it meant anything," Summer said doubtfully.

"He kissed you. That had to mean something. Adam isn't a total dirtbag who runs around kissing girls. Unless he's gotten worse since last summer. You know, someday he may be senator or governor. Or president."

"He used to go out with my cousin," Summer pointed out. The thought had just occurred to her, probably because her mind was just coming out of brain lock.

"Ancient history," Marquez said. "Come on, you don't want to hang around looking like you're waiting for him."

"I'm *not* waiting. I don't even know him."

"Yeah, yeah. Either way you don't want to just stand here, do you?"

"No, I guess not."

"Come on, let's dance."

"The two of us?"

"I have to dance," Marquez said, as if that were obvious. "And I don't see any guys asking either of us right this minute. Besides, they're starting to play some better music. Rap is cool, but I feel like totally thrashing out with some serious rock."

From the speakers the Ramones began roaring

through "I Wanna Be Sedated." For Marquez, the transition from standing around to dancing was instantaneous and total. It wasn't about looking cool, it was about losing all contact with the normal world, going away to a place where her body and mind and the music were all the same thing.

It was impossible for Summer to resist. Impossible not to be drawn in. The night was hot, and Marquez was dancing like someone possessed, and Summer could still feel Adam's lips on hers, could still recall the shock when his arm had gone around her in the water and the contact of flesh against flesh.

She had just been kissed by a guy. Kissed by a very cute guy, and she wanted to be kissed again.

As long as it didn't turn out that Adam had his own Lianne hidden away somewhere.

The music throbbed through her as Marquez guided them toward the speakers like a moth drawn to a candle, louder and louder till the music wasn't a sound anymore but something that came from inside her.

She'd been kissed by a complete stranger, and she had liked it. Held by a guy she didn't know and had liked that too. And worst of all, it was the second time in less than a week. Ha! Try calling *that* "nice."

The *nice* Summer Smith was dead and lying in her grave while the new, improved, bolder, wilder, goes-to-parties, kisses-guys-she-hardly-knows Summer Smith shoveled dirt over her.

Summer closed her eyes and danced.

When she opened her eyes again Adam was there, as if in answer to a wish. He smiled and she smiled back. She closed her eyes again, afraid that looking at him might cause her to feel the edge of self-awareness return, the sense of eyes following her, judging her.

With her eyes closed Summer had the feeling that she could dance like Marquez. She'd forgotten that she was surrounded by strangers and was dancing in a two-piece bathing suit. She felt drunk, though she'd had nothing to drink. She peeked from under narrowed lids as Adam danced closer, so that now she could reach out and touch him if she wanted to, touch his smooth chest.

The music slowed from its exhausting pace into a gentler but still intoxicating reggae song. This, at last, was the right music, she thought. The melody of sun-baked islands and warm nights and people who never, ever wore parkas.

Summer realized they were no longer on the floor. There was grass under her feet as she danced, and the music, though still loud, had softened a little. It was darker now, and Adam was closer. Inches separated them, and his eyes were focused on hers. She looked down, embarrassed, but this time she didn't feel like being embarrassed, so she looked up and met his gaze.

The music paused between songs. Summer felt something rough at her back and leaned against the tree. Adam came closer.

"You are very, very beautiful," Adam said. He made no attempt to hide the fact that his eyes were taking in her entire body. "Are you sure you don't have a boyfriend?"

"I'm sure," Summer said, her voice a distant, Minnie Mouse squeak.

Adam leaned first one hand and then the other against the tree, imprisoning her.

Now would be the time to say, "Hey, hold up, I barely know you," Summer told herself. Yes, now would be the time. Right now, before he leaned any closer.

This time when he kissed her it wasn't the quick, almost playful kiss she'd felt earlier. This time he really kissed her. And the music started up again, soft but insistent. He kissed her and to her utter amazement, Summer kissed him back.

Something hit Summer on her right side. She staggered and nearly tripped over a body.

"Whoa, sorry." A guy scrambled up, standing awkwardly in the very small space between Summer and Adam. "I tripped. Over a root or something. Adam, dude, you ought to talk to your gardener about that. A guy could get killed."

"You been drinking, Mr. Moon?" Adam asked, taking a step back.

Summer peered through the darkness. Yes, it *was* Seth. *Seth!* Possibly the last person on earth she wanted to see right at this moment. What was he doing here?

"Hey, it's Summer," Seth said. "Summer from Minnesota."

"Hi. Again," Summer said. For reasons she couldn't immediately explain, she felt guilty. Feeling guilty just made her feel angry.

Seth smiled a little lopsidedly. "So, I see you're getting to know people, making friends and all." He rolled his eyes exaggeratedly at Adam.

"Good-bye, Seth," Adam said tersely. "Great seeing you again, welcome anytime and so on."

"I was just going to ask Summer to dance," Seth said.

"She's busy."

"That's very disappointing." Seth shrugged.

Suddenly a new sound mixed in with the music, then rose louder still. Shouting, one voice loudly enraged and other voices trying to instill calm. Summer saw a disturbance on the far side of the dance floor.

"Sounds like Ross has gone off again," Seth said, not unkindly.

Adam bit his lip and glanced uncertainly at Summer.

"Go on, deal with it," Seth said to Adam. "Don't worry, I'm not going to take her anywhere."

The noise was beginning to sound like a fight, with shouts of encouragement from at least two sides.

Adam cursed. "I'll be back. Don't let Mr. Moon here give you any crap."

"What's happening?" Summer asked Seth.

Seth shrugged. "Oh, Ross is drunk and picking fights. Drunk or high, or maybe E: all of the above."

"Adam's brother?"

"Yeah. It happens." Seth looked uncomfortable. "So, um, sorry if I broke anything up. Not real sorry, though."

"I'm not sorry," Summer said before she'd had a chance to think about it. "Not that . . . I mean . . ." She sighed. "Forget it."

"Okay. Forgotten. So, you want to dance? It looks like the fight is getting under control. Besides, it's way over there."

"I don't know if I should dance any more," Summer said. She felt as if she were coming out of a trance. It was a disturbing feeling, like thinking you'd been talking in your sleep and wondering what people might have heard.

"Take it slow, Minnesota," Seth said kindly. "You know, all this down here gets to people sometimes. Warm nights, ocean breezes in the palm trees, that whole tropical thing . . . you might just forget who you are. Forgetting who you are is the whole idea of Crab Claw Key."

Summer blushed. "I did not forget who I was," she said. She said it with extra conviction because it wasn't true. "And unlike certain people, I don't forget I have a girlfriend I've been going with for four years."

Seth winced. "Look, what I told you was true— I *did* break up with Lianne. Only . . . I guess she doesn't want to accept it."

"Poor you," Summer said sarcastically. "I guess she can't give you up because you're just so wonderful. And you say *I'm* the one who's forgetting who they are?"

Seth nodded glumly. "Yeah, I guess I deserved that. Okay. Cool. I'm just saying look out for that tropical effect, that tropical rot. It eats away at everything, so that things here deteriorate faster, fall apart faster, and then it all grows back faster and wilder than before. The old stuff disappears." He snapped his fingers. "And before you know it, something new has shot up overnight to take its place."

"I'm a grown person," Summer said sharply. "I think I can make my own decisions."

Seth pulled off his cap and made an exaggerated bow. "I apologize. None of my business."

"That's right, *none* of your business," Summer said.

He started to walk away, then he turned back.

"Just for your information, I didn't lie to you."

Summer met his gaze, and suddenly she was back in the airport, with his mouth on hers, feeling a surge of something she'd never felt before that moment.

He looked as if he was telling the truth. His eyes didn't waver or turn away.

Adam had asked her to wait for him. Seth was drawing her closer with just his gaze. . . .

Suddenly there was a loud, feminine squeal. A look of confusion clouded Seth's face, then was quickly replaced by dread or embarrassment or both.

"Sethie!" the voice squealed again.

"Lianne?" he said in a whisper.

A girl appeared, running joyfully, arms outstretched like something from a slow-motion movie. She was short, but with that uniquely petite perfection. Pale, almost translucent skin. Dark red hair that fell over her shoulders in a luxuriant wave. She was wearing shorts and a cropped top.

She leapt on Seth, wrapping her bare legs around his waist, her arms around his neck. He supported her minimal weight by linking his hands beneath her bottom.

"Are you surprised?" Lianne asked gleefully. "I decided to come down a few days early. I just couldn't stand to be separated a minute longer."

She kissed him, a peck on each cheek, then a long, slow kiss.

It may have been that Seth was trying to push her away. It may have been that he tried to avoid her kisses. But Summer had seen enough. She turned on her heel and walked away.

At a safe distance, from under the dark shadows of the trees, she looked back. Seth and Lianne were standing close, deep in conversation. Then Seth turned and walked a short distance. He hesitated. Summer saw his shoulders sag.

Lianne went to him and looked up at his face. A red lantern was just above them, and it cast a shadowy pink light on Lianne's pretty features.

Lianne put her arms around Seth. His arms hung limp. And then, just barely tall enough to look over Seth's shoulder, Lianne aimed her gaze directly at Summer. It was impossible at that distance to read her expression.

Summer shrank back against the nearest tree trunk. Lianne couldn't possibly see her even there in the dark, could she?

And yet, for just a fleeting moment, despite the hot night, Summer felt a chill.

She spotted Seth a few times after that, drinking soda, talking to people, dancing a little with Lianne and other girls. But he said nothing to Summer.

And Summer said nothing to him. She didn't care

about Seth Warner. And now, she assured herself, she would be able to put the airport incident behind her for good.

She was wandering around on the steps leading up to the main door of the estate house, hoping for a clue to the nearest bathroom, when she ran into Adam.

"*There* you are," Adam said, appearing at the bottom of the stone steps. He was wearing a shirt now, and he looked subdued.

"Hi," she said.

"Were you looking for me?" Adam asked.

Summer hesitated and Adam laughed. "I guess not," he said ruefully.

"I was sort of looking for a bathroom, but I'd rather find you," she said hastily. She winced. "I don't think that came out exactly the way I meant it."

"You meant I was second runner-up behind a bathroom. That's okay," he said. "I can live with that. Come on."

He trotted up the stairs and took her hand. He led her to the door and used a key to unlock it. "We usually just let the party guests use the bathrooms by the pool house. I have to keep the doors of the main house locked or Manolo will kill me. He's the butler, all-around guy in charge of the house. He's the *real* boss."

They entered an arched atrium and set off down a long hallway. It was like stepping directly out of

Florida and clear across time and space to nineteenth-century New England. The senator's tastes obviously didn't embrace the lighter, looser Florida look. The walls were lined with alternating gilt-framed floor-to-ceiling mirrors and paintings, all more or less gloomy portraits of stern-looking men.

"The Merrick clan," Adam said, noticing her awed expression. "There's a set just like them in the New Hampshire house. All the dead Merrick men. Some-day I'll be there too, looking old and serious. That guy there?" He pointed. "That's Aubrey Merrick. He used to import slaves, back in like 1795 or something. He didn't *approve* of slavery, of course, but business was business."

"Wow" was all Summer could think to say.

"And that guy, the guy with the whiskers, he was cool. He sort of made up for old Aubrey. That's Josiah. He died with the Maine boys on Little Round Top at Gettysburg. Took three bullets and was still yelling and shooting rebels when he keeled over dead."

"I saw that movie," Summer said. Her eyes met Adam's and they both laughed. It was a relief to laugh.

"Someday in the year 2090 or whatever, some young Merrick guy will be walking along with some girl he's trying to impress and point to me. 'That's Adam Merrick. Never did a damned thing.'"

"Maybe you'll do something," Summer said.

Adam smirked. "Yeah, maybe. If they decide to hold another civil war, I'm there."

"And then you'll be in the new movie. Played by Josh Hartnett or someone."

"Do you like Josh Hartnett?" Adam asked.

"Yeah. He's cute, I guess. I mean, um, he's a good actor."

"You know, when you blush like that it makes me want to kiss you again," Adam said.

"I thought you were showing me a bathroom."

"Oh, right." They reached the end of the hallway and entered a vast, open room, two floors high. Rough wood beams, each as big as a full-size tree, supported the ceiling. The walls were paneled in dark wood. The furniture, though there was a lot of it, seemed lost in the space. At one side of the room was a fireplace, fire roaring under a granite mantel that reminded Summer of pictures of Stonehenge.

"You must have the only fireplace in this state," Summer said.

"Certainly the only one in use when it's in the high eighties outside," Adam agreed. "My dad likes fires. So the staff lights it every night, whether he's here or not, no matter how hot it is outside." He laughed. "Seems slightly absurd, right?"

"Maybe. But I'm starting to get the feeling that it

takes an awful lot to seem absurd around this place."

Adam laughed his easy laugh. "Ah, you're starting to get the picture. See, I know what you mean. I guess New Hampshire is similar to Minnesota in a lot of ways. It makes you slightly schizo going back and forth between the 'normal' world and this island."

"Seth said something kind of like that," Summer said. She instantly regretted mentioning Seth.

Adam just rolled his eyes slightly. He pointed to a small door, almost invisible in the paneling. "There you go. At least I think that's a bathroom."

"How many are there in this house?"

"Twenty-one, I think. We have like twenty-six at the New Hampshire house. We thought that many would be too ostentatious for Florida, though." He laughed to show that he was just kidding.

But somehow for Summer, the fact that this one family had a total of forty-seven bathrooms (possibly more because who knew if they owned other houses?) was deeply impressive. Forty-seven bathrooms. Forty-seven rolls of toilet paper. They must buy it in truckloads.

When she came back, she found Adam standing a few feet from the fire. It made a dark silhouette of his body, accentuating the heavy shoulders, the muscular torso. Even in silhouette he exuded easy confidence, something bred in him, something that announced to the world that here was a person without self-doubt, without awkwardness, without self-consciousness.

It drew Summer to him, and yet frightened her just a little. He was so different from other guys her own age. He could easily be twenty-five, or even forty.

Maybe being rich made it possible to just sort of glide by all the little tortures of teenagehood. After all, Summer realized, Adam didn't worry about getting work, or getting accepted to college, or paying for college, or whether he could afford to buy cool clothes, or if his folks would get him a car. If he ever got a zit, they probably flew in a whole team of dermatologists to get rid of it.

He noticed her and turned. "Was it a bathroom?"

"No, it was a closet, but I went anyway," she said, and he laughed. She wasn't going to act all impressed and inferior with him. Just because he could probably buy her entire family with his weekly allowance.

"Would you like a drink?" he asked.

"I don't drink very much," Summer said.

"That's probably good. Booze is our favorite family vice. I don't drink because it makes me break out in hives." He laughed. "Seriously. It's not a pretty sight."

"I guess I should get back outside and see what Marquez is doing," Summer suggested.

"Marquez can take care of herself." He shook his

head slowly, amused. "She's very cool. Just don't ever make her mad. The girl has a temper. One of those ice-cold tempers, you know?"

"She's been really nice to me," Summer said. "Like bringing me here."

"I'm very glad she did that," Adam said.

Summer debated whether to ask the next question. It could ruin things instantly, and her impertinent questions had ruined other relationships before. "Do you try to pick up just any new girl that shows up around here?"

He looked startled. "You mean you think I'm trying to impress you and score with you so that I can add another notch to my belt?"

"I guess that's what I mean," Summer said. "Some guys *are* like that." She could think of at least one by name.

"Maybe I should ask you a question. Are *you* trying to make it with me so that you can tell all your friends you dated Adam Merrick? Or perhaps even go to the *National Enquirer* and sell the story: 'My Hot Affair with Boy Billionaire'?"

Summer recoiled. "Why would you think *that*?"

"It happens," Adam said. "Just like it happens that some guys, whether or not they happen to come from a wealthy family, try to see how many girls they can pick up."

"Oh. I guess you're right. I guess that is true, isn't it?"

"I'll tell you the absolute truth, cross my heart and hope to die. I saw you sitting there, looking lost on that Jet Ski, and I instantly thought 'What an idiot. How could she manage to get stuck out here like this?'"

"That's very flattering."

"Then I jumped in to help you—admittedly I was happy to have an excuse to put my arms around you, since we're being honest here—and . . ." He made a wry face. "And something just happened. It felt like something I wanted to do again. And when you talked, it was this voice that I wanted to hear again. And when you spit seawater out of your mouth, it was a mouth I wanted to kiss. And then I did kiss you, and wanted to kiss you again. Like I do now."

Summer swallowed once. Twice. "We'd better not," she said. "It's all kind of . . . tropical."

"Tropical?"

"I mean, we haven't even had a date or anything."

Adam slapped his forehead. "I knew I'd forgotten something! Would you go out with me? Tomorrow? No, wait, day after tomorrow." He took Summer's hands in his. "Would you go out with me?"

"Yes," Summer said, sounding weirdly stiff. "That would be excellent."

It was about one in the morning when Marquez finally tired out. Half the people at the party had already left, and Marquez found Summer asleep, leaning back against a tree trunk with an empty Mountain Dew in her hand, her now dry but still misshapen dress laid over her like a blanket.

For a moment Marquez considered playing some prank on the gently snoring girl, but she was too weary to think of anything and besides, Summer wasn't a person you could be mean to.

She knelt and shook Summer's arm.

"What?"

"Time to wake up. We should get going. This guy I know with a truck said he'd give us a lift."

"What?" Summer repeated. She was looking around with that confused where-am-I look.

Marquez took her hand and pulled her to her feet. They headed for the driveway, where a battered red pickup truck was idling. In the cab beside the driver were two other guys Marquez knew from school.

"You're going to make us ride in the back?" Marquez asked. "What gentlemen."

"James here is probably going to hurl," the driver pointed out. "You'll be safer in the back."

"Don't say 'hurl,'" a voice groaned.

She and Summer climbed over the tailgate, and

Marquez pounded twice on the roof of the truck, signaling the driver that he could go.

They took off down the winding, wooded path through the Merrick estate.

"I didn't say good night to Adam," Summer said.

"Too late now," Marquez said. "Besides, I think he disappeared around midnight with a bunch of guys who said they were going to drive to some club down in Key West."

"Oh."

Marquez rolled her eyes. "If you're going to hang around with Adam Merrick, you have to deal with the fact that he and his buds move kind of fast."

"Oh," Summer said again, nodding vaguely.

"So, you going to see him again?"

"I don't know. I think so. I hope so. He said he'd like to take me out on a real date. You know, dinner and all that. Day after tomorrow."

"You don't sound totally psyched."

"I'm just tired," Summer said. "And it seems unreal, you know? This whole place. All of a sudden I meet a bunch of new people and go to a big party at a senator's house and kiss this guy I barely even met."

"Uh-huh. So, it was good, right?"

Summer giggled unexpectedly. "The first one was too quick, and I didn't even know what was happening. Later we had a longer one. That was kind of nice."

"Kind of nice?" Marquez made a face. "Don't tell that to Adam. He thinks he's the stud prince of planet earth."

"It's not that," Summer said. "It's just that I don't have all that much to compare it to. I mean, half the time I was just scared that I would do something stupid, you know? Like burp or suddenly develop insta-zits. I've never kissed someone famous before."

Marquez smiled. "But how did it make you *feel*?"

Summer nodded her head from side to side and scrunched her face up, struggling for some definition. "It made me feel slightly sick. Like maybe I was getting the flu. Or else like the time I visited my grandmother in Virginia and we went on a roller coaster at King's Dominion. It was my first ever roller coaster, and I felt sick but also giddy and wobbly. It was fun, but I wasn't sure I wanted to go on it again. Do you know what I mean?"

Marquez nodded knowingly. "You'll go on it again."

12

Video Blog

Hi, Jennifer. Sorry I'm whispering, but Diver is asleep up on the roof and I don't want him to hear me. Yes, I know, I need to explain about that. I guess a lot's been happening even though I feel like I just got here.

Anyway, it's almost two o'clock in the morning, but I couldn't fall asleep mostly because I'm kind of excited. I mean, I'm really excited, I guess. You know what happened tonight? This guy kissed me. This guy named Adam. Not Seth. Seth is the other one I told you about, the using creep with a girlfriend.

Forget him. This is Adam I'm talking about now. Totally different situation. I hope.

Now I'm going to tell you his last name, but you

have to swear, absolutely swear, you won't tell anyone, and I mean it. Okay. Did you swear?

Adam *Merrick*. You know, like the senator? His son. They have a house you would not believe. You'd faint if you saw it. It's the size of a castle. Diana's mom's house is like one tenth the size. Anyway, we went to a party there, me and Marquez.

Wait, I haven't told you about Marquez, either. Marquez is this girl I met here. She's very cool and dances really well. Anyway, we're going to this party at the Merrick estate, right? And we fall into the water. I mean, *I* fall into the water, being the klutzoid one. And Adam jumps in and gets me, not that I was drowning or anything, but he didn't know that. So later he says I should let him kiss me because he rescued me, right? So, he did. Just a little kiss, only later we danced and then we ended up making out. For kind of a long time.

It was just like you told me it was with Blake, so now I guess we're equal. Unless you've been doing something you shouldn't, you bad girl. And if you have, you'd better tell me because I'm telling you *everything*.

Except for Diver. Which is complicated. See, he kind of lives here. He's very nice but a little strange. I mean, he thinks he can communicate with Frank, and Frank is a pelican.

I don't know why I'm letting him stay here. He

just comes in to use the kitchen or the bathroom, so it's not like he's really living here. Just do not ever tell Mom about this or I'll kill you. I'm serious.

I don't know what I'm doing anymore, Jennifer. It's weird, almost, because it's like I just get here and boom! I'm kissing this guy in a photo booth at the airport, and then boom! I have this other guy practically living in my house, and then boom! I'm at a party making out with Adam Merrick.

Seth said it's an effect of the tropics.

Maybe he's right, Jen. I don't know. I don't feel like I'm any different, you know? Not inside. Maybe it's just when you take your same, normal self to a new place and are around new people that everyone else sees you differently. That's my theory, anyway. Or is it a hypothesis?

I know, you're thinking: typical Summer, trying to analyze everything when she should just be enjoying it. But I have to think about it, at least a little. It's like if I'm still me, why are people acting differently toward me? And if I'm *not* me, then . . . who am I?

And if I don't know who I am, how am I supposed to know how I feel about things? I tell Seth to take a hike because he's got a girlfriend already and because I'm not the kind of girl who goes out with guys who

already have girlfriends. But who says I'm that kind of
girl? Maybe I'm not. Or maybe in Minnesota I was,
and here I'm not.

I am totally a mess. Lost and confused.

Or maybe I'm just sleepy.

13

Fishnets, Reeboks, and Lost Loves

"Good morning, Frank," Summer said. The bird gave her a fishy look and turned away.

"Must be the uniform," Summer muttered. She was dressed in her brand-new Crab 'n' Conch uniform, consisting of a too-short white-and-blue sailor-suit dress, a white apron with a huge starched bow, fishnet panty hose, a really dorky sailor hat, and her own black Reeboks.

"What would *CosmoGirl* or *Seventeen* say about combining black leather running shoes and fishnets?" she asked Frank. "I'm thinking it's a major 'fashion don't.'"

Frank spread his wings and flapped off.

Pretty much the same reaction as the one she'd gotten

from Diver that morning. She'd gone into the bathroom to change and had emerged as he was eating a bowl of cold cereal. She'd been hoping for some sort of reassurance, but he had almost shuddered at the sight of her.

Like a guy with exactly one piece of clothing in the world was one to criticize.

Summer was too tired to care. Between the party, doing the latest installment of the video blog for Jennifer, and trying through bleary eyes to read at least some of the employee manual, she'd had very little sleep.

She ran into Diana on the lawn of the main house. Diana was in a fully reclined lawn chair, wearing a bathing suit showing off a disgustingly tan body, talking in a low murmur on a portable phone from the house. She glanced up almost guiltily at Summer. "No, she's not here," Diana said into the receiver. "She went to work."

A pause while Diana listened, eyeing Summer's outfit pityingly.

"The Crab 'n' Conch, from the look of the uniform she was wearing," Diana told the telephone. "Yes, she looked very cute in the uniform." Rolled eyes.

Summer gave a little wave.

Diana returned her attention to her mother, a somewhat shrill voice in the phone, long distance from Ohio. "Sorry, what did you just say?"

"I asked if Summer likes the room."

"The room? The room. Oh, well, she decided she didn't want to stay in the room."

"What are you talking about, Diana?" Her mother was using her dangerous I-suspect-you've-been-up-to-something voice.

"You know what happened? She saw the stilt house and absolutely fell in love. *Her* words—'fell in love.' So she's staying out there."

Diana held the phone several inches away from her ear, anticipating the response.

"Little Summer is out in that pile of rotting wood?" Mallory shrieked.

"I know, I was surprised too," Diana said blandly. "Different people have different tastes, I guess."

"You *guess*? Why do I have the feeling you had something to do with this?"

Diana tried her best to sound outraged, but she hadn't been expecting the phone call and was unprepared. "Me? Why would I have anything to do with Summer being out in the stilt house?"

"I don't want to go into this over the phone, Diana. Just get your cousin moved into the house."

"I think she actually does prefer it out there," Diana said stubbornly. "She's kind of a private person."

"Uh-huh. I have a pretty good idea who the private person is behind this," Mallory said.

Diana offered no response. Giving her mother the silent treatment was often the most effective thing to do. Then Diana noticed with a shock that Summer hadn't left yet. She was still standing a discreet distance away, looking as if she wanted to talk to Diana.

Oh, man, had Summer been able to overhear? Maybe not—the gardener at the house next door was running electric hedge clippers. Diana hoped she hadn't heard.

"Well, what's done is done, I guess," Mallory said in Diana's ear. "But there is one thing I absolutely insist on."

"What's that?" Diana asked guardedly.

"Get someone down to make that stilt house livable. Get her a decent bed, at least. You can move the one out of the guest room. And have someone make any other repairs. Call what's-his-name. The old man."

"Mr. Warner?" Diana suppressed a smile. Mr. Warner was Seth's grandfather. Seth worked for him during the summer. She liked Seth—it was almost impossible not to. He was a little like Summer in that way. The two of them should get together. They would represent more concentrated wholesomeness than existed anywhere else in the Keys.

"Yes," Mallory said, breaking into Diana's cynical reverie. "I want that stilt house made fit for a human being. Summer's mother would kill me if she saw where her daughter is living."

"Okay," Diana said. "I'll call Mr. Warner right away. Bye." She pressed the disconnect button and put down the phone.

Well, the situation wasn't ideal. Ideal would have been scaring Summer all the way back to Minnesota. But at least this way she wouldn't really be a part of Diana's daily life.

"Diana?" Summer came back over and stood in front of Diana.

"Uh-huh? Don't you have to get to work?" Diana asked. "Black fishnets with running shoes?"

"That's the uniform," Summer said, blushing a little. "I have kind of a stupid question to ask you. I mean, maybe it's stupid, I don't know."

"What is it?"

"Well, I went to this party last night. You know, over at the Merrick estate?"

"So?"

"Well, it's just that you used to go out with Adam."

Diana's heart skipped several beats. What did Summer know about that? Had Adam actually told her something? "Used to," she said guardedly.

Summer dug her toe into the grass awkwardly. She stared down at the ground, looked up, smiled her big smile, then looked down at the ground again. "It's just that, what would you think if he was going out with someone else?"

"I guess I'd have to think something like 'life goes on,'" Diana said, sounding much cooler than she felt. In fact, her heart was pounding at near-panic intensity.

"So you don't mind if, like, I—"

"*You?* You and Adam?"

"I don't have to if it would upset you," Summer said quickly.

"Why should it upset me?" Diana asked. "It's all in the past." All of it. In the past.

"Cool," Summer said. Again the smile. "I'd better get going. Don't want to be late my first day of work."

"Have fun."

Summer trotted off across the grass, hurrying to make up for lost time.

Summer and Adam. Adam and Ross.

Diana shuddered and tried to thrust away the memory. It had all happened last summer, a year ago, a long time. And Ross had been doing a lot of drugs back then. A lot. And everyone said he'd calmed down quite a bit, had spent six months in rehab.

Nothing to worry about. Summer was a big girl. She could take care of herself.

In which case Summer would have Adam, Diana

realized with a wrenching feeling that brought a grimace to her face.

And if Summer *couldn't* take care of herself?

"Not my problem," Diana told herself firmly. "I didn't even want her here."

"Hey, everybody, this is Summer Smith!" Marquez announced in a brassy yell that managed to carry over the roar of the dishwashing machine, the clash of plates, the pounding of knives on cutting boards, and a radio that was blaring salsa music. "She's a new waitress."

"Poor kid," another waitress remarked.

"She have a boyfriend?" the dishwasher yelled.

"Yeah, *me*," the smaller of the two male cooks replied, laughing.

"She doesn't date outside her species, Paulie," Marquez shot back.

"Good one, Marquez," offered a female cook with a nearly shaved head and a long tail of hair down the back. "She don't need none of what passes for males around here."

"Wait a minute, Skeet, *you* pass for male around here," the taller, cuter cook said.

The woman named Skeet Frisbeed a slice of tomato at him.

Marquez took Summer's arm. "The tall one who

thinks he's funny is J.T. The stupid-looking one is Paulie, and that's Skeet."

"We may be stupid, but we have knives," J.T. said. "So you have to obey us in all things. Just pick up your food when it's hot and we won't have to hurt you."

Skeet and Paulie both laughed.

"Ignore them," Marquez said. "Cooks are all crazy."

They stepped out of the loud, boisterous, and brightly lit kitchen into the dining room, an area as big as a football field with what looked to Summer like a thousand tables.

"Okay," Marquez announced, "so you read the employee manual, right?"

"Yes, last night." Summer yawned.

"Cool, now forget everything in the manual. All that stuff is bull. Just follow me around and I'll teach you what to do."

"Thanks."

"Don't thank me," Marquez said, laughing. "You're my slave for the day, honey. Good thing, too, because I'm beat. I'm all sore, especially my legs from dancing."

Summer nodded. "Now what?"

"Well, we've done our setup work, we've introduced you to everyone. Now we stand around and wait till the customers start to show up. And while we're doing that, we gossip. Like you tell me more about Adam."

"Today I asked Diana if it was okay for me to go out with him," Summer said.

Marquez nodded. "That was a stand-up thing to do. I have this guy I was seeing for a long time. We just broke up a couple weeks ago, and I don't know if I'd want my cousin going out with him. What did Diana say?"

"She said she didn't care because it was all in the past."

Marquez nodded. "Yeah, she's right. Past is past."

"Tell me about this guy. The one you were going with?"

Marquez sighed. "He was okay, I guess. Only, he was screwed up in the head. His family is totally screwed up. I mean, like his mom is completely weird."

"Why did you break up?"

"Found out he was going out behind my back."

"With another girl?" Summer asked.

Marquez rolled her eyes. "Actually, it wasn't any-one, that I know of. It's just that he suddenly says he's not happy and wants to start seeing other girls. The jerk."

"Wait, so now you don't see this guy anymore?"

"I see him around," Marquez said with a shrug. "It's J.T., okay?"

"The cook? The tall one?"

"Yeah, that's him."

"But neither of you acted like . . ."

"Hey, we're at work, right? We have to deal with it, so we both act like it's no big deal."

Summer noticed a waitress crossing the dining room toward them, swinging her petite hips through the close-packed tables with practiced ease. Her red hair was swept back in a ponytail held in place with bright scrunchies.

Lianne.

"Hi, Marquez," Lianne said.

"Hey, Lianne. Back to the grind, huh?" Marquez said.

"Just like last summer," Lianne said. "This place hasn't changed. You have, though. You look wonderful, Marquez. I love your hair."

Marquez nodded noncommittally. "You two met at the party last night, right?"

"We didn't actually meet," Lianne said. She flashed a killer smile at Summer. "I was so excited to see Seth again, it was hard to concentrate on anything else. It's been *days*."

"Uh-huh. Well, Summer, meet Lianne, and vice versa. Lianne waited tables here last summer, like me," Marquez explained.

"Summer? I think that is the most beautiful name," Lianne said. "It must be great. Every time anyone thinks of you they're going to think of sunshine and warm breezes. And you have the looks to go with the name."

Summer was a little taken aback. Lianne seemed very sweet. "Thanks," Summer said, feeling flustered because she couldn't think of a way to return the compliment.

"I've heard of you, you know," Lianne said. "From Diana. She and I are good friends."

"Still?" Marquez said skeptically.

Lianne looked sad. "We *have* grown apart, I'm afraid. I suppose Diana has outgrown me." She made a wistful, bleak smile. For a moment Summer thought Lianne might actually cry.

"Diana has outgrown everyone," Marquez said.

Lianne put on a brave face and directed her smile at Summer. "Anyway, now I feel like I have a new friend. At least I hope we'll be friends, Summer."

"Sure," Summer blurted.

"Well, happy happy, joy joy," Marquez said dryly. She peered across the dining room and became more serious. "Okay, we have a party of two. We call that a deuce. Deuce, three-top, four-top, et cetera. Pour two glasses of water, Summer. Gossip time just ended."

Marquez took off and Summer started after her. But then she felt a hand on her arm, holding her back.

Lianne pitched her voice low, so no one else would hear. "Summer, since we are going to be friends, I should just warn you about one thing. It's Seth. I know he's pretending like we broke up, but we didn't. Seth has a little problem with the truth sometimes. And if you get in the middle, you're just going to get hurt, because Seth really does love me."

"I'm not in the middle of anything," Summer said stiffly.

"Good," Lianne said. She exhibited a brilliant smile that never reached her eyes. "Seth may not be perfect, but he's all I have."

14

The Mysteries of Paint

"My feet hurt." Summer was practically limping through the town, across mostly empty streets baked by the terrifying late-afternoon sun.

Marquez had volunteered to take her shopping for a few necessities that the stilt house lacked, like towels and toilet paper and food. But first they had to change out of their uniforms, which smelled of cocktail sauce and cigarette smoke. That meant walking from the restaurant to Marquez's house and then to Summer's house, all on painful feet and pavement that was approximately the same temperature as the surface of the sun. Marquez said she might be able to borrow her parents' car for the rest of the trip.

"My feet hurt too," Marquez said, "but you'll get used to it. At least it isn't hot out."

"It isn't?"

Marquez grinned. "It's only early June. Now, August . . ." She laughed an evil laugh. "August afternoons, I've seen people burst into flames."

"You have not."

"If you say so. All I'm saying is, don't wear polyester—that burns too fast. Come on, we're almost there."

"There" turned out to be a genteelly seedy three-story building just off the main drag. The bottom floor had once been a store. It still had a huge plate-glass window with a faded, old-fashioned sign painted on it.

"Ice Cream Parlor?" Summer read.

"Yeah, it used to be an ice cream parlor, back like fifty years ago. Upstairs was offices. My dad bought the building after he got settled in this country."

Marquez opened a side door that gave onto a narrow stairway. The entrance was made more narrow by the three bikes that were parked there. From up the stairs Summer could hear a TV or radio, the announcer speaking Spanish.

"My folks speak English too, but they like Spanish sometimes," Marquez explained, not exactly self-consciously, but as if she were waiting to see how Summer would react.

"So do you speak Spanish?" Summer asked.

"Sure. A little, anyway, just so I can talk with my grandma. My older brothers still speak it pretty well because some of them were older when we left Cuba. Well, here goes." Marquez opened a second door that led from the landing. "This is my room."

Summer stepped through the door and gasped. Then she laughed. Then she just stared, mouth hanging open. "This is your room?"

"Yeah. Different, huh?"

The room was huge, a vast, open space. Most of one wall was mirrored, with gleaming chrome shelves where Coke glasses and banana split dishes had once been stacked. Now the shelves held folded T-shirts and sweaters and shorts. Panties spilled out of a former hot fudge warmer. A menu on the wall showed the price of hot fudge sundaes as fifteen cents.

Down the middle of the room was the Formica-topped, chrome-trimmed bar, fronted by half a dozen stools bolted in place and upholstered with red plastic. The bar was cluttered with a boom box and a disorderly mess of CDs and at least a dozen spray cans of paint.

But the most amazing thing about the room was the walls. They were bare brick—or had once been bare. Now they were coated an inch thick with wild graffiti, words a foot tall in places. There were strangely beautiful pictures, like murals, showing dazzling mountain scenes and rain forests and sunrises. In one corner of the room a palm tree had been painted all the way up the high wall, with fanned branches spreading out across a corner of the ceiling.

"You like my tree? Don't even have to water it," Marquez joked.

"Marquez. This. Is. The most *amazing* room I've ever seen. This is so excellent. This is so far past just being cool. This is a whole new planet of coolness."

"I'm glad you like it," Marquez said. "If you didn't like it, we couldn't be friends."

"Like it? It's a total work of art. You're an artist."

"No, it's just playing-around art. I got this room because I'm the only girl," Marquez said. "I have five brothers. My older brothers got rooms with views of the water, and my younger brothers share a room whenever my older brothers are around, which they are only sometimes." She counted off on her fingers. "Tony is in the army and he's in Germany. Miguel and Raoul are in college, only they're home for the summer now. Ronnie is going into tenth grade and he's a monster, and George is going to start eighth."

"How come everyone got Spanish names except Ronnie and George?" Summer asked. "Is it okay if I ask that?" She was still walking around, head tilted back, taking in the amazing details.

"Sure, why not? Ronnie and George were the first ones born in this country. So they got named after, guess who? *Ronald* Reagan and *George* Bush."

Summer smiled. "You guys sound so interesting. I mean, escaping from Cuba and this room and all. My family is so boring. Plus five brothers. I never had any siblings. You know, except for Jonathan, and like I said, I never knew him except from some pictures."

"Have a seat on the bed," Marquez said, nodding toward the king-size bed in front of the curtained shop window. "I just want to change out of this uniform and we can go."

Summer sat and let her eyes wander over the walls. Much of the graffiti was names. Names of TV stars and musicians, names of fictional characters from books, names that could be anyone. And what could only be called thoughts or slogans.

"'J.T.,'" Summer read out loud. "Is that the same J.T.?" The letters were about three feet tall, red and rimmed with black so they stood out as though they were three-dimensional.

"Yeah, that's him." Marquez was stripping off her uniform, showing none of the modesty Summer would have, even in front of another girl.

"I would have thought you'd paint over it."

"No, that's not the way it works. Once something goes on the wall, it never gets deliberately painted over.

Maybe over time, months and months or whatever, a little gets covered here, and a little more there until it's almost all gone. But you can't just wipe out the past."

Summer grinned. "Very deep."

Marquez laughed. "You probably didn't know I was so philosophical, right?"

Summer was about to ask whether she would eventually be invited to add her name to the wall. To be added and never deliberately erased or painted over. A strange kind of immortality, like something permanent left behind when she left Crab Claw Key.

"Ready?" Marquez asked. She had slipped on a tube top and shorts. "I'm ready to shop. Our car's out front. Let me just run upstairs and see if we can take it."

Diana saw them pull into the driveway in the Marquez family's huge, aging Oldsmobile. She was upstairs assembling a pile of washcloths, towels, and sheets to carry down to the stilt house. It was a shame Summer was home so early. It would have been better to have everything done. Diana was prepared to comply with her mother's orders to make the stilt house comfortable. She just didn't want to be seen acting generous.

Summer was wearing her absurd uniform. Marquez was dressed like a slut, as usual. As they got out of the car they both started giggling, sharing some joke.

Diana felt a stab of jealousy. At this moment Summer was already more a part of life on Crab Claw Key than Diana, though Diana had lived here most of her life. Summer had a job, a friend—probably a boyfriend, soon, if Adam really was interested in her.

Diana remembered when her own life had been more that way. When there had been friends, boyfriends, reasons to start giggling over nothing.

Diana headed down the stairs and caught up with them as they were heading down the lawn toward the stilt house.

"Hey, Summer," Diana said.

Summer and Marquez turned.

"Hey, Di-*Anne*," Marquez said.

"Hello, *Maria*," Diana answered. She hated when people mispronounced her name. Almost as much as Marquez hated being called Maria. "So nice to see you again. I was afraid that now that I've graduated, I wouldn't see you anymore. Terrified, in fact."

"I've been thinking about you, Di-*anne*. See, I heard this guy was found dead over on the new side, right? And there were these two little holes in his neck, and all the blood had been drained out of him, so naturally, I thought of you right away."

"Amusing as always, Maria. Those paint fumes in your room blurring your vision again? Or is there some other reason for the way you're dressed?" Diana turned quickly to Summer before Marquez could come up with a reply. "I just wanted to tell you, before you go down to the stilt house, that someone's there."

Summer's response was surprising. Her face went blank and her eyes grew wide. "No, there isn't," she said quickly.

"Yes, there is," Diana said.

Summer shook her head almost violently. "There's no one there that I know about, and I would know, right? If you found something there that looked like there was someone there, then maybe it was something of mine and just looked like somebody else's."

Diana looked at Marquez. "Did you understand that?"

Marquez shook her head, equally puzzled.

"Summer, let me try it more slowly this time." Diana sighed. "Seth Warner is down at the stilt house. He's doing some work on it, fixing it up."

"*Seth!* Oh, Seth," Summer said, looking inexplicably relieved. "Seth. Okay, Seth is down there. Not anyone else though, right?"

"Who were you expecting?" Diana asked sourly. "Adam?"

"No, I'm not supposed to be seeing him till tomorrow night."

Summer and Marquez started again for the stilt

house and Diana fell in step behind them, still carrying her gift of towels.

Summer found the house looking strange. Water was dripping from the eaves and from the railing and was puddling on the deck, though it hadn't been raining. Plus, something was missing.

"The bird crap!" Summer said. "It's gone." The pelican was sitting on his usual corner but was looking disgruntled. "Frank, you okay?"

"Frank?" Diana asked.

"Um, well, that's what I call him," Summer said quickly. "You know, just a name I made up."

Summer stepped over a toolbox and paint-splattered canvas drop cloth.

From inside the house there was the sound of a radio or stereo playing. The Breeders. And a male voice was singing along, changing the lyrics. "I'm just looking for the div-i-ne paintbrush. One div-i-ne paintbrush. I'd brush it all day. . . ."

Instantly, as if on command, the three girls froze and fell silent. Marquez raised one eyebrow, playfully suggestive. She quietly opened the toolbox and extracted a hammer.

Stifling giggles, they tiptoed to the door.

"One divine paintbrush, one div-i-ine paintbrush . . ."

Diana opened the door. Seth was standing on a

short ladder, his bare shoulders splattered with little drops of white paint, wearing shorts and work boots. He was using a roller to apply paint to the ceiling.

"We couldn't find the divine paintbrush," Diana said.

"But we have the divine hammer," Marquez said, holding it up.

"That was just the DJ singing along," Seth said lamely.

"Oh. I believe that," Marquez said. "Don't you believe that, Diana? Even though it's a CD, not the radio."

"I didn't know Mr. Moon could sing," Diana said. "I knew he had other attributes, but I didn't know he could sing."

Seth climbed down off the ladder and rested his roller in the paint pan. "Okay, I'll ask you again, Diana, what will it take to get that picture from you? And the negative, too."

Summer noticed the paint splats on his skin. Some had dried already, and the effect made the skin itself look soft and warm.

"I thought I'd give that picture to Summer," Diana said. "She could hang it on these nice white walls."

Summer blushed as badly as Seth did.

"The two of you, you're both so sweet," Marquez said. "Look at them blush."

"So is white paint okay? It's off-white, actually," Seth said to Summer, clearly trying to change the subject.

"It looks great," Summer said coolly. There had to be other people who could do this work. So why was Seth there?

"I did the walls earlier, so they're almost dry. Then I hosed off the outside, and I figured I might as well start on the ceiling. And there's the bed," Seth said, pointing, as if a new double bed could somehow be invisible in the small room. He seemed to be trying very hard to act professional. "You want to get rid of the old one?"

Summer looked inquiringly at Diana. Had this repair and cleanup work been Diana's idea?

Diana shrugged. "I thought since you *insisted* on staying down here instead of staying in the main house that at least we could improve things a little. So I called Mallory and asked her if I could have the place fixed up for you."

"That was awfully nice of you," Summer said dubiously. She wasn't normally a skeptical person, but Diana's story sounded slightly unlikely. That morning it had sounded as if Aunt Mallory was yelling at Diana on the phone.

Seth laughed. "Yeah, and then Diana's mom called my grandfather long distance and said we should do the work regardless of what Diana said or did to stop us."

"Must be the paint fumes, Seth," Diana said without much sincerity. "You obviously misunderstood."

"You're getting a new paint job, bird crap removal, and some new flooring in the bathroom and the kitchen," Seth told Summer. "You can come with me and pick out the tile after I get cleaned up. If you'd like. You don't have to, but you could have your choice, and there's lots of kinds of tile. Also we're going to run cable down from the house." He put a finger to his lips. "Only don't tell anyone about that, because it isn't exactly legal."

From outside came the sound of a boat motor, loud at first, then gentling to an idle. A horn sounded.

"Anyone home?" a voice called.

"That sounds like Adam," Summer said. Her heart began beating very fast.

Again she felt an inexplicable sense of guilt. As though there was something wrong in letting Seth know she was seeing Adam. Or the reverse.

"*Is* that Adam's voice?" Marquez asked Diana, batting her eyes provocatively.

Diana said nothing. Summer opened the door and went outside. A large motorboat had nosed under the house. Behind it trailed the two Jet Skis, bobbing on the wake.

"Adam?" Summer called, but he was concealed from view beneath the house. She went back inside as the floor hatch opened and Adam climbed up, smiling his seductive, mocking, maximum-power smile, until his eyes fell on Diana. Something dark and unfathomable passed between Adam and Diana.

"Hi," Adam said, in a general sort of way. Then, "Hi, Summer."

Summer saw his eyes dart to Diana again and then away. Diana crossed her arms coolly. No matter what Diana said, there was something powerful between the two of them. Some potent, disturbing emotion that Summer couldn't read.

"I was going to ask what had happened to the Jet Skis," Diana said. "I noticed they were gone."

"They left them at my place," Adam said curtly. "Seth, my man, what's up?"

"Just doing some work. You've heard of work, right?"

The two guys were eyeing each other warily, Summer noticed, but without hostility.

"I may have heard something about it," Adam said, smiling good-naturedly at the sort of teasing he'd obviously heard many times before. "Work. Yes, I think one of the servants may have mentioned it once. Speaking of which, want to give me a hand getting those skis tied off?"

Seth headed below with Adam.

Marquez shook her head. "You are something, Summer," she said.

"What? What do you mean?"

"You just breeze into town and already you've got two A-list guys interested in you," Marquez said. "Not that either of them is my type, so what do I care."

"No, your type would be more the slightly deranged, mentally unstable type, *Maria*," Diana said with surprising intensity.

"I don't think either of them is interested in me," Summer protested weakly. "I *know* Seth isn't," she lied. "He has a girlfriend. Maybe Adam . . . Oh, you guys are just teasing me."

"Are you blind?" Marquez demanded in a loud whisper. "Of course Seth is interested in you. Didn't you see that little guy thing between him and Adam?"

"You're crazy," Summer said, a little too forcefully.

"Seth is a nice guy," Diana said, almost to herself. She chewed a fingernail.

Marquez sent Summer a significant look. "Oh, *Seth* is a nice guy, huh? As opposed to Adam? Hmmmm."

Diana narrowed her eyes and seemed to snap back to the present. "Shut up, *Maria*. It's totally over between me and Adam. Just because you can't get over J.T. doesn't mean I have the same problem."

"I repeat—hmmmm."

The hatch in the floor opened, and Adam emerged, followed by Seth. For a moment they formed a single picture, framed against the dark opening. Seth thinner, perhaps a little taller. Adam darker, more muscular. It was amazing to think that they *were* interested in her, Summer thought. Amazing and disturbing in a way, like maybe it was all some elaborate practical joke.

"So what are you girls up to?" Adam asked.

Marquez answered. "Summer and I were going to do some shopping in town, or else drive down to Key West and hit some stores there."

"Cool," Adam said. "Why don't I give you a lift down to Key West in the boat? It's as fast as driving there, and no traffic."

"Um, look, um, Summer," Seth began, "if you want to look at some tiles, you know . . ." He let the question peter out and made a wry face. "Let's see. Go to the hardware store to look at tiles or boat down to Key West. Wow, tough choice."

"Actually," Summer said, a little too quickly, "Marquez and I are going shopping for girl-type stuff, so it should probably be just a girl trip."

"Yeah, besides, guys don't know how to shop," Marquez said, picking up on Summer's hint.

"Diana, would you come with us?" Summer asked.

"What are you shopping for?" Adam asked suspiciously. "I know how to shop just fine."

"Let's see," Marquez said, "what was on our list?" She began counting off on her fingers. "Oh, yeah, makeup and shampoo, and of course lots of tampons."

"Oh. You know, we could look at tiles another day," Seth said quickly.

"The thing is, I just remembered I have to get home," Adam said just as quickly. "But I'll pick you up tomorrow evening, Summer, okay?"

"And I'll be by to finish the painting tomorrow," Seth said.

"I can drop you at the dock," Adam offered to Seth.

"Cool. Later, everyone."

"That worked pretty well," Diana said when the two guys had escaped down through the hatch. "Nothing like the word *tampon* for clearing guys away. What are you two really shopping for?"

"Whatever," Marquez said.

"Come with us, Diana," Summer said again.

"I don't think so," Diana said.

"Doesn't want to be seen with the riffraff," Marquez muttered.

Summer took Diana's hand. Something made Summer feel Diana wanted to go with them. "Come on. You have to come."

"Well, if I have to," Diana said testily. "If I *have* to, I guess I will."

15

Purchases

SUMMER

(using the spending money her parents gave her)

BufPufs

Sea Breeze

Hawaiian Tropic SPF 8–10

Dove soap

Generic disposable razors (5 pack)

Bare Assets two-piece bathing suit

Pepperidge Farm raisin bread

Skippy Extra Chunky

Oreos

Milk 1% fat

2 Dannon yogurts (blueberry and raspberry)

Ben & Jerry's Cherry Garcia frozen
  yogurt
Jiffy Pop
Advil
Breeders CD
July issue of *Seventeen*
TOTAL: $90.14

MARQUEZ
(*using the tip money from the lunch shift*)
Express Ltd. white denim shorts (on
  sale)
Snickers bar
TOTAL: $19.55

DIANA
(*using her mother's Visa Gold Card*)
Lancôme Bienfait Total
Jean Paul Gaultier bra top and sarong
  skirt
Abe Hamilton linen gauze dress
Crest Fresh Mint Gel
July issue of *Seventeen*
TOTAL: $532.35

16

Summer's Heinous Truths and Diana's Little Pills

"Your calves are not chunky, for heaven's sake," Marquez said, throwing her hands up in exasperation. "Your little Minnesota calves are perfect. You have the calves of Hillary Duff. And she's probably wanting them back."

Summer turned sideways to check the effect of her new bathing suit in Diana's full-length mirror. For the twentieth time. "But it does make my butt look huge."

"Your butt wouldn't look huge if you stuffed a pair of beach balls back there," Marquez said, thoroughly disgusted. She slapped her own rear end, barely contained within the very short shorts she'd bought. "Now, *this* is a big butt."

Diana emerged from the bathroom, wearing the white gauze dress she'd bought for more than the cost of Summer's entire wardrobe. She stood thoughtfully in front of the mirror and looked at herself critically.

"Don't *you* even start," Marquez warned.

"It looks okay," Diana allowed.

"For what it cost it should look okay," Marquez said.

Diana nodded. "We used to not have any money back when I was in junior high. Before Mallory started writing her trashy books, back when it was just my dad trying to support us. So I've done the life-on-a-budget thing." She made a wry smile. "Lose a father, gain really good clothes."

"Is that why your parents broke up?" Summer asked.

"Who knows," Diana said. "That's what most of the arguments were about. That and sex."

Summer winced. "They talked about that in front of you?"

"No. They just talked in very loud voices so that even people who lived on the next block got to hear."

"Gross," Summer said, making a face.

Marquez flopped back on Diana's bed. She rummaged in the package of Oreos Summer had bought and twisted one open. "Truth or dare?" she said suddenly.

"Forget it," Diana said flatly. "If you two start

that junior high stuff, I'll kick you both out."

"I can't believe you haven't kicked us out already, Diana," Marquez said. "Is this like reverse PMS or something? Your hormones are making you be nice?"

"Don't put your shoes on the bedspread, *Maria*."

Marquez grinned, threw back the covers, and stuck her shoes under the sheet. "This better?"

"Are you *trying* to annoy me?"

"Come on, you guys," Summer said, "don't fight." It was a phrase she'd had to use at least half a dozen times during their shopping excursion. And though Diana and Marquez had sniped at each other in one store and out another, Diana had seemed happier than she had since Summer had arrived in Florida. She'd been almost giddy at times.

But since they'd returned home, Diana's mood seemed to have grown darker. It was as if she was making up for the fact that she'd had a good time.

"Okay, truth or dare," Diana said suddenly, her eyes lighting up. "For you, Summer."

Summer sat down on Diana's desk chair and put her hands on her knees. "Truth, I guess. But throw me an Oreo first, Marquez." She hoped Diana wasn't going to ask her about Adam.

"Good. Here's the question, and I want the truth." Diana was fixing on her with way too much intensity. "Why did you come down here?"

Summer sighed with relief. "Because it sounded cool. I mean, the beach and everything."

"Yeah, yeah, but why, really?" Diana pressed. She was standing over Summer, looking simultaneously imperious and very much like an angel in her gauzy dress.

"That's it. When your mom called my mom I was having this terrible day. I was freezing—which is pretty much every day in the winter in Minnesota—and my friend Jennifer was going away to California for the summer, and this guy, this jerk named Sean Valletti who I thought I had a crush on, had started going out with this other girl just because she has massive . . . Never mind."

"What did Mallory tell you?" Diana pressed. "Didn't she tell you that I was being a pain or something?"

Marquez jumped in. "Why would she have to tell Summer that? Everyone who knows you knows you're a pain, Diana."

"Diana, what are you saying?" Summer asked. "You think this was some kind of a conspiracy or something?" Summer would have laughed, only Diana looked so serious.

"I *know* what Mallory was thinking. I'm just wondering if she told you."

Summer shook her head solemnly. "No one told me anything. Why? Is something the matter?"

Diana looked nonplussed. She shook her head distractedly. "Oh, my mom, I mean, Mallory, thinks I'm depressed or using drugs or something. She wanted you to come down and cheer me up, because she can't be bothered to worry about me herself."

"*Are* you depressed?" Summer asked.

"Of course not," Diana said quickly. Her words gathered momentum. "Why would I be depressed? I'm *not* depressed. Besides, it's none of your business, Summer. Believe it or not, we all had lives going on here even before you showed up."

There was a shocked silence.

Diana took a deep breath. "Sorry. I have this headache."

Summer shook her head and sent Marquez a sad look. She held out an Oreo for Diana. "Here, don't be depressed."

"I'm not depressed," Diana snapped. "It's not like I'm lying awake at night thinking about ways to kill myself."

For several seconds her statement hung in the air between them, and no one spoke. They had all three heard something false, something ragged and raw in Diana's voice.

"Okay, my turn," Marquez said, breaking the silence. "Also for you, Summer. Truth or dare?"

"Truth. I don't trust you with a dare." The moment

was past. Maybe it had never even occurred. How could she hope to read Diana's thoughts? Summer asked herself. She barely knew her cousin.

"You're a smart girl," Marquez told Summer. "Never trust me with a dare. Here's the question. Are you really as sweet as you seem or is there some dark, twisted inner core of hostility inside you?"

Summer laughed. "Definitely dark and twisted."

"Oh, there is not," Marquez said. "If you were really dark and twisted, like a certain person in this room who shall remain nameless but whose name rhymes with banana, you'd never admit it."

Diana managed a wistful smile. "That's right."

"I'm not totally sweet," Summer said defensively.

"Sure. Right." Marquez grinned expectantly.

"I'm *not*." Summer was beginning to get annoyed. *Sweet* was something she'd left behind in Bloomington.

"Okay, then prove it. What's the sleaziest, most heinous thing you've ever done?"

Summer thought frantically. Marquez and Diana were both eyeing her doubtfully, waiting for her to admit that she couldn't think of anything. "Do dreams count? Because I have great dreams. And I usually remember them."

"No way," Marquez said. "If dreams counted, I'd be arrested."

"How about this?" Summer said with sudden defiance. "I kissed a total stranger once." She saw Marquez dart a glance at Diana. Oh, no, Marquez was thinking of Adam! "Actually, it happened twice," Summer said quickly, "and the first time was the most heinous." She hoped Marquez would get the message.

She did. "Drunk or sober?" Marquez asked.

"Sober. So I had no excuse. I just let him kiss me. It was in a photo booth."

Marquez shrugged. "That's not heinous, Summer. It sounds like fun."

"It was heinous enough," Summer said. But clearly neither girl was impressed. "Okay, fine. Try this. I let a guy spend the night with me."

Marquez and Diana both snapped to attention.

"I mean, we didn't do *it* or anything. It wasn't like that," Summer said quickly.

Both Marquez and Diana relaxed.

"Actually, he kind of spent the night outside my room." On the deck over her roof, to be exact, and nothing whatsoever had happened between them. He wasn't even interested, because it would disturb his *wa*, whatever that meant. But there was no reason to tell that to these two.

"So, some guy slept outside your room in Minnesota? Hope it wasn't winter," Diana said.

"No, it was summer," Summer said evasively. She

wasn't ready to tell anyone about Diver. Or Seth.

But she couldn't help wondering that the only remotely heinous events she could think of happened during the few days she'd been in Florida.

Marquez sighed and shook her head in disappointment. "Well, that was pretty heinous, Summer. I'm horrified. Aren't you horrified, Diana? Call 911."

"It was the most terrible thing I've ever heard," Diana said. "I don't know how I'll ever be able to sleep tonight."

Summer stewed resentfully. Maybe if she could have told them all the details, that the first guy had a girl-friend already. Ha! Or that the second guy was totally awesomely cute. That he never wore any real clothes. That he appeared in her bedroom while she was asleep. That he talked to pelicans . . . no, that wouldn't help.

"Fine, now it's *my* turn," Summer said. "For you, Marquez. Truth or dare?"

"Dare."

"No, say truth, I don't have a dare," Summer said.

"Okay, truth."

"I want to know two things. Why did you break up with J.T., and were you doing it with him?" Ha, that would show Marquez. Maybe she wasn't heinous, but she could ask heinous questions.

"It?" Marquez repeated with a slow drawl. "What can you possibly mean by *it*?"

"Just answer the question."

Marquez put her hand over her heart. "I am still a virgin, if that's what you mean." She batted her eyes. "Why did I break up with J.T.? Because he's crazy, I told you."

"Crazy is kind of vague," Diana offered.

Marquez shrugged. "Okay. Okay. Fine." She stood up, evidently enjoying being the center of attention. "See, he got cut pretty bad at work, right? This is like three weeks ago, right? Maybe a month. Some of the cooks were screwing around throwing knives like idiots, which is what cooks are. So he's gushing out blood from his neck and they rush him to the hospital and they're saying he may need a blood transfusion, right? He didn't, but that doesn't matter."

"It doesn't?" Summer asked.

Marquez waved her off impatiently. "No, it doesn't matter. Anyway, his mom is there by this time. So they're going to use her blood if it's compatible. Only it isn't. And his dad gets there, and they check him, and *his* blood isn't right, either."

"So?" Summer asked.

"So? So it turns out J.T.'s parents aren't his parents. He's adopted. He finds this out while he's lying there bleeding." Marquez shook her head sadly. She was no longer pretending to enjoy the story. Her voice grew softer, till it was hard to hear her. "I guess he couldn't handle it. After that he started getting weirder. At first I thought it was because he got cut so bad. I mean, he said while he was unconscious he was having all these visions and things. Anyway, he got distant and wouldn't talk about anything. Then he tells me out of the blue that he wants to see other girls." Marquez flopped back onto the bed.

Summer was sorry she'd asked. Marquez was so down now, and she'd been so happy. "This is a stupid game," she said.

Marquez made a noise deep in her throat and wiped at a tear. "Don't worry, Summer. It isn't your fault."

Diana looked almost as depressed as Marquez. And the mood was hard to shake off.

"Great. Now we're all feeling lousy," Marquez said. "There's only one way to get over this. Diana, we need some entertainment."

"What?" Summer asked, ready for any help.

"Ah, yes, Maria," Diana said. "I'll get my photo album."

"I don't know, Diana," Marquez said. "Summer may be too sweet."

"I am *not* sweet," Summer said. "Besides, what does looking at pictures have to do with being too sweet? Pictures are . . . Oh. *That* picture."

֍

After they had gone, Diana lay in her bed, holding the photo. Not the infamous one of poor Seth, but the picture she had taken of Adam. In it he was just waking up, looking confused, with his hair tousled, one eye closed. In the photo, taken aboard his father's yacht, he looked vulnerable, something he never looked the rest of the time. He'd been water-skiing earlier in the day, and the sun and exercise had made him sleepy. Diana had gone below and spent an hour just watching him sleep, while up on deck the usual loud Merrick family party was under way.

She remembered the moment perfectly, every detail. How she had silently wound her camera and taken shot after shot of Adam sleeping, curled in a ball on the narrow bunk. She had kissed him ever so gently on the lips, and, as he had awakened, taken the last shot on the roll.

That had been two days before the last day with Adam.

She had developed the film a week after. She had taken scissors and cut each of the other pictures into tiny pieces and burned the pieces in a trash can, causing an awful, oily smoke.

She had saved this one picture. She hadn't been able to destroy it.

Summer had seen the picture an hour before, and

Diana had easily read the look in her eyes, the interest. Summer had looked guilty, realizing somehow that this picture meant something to Diana.

Was that why Diana had shown it to her? Was that why she had spent the afternoon shopping with Summer, and hanging out with Summer? So that she could find a way to let Summer know how she still felt about Adam?

Diana put the picture back and hugged the album to her chest.

She had tried to bury those feelings. She had wanted to forget the sick mixture of love and contempt, desire and betrayal. But Adam had gone after Summer and stirred the feelings up again.

Diana got up, set the album aside, and walked down the hall, down the curving staircase to her mother's wing of the house. Through the ludicrous *Gone with the Wind* bedroom with its canopied bed and frills. To the vast bathroom, with the oversize marble tub raised on a platform and surrounded by lush plants. Mallory had had herself photographed there in the tub, just her head and shoulders visible through discreet clouds of bubble bath. Printed in *Romantic Times* magazine, the photo was supposedly a portrait of the romance author dreaming up her newest hero.

Diana opened the medicine cabinet. The bottle was still there, on the middle shelf. Twenty-three pills. She spilled them into her palm and counted them again. Yes, twenty-three. More than enough.

She could do it tonight. The maid would find her in the morning. Her mother would have to rush home from her tour.

Where? At the bottom of the stairs, perhaps, dramatically sprawled there? On her mother's bed? And the note—should she leave a note? A note telling the world what had happened that night, one year ago, at the estate of the famous and wealthy Merrick clan?

Not tonight, Diana decided. She was due to go to the center tomorrow. Lanessa would be expecting her. Lanessa, the helpless little girl who couldn't even speak of what had been done to her.

Diana put the pills carefully back in the bottle, returned the bottle to the shelf, and closed the mirrored door.

17

Bubble Baths and Dreams of Sunrise

Summer was in the bathtub, lying with her head back, eyes closed, and a magazine hanging from one limp hand, when she heard the knock at the door. Her first thought was that it must be Diver. But Diver didn't knock. Diver just appeared.

Her second thought was that she wasn't going to answer it. It had been a long, tiring, emotional day. The hot water felt good. The white mountain of bubbles smelled like vanilla and melon.

Again the knock came, loud but not aggressive.

Summer sighed, which sent a little flurry of bubbles flying. "I'm coming!" she yelled grumpily.

She climbed out, wrapped her terry-cloth robe around her, and padded on wrinkled bare feet to the door. "Who is it?"

"It's Seth."

Summer's breath caught in her throat. She clutched the robe securely, cursing the fact that she'd lost the belt.

She opened the door. Seth was standing close, almost as if he'd had his nose pressed against the door. Summer was surprised by his nearness and clumsily backed away, waving her hand in a vague invitation to come inside.

Seth stepped past her. He looked at her, taking in the robe and the wet strands of her hair, and winced. "Oh, sorry. You were taking a shower, I guess."

"A bath, actually," Summer said.

"Be careful in there, by the way. The floor isn't in great shape."

"Is that what you came by to tell me?" Summer wasn't in the mood to be hospitable. She felt at a disadvantage, wearing only a robe.

"I was hoping I could, you know . . . talk to you. About . . . stuff." He swallowed hard, clearly unsure of what to say. "Is it okay if I sit down?"

"Seth, I'm kind of in the middle of taking a bath, and I'm tired, you know?"

Suddenly, as if he were being propelled by some

outside force, Seth came toward her. He put his hands on her upper arms and drew her close.

"No!" Summer pushed him away with a hand on his chest.

Seth looked stricken. "I just wanted to . . . I thought . . . everything was so perfect the other day, in the airport."

"What do you think you're doing?" Summer demanded.

"I just thought if we kissed again, that everything would be fine."

Summer almost laughed. "That's what you thought? Um, excuse me, but it isn't that easy."

He ran a hand through his hair. "I guess not. I guess not. Look, the thing is, I keep thinking about you. And today when you came back and I was here, it was the same feeling, like I couldn't forget you. Like you were all I could think about."

"Seth, we don't even know each other. All we did was kiss once."

"We talked at the party," he said.

"You told me I was losing control. That wasn't exactly talking. And, oh, by the way, the conversation ended when Lianne showed up."

"I couldn't help that," Seth said.

"It didn't look to me like you were trying to help that."

"What was I supposed to do? Shove her away and make a big scene in front of everyone? We may be broken up, but we were together for a long time and I'm not going to be mean suddenly. I don't *hate* her."

"Look, forget it. This is silly, this whole thing. We kissed, so what? You don't even know me."

He started to say something, then stopped himself. "Okay, maybe you're right. That doesn't change how I feel about you, though. Ever since that day in the airport . . . It's like, like something I can't explain, Summer. But there's just this feeling in my head that you're the one."

"What one?"

He shrugged and looked miserable. "I don't know. Fate or something. Like you and I belong together."

Summer swallowed hard. "Did you use this same line on Lianne?"

"No," he said. "I never felt this way about her."

"Yeah, right," Summer said weakly.

Silence fell between them.

"Sorry. I'm putting too much pressure on you, aren't I?"

"A little," Summer said. "I mean, look, you seem very nice, and we had this one kiss—"

"Two kisses," he interrupted.

"Even if it was ten, that doesn't mean we're anything special to each other," Summer said.

"So if that doesn't mean anything," Seth asked, "what does?"

"I don't know," Summer said softly. She felt worn out. Dead beat. She had the feeling she was winning an argument she didn't really want to win.

Again silence fell.

"All I want is a chance. I see you going with Adam and think I'll never even get a chance. And this is important to me." He hesitated again, then forged ahead in a flurry of words. "I know you think I'm nuts or just feeding you some line, but this feeling I have is so incredibly powerful and so real . . . I can't believe you don't feel it too. I can't believe the . . . that the walls aren't vibrating with it, that the . . . that the air around us doesn't just catch fire."

The air may not have caught fire, but a prickly blush began to crawl up Summer's neck. For a moment she *did* feel it—a feeling like gravity, like magnetism, a strange craving drawing her to him. The distance between them seemed to warp and shrink.

Summer made a noise like a whimper. It was a whimper, but she tried to disguise it with a cough.

"Summer, all I want is a chance. I'm not saying *don't* go out with Adam. I'd like to be able to say that," he added with a rueful half-smile, "but I know I don't have the right. Just don't shut me out, okay?"

"What does that mean?" Summer asked.

"It means give me a chance. You said we don't know each other, so let me get to know you better."

"Uh-huh, okay," Summer said. This at least was safer ground.

"Okay? Really?" he said. He looked awfully sweet when he smiled that way. "Look, we'll do something that isn't like a real date, okay?"

Summer almost laughed. "Maybe we could go pick out some tile together."

"Perfect! When?"

"I have to work tomorrow, and I told Marquez I'd hit the beach with her for a while. How about tomorrow evening? I'm free till around eight."

"Excellent. Excellent. What happens at eight? Oh. Adam, huh?" He digested the import of that. "That's okay. Come to my house, all right? My house is nearer the beach."

"Your house, after the beach. Now can I go back to my bath?"

"Sure. Only step lightly around that part of the floor where the linoleum is all cracked, okay?"

Summer put her hand over her heart. "I promise."

He seemed unable to stop grinning. "I'll just leave, then."

"Goodnight."

He started toward the door, practically dancing over to it.

"Just one thing," Summer said. "You're telling me the truth about you and Lianne, aren't you? It's really, really important."

He held up three fingers close together. "Scout's honor."

She laughed. "You weren't really a Boy Scout?"

"Absolutely."

Summer heard him whistling as he walked away down the planks of the pier.

Summer fell asleep early. She was unbelievably tired. Tired of laughing and arguing with Marquez and Diana. Tired of turning Seth and Adam and Diver over and over in her mind. It had been a very, very long day, full of new experiences.

The room still reeked a little of paint fumes from the work Seth had done earlier. She'd opened all the windows, but the smell was still there, trapped in the house.

She lay there in the dark, on the new, soft bed with pillows that smelled of fabric softener, not mildew, and listened to the water slapping the pilings outside.

Sometime in the night, rain began to fall loudly on the roof, dripping from the eaves outside the window.

Summer woke when hands reached under her sheet and gently lifted her up. There were lots of hands, and as she looked around her she saw Diver and Seth and Adam. They were raising her from the bed and carrying her between them as if she were paralyzed and they were taking her to the hospital, or perhaps like she was a sacrifice and they were carrying her to the altar.

Each of them had a tarot card hanging on a string around his neck. Summer focused and she could see the cards, but for some reason couldn't connect them to the faces. At a distance stood a fourth guy, face in shadow, laughing and dressed all in white.

Summer wasn't scared, not quite. She felt giddy and sick, like she might throw up. They held her by her arms and legs, and one held her head supported in his hands and bent low to her—for a kiss? No, because they had carried her right back to her bed and now could no longer be seen.

Instead there was Marquez, her body painted in serpentine scrawls of color, dancing all alone.

And in her bed Summer was being drawn by the music, disturbing music that was all shifting tunes and melodies that never seemed to coalesce.

Then the room was silent and Diana was there, a faraway figure dressed like an angel. Summer got out of her bed and tried to go to her, but Diana kept receding, growing smaller and farther away.

A face, very near her own. Adam? Seth? A little of both. And Diver.

A kiss, the most fleeting contact, not on her lips, but on her forehead. Something wet.

Diver, barely visible in moonlight, at the side of her bed, holding the framed photograph of Summer's parents. Looking thoughtfully at them, sad, it seemed to Summer, faraway and sad.

At some point, Summer realized, she had slipped over the line to consciousness, but when exactly she couldn't say.

She only knew that the sounds she heard now were the sounds of reality. The drip of water from the eaves. The sound of her own breathing.

"Hi," she said.

"Oh," Diver said. "I didn't mean to wake you up." He replaced the framed photograph on the stand beside Summer's bed. "It's raining, so I came in."

"Good," Summer said.

"New bed, huh?"

"They left the old one. Anytime you want to use it . . ."

He shook his head. "Only when it's raining."

"I know. I would disturb your *wa,* right?"

He smiled.

"This is the second time I've gotten up from a dream and seen you. Sometimes I'm not sure you're real. Maybe you're part of a dream," she said softly.

He shrugged. "Could be."

"What time is it?" Summer asked.

"The sun is just ready to come up."

"I've been having some very strange dreams."

"This place is full of paint fumes. They're not good for you, you know. You should come outside, get some oxygen. That will clear out your brain."

Summer nestled down under her sheet. "Too sleepy."

He reached out a hand, and without thinking, she took it. She had never touched him before. He felt real.

"Come on," he said. "You're polluted."

He pulled her from the bed and drew her to the door. Outside the world was gray, with shapes barely distinct. Frank refolded a wing and snuggled his neck back against his feathers. The air was almost cool and very wet. Summer's baby-tee clung to her clammily.

Diver ascended the ladder that ran up the side of the house to the flat part of the roof, just over her own bedroom.

"Is this where you sleep?" she asked when she had joined him.

He nodded. "Here, sit. This way, toward the east."

Summer obeyed and folded up her knees, wrapping her arms around them. The baby-tee and boxers were thin and insubstantial, but the warmth of her bed still clung to her.

A faint, reddish glow could be seen on the horizon. The stars were retreating into the west. The water of the bay, so vividly green in the daylight, was black still. Here and there a light blinked from the homes across the bay. One of those lights was in the Merrick estate. Perhaps Adam, awake in his room.

Adam in his room, in a huge mansion. Seth, somewhere to the north, in his grandfather's modest house. And Diver, so close beside her.

Images from the dream surfaced in Summer's consciousness. Unsettling images that carried unfamiliar emotions in their wake.

Summer shifted uneasily. "My *wa* is disturbed, and I don't even know what it is," she said.

"Just watch," Diver said. "Soon."

"Do you have a name? A *real* name?"

Diver put a finger to his lips. "Here he comes."

The horizon had grown rapidly brighter, violet and red and yellow. Scattered clouds were etched in orange. Then . . .

"Oh!" Summer pressed her hand over her heart. It had been so sudden. A brilliant, blinding arc of fire peeking over the edge of the world.

Diver smiled.

Down below on the railing, Frank turned his head, facing the rising sun.

And now the sky overhead seemed to ignite, to

burst into flames, an impossible, overwhelming display. Colors beyond description. Colors that memory could never recall. The sky was everywhere. The sky had become the entire universe. And the two of them were the smallest, least significant specks, floating upward toward magnificence.

Summer realized that tears were coursing down her face.

Diver was looking at her, watching the tears. He nodded. "Frank was right about you. He said you were all right."

18

Diana Lies, Summer Cries, and Marquez Takes No Crap from Guys.

Diana spotted Summer on the road to town, walking along in her work uniform as though she didn't have a care in the world. Diana considered just driving on past, but as much as it made her uncomfortable to admit it, Summer had crossed a line of some sort yesterday.

You couldn't just drive by and ignore someone you'd shopped with, could you?

Diana pulled the Jetta to a stop beside Summer. "Hey. Want a ride into town?"

"Sure." Summer climbed in, careful not to crush her apron bow. She had a copy of the menu on her lap.

"Off to work, huh?"

"Yes. I think they're going to let me have some tables on my own today."

"Please don't tell me that excites you," Diana said.

"I have to make some money this summer," Summer said. "I wish I didn't, but I guess it will be good experience. When I go to college I'll probably have to earn all of my spending money, even if I get a scholarship. I don't know what I'll do if I don't get a scholarship. Have you ever had a job?"

Diana shook her head. "Nope. Haven't needed one, I guess."

"Must be nice," Summer said. "You'll be able just to concentrate on classes when you go to college."

"I don't think I'm going," Diana said.

"Oh."

"It's not my grades or anything," Diana said, detecting what she thought was pity in Summer's eyes. "I got accepted all over the place. Mallory forced me to apply. But she can't force me to go."

"I have to go. I mean, if I want to get a job."

Diana smiled condescendingly. "What are you going to be when you grow up?"

"I don't know. Lately I've been thinking I could be a TV reporter. Only, I don't really enjoy having to be rude and ask people lots of questions. Where are you going?"

"I thought you didn't like asking questions. I'm just going shopping."

"I would have figured you were all shopped out after yesterday," Summer said.

"Here we are," Diana said, sidestepping the question. The institute was her own private place, not for anyone else to know about. Even her mother had no idea. She idled the car in front of the restaurant.

Summer climbed out. She hesitated, as if about to ask Diana something, then decided against it.

The manager gave Summer three tables. The first party went fine, with Marquez looking over her shoulder like a protective big sister. Then the place went wild. People seemed to be coming from everywhere, filling every table and standing ten deep at the hostess stand.

"One more piece of restaurant language you need to know," Marquez said as she bustled past Summer, carrying a huge trayload of food.

"What?" Summer asked anxiously. She was trying desperately to make sense of the insanely beeping computer precheck machine.

"In the weeds," Marquez said over her shoulder.

"What's that?"

"That's what we're in right now," Marquez said. "We are deep in the weeds."

Fill waters. Fill bread basket. Carry away dirty dishes. Check kitchen for order. Punch in drink orders on the machine. Ladle soup into bowls. Clean soup off underliners. Get yelled at by Skeet for making a mess of the soup area. Find cocktail sauce. Stand around with a ten-pound tray looking for a tray stand. Nearly drop tray. Consider bursting into tears. Back to the kitchen to find cooks screaming your name at the top of their lungs. Realize you've forgotten to pick up drinks. Tray up food. Return to grab lemon. Avoid meeting the eyes of the people whose drinks you'd totally forgotten. Slip on a piece of lettuce. Pick up drinks. Wrong drinks. Return to bar. Pick up the right drinks. Answer questions from one table about where you were born while another table gives you death looks. Wait in line at the precheck while another new girl punches buttons randomly. Race to the kitchen, get yelled at by J.T. for not picking up orders. Definitely consider bursting into tears.

And suddenly it was over, and two hours had passed. The other waitresses were grinning and looking like the team that had won the Super Bowl. Everyone was drinking coffee and Pepsis. The smokers were sneaking forbidden cigarettes in the waitress station, waving the smoke away with menus.

Summer went to the kitchen. The cooks were

cleaning up their stations and rocking out to Plain White T's.

Summer went to Skeet. "I'm sorry about messing up the soup," she said, practically sobbing.

Skeet looked amazed. "What?"

"And I'm sorry I didn't pick up my orders in time," Summer told J.T.

The cooks exchanged a look. Skeet said, "Aww, isn't that sweet? J.T, you a–hole, you got her all upset."

J.T. laughed, but not unkindly. "Come here." He motioned her down to the end of the line. He leaned back against the walk-in refrigerator door and sucked on a huge iced tea. His white uniform was stained and greasy. But he had nice, light brown hair pulled back in a ponytail and an open, somewhat lopsided smile. Summer could see why Marquez had been attracted to him.

"Summer," he said, "you don't pay attention to what we all say when we're in the weeds. When we're weeded, we get cranky. We have to yell at someone, and the waitresses are the traditional people to abuse."

"Oh. Who do *we* get to abuse?"

J.T. laughed. "Right back at us. Now, Marquez, when she gets yelled at, she throws it right back. She can curse in two languages. Three sometimes." He wiped the sweat from his forehead with a towel. "You did all right today, especially for it being only your second day."

"Thanks. I was kind of panicky, really."

He looked at her thoughtfully. "So I guess you and Marquez are hanging around together, huh?"

"Yeah, I guess so. I really like her."

He nodded and glanced across the room toward the dining room door. "I guess she told you about us?"

Summer tilted her head back and forth, an admission.

"Hope she didn't tell you too much bad stuff. How is she, anyway?"

"Marquez? She's great, I guess. She's the most totally unique person I've ever met."

His blue eyes were soft. "Yes, she is." He laughed. "Have you seen her room yet?"

"Isn't it great?"

"She created that room, and she thinks she's going to be a lawyer someday," J.T. said. "My name used to be up on her wall, bigger than anyone's."

"It still is. I saw it."

He stood away from the walk-in. "It is? *My* name? I was sure she'd have painted it over."

"She said that's how it is, that she never paints over something."

J.T. shook his head in amazement. "When she broke up with this guy named Juan, his name was gone under three coats of white enamel before he managed to walk home." His eyes were bright. "J.T., right?"

"Big red letters," Summer confirmed.

Skeet yelled something rude, suggesting that J.T. might want to help do some of the work. "I gotta get back. Just remember, don't be sensitive around here. No one else is."

Summer saluted solemnly. "No more sensitivity. Absolutely."

Marquez was waiting for her as soon as she passed through the swinging doors to the dining room. She gave Summer a look and seemed about to ask a question, but stopped herself.

Summer suppressed a grin. Marquez wanted to know what she'd been discussing with J.T. That was obvious. And she didn't want to have to ask. Well, too bad. She'd just see how long Marquez could hold out.

"What's my side work?" Summer asked innocently.

Marquez glared at her through narrowed eyes. "You have sauces with me."

They dragged big plastic jars of cocktail sauce and tartar sauce out of the walk-in to the waitress station, where they stood side by side dumping spoonfuls of each into small dishes.

"So. Tonight's the big night," Marquez said. "You and Adam."

"Uh-huh. Actually . . ." Summer paused and looked

around guiltily. Lianne was nowhere in sight. "Actu-ally, after we do the beach thing I have to go run an errand with Seth." She said it as casually as she could.

Marquez was nowhere near being fooled. "An *errand.* She's running an *errand* with Mr. Moon. Did that picture of Diana's have anything to do with this?" Marquez giggled gleefully.

"Why did I even tell you?" Summer fumed. She slopped more tartar sauce. "It's not that, just for your information. It's—" Again she looked over her shoulder. No Lianne. Summer lowered her voice. "Look, remember at Diana's how I said there was this guy—"

"—that spent the night with you! That was *Seth*?"

"No, no. Keep it down, Marquez."

"The kiss! The guy you kissed in a Laundromat who you didn't even know."

"It wasn't a Laundromat. It was a photo booth. At the airport." Summer sighed. There. She had told someone.

"How was it?" Marquez asked.

"The point is, Mar-*quez,* that I am just going with him to buy some tile this evening, after we go to the beach. That's all. I'm meeting him at his house."

"After we go to the beach and *before* you go out tonight with Adam. Summer, Summer, Summer. I used to think you were such a nice, sweet girl." Marquez laughed. "I have to work a double shift, but I am coming over tonight after your date to get the complete story. So be prepared. This is not gossip that can wait."

Summer was feeling sort of pleased with herself, enjoying her new image as maybe-*not*-totally-nice, when Lianne came around the corner into the waitress station. She seemed to have appeared out of nowhere.

"Hi, you two," Lianne said. "Did I hear something about gossip?"

"This is my first time actually lying out in the sun," Summer said. "I figured when I came here I'd be spending every minute out on the beach. Look at me, I'm still white as snow." Summer adjusted her top and pried open one eye. Even through the sunglasses, as dark as she could find, the sun was still too intense. Her skin was hot on her exposed front, her back only slightly cooler on the towel laid out over sand the color of powdered sugar.

"Everyone thinks that," Marquez said, her voice slurred with sun sleep. Her reply came about two minutes late, as if the words had taken a long time to get to Summer, lying just a foot away. "I mean, when you're here on vacation, sure. But when you live here, you have other stuff to do. Like work."

Several minutes later Summer said, "Yeah."

The beach spread down the western edge of Crab Claw Key, facing the Gulf of Mexico. The water was pure translucent green, and as warm as the air. Summer had gone in up to her knees, and now there was sand stuck to her calves. The rest of her was coated with Hawaiian Tropic.

"How does sunscreen work?" Summer asked. No answer. "I mean, how does it keep . . . light? How does it keep sunlight from . . ." She couldn't think of the word. No point in wearing herself out thinking.

"Penetrating?" Marquez said eventually.

"Huh?"

"Penetrating. That's the word you wanted."

"Okay." Summer heard Marquez rolling over. She rolled over herself. They were pointed with their heads toward the water, the theory being that they didn't want to sunburn the bottoms of their feet as the sun crossed the line from east to west.

Summer opened her eyes again and looked out across the water. Far in the distance pillars of clouds rose, looking like fantastic islands of snow-covered peaks. It reminded her of watching the sunrise with Diver that morning.

Sunrise with Diver. Sunset would be with Adam. And in between, a little quality time with Seth. This vacation would be working out great if she could just lie back and enjoy it.

She must have been smiling, because Marquez said, "What's that grin all about? That looked lecherous."

"No, not lecherous," Summer said.

"Adam?"

Summer made a "maybe" look.

"Seth?"

"We're just shopping for floor tile."

"Uh-huh. You know, you two just look right for each other," Marquez said. "Like you could get married someday and have a bunch of wholesome children and a minivan."

Summer made a face. "That's how you see me, huh? A mommy with a bunch of kids?"

"Don't get pissed off," Marquez said. "It's just that he's a nice guy—not to mention the godlike body—and you're a nice girl. Nice in a good way."

"Maybe I don't want to end up with a nice guy," Summer said.

"Maybe you'd like a certain cute, very rich guy?" Marquez suggested.

"Maybe," Summer said, drawling the word and wiggling her eyebrows in a parody of seductiveness. "Did I tell you about the woman on the plane? The woman who did tarot cards? She told me I was going to meet three guys."

Marquez looked interested. "I don't believe in any of that superstitious junk."

"Me neither."

"So? What did she say?"

"She said I'd meet three guys here. One would seem to be a mystery, one would seem to be dangerous, and one would seem right."

"*Seem?* That's kind of weasely, isn't it?" Marquez asked. But she was looking thoughtful. "So far you've met Adam and Seth, right? Are they supposed to be two of the guys?"

"How am I supposed to know? Maybe. Not that I believe any of that stuff. I mean, cards? Puh-leeze."

"You excited about seeing Adam tonight?" Marquez asked.

"As long as I can get a totally perfect tan between now and then I'll be happy." Summer twisted her head around to try and see the back of her legs. They looked pretty white. She was still an official chalk person.

"Where's he taking you? Somewhere *dangerous*? Somewhere *mysterious*? Or somewhere just *right*?"

Summer shrugged. "I don't know. He didn't say. I asked and he said just to leave it to him."

"Oh, the mighty macho man in control," Marquez mocked.

Summer flicked sand at Marquez. "That kind of reminds me of something. Guess who I talked to."

"Do I care?"

"I think you will," Summer said cockily. "I think

you've been wanting to ask me all afternoon."

"I saw you," Marquez said, sounding utterly bored. She pretended to yawn. "I saw you talking to J.T. I was wondering if you were going to bring it up."

"He seemed very interested in *you*," Summer said.

Marquez sighed dramatically. "Okay, you might as well tell me what he had to say."

"I wouldn't want to bore you. I can tell you're not really interested."

Marquez pointed. "See that guy down there? The big hairy old guy? If you don't tell me exactly what J.T. said, I'm going to tell that guy you're hot for him."

Summer related the conversation with J.T. as accurately as she could.

When she was done, Marquez slapped Summer's arm. "You weren't supposed to tell him his name was still on my wall."

"Oww. Why not?"

"He'll think I still like him."

"Do you?"

"Duh. I'll tell you one thing—he'd better not be your third tarot card."

"He's cute," Summer said. "But you know how sometimes a guy will be cute, but you don't react in *that* way?"

"No. Absolutely not. Okay, sure, I know what you mean."

"J.T. is cute, though," Summer repeated. "And he seemed nice."

"Yeah. He is cute. And he knows it. He has that Anglo, Nordic, blue-eyed thing going for him. Also, he's excellent at kissing. The creep. The subhuman." Marquez pounded the sand, but not so much in anger as in frustration. "He reminds me of you that way."

"What, you mean *I'm* a subhuman? Or has someone told you I'm excellent at kissing?"

Marquez laughed. "No, I mean the blue-eyed Nordic Midwestern guy or girl next door thing. Speaking of which, we'd better get out of here before you get burned." Marquez stood up and began brushing sand off her stomach.

"So how come you and J.T. don't just make up?" Summer asked.

Marquez gave her a look that was cold as ice. "Because no guy ever gets to treat me like crap twice. Once. That's the limit. I don't hang with people who mess me up. I have more important things in my life, you know?"

The look surprised Summer. "More important than true love?"

"It isn't about what happens *now,* Summer. I'm just having fun now, but my life is about succeeding and making something out of myself and making my parents and my brothers proud of me. I'm not going to waste my mental energy dealing with jerks."

Summer stood looking at her.

"Sorry," Marquez said, rolling her eyes. "Sometimes I get this sudden attack of seriousness." She pointed up the beach. "See that point there? Up by the rocks?"

"Sure."

"That's the spot where my parents and my big brothers and little tiny Maria Marquez landed in this country." Marquez measured with her hands how tall she was at the time. "My dad was three years in prison in Cuba for complaining about the government. When he got out, we left. We were in a rowboat at night, and a Cuban navy patrol boat passed by only about a hundred yards away. If they'd spotted us, my dad and mom would have been thrown into prison and all us kids would have been taken away from them. We got blown around in the sea. I mean, I can still remember it a little. My mom was trying to act like it was this big family picnic, right? So eventually we bang right into good old Crab Claw Key in the good old USA. We had the clothes we were wearing. That's it. No money. My dad and mom couldn't speak any English. Now my dad owns the gas station." She made a self-deprecating face. "Big deal, right? A gas station."

"Yes, a big deal," Summer said softly.

"He loves it, I can tell you that. You'd think that one gas station was the whole Shell Oil Company."

They began to cross the beach, feet sinking in the burning sand.

"Well, anyway, the thing is that I have to do better. Better than a gas station."

Summer gave her a quizzical, skeptical look. "Wait, so you can't forgive J.T. because you have to succeed?"

"That's right," Marquez said firmly. Then she made a sly grin. "You know, unless he begs. And crawls." She nodded thoughtfully. "Crawling would be good."

19

Finally—the Naked Truth

Lianne Greene watched from cool, air-conditioned comfort as Summer and Marquez made their way across the beach and paused at the low seawall to brush the sand from their legs.

She sat in the window of a small café, sipping an iced tea with mint. A raucous, Spanish-language game show was playing on the TV over the bar. Lianne had been there since the girls had arrived, having followed them from work to Marquez's house and then to the beach. She didn't mind waiting. It was boring, but she knew the next act in the little drama would make up for the long, dull wait.

Lianne left two dollars on the table and went outside.

The heat seldom bothered her the way it did so many other people. It was all a trick of the mind, she believed. Stay calm and cool inside, and the sun couldn't reach you.

She followed Summer and Marquez at a safe distance, not that they would have noticed her had they turned around. She was wearing big sunglasses and a white cap with the bill low over her forehead.

Several times Summer and Marquez would stop just to laugh or playfully slap at each other. They were having a fine time. Especially Summer. And why shouldn't she be? She was on her way to pick up Seth.

A little knot of rage burned in Lianne's stomach. Seth was just a fool to fall for a girl like that. But then, that was Seth all over. He was too kind and decent to realize how people used him. He was too sweet to understand what a two-faced little manipulator Summer Smith was. And it was so obvious. Lianne had recognized her type right from the start.

They stopped at Marquez's house again, presumably so Summer could change clothes. Good. Lianne had plenty of time.

She knew Seth's house, inside and out. And she knew Seth better than anyone. That would make it all work. Then it would be bye-bye Summer.

And Seth would be right back where he belonged. Right where he would stay.

With her.

⚘

At four in the afternoon, the sun was still high and
hot. The same clouds Summer had watched from the
beach were darkening and building up over the water,
threatening an afternoon thunderstorm.

Summer had showered quickly at Marquez's house
and changed clothes. Marquez had turned up her nose
at the top Summer was wearing and convinced her to
borrow one of hers instead. Now Summer was walking across Seth's lawn, feeling conspicuous and worried that she was sending a message Seth might easily
misinterpret.

"Yes," Summer muttered under her breath, tug-
ging at the tight top, "this is how I always dress when
I go to hardware stores."

Seth's grandfather's house was a low, flat-roofed
bungalow, dwarfed by massive shade trees on all sides.
One was a banyan, a tree that fascinated Summer. It
looked like something from another planet, but its
leaves defeated the sun and spread a welcome coolness.

There was a screened porch that went around two
sides of the house. The screening was old and nearly
opaque in the shade.

Summer was confused. There was a regular door on
the left side and the screen door on the right. Which
was the front door?

Then she heard a sound, the creak of springs, as if someone was sitting down in an old chair. The sound came from the porch. Summer headed toward the porch, still feeling ridiculous in the gaudy top Marquez had loaned her. Still feeling a quaking in her stomach, a feeling of uncertainty mingled with anticipation.

"Seth?" she said as she neared the screen door. No answer.

She climbed three stairs to the door. She cupped her hands around her face and pressed her nose against the screen to see inside. There was a rocking chair. Laid across the rocker, a pair of men's jeans. And over the jeans, Summer saw a white lace bra.

Close against the wall of the house, there was a bed. The bed wasn't empty.

"Oh, my gosh!" a female voice yelped. "Summer! What are you doing here?"

Lianne leapt up from the bed, snatching thin covers around her bare shoulders.

Summer could only gape, openmouthed.

"What are you doing here?" Lianne demanded again.

From inside the house, Seth's voice. "Lianne? *Lianne?*"

Summer stumbled back down the steps. "Sorry. I'm really, really sorry." She turned and ran as fast as she could back to the road.

Summer was nearly home by the time Seth caught up with her. She had been walking fast. Very fast.

She noticed him when he was still several blocks behind, trotting along in her wake, dodging the occasional car. He called to her to wait, but she continued doggedly. She was dangerously near tears.

They were both panting when she felt his hand seize her arm. "Leave me alone," she snapped, shaking him off.

He fell in step beside her. "Look, Summer, that was not what it looked like."

"No? You mean that wasn't Lianne, lying in your bed when you knew I was coming over?" Summer wished she didn't sound so much like she cared.

"Will you hold up a minute? You're practically running."

"Go away."

"Come on, Summer, you at least owe me a chance to explain," Seth said angrily.

"Explain what? Why should you explain? You tell me it's over with Lianne, and then, whoops! Surprise! She's in your bed. While her clothes are not. No, her clothes are over with your clothes on the chair. What happened, you got up to get a drink?"

"Summer, this whole thing is just a setup. Lianne can't accept the fact that it's over," Seth said.

"You can't accept the fact that it's not," Summer shot back.

"That was low," Seth said.

"Don't tell me what's low," Summer muttered. Diana's house was just ahead. She raced up the drive-way, around the side of the main house, down a narrow walkway lined with rosebushes.

Seth followed her, saying nothing while they were under the shadow of the main house. But out on the back lawn he exploded. "This is not fair, Summer. You have to give me a chance to explain."

"No. I don't."

"You *want* to be mad at me," Seth accused. "You want to believe what you think you saw is true so you can push me aside and go off with Richie Rich. Now you've had a good look at my house compared to Adam's house. I guess it's cooler to be going with a billionaire, huh?"

They had reached the walkway out to the stilt house. Suddenly Summer stopped and turned to face him. "This is my home, at least for now, and I don't want you in it. You can finish the work you have to do, but that's the end of our relationship."

She stomped several paces down the walkway, struggling to control her anger. She lost the struggle and turned again. "You talk about Adam's house and your house? The difference is that Adam doesn't have his girlfriend in his bed at the same time he's giving me all kinds of lines about . . . about air catching on fire and people being meant for each other."

Seth shook his head bitterly. "I was wrong about you. You're not so special."

"Jerk."

"Jerk."

"Go back to Lianne and leave me alone, you low-life."

"Maybe I should," he said.

"Great, because I have better things to do. I have a date tonight."

"With Adam, I know."

"That's right, with Adam."

"Fine, go with Adam. I don't even care."

"Run home to Lianne, Seth. If you hurry, maybe you can get back *before she gets dressed*!" The final shout echoed off the water.

This time Summer didn't turn back. She blew past Frank like a storm cloud, causing him to spread his wings and glide off toward a more peaceful perch.

20

Big Date, Big Questions, and Diver for Dessert

The time Summer had allocated to be with Seth, to get to know him and to decide whether there was anything real between them, was spent instead on crying, storming around the house, wondering whether he was telling the truth somehow, and ultimately deciding to put him out of her mind for good.

By eight o'clock the swelling in her eyes had gone down with the help of two ice cubes. The anger was gone, too. It was all silly, she told herself. One of those things she'd look back on someday and laugh about. Ha ha. Seth wasn't the only guy in history to lie about having a girlfriend. He was a low, scum-sucking snake who masqueraded as a nice guy so he could seduce girls at the airport, but hey, Summer could handle it.

Ha ha ha. Just another jerk. He wouldn't be the last she'd run into. But being cool—as she was—she'd just laugh it off. Ha ha.

She was dressed and ready and completely *not* angry anymore by the time she heard the engine of Adam's boat on the water outside.

Adam was standing at the wheel of the boat. Its long prow nosed in under the stilt house as Summer descended slowly, a bit cautiously, through the hatch.

He had an almost dreamy smile on his face and was shaking his head admiringly. "That was a very nice start to the date," he said, offering his hand to help her aboard.

"What was?" she said, with just a trace of a snap in her tone.

"Watching you come down the stairs. Like an angel descending from heaven to visit earth."

"White as an angel, anyway," Summer said, blushing in a mixture of pleasure and embarrassment.

She stumbled a bit as the boat rolled. Adam caught her easily. He kissed her, just a playful kiss on the forehead. Then the playfulness went out of his eyes, and he kissed her lips.

Summer gasped when he pulled away.

"I've been wanting to do that since the other night," Adam said. "I've been thinking of nothing else."

"Sure, right," Summer said. It had been a very nice kiss. She would have enjoyed it even more if she hadn't still had half her mind on Seth.

"Cross my heart," Adam said. "This morning I woke up thinking of you. I was imagining you here, in this house, warm and cozy in your bed. By the way, what *do* you wear to bed, just so I can be sure I had the picture right in my mind?"

"At home in Minnesota I wear a flannel shirt I got from my dad. And socks."

Adam grinned and gunned the engine a little, backing the boat away from the house. "I wasn't picturing you in Minnesota."

He steered the boat toward the open sea. Even at eight o'clock the sun was still bright, though it hung within inches of the horizon. "I guess you don't want to know what *I* wear to bed, huh?" Adam asked.

"Not especially."

"Pajamas with feet on them. And the little flap in back." He said it with such absolute sincerity that for a moment she believed it.

"Uh-huh. Right."

Summer drew a deep, steadying breath. Wait a minute, she told herself, she was letting Seth ruin her time with Adam. And that was stupid. She slid her hand into his as he opened the throttle. He squeezed her hand.

They motored clear around the circumference of

Crab Claw Key, rounding the old side point, following the line of beach where Summer had sunned that
afternoon with Marquez, gliding under the causeway, past the marshy, uninhabited north end of the
island.

"What's all that white stuff in the trees over there?"
Summer asked.

Adam turned the boat closer to land, and Summer
could see that the "white stuff" was actually dozens,
maybe even hundreds, of wood storks. The birds seemed
too large to be resting in trees, but there they were, looking like snow where no snow had ever fallen.

Slowly the last thoughts of Seth really did fade away,
perhaps some effect of water and salt breezes. It was
amazing how quickly every problem that existed on
land seemed to evaporate, how alien the land seemed as
they rode over gentle waves. It was as if the land were
just some curiosity, a zoo filled with familiar creatures
in familiar cages of stucco and wood.

From the sea, the interesting parts of the land
weren't the things made by people, but the trees—tall,
pencil-thin palms that swayed on the slightest breeze;
stunning trees that were an explosion of garish red or
lavender flowers; mangroves that grew right from the
edge of the water.

They rounded the north end and again passed
under the causeway, now cruising south along the

new side's outer shore. This shore was lined with a mix of fantastically large new homes and smaller, humbler bungalows. Then the homes stopped abruptly and gave way to manicured grass and perfectly formed oaks fronting a stretch of pristine beach.

"This is the beginning of the estate," Adam said.

"Does it ever seem weird to you having all this land and this monster house?" Summer asked.

"I guess not. I guess it would seem weird to me if I just had a normal house. You get used to what you know."

"Must be nice," Summer said. "Everything always perfect and beautiful."

"Not *always* perfect," Adam said. "Even rich people have problems."

Summer laughed. "Sure. Look at the Quartermaines."

"Who?"

"They're the rich family on *General Hospital*. Divorces, murders, evil twins, all kinds of problems."

"We haven't had any murders yet," Adam said dryly. He looked at Summer closely. "What did Diana tell you about me?"

"Nothing," Summer said. "Diana and I don't talk all that much. I think she's—Never mind."

"What? What were you going to say?"

"Just that she seems very sad to me. I'm probably

wrong. Even Marquez says Diana always used to be a little antisocial but that she's gotten a lot worse. But I guess you know her a lot better than I do."

"I don't think she's gotten any worse," Adam said shortly. He was twisting the wheel in his hands. "I think she's the same as always. She was always a little different."

"It's like you can't quite communicate with her," Summer said. "Like you reach out to her, but she's never exactly there."

"Whatever it is, she'll get over it," Adam snapped. Then he forced a smile. "Let's not talk about old girl-friends or old boyfriends."

"I don't have any old boyfriends," Summer said.

"Maybe that's about to change," Adam said. The usual cocky yet self-mocking grin was back.

The boat rounded the point and entered the bay again, sidling up to the Merrick estate dock. Summer glanced across the water. The little stilt house stood out quite clearly, as did Diana's house.

"Thanks for the ride," Summer said as she climbed over to the dock.

"Anything in particular you'd like to do now?" Adam asked.

Summer shrugged. "Whatever you want."

"I wanted to check first because I didn't want to just be taking charge," he said.

"That's okay. If there's anything I don't want to do, I'll tell you," Summer said. She was feeling mellow to the point of dopiness after the boat trip.

"Well, I was just going to do some horseback riding, have dinner, watch a movie . . ."

"Wow."

He looked doubtful. "Too much for a first date? Does it look too much like I'm trying to impress you? At least I decided against trying to get the use of the helicopter to take you to a club in Miami."

"Now, that would have been too much," Summer agreed. "I don't have the clothes for a club."

"But how about the rest? Have you ever ridden a horse?"

"A horse?" Marquez asked, curling her lip in disgust. "Have you ever ridden a horse?" She took another of Summer's potato chips and crunched it noisily. She was still wearing her work uniform, having come straight over from finishing her dinner shift.

"I told him I hadn't," Summer said. "I wanted to make him tell me all this stuff about how to ride and all. Then I showed him." Summer giggled at the memory of Adam's face.

"Showed him what?"

"I started riding when I was like six years old," Summer said. "My grandmother owns a stable outside of Owatonna. That's a town in Minnesota," she added, noting the blank look on her friend's face.

"Of course. Who hasn't heard of Owatonna?"

"Anyway, it was good to be better than him at something. He's so sure of himself."

"So you rode, then what?"

"We had dinner. It was amazing. We had a picnic in this tower they have with windows all around, where you can see everything. We ate all this cool stuff that their cook made up. Little tiny sandwiches and shrimps and dessert."

Marquez crunched another chip. "Are you going to get to the good part? I just got done waiting on about a thousand tables. I don't want to hear about food."

"That *was* the good part. We had all this excellent food and watched the sun go down, only there weren't enough clouds to make a really excellent sunset."

Marquez looked shocked. "What? The Merrick family can't control the sunset?"

Summer sent her a pitying look. "Envy is so beneath you, Marquez."

"Come on, let's get on with the story. I didn't come all the way over here at practically midnight to hear *this* stuff."

"So then we watched a movie in their theater. Their own theater, with a projector and a screen and a popcorn machine."

"What movie?"

"That new Orlando Bloom movie."

Marquez closed her eyes and let her head float back and forth dreamily. "Orlando Bloom. That boy could get his name on my wall in very, very big letters."

Summer shifted uncomfortably on her bed. "Then we made out a little."

"How little?"

"A lot."

"Oh, a *lot* little." Marquez leaned close. "Okay. How was it?"

"It was excellent and fantastic, and I was scared because it was like if he'd tried to do anything more I don't know what I would have said, all right? It was like, so *much,* you know? The boat and the horses and the food and this romantic movie . . ."

"You were seized by the moment," Marquez said eagerly. "You were caught up, overwhelmed, carried away!"

"I wasn't carried away," Summer said. "I maybe could have been carried, though." She shook her head and rolled her shoulders to get rid of some tension. "I guess it's like Seth was saying about people coming here and losing their minds. I think I'm losing mine."

"So you're falling big time for Richie Rich, huh?"

Summer jumped up and walked nervously across

the room. "I don't know, Marquez. Yes. Maybe. I
mean, when I was with Adam, the answer was yes,
definitely."

*And when I'm with Diver . . . and with Seth, even
though he's a toad . . .*

"Well, you could do worse. Adam is major *A*-list
material. He's beyond *A*-list. But speaking of which,
what about Seth? Did you guys go to the hardware
store?"

Summer told Marquez what had happened that
afternoon. Marquez reacted with exactly as much sensitivity as Summer expected—she let out a loud whoop
of delight.

"Oh, man, why don't things like this ever happen
to me?" Marquez wailed.

"It wasn't exactly a good time, Marquez," Summer
said.

"Not a *good* time, no," Marquez allowed. "But so
extreme! Who'd have ever figured Mr. Moon was so
twisted?"

"He hides a lot behind that innocent, Midwestern
face," Summer said darkly.

"Unless he's telling the truth," Marquez said.

"Oh, puh-leeeze."

"I'm just saying, it could be." Marquez shrugged.

"How do you figure that?" Summer pressed.

"Does it matter? Don't be worrying about two guys

at once, Summer. One guy is already too many. Two is *way* too many."

How about three? Summer couldn't help adding silently.

She turned things over in her mind, biting an uneven fingernail. It was possible Seth was telling the truth, she supposed. Just barely, slightly possible.

"It's not *my* fault," Summer said at last. "I just don't know what to do. I mean, Adam, Seth . . ." *Diver,* she added to herself. "How are you supposed to know?" Summer said. "How are you supposed to figure out the truth? How do you know if guys are interested in you or not? And how are you supposed to know if you really like them? How do you know if it's real?"

"I don't know," Marquez admitted. "I guess you should go out with both of them and see how you feel."

"What if one of them won't even go out with you?" Summer asked, voicing the question before she'd thought about it.

"Seth won't go out with you? Sure he will. Don't be stupid." Marquez stopped. "Wait a minute. Are you telling me there's a *third* guy? You're not, are you, because I can't take any more complications."

Suddenly, to Summer's horror, the hatch in the floor began to open.

Diver's head appeared. "Um, hi. I didn't want to interrupt when you have people over," he told Summer. "But I'm really thirsty. Maybe I could just get a drink of water and then I'll bail."

Summer froze. Marquez froze with her mouth wide open. Only her eyes moved, going from Summer to Diver and back again.

"You might as well come in, Diver," Summer said. She covered her face with her hands. Why had she for a moment believed Diver would be able to keep himself a secret?

"Just a drink and I'm outta here. Hi," Diver said to Marquez.

For once Marquez seemed to have nothing to say. Diver cupped water from the sink faucet. He grabbed a soda from the refrigerator. Then, with a last wave, he disappeared back down the hatch.

At last Marquez found her voice. "Summer, Summer, Summer. I am really glad I met you, girl. I have a feeling nothing is going to be boring as long as you're here."

21

Video Blog

Hi, Jennifer. Here I am again.

I was going to use the video camera to make this diary into kind of a cool documentary, you know? But as you can see, it's just me again. Hi. It's dark because I don't want to turn on the light because Diver's outside on the roof and he might see it. Which is also why I'm whispering.

My life is such a mess. I mean, it's a good kind of mess. It's just very confusing. I guess it's better to have three guys to worry about rather than none, which is how many I had before I got here. It's like God suddenly realized I'd managed to get through my whole life without very many romantic problems and decided to make up for it all at once.

I went out with Adam tonight. You would not believe it, Jen. It's too dark for you to see my face, but I have this silly grin on it because it was this totally excellent evening.

But right before I left, I had this huge dumb fight with Seth. So, even while I was with Adam, sometimes even *while* Adam was kissing me, I would be thinking about Seth. Or other times Diver would suddenly pop into my head.

What is going on with me? You know me better than anyone. I'm just me. Normal old me. This is too much.

I asked Marquez about it, you know, how you can tell who is the *right* guy? I figured she would know because she had this long-term one-on-one thing with this guy named J.T. But that's when Diver poked his head through the floor and that was the end of *that* conversation.

So, I'm sitting here, whispering like an idiot, talking to a little camera with a stupid blinking red light on it, trying to figure things out. How can I feel so . . . so wonderful when I'm with Adam? And at the same time be feeling mad and guilty because of Seth? And at the same time wondering, Hmmm, I wonder if Diver has a real name, and I wonder if he ever wears real clothes? It doesn't make sense, does it?

Aaargh! This is so confusing. Why aren't you here to straighten me out? You always know everything.

All I know is that this vacation is working out very differently than I expected. It's like I got on the plane at the airport *there,* normal Summer Smith, and by the time I stepped off the plane *here* I was someone different. Like not only did the place change, but I changed too.

Maybe that's the way it always is, Jen. Maybe when I'm in Bloomington, I'm part of Bloomington. And when I came here, I had to be part of this island.

Or maybe I'm just this wispy little wimp who gets blown back and forth depending on who I happen to be with.

Or maybe everyone there in Bloomington is just so used to me being a certain way that I was *already* different, only no one there noticed. See?

I know what you're saying, Jen. You're saying, "Summer, shut up already, you're giving me a headache. Quit all your whining and just go for it, girl."

That's easy for you to say. You're more experienced than I am. Maybe I'm just emotionally retarded. Remember how you got your period six months before I did? Maybe I'm just slow at everything.

Shhhheeeeesh. Ghaaaarrrr. Aaaaaaaargh.

There, I feel better now. Now you can see just how insane your best friend has become.

22

All About Deep Holes and Cold Hearts

Diana woke in the hole.

It happened sometimes. Sometimes not. But she could always tell, as soon as her eyes opened.

The hole was blackness inside of blackness. It was a place where no light entered. It was a place of dull, relentless pain.

It happened sometimes. She wished she knew why. Why one day she felt okay, and the next she felt hopeless. The night before she had watched from her balcony as Adam had driven Summer away in his boat. And returned her hours later.

But that wasn't why she was in the hole. She wasn't jealous. Jealousy was too active an emotion to exist in the hole. There had been another emotion that came from watching Summer with Adam—a sense of loss, a realization that Diana had once been . . . *happy?*

Maybe not happy. Certainly not for a long time.

She kicked at the sheet that covered her, but it just tangled around her legs. She didn't want to get up, but she had to pee. Peeing right there in the bed was a bad idea. She would have to get up. Eventually.

If she just stopped eating and drinking, she could lie there without having to get up. If she did that, though, she'd die.

Yes.

After a while she got up and slumped toward her bathroom.

She saw herself in the mirror and leaned close, closer, till the outlines of her face blurred and all she could see there was the reflection of her own eyes. Eyes looking at eyes looking at eyes.

"Hi, there," she said to the reflection. "Having a good time? No? You're in the hole today? Me too."

Eyes looked at eyes looking at eyes.

"You're pathetic, you know that, right? Pathetic. You make everyone sick. You make *me* sick."

The eyes were crying now. Tears were welling and spilling, welling and spilling.

And Diana didn't care.

There was a knock.

"Go away," Diana whispered.

The knock came again. "Hey, Diana? Are you up?"

"Am I up?" Diana asked herself, viciously parodying Summer's chipper voice. "Am I up? No, I wouldn't say *up*."

"Diana? Are you on the phone? Can I come in? I just want to ask you something."

"I just want to ask you something," Diana muttered. "I just want to ask you something."

Now there was a knock much closer, louder. She was knocking on the bathroom door.

"Diana, are you okay?"

Concern now. Definite concern in Summer's voice. And just what the hell was little Summer going to do if cousin Diana wasn't okay?

"Go away," Diana said.

"Diana, are you all right?"

"I said go away. Leave me alone."

Silence. But not the sound of a person walking away.

"Look, Diana, I'm not going away till I'm sure you're all right."

Diana snatched at the door handle and threw it open. "Here I am, see?" Diana said. Her voice was guttural. "You happy now?"

Summer's eyes were wide with shock. There was fear there, too.

"Get out," Diana snapped. "Just get out. Go away."

Summer didn't move.

Suddenly Diana emitted a short laugh. "Fine. Stand there. I don't care. This is what you came to see, all the way from Cowtown, all the way from the biggest mall in the whole wide world, *Summer*? Great, now you've seen it, *Summer*. You can go tell my mother, 'Yes, Diana looks like she might be a little strange,' *Summer*."

"Diana, what's the matter?"

"What's the matter? What's the matter?" Diana mimicked. Then her voice became low, almost sultry. "You want to know what's the matter? I'm in a big, deep hole, and no matter what I try, I can't get out."

"What are you talking about?"

Diana felt the energy drain out of her. Her shoulders sagged. She hung her head. She ran her fingers back through her lank hair.

"Diana?" Summer said. She reached out and took one of Diana's hands.

Diana stared blankly at her own dark hand, held in a web of Summer's almost translucent white fingers.

"It's just PMS," Diana said. She managed to plaster on a false, shaky smile. "Sorry. I didn't mean to yell at you. I'm just not feeling all that great this morning."

Summer didn't look convinced. She kept her grip

on Diana's hand, and Diana didn't have the will to pull away.

I would give anything to be you, Diana thought. To have those contented blue eyes, even now touched by concern. To be a creature of light and sun and hope.

"Are you upset over Adam?" Summer asked. "I mean, because I'm seeing him?"

It was almost funny. Another time it would have made Diana laugh. "I think I'll just go back to bed." She disengaged her hand.

"I really like him, but if it's hurting you . . ." Summer said.

Diana took a closer look at Summer. She was wearing her stupid waitress uniform. She must be on her way to work or else on her way back. "It's over with me and Adam," Diana said wearily.

"But you still care about him, don't you?"

"No."

"I don't believe you."

"I don't care what you believe." Diana walked to her bed and flopped facedown, arms at her side.

"I have to get to work," Summer said. "But I want you to tell me something before I go. I want you to tell me why you and Adam broke up."

Diana stared at the pillow an inch from her face. It was a color called salmon. Fish-colored pillow.

Summer came and sat beside her. "Tell me."

"Tell you?" Diana muttered. "Tell you. I'll tell you just one thing."

"What?"

Diana sat up, hunched over the pillow, hugging it to her. "Just remember you're nothing to any of them. Just remember that. You're nothing. Not to Adam Merrick, not to his father, not to his . . . any of them. You're less than nothing."

Summer looked disappointed. Her mouth was in a tight line. She stood up. "I don't know why you're so mad at me, Diana. And I don't know why you're so sad. If you won't tell me anything, how am I supposed to help?"

"You're not supposed to," Diana said. "You can't."

"I have to go to work." She headed for the door.

"Summer," Diana called suddenly.

Her cousin turned back, questioning.

Diana felt her throat clutching up. The panic feeling was rising in her. Soon it would sweep over her. She tried to speak and nothing came out. She took a deep breath and tried again. Her voice belonged to someone else, but the words came out. "Look out for Ross," Diana said.

"The soup is conch chowder, and we have blackened redfish for the special, $10.95," J.T. said.

Marquez dutifully wrote this information down with a red dry marker on a white board.

"Make sure everyone knows we only have three lobsters. We didn't get the shipment today," J.T. added. He was standing behind the line in the kitchen, arms folded over his white cook's shirt.

"Anything else?" Marquez asked.

"You're so tough, aren't you?"

Marquez looked up from the board. She could feel the blood rushing to her face. "Excuse me?"

"I said you're real tough, real cold, Marquez."

"We are not going to do this here in front of everyone," Marquez said firmly.

"Walk in," J.T. said, pointing toward the walk-in refrigerator.

"This is work here," Marquez said. "You want to talk to me, maybe you should do it some other time."

"I've had almost two weeks of your attitude," J.T. said.

Marquez saw Summer come into the kitchen. Skeet was looking down at her work, pretending to be totally absorbed in wrapping bacon around shrimp.

Without a word Marquez stomped to the walk-in. It was chilly inside and not exactly roomy as she stood between bins of chopped lettuce and shelves loaded with salad dressing, sliced vegetables, and trays of fish filets lined up in neat rows.

J.T. closed the walk-in door and stood there, glaring at her. "You didn't take my name off your wall."

"I haven't gotten around to it yet," Marquez said. "But if it bothers you, I'll make sure I paint over it this afternoon."

"Yeah, you would," he said.

"You're the one who started this, J.T.," Marquez pointed out. "Was it *me* saying I wanted to see other *guys*? No."

"I told you I was sorry about that. It was just something I said because I was upset." He straightened a tray of tomatoes. "I was freaked, and you were giving me nothing. As usual."

"Oh, and so I'm supposed to just forget it?"

"No, you're supposed to realize that I've been going through some stuff, all right?" he said.

"Why is that *my* problem?"

He rolled his eyes. "Why is it your problem? I don't know—maybe because you supposedly love me."

Marquez winced. She rubbed her bare upper arms. The cold was beginning to have an effect. "Look, J.T., I'm sorry, all right? I'm sorry you found out some stuff you weren't supposed to know. If it hadn't been for bad luck, you'd be happy and normal, right? Your mom would be your mom, your dad would be your dad. So why not just forget it? Lots of people are adopted."

"Man, Marquez, is that really the way you think? Are you really that cold?" He threw up his hands. "Of course you are. How stupid of me."

"Are you done? Because, speaking of cold, this *is* a refrigerator."

"I just wanted some sympathy, you know?" he pleaded. "I wanted you to be there for me."

"Yeah? When was I supposed to *be* there for you, J.T.? When you were throwing things around my room and yelling about how you were going to go find some other girl? How easy it would be for you to find someone else?"

"I told you, I was freaked. I was messed up. I needed some understanding from you, and I wasn't getting it, so what else was I going to say?"

"Great. Cool. No problem," Marquez said. "You want to talk a lot of crap, fine. Only don't expect me to take it."

J.T. was silent, hanging his head. He picked at a loose label on a jar of blue cheese dressing. Marquez shivered and stopped her teeth from chattering.

"There hasn't been anyone else," J.T. said. "You know that, right?"

"How would I know that?" Marquez said. But her anger had begun to ebb.

"Well, I'm telling you. There hasn't been anyone else." He looked at her with a question in his eyes.

"I haven't had time to be out picking up new guys," Marquez admitted.

His answer was a gentle wisp of a smile.

"J.T., you have to get over this now. Your parents lied. It happens sometimes. They didn't lie in order to hurt you. You should be proud you're adopted. That means they had to really want you."

J.T. nodded. "I don't have a birth certificate," he said in a conversational tone. "I needed one to get a social security card, right? Last summer, when I first started here. So I asked my mom. She gets me down a baptism certificate instead. She says that will do just as well, and she was right, they accepted it."

"So?"

"So I was two and a half when I was baptized," J.T. said. "In our religion you get baptized when you're a few days old."

"Maybe your real mother, your birth mother, didn't baptize you and your mom and dad wanted to make sure."

He nodded. "Yeah, that's what I figured. But after I found out, you know, about all this, I checked. See, when you get adopted, they issue you a new birth certificate showing the names of the adoptive parents. It's like they rewrite the record, so that adopted kids have a birth certificate."

"Is there a point to this story? I have side work to do."

"The point is, why don't I have a birth certificate? Why isn't there a record of me until I was more than two years old?"

"I don't know," Marquez said impatiently.

J.T. nodded. "Sorry to lay it on you. I know you don't give a damn." He forced a grim, angry smile and threw open the walk-in door.

23

Marquez's Walls, Summer's Floor, and Adam's Many Bathrooms

"Twenty-seven dollars even," Marquez said. She had the money arranged in neat stacks on the counter in her room: two fives, a number of singles, quarters, dimes, and nickels.

"Thirty-four dollars and forty cents," Summer reported. Her stack was mostly singles.

"You made more than me?" Marquez demanded. "On your first real day?"

"I guess so."

Marquez shrugged. "Well, I was in a lousy mood. People may have picked up on that."

"I wasn't in a great mood either," Summer said. "I told you about my little encounter with Lianne at work. She just kept apologizing, like it was all her fault, and *I'm* the one who was barging in on her."

Marquez gave a noncommittal nod.

"And the day started out even worse," Summer said. "Diana yelled at me this morning before I went to work."

"Diana yelled?" Marquez asked sharply. "Why?"

"I don't know. She said it was PMS. But I think she may be messed up over something. I mean, *real* messed up."

Their eyes met. Summer could see that Marquez didn't dismiss this possibility.

"She shouldn't rag on you about it," Marquez said. "You bring a suit?"

"In my bag," Summer said. She began stripping off her uniform. "Maybe she had to take it out on someone. Her mom isn't around for her. She doesn't seem to have a lot of friends."

"That doesn't mean it's *your* problem,"

Summer was looking at her thoughtfully.

"What?" Marquez demanded.

"I'm wondering if Diana's PMS is catching."

Marquez rolled her eyes but laughed. "I guess you heard about me and J.T. playing rock-'em sock-'em robots in the walk-in."

Summer wasn't sure how to answer that question. The gossip machine at the restaurant worked at the speed of light. "Skeet may have mentioned something about it."

"Uh-huh. Skeet's your friend now, huh? Don't go leading her on."

"Very funny." Summer tied on her bathing suit top. She pulled the side of her suit bottom away an inch, hoping to see some evidence that a tan line was developing. There was none.

"I can't believe how polite you are," Marquez said. "You aren't going to ask me what J.T. and I were fighting about?"

Summer batted her eyes. "I'm too polite."

"It was the same stuff. He did apologize for what he said about wanting to see other girls. He said it was because I wasn't supportive. Do you think I'm not supportive?"

"I don't really know you all that well, Marquez," Summer said, evading the question.

"Don't give me that. You don't think I'm supportive?" Marquez was standing with hands on hips, looking intense.

"I don't know about supportive. I know you kind of intimidate people. At least me you do. Not that you *try* to intimidate, it's just that you're so—"

"So *what*?"

"You're just so you. It's like you always know

who you are and what you're doing. Some people aren't that sure, I guess. *I'm* not."

Marquez looked troubled. "I'm not *always* sure. Yeah, I know *who* I am, like you said, but everyone knows who they are."

"No, they don't," Summer said. "Lots of times I don't. Lots of times I'm like a cloud changing shapes with the wind. It's like people look at me and some think I look like a rabbit or a squirrel, and others think, no, that cloud looks like a map of Australia."

"Australia?"

Summer was beginning to feel foolish, but she wasn't going to be cowed. "I'm just saying, how do you know what you are or who you are? I've been thinking about it a lot lately."

Marquez didn't laugh. Instead her eyes drifted toward the big red letters that spelled out *J.T.*

"Like if you suddenly found out your parents weren't your parents," Marquez said. "I guess that could make you confused about who you are."

Summer decided against saying anything. She hadn't said what she'd said in order to make Marquez feel bad.

"Ready to go?" Marquez said, suddenly switching on her cheerful voice.

"Ready. I'm not going to get tan hanging around in here."

"Tourist." Marquez laughed. "Come on, we'll turn you nice and dark, little Minnesota person." They went outside into the blistering sun and started toward the beach.

"By the way," Marquez said, sounding a little too casual, "not to bring up unhappy things . . . I was just wondering, Summer. I mean . . . you have such a cool name and all. *Summer.* What was your brother's name? I know you told me already, but I wasn't sure. It wasn't *Winter*, I guess? Or *Spring*."

"No, it was Jonathan," Summer said. Why did Marquez care?

"Jonathan," Marquez repeated the name slowly. "Jonathan. Pretty common name. Not like Summer."

"It is pretty common, yeah."

"Good evening, Frank. How's fishing?" Summer said when she arrived back at the stilt house. "I see you've started replacing the bird poop that was washed away."

Frank spread his wings, startling her.

"Just a joke," she said.

She opened the door of the house and gasped. The cheesy indoor/outdoor carpeting had been ripped up off the floor, which was now bare wood, studded with the protruding heads of nails. In the kitchen the linoleum was off the floor. It was off in the bathroom, too, revealing some unpleasant-looking wood subflooring. In one place she could look straight down through a crack widened by rot and see the water beneath the house.

She found the note from Seth resting on her table.

Summer:
Sorry to leave such a mess, but I wanted to get all the old linoleum up at once so we could make just one trip to the dump. Be back tomorrow to start laying the carpet and the tile. By the way, don't use the bathroom; the floor is too dangerous in here. You'd better use one in the big house.

Sorry. Right. *Right.* He had made a total mess of the place. A *total* mess. "Don't use the bathroom?" she muttered. It was hard not to suspect that Seth was being slightly spiteful. *Don't use the bathroom.* Oh, sure, no problem.

She crumpled the note and threw it at the wastebasket. She missed, so she kicked it and missed again, banging her toe into the table leg.

She was cursing Seth when there was a knock at the hatch in the floor.

"Who is it?" she snapped.

"Adam. But I'm not coming in if you sound like that."

She hobbled over to the hatch and raised it. "Sorry, I banged my toe." She must have been cursing too loudly to notice the boat's engine.

Adam stuck his head up through the floor and whistled. "Is Mr. Moon pissed at you or something?" He climbed the rest of the way up.

Summer tried to massage her toe and started to tip over. Adam grabbed her and steadied her. "You want me to kiss it and make it better?"

"My toe?" Summer laughed.

"How about this instead?" He wrapped his arms around her and kissed her, lightly once, and then, when she stopped holding her toe, more deeply.

"That helped," Summer said breathily.

"A definite mess," Adam said, releasing her. "Good thing I'm here to take you away from all this. I just stopped by to see if you had anything planned for tonight."

"We're going out tomorrow, I thought."

"Yeah, I know. But I couldn't wait till then to see you again."

"Really?" Summer asked, wanting to hear him say it again.

"Really. I was sitting around doing nothing, and I kept thinking 'There she is, just across the bay.'"

"I just got home myself," Summer said, feeling very

pleased with herself. "Marquez and I went to the beach again, in search of the perfect tan. As you can see, I didn't get it."

"You don't need a perfect tan. You are perfect."

Summer felt warmth suffuse her body. But at the same time, she was acutely aware that she was wearing nothing but a bathing suit, and that his gaze was very attentive.

"I was, uh . . ." She completely forgot what she was going to say.

"Look, this place is trashed. Where are you going to stay tonight? You can't stay here."

"I guess I'll go barge in on Diana," Summer said. The thought wasn't pleasant. Diana wasn't exactly hospitable at the best of times. And judging by this morning, this was not the best of times. "She has all kinds of room there. I'd stay here, only Seth says I shouldn't go into the bathroom."

"That's certainly convenient. Just hold it till tomorrow. Look, I know a place with lots and lots of bathrooms," Adam said. Then, seeing her reaction, he hastened to add, "No, no, it's not what you think. We have guests staying there all the time. We had the ambassador of France and his wife there, we've even had a bishop stay there. No wife, of course. But if it's safe enough for a bishop . . ."

Summer could see a clear picture in her mind of

Adam's house. And an even clearer picture of the mess that Seth had left her. "It wouldn't be like I was staying *with* you," Summer began. "I mean—"

"I *know* what you mean," Adam said. He pretended to be offended. "What kind of dog do you think I am?"

"Okay," Summer said dubiously. It gave her some pleasure to think how annoyed Seth would be that by tearing up her house she would end up sleeping at Adam's house. "Let me change and get my stuff. Which means you'd better wait down in your boat. I can't go into the bathroom to change."

"Yes, ma'am," Adam said.

As Summer quickly changed out of her suit, two thoughts struck her with sudden force:

1. She had to let Diver know about the bathroom floor situation. What if he fell through?

2. She was spending the night at a guy's house!

Her stomach did a quick turn. She hadn't thought this through. She had barely hesitated. What was the matter with her? Was she crazy?

She was about to tell Adam she had reconsidered but stopped herself. Why should she? Adam's house was as big as a hotel, wasn't it? It wasn't like they would be sharing a room. They would probably end up as far apart as two people at opposite ends of a football field.

"Are you coming?" Adam called up through the floor.

"Right there!" Summer yelled back.

Okay, a note to Diver. But where to leave it? On the floor by the hatch. That way he was sure to see it.

She grabbed a piece of paper and a felt-tip pen.

Dear Diver,
The place is a mess because Seth is supposedly
fixing it, so you can't use the bathroom or you
might fall through the floor. Be careful.

Now to sign it. Her pen was poised over the sheet. "Summer?" she asked herself. "Love, Summer?" No. Not love. He'd get the wrong idea. His *wa* might be disturbed.

"Sincerely?" Yeah, right. She'd said "dear." Not that it meant anything because that was how you always started a letter.

Love, Summer

What if Diver didn't see the note, but Seth did when he came in the morning?

She shook her head. Marquez was right. She *was* in trouble.

She rested the note beside the hatchway. *Love, Summer* was just the same as *Dear Diver*. No biggie. Forget it. And staying at Adam's house was just like staying at a hotel. Also no biggie.

Oh, man.

24

Old Fear, New Passion, and Dana's Sadness

By the time the sun set and darkness fell, Diana was tired of her bed. She had been there from sunrise to sunset. And now, suddenly, a restless nervous energy was rattling her legs, making her feel twitchy.

She had to get out. The house was too quiet. Too big and empty.

She showered, scrubbing almost violently at skin tattooed by the pressure of crumpled sheets. She shampooed her hair and left it wet and combed straight back. She avoided looking at herself in the mirror and dressed with feverish haste.

She was in her car, sitting in the driveway with the engine running, before it occurred to her that she really had no place to go. The kids at the institute would all be in bed. Besides, volunteers were asked not to disrupt the comforting regularity of the schedule there. Too many of the kids associated any change in routine with something bad.

She had no friends. Not anymore. The stores were mostly closed.

She could drive down to Key West. There were plenty of restaurants open there, places where she wasn't likely to run into former friends.

She pulled out onto the road and headed toward town. Yes, some serious, speed-limit-busting highway driving. That's what she needed to burn off some of this manic energy. Maybe she should have taken Mallory's Mercedes. It was faster.

She was pulling through town when she saw him. She had stopped for the light. He was with two other guys, crossing the street, right in front of her.

Ross Merrick.

Diana stopped breathing. She'd guessed he was back in town. The six months in rehab had been up a while ago. The *second* six months in rehab.

Diana recognized the other two guys, both hangers-on, the kind of creeps who hung out at the fringes of the Merrick family, sucking up to Ross and Adam, looking for the free plane trips and meals and parties.

They were right in front of her. If he turned, he would see her.

Diana shrank behind the wheel. If only the light would change.

There was a muffled bang. Something had hit the car. Ross.

He turned slowly, eyes trying to focus.

The look sent a chill of terror through Diana. It was that same look. He was drunk. Drunk and with that same dangerous leer.

He waved her off, a bleary apology for staggering against her car. Then he stopped. He bent down to peer inside the car.

And then he grinned.

Their eyes met.

He looked at her and silently mouthed words that were all too easy to read.

The light turned green.

Ross and his toadies headed off down the street, hanging on to each other, swaggering and shouting into the night.

Diana gripped the wheel with white fingers. She waited there through the next cycle of the light, ignoring angry horns blowing behind her.

"It's catching fire!" Adam warned.

Summer pulled the marshmallow from the fire but

let it burn till the outside was crispy black, caramelized all over. It hissed as it burned, louder even than the crackle of the fire.

She raised the straightened coat hanger and held the burning marshmallow against the black sky overhead. "Look, it's a comet," she said.

"Yeah, but now you can't eat it," Adam said. He was toasting his own marshmallow more carefully, trying to get it an even brown all the way around.

"This is just how I like them." Summer blew out the flaming marshmallow comet and gingerly drew it off the end of the hanger. She popped the whole sticky mess in her mouth.

"That's disgusting, you realize," Adam said. He pulled off his own marshmallow and scarfed it up.

"Itf perfek fis way," Summer mumbled.

"Mime is beher," Adam argued.

They were on the Merricks' private beach, a neatly groomed stretch of sand bordered by palm trees. A pair of Hobie Cats were pulled up on the sand nearby. Just down the beach was a cabana and a barbecue grill.

As usual the gulf was calm, lapping in a restrained way, soft crashing noises followed by the rattle of a million tiny shells. Each foamy curl came a little closer to their small bonfire.

Summer set her marshmallow stick aside and leaned back against Adam. He cradled her head on his lap and looked down at her with eyes that reflected the fire's light.

"This is just exactly the reason why I wanted to come here to Florida," Summer said.

"What? You don't have marshmallows in North Dakota?"

"You *know* it's Minnesota," Summer said complacently. "I meant this night. Stars and warm breezes and the sound of the water."

"And?"

"And the sand and the bonfire."

"And?" he insisted.

"Did I mention the stars?"

He playfully pushed her head away.

"Okay, okay," she said, giggling and reclaiming her warm spot on his lap. "I did leave out the best thing of all."

"Which is . . ."

"You know it's *you*," Summer said. "Although even in my best daydreams about how cool it would be, I didn't imagine you."

"You didn't expect to meet guys?"

Guys, plural, Summer thought. If only he knew. But she was putting that behind her. This was the time to feel very content to be here with Adam, to savor the way he looked at her, the hard muscles of his thigh under her neck, the way he rested his arm across her bare stomach.

She had made a decision. She'd made it without even knowing it. She couldn't look back and point to the exact time. Maybe it had been at the moment when she agreed to spend the night at his house. Maybe it had just happened a moment ago.

He wanted to kiss her, she was certain of that. And she wanted to kiss him. Yet neither of them had since coming out to this perfect beach, and the tension over when they would was sweet and agonizing at the same time.

"How could I have expected to meet you?" Summer said, with wonder in her voice. "I didn't even know guys like you existed. All the other guys I ever knew were so dorky and immature compared with you." She grimaced. "*That* sounded dorky and immature, didn't it? I just meant that you're so different."

"That's because I'm really thirty," Adam said. "Didn't I mention that? People just think I'm eighteen."

"You like much younger girls, huh? What are you, some kind of perv?"

"I just like one younger girl," Adam said, and his voice was low with emotion.

He slipped his hand under her head and raised her slowly, ever so slowly, till her lips met his.

They kissed for what might have been minutes or hours. She felt his lips on hers, on her throat, on the back of her neck, making every hair on her head tingle. With his fingers he stroked her cheeks, and smoothed back her hair, and sometimes just touched her lips, as if he couldn't believe they were real.

Her mind was firing away, thoughts flying back across time and forward to some imagined future. And through it all, the realization that she was feeling things she had never before felt with such intensity. Pleasure and fear and guilt and anticipation and desire. And a new emotion that was some blending of them all.

Love? Was this love? Or was it an illusion woven together out of gentle touches and slowly dying fires and bright clouds scudding swiftly across the moon and infinitely sweet kisses?

She heard a loud hiss, and the firelight was gone. A second later the warm foam covered her feet.

"Oops, tide coming in," Adam said. "Stay here any longer and we'll get swept out to sea."

Summer sat up, reluctant to break the contact with him. Far out to sea there was a prolonged flash of lightning.

Adam helped her to her feet and took her in his arms again. "I guess we should go inside," he said. "If the tide doesn't get us, that storm out there will. It's blowing this way."

They walked slowly back to the house, following

the beach, holding hands. Adam stopped at the cabana and hosed the sand off their feet.

"Manolo sees sand in the house, he threatens to quit," Adam explained. "Although he's off tonight, so I guess we could be brave and track in two or three grains."

They held hands and laughed quietly all the way to the house and down the long, gloomy hallway of dead ancestors.

"Aww, isn't that sweet?" A voice spoke from the darkness of the big common room. It was impossible to tell where it had come from in the maze of couches and chairs. The fireplace fire had been allowed to die down and was just embers now, like the fire they'd left on the beach.

Summer felt Adam's muscles stiffen as he squeezed her hand.

"Home early, aren't you, Ross?" Adam said.

Summer peered and could see a shadow. In this light he could have been Adam, the resemblance was so close.

"Bartender at the Pier actually had the guts to card me," Ross said. "So I came home to raid the domestic stock." He held up a glass. "Would you two lovebirds care to join me?"

"No, thanks," Adam said evenly.

Ross came closer, holding himself up by resting

against a couch back. He peered at Summer. "Do I know you?"

"Summer Smith," Summer said. "We kind of met at the party."

"What party? Never mind. It's all the same party." He took a longer look and then glanced at Adam. "You do have good taste, little brother," he said.

Adam pulled Summer toward him. "Good night, Ross."

"Where are *you* going?"

"To show Summer her room. She's spending the night. Her house is having repairs done."

Ross started to say something, looked at his brother, and decided to take another drink.

"Come on, Summer," Adam said gently.

"Good night," Summer said to Ross.

Ross said nothing, but as she walked away, Summer could feel his eyes on her.

It would have been impossible at that moment not to see Diana's face in her mind's eye. A sad, haunted-looking Diana saying, "Look out for Ross."

Marquez was half asleep, staring blankly at Letterman's Top Ten list on the TV, when she jumped at the sound of something rapping at her window.

"Madre de Dios!"

She seldom spoke Spanish unless cursing. She

climbed out of bed and pulled back the edge of the curtain that blocked off the big shop display window.

"Seth? Diana?" *Diana? Here?*

"Let us in," Seth said tersely.

Marquez let the curtain fall back. Midnight, and suddenly Diana shows up with Seth?

It had to be bad news of some kind. She dug around in a pile of clothes, found a bathrobe, and let them in. Both were soaked through, clothing clinging to their skin, hair matted.

Seth was hovering at Diana's side, too close, as if he were afraid for her. He kept glancing at her with worried, wary eyes, as if ready to spring to her side and prop her up.

But Diana didn't look as if she were going to fall. She was nearly vibrating with electric energy. She pushed past Marquez into the room, looking around with quick, jerky little bird movements.

"Good evening to you, too," Marquez said huffily. "You know it's midnight?"

"Is Summer here?"

"No. What would Summer be doing here?"

"Do you know where she is? I banged on her door for about an hour and she's not at home. I went in and I found a note on her floor."

"What note? What are you talking about?"

"I found Diana wandering around in the rain downtown," Seth said, speaking for the first time. "She said she was coming here, so I offered to take her."

"Is she high or something?" Marquez asked Seth in a quiet aside.

He shrugged.

Diana had stopped pacing and was staring at her own name on Marquez's wall. "We used to be friends, didn't we, Marquez?" she said.

"Did we?" Marquez asked archly.

Diana was unaffected by the sarcasm. Marquez had never seen this side of Diana. If it wasn't drugs, it was way too many cups of coffee.

"You know, I never wanted her to come here," Diana said. She was picking through the CDs on the counter.

"What?"

"Summer. I never wanted her to come here."

"I think we all kind of figured that out," Marquez said.

"It's not my job to take care of her," Diana said.

"Diana, why don't you sit down and tell me what's going on?"

"I'm wet. I don't want to get everything wet. I'll go. I just was wondering if Summer was here. You don't know where she is, do you?"

Marquez shrugged. "The only other person she knows around here is Adam."

"Who's the diver?" Diana asked suddenly.

"The diver?"

Diana shook a damp note in Marquez's face. "She wrote a note to some Diver person. Told him to be careful because Seth had torn up the place."

Seth winced.

"Seth tore up the place?" Marquez asked, arching an eyebrow at Seth.

"I had to take up the—" Seth began, but Diana cut him off.

"He's fixing her place, Marquez. Don't act stupid!"

Marquez would have been offended, would have lashed back, but there was something frightening in the way Diana was acting. She hesitated for only a moment. If she guessed wrong about Diana, then Summer was going to be mightily pissed. "Diver is a guy Summer knows."

"Maybe she's at *his* house, then," Diana said eagerly.

"No. He lives at the stilt house. He sort of lives with Summer."

"What?" Seth demanded.

Momentarily Diana snapped out of her frenzy. "She has a guy *living* with her? She just got here."

"It's a long story. Look, Diana, you're starting to scare me."

Diana waved her off impatiently. "Nothing to be scared of. I'm sure she'll be fine. I told her to look out for Ross. I mean, I did warn her."

Marquez had had enough. She grabbed Diana by her shoulders and forced her to sit down on the bed.

"I'll get it wet."

"Tell me, Diana. Why did you warn Summer about Ross Merrick?"

"He was supposed to be rehabbed," Diana said bitterly. "But I saw him, and he was drunk."

"He was drunk at the party the other night, too," Marquez said impatiently. "What else is new?"

Diana was biting her knuckles. Marquez was afraid they would start to bleed. "I didn't know."

"Diana . . ."

"It's no big deal. He tried to rape me, is all, but he was drunk, and . . ." She faltered, unable to go on.

Marquez felt like the floor was moving. Like she might lose her balance and fall.

On the television, Letterman was interviewing Charles Grodin. Seth had turned to stone.

Diana had become very small, a tiny, shivering wet figure, lost in a vast room.

"Adam said I shouldn't make a big deal out of it. I mean . . . you know, the family and all. And there would be all this mess. Besides, you know, Ross was going to get help."

Diana dug her fingernails into her arms, clawing herself almost violently.

Marquez drew back instinctively. She looked for a place to go, to pull away. Her gaze fell on the big red letters. *J.T.*

She looked back, unwillingly, at Diana, lost and alone and so filled with self-loathing that it was like a force field vibrating the air around her.

Not my problem, Marquez told herself. *Not even close to being my problem.* But Seth was too stunned, too paralyzed to help. And Diana needed someone. Anyone.

Marquez walked back to the bed. She sat beside Diana and put her arm around her quaking shoulders.

25

What Summer Knew

Adam and Summer sat side by side on the floor of his room, talking in soft voices, kissing, sipping sodas, and intermittently watching MTV.

Letterman was on when Summer started to yawn.

"Sleepy? I'd better show you your room," Adam said. "Unless . . . It's such a long walk." He flinched, as if he were waiting for her to throw something at him.

Summer smiled and yawned again. "You'd better show me *my* room. No matter how long the walk is."

He held up his hands in surrender. "I had to try."

She took his hand and pulled him up off the bed. "Come on." She grabbed her bag and followed him down the corridor and around a corner.

He opened a door and reached in to flip on a light.

Summer groaned. "Look at this room! Oh, I could get used to this very easily."

"Your own bathroom right there." Adam pointed. "TV there, radio alarm clock. What else?" He looked around. "Oh, yes. Bed. Big, lonely, empty bed."

"Thank you," Summer said primly.

"Hey, where's my tip? I showed you to your room."

"Like *you* need me to give you money?" Summer said.

"Who said anything about money?" He put his arms around her and kissed her till she was gasping for air and feeling weak.

"I'll let you get some sleep," he said.

"Good night."

He turned away.

"Adam? It was a really beautiful evening. The stars, the ocean, the marshmallows."

"And?"

"And you," Summer said softly. "Definitely you."

He swallowed. "I am leaving this minute, and you might just want to lock your door after I'm gone. Because I don't know how long my decent impulses will last."

Summer laughed. "Get out of here."

When he was gone, she explored the room for a little while and washed her face. Her hair smelled of wood smoke and sea salt, but she decided she didn't want to wash that away, not yet.

She climbed into the bed and flipped on the TV. Sleep overtook her quickly, even though moments before she had felt too excited to even think about falling asleep.

She dozed and woke just long enough to turn Letterman off.

She slept. For how long she didn't know. She slept and dreamed of things that brought a smile to her lips, of tarot cards and three guys. In her dream she knew which was which—the right one, the mystery, the wrong one. She knew the choice she would make, as if she could see far, far into the future, past many months and years. In her dream she laughed and said, "Oh, of course, it had to be you all along."

Summer awoke, aware of a noise. A soft, imperceptible noise. She opened her eyes and saw the door of her room opening.

Adam, silhouetted against soft light. He had come back. Maybe she *should* have locked her door. He sagged against the doorjamb, and in an instant Summer knew.

From far, far off there was a faint, insistent pounding noise.

july

The Incredible Shrinking Adam

"Adam?" Summer said, tentative, doubtful.

"I could be," he said. It was a voice heavy and slow with alcohol. "You could close your eyes and you'd never know the difference."

In an instant the meaning of what she was seeing changed utterly. She sat up and drew the covers close around her.

"Ross," Summer whispered. "What are you—" Her cousin Diana's warning came back to her. Fear's cold fingers climbed up her spine. *Look out for Ross.* Diana had been strange at the time, almost terrifyingly sad and angry, all at once. *Look out for Ross,* she'd said.

Summer realized her mouth was dry. Her heart seemed unnaturally loud in her chest.

"Thought you might want a nightcap," Ross Merrick said. "You know, little drink before bed. Help you sleep. Maybe . . . loosen you up a little."

"No, thank you," Summer said, her voice a quivering, uncertain whisper.

Ross came into the room. He staggered and cursed as he banged his knee against the side of her bed.

Summer crept back to the far corner of the bed. She had stopped breathing. Her eyes measured the distance to the door, the possibilities of racing past Ross and running down the hall.

"I'm tired. I'd like to go to sleep," Summer said as firmly as she could manage.

"You don't really want me to leave," Ross said softly. He reached toward her.

Summer slapped his hand away. "Get out."

"Oh, you can be a little more friendly than that," Ross said.

They both heard the noise in the hallway at the same time—rapid footsteps.

Summer breathed again.

"Another time, sweet little Summer," Ross said. He got off the bed and went back to the doorway just as Adam arrived.

Adam glanced anxiously from Ross to Summer.

He seemed relieved, but when he turned back to Ross his voice was tight and angry. "What the hell are you doing here, Ross?"

Ross shrugged. "I heard the pounding downstairs. I came to make sure our house guest was safe."

Adam was wearing boxer shorts and an open robe. His short dark hair was uncharacteristically messy, tufted and flattened by sleep. He stood just inches away from his brother. It was so easy to see the similarity between the two of them. And yet, there were differences, too. Adam was larger than Ross, more muscular, and several years and many hangovers younger. She should have known immediately that it had been Ross and not Adam.

"You're a liar, Ross," Adam said. "You're a drunk and a liar."

Summer was shocked at the venom in his tone. She had never heard Adam angry before. His usual tone of voice was gentle and amused. Now he almost seemed to vibrate with suppressed anger.

"Get lost, little brother," Ross said contemptuously.

Adam grabbed his brother, bunching the front of Ross's shirt between his fists. He slammed Ross against the doorjamb with surprising violence. "That pounding noise was Diana," he shouted. "She's downstairs with Marquez and Seth Warner right now. You want to guess why they're here at two in the morning, Ross?" Adam slammed him again. "You want to try to guess?"

"Get your hands off me," Ross snapped.

Adam hesitated. Then he threw Ross back, as if he were throwing away a piece of garbage. "Get out of here," he said. "Get out and let me clean up your mess. As usual."

Ross straightened his shirt, turned halfway to send Summer a leering wink, and shambled away.

For a moment Adam refused to look at Summer. He passed his hand back through his hair several times. He shrugged, as if trying to shake off the tension. At last he looked at her, then looked down at the floor. "I guess you heard," he said. "Marquez and Seth are with Diana downstairs. They want to see you."

"Why?" Summer was trying to act cool and calm, trying to reimpose normalcy on the insanity.

Adam sighed. "I guess I'll let Diana tell you," he said at last. "You'd better come down or they'll come up here."

Summer climbed out of the bed, feeling conspicuous and vulnerable in her baby-tee and boxer shorts. Lying atop her overnight bag was a robe. She put it on, grateful for the sense of warmth it conveyed, though the air was not cold.

Adam kept his eyes on the floor. "Look, Summer, I

just hope . . ." He sighed again, sounding like a person who had no reason to hope. "I hope you'll hear my side of things, okay? I mean, before you make up your mind completely."

Summer went down the wide, plush-carpeted stairs, sliding her hand along the polished surface of a carved walnut banister too massive for her to really hold. Adam was a few feet behind her, the two of them a wildly incongruous sight, half-dressed amid the stifling grandiosity of the Merrick mansion.

In the huge common room below she saw Diana pacing, agitated, dripping rainwater from her sleek dark hair, leaving damp footprints on the Oriental rugs.

It must be raining outside, Summer realized. Deep within the hushed heart of the mansion she'd never even heard the thunder.

Diana Olan was wringing her hands like some over-the-top parody of worry. She slapped her hands down to her sides, but they didn't stay there for long. Her usual mask of cool, distant boredom was gone. She looked as if she would scream at the first unexpected sound.

The sight of Diana this way was deeply shocking. Summer had glimpsed *this* Diana only once before, briefly, before the mask had come down again.

Summer looked at Marquez, perched edgily on a couch, wearing too-loud clothing, her buoyant brown ringlets matted and messy, her leg bouncing nervously, dark eyes glancing around the room, as if she were planning her escape. *Poor Marquez,* Summer thought. *She hates getting dragged into other people's psychodramas.*

Seth stood, almost completely still, within a pool of shadow thrown by a huge potted tree. He tended to seem serious, even at the best of times, but now he was grim. He looked up at her, saw her, and a slight smile softened his face for a moment.

Summer gave a wave, a small, sheepish gesture. "Hi," she said. This must look like something more than it was, with her dressed for bed and Adam wearing nothing but boxer shorts. She looked around the group as their eyes found her. "Why are you guys here?"

Diana seemed to be transfixed, ignoring Summer, staring at Adam. What was in that look? Hatred? Fear? Even some lingering echo of love?

"What did you tell her?" Diana asked Adam.

"Nothing," he said. His voice was empty of any emotion. Flat. "This is *your* party."

Diana hesitated. She looked at the others, as if they would handle the situation for her. "Where's Ross?" she asked at last.

Adam said nothing, just lowered his eyes and stared down at the floor.

"What's all this about?" Summer asked, growing impatient. The fear she'd felt had lessened. Her friends were here. As ominous as they all looked and as embarrassed as she felt, their presence was comforting just the same. Especially Seth's. Nothing bad could happen with Seth there. Seth was like her—an intruder from the normal world beyond Crab Claw Key.

Marquez jumped up from the couch. "Diana, you'd better tell her, all right?"

Diana shook her head. "I just wanted to make sure Summer was okay," she said in an almost inaudible whisper.

"Diana!" Marquez exploded. "You can't start this and not finish it. Look, we're here, right? So spit it out and we can all get out of this museum."

"This is about Ross, isn't it?" Summer said to Diana. "About you warning me the other day." She could feel Adam tensing up beside her.

"Not *just* Ross," Diana cried, so suddenly she seemed to shock herself.

"What about Ross?" Summer demanded sharply. She turned to Adam. "Adam, will you tell me what's going on here?"

But Diana had fallen mute again. Her hands were working convulsively at her sides. Her eyes were downcast, hidden in shadow. Adam said nothing.

Marquez lost patience. "Ross tried to rape Diana last summer. That's what this is about, Summer. Ross tried to force Diana."

Still Diana was silent. She just hung her head and nodded, almost invisibly.

For a moment Summer didn't react at all. The words just hung in the air. *Ross tried to rape Diana.*

Then she began to see pieces of a puzzle falling into place. The anger in Diana's voice whenever she'd spoken of Adam or his family. The distant sadness she'd so often seen in Diana's eyes. The curt, dismissive way Adam spoke of Diana. The tension that crackled between them whenever they met.

"What happened?" Summer asked. She wanted to go to Diana, put her arms around her cousin, and try to penetrate the wall of sadness that surrounded her. But something was still unspoken. Summer could sense it. The story was not over, not yet.

"Right there, on that couch." Diana pointed. "Adam and I had been out together, dancing. That's right, isn't it, Adam?" she asked, suddenly raising her voice. "Because I have such a hard time remembering the truth, what with so many lies."

When Adam remained silent, she went on. "I was tired. Adam had some friends down from New Hampshire, and he wanted to show them around town. So I said I'd just crash on the couch for a while till he got back. It was a pretty normal thing. Adam and I were close then. I was here a lot." She waited, as if expecting an argument. "Oh, I see—Adam has nothing to say. Fine. Anyway, I was tired, like I said, and I fell asleep. When I woke up, Ross was all over me. He was stinking drunk, but he was still strong. . . ." Her voice faltered.

"I don't think you have to tell us any details." It was Seth, speaking for the first time. Summer had almost forgotten he was there.

Diana seemed grateful. But she plowed ahead in her low, bitter voice. "Most of my clothes were torn. I had . . . he hit me, so I had a black eye." She pointed to her left eye and pressed it tenderly as if somehow it still hurt. "Anyway, that's when my hero came riding to the rescue. Adam came back. He pulled Ross off me. Isn't that right, Adam?"

Adam remained perfectly still, arms crossed over his bare chest, looking down as if vaguely concerned by some pattern in the rug.

"What did you . . . did you call the police?" Summer asked. She felt herself draw slowly away from Adam.

"The police?" Diana echoed hollowly. She raised her face and shot a look of cold disdain at Adam. "Did I go to the police, Adam? No, I didn't go to the police," she said. "How could I? I had no witnesses. It would have been my word against Ross's." She made a twisted, bitter smile. "My word against Ross's . . . and Adam's. See, Adam was very sorry about what had happened." Diana slipped into an anger-drenched parody of Adam.

"He was so sorry. He felt my pain, really he did. But, see, I had to understand how it would be if I accused Ross Merrick of trying to rape me. See, the Merrick family, well, gosh, it has so much influence, and darn it if Senator Merrick wasn't the kind of loyal father who would stand by his son. And really, after all, what choice would Adam have but to stand with the family, to deny anything had happened? Good old Adam, my one true love, well, he'd have no choice but to back up Ross."

Throughout Diana's story, Summer had felt a growing chill, a grim feeling that seemed to radiate from her heart and spread over her. She wanted not to believe Diana. But Adam stood silent. And Diana's words were too loaded with hurt and betrayal and anger and . . . some other feeling. Some feeling that made her look as if she were being eaten away inside.

Guilt, Summer realized. Guilt. Diana blamed herself somehow. And that lit the fire of Summer's own anger. She'd seen this kind of guilt before. It had never stopped eating away at her own parents.

"Is this true, Adam?" Summer asked.

Adam stuck to his silence.

"I said, is . . . it . . . TRUE?" she snapped.

The others all looked at her in surprise. No one could quite believe that tone of voice could come from Summer Smith. Adam looked stunned. His eyes met

Summer's gaze, then flickered and darted away.

"It's *still* true," he whispered.

"What?"

"I just told Diana what would happen if she attacked the Merrick family. It's not my fault. It's just the way things are. If she attacks us, we'll end up destroying her. I don't like it, Summer. But I have no choice."

"If *she* attacks *you*?" Summer almost laughed. "She attacks you? I think you have it backward, Adam."

But Adam had relapsed into silence.

It was as if he were shrinking before Summer's eyes. As if he had grown small and far away. Miles separated them already, light-years, compressed into just a few feet. She almost felt dizzy, disoriented. The world had shifted around her, and nothing was what it had been just moments before.

The silence stretched for a long time. Finally it was Seth who spoke. "Let's just get out of here."

Marquez nodded agreement. "Yeah, this place stinks. It smells like a pathetic little boy who doesn't have the *cojones* to be a man."

"You don't understand," Adam said, almost whispering.

"I think Marquez understands perfectly," Seth said evenly. "I think we all do. Summer? Are you ready?"

Summer looked pleadingly at Adam. Wasn't there something he could say to make everything all right?

Just hours before, she had gone to sleep thinking that maybe she was in love with him. Now, in the blink of an eye, he seemed to have become a completely different person.

Then she remembered Ross, leering and drunk at her door. She shuddered. Adam had known what Ross was capable of. And he had brought Summer here, just the same.

"Yes," she said, with a heavy feeling in her chest. "I'm ready."

2

Aftermath and Before Morning

"So, I'm guessing no one wants me to put on any music," Marquez said, joking lamely as she started the engine of her parents' car.

Summer didn't answer. No one answered as they drove down the long, winding crushed-shell driveway.

"No, guess not," Marquez answered her own question.

Summer had ended up in the front, with Marquez, thinking only that she didn't want to be near anyone. Marquez would leave her alone. Alone was good at the moment.

Diana was in the back with Seth. When Summer

glanced up in the vanity mirror she could see that Diana was leaning against Seth, her head buried in the collar of his shirt. His arm was around her.

Summer felt like a fool. Now that the initial shock was beginning to wear off, she felt like an idiot, like a not-very-bright kid who gets into trouble and has to be rescued by the adults. She knew she should be feeling sorry for Diana, or perhaps raging at Adam, but what she felt most was humiliation. To be dragged out of her bed, away from Adam's house, jerked out of her ridiculous romantic daydreams and be given this nasty, hard slap of reality . . .

Part of her was angry. She knew it was unreasonable of her, but she felt as if Diana had maliciously stolen something from her. Summer had been on a wonderful ride, floating along with Adam. It had been a great story. Here she was, the inexperienced, average girl from an average town who'd ended up going with the handsome, sexy, charming billionaire. It was as close to becoming a princess as was possible in a country without royalty. It was as if she were Princess Di, chosen by Prince Charles.

Bad example. Another unhappy Diana.

Now the big fantasy was over. Crash. Bang. Over.

Even in the soap operas it didn't happen this fast. The reality shift was never this total. How could she have been such a fool? How could she have fallen so far for a guy without ever seeing what he was?

And now Diana was crying in Seth's arms, and Summer had no one's shoulder to cry on. It was unfair. It was . . .

Summer grimaced, angry at herself for having these thoughts.

It was sickening. She was actually resentful of Diana for coming to rescue her. And Diana *had* come to rescue her, despite the pain it had forced her to face.

Summer felt the sting of the humiliation fade, a little at least.

That Diana had come to save her was something not to be forgotten, Summer knew. Not ever.

However humiliated Summer felt, Diana had to feel worse. This wasn't the time for self-pity. She took a couple of deep breaths and brushed off the beginnings of tears.

Summer turned in her seat. She reached back and placed her hand on Diana's arm. "Thanks," Summer said. "Thanks for coming to get me. I know . . . I mean, I can guess how hard it was."

To Summer's surprise, Diana put her own hand over Summer's. It touched Summer's heart. She and Diana had never exactly been close.

Summer's gaze met Seth's. He still held Diana close, offering his shoulder to cry on, knowing that she needed one.

He mouthed a soundless question—*are you okay?*

For some reason, at that moment, the tears she had held back began to fall. Was she okay, he wanted to know? Seth still had another shoulder, if Summer needed to cry about losing the guy she had chosen over him.

Many perceptions had changed in an instant. Diana was not the person Summer had thought she was. Neither was Adam.

And Seth?

Summer looked past him out through the rear window, watching through blurry tears as the Merrick estate, big as a castle, receded into the night.

Marquez dropped Summer and Diana at the Olans' big house, then took Seth to his own more humble house. She parked in the alley behind her home. She closed the car door carefully, not wanting to wake anyone upstairs. All she needed now was for one of her older brothers to start cross-examining her about why she was out so late. Her younger brothers wouldn't care, but her older brothers were not quite as Americanized as she was. There were some habits—overprotectiveness being one annoying example—that they had retained from their childhoods in Cuba.

Marquez went in through the front of the house. It was a three-story brick building. Her own room was on the ground floor, a huge expanse of territory that had once been an ice cream parlor. She still had a plate-glass display window at one end, and the long, low soda counter fronted by round upholstered stools. Down one wall were the glass and mirror shelves that had once held banana split bowls and milkshake glasses and now held her books, CDs, and assorted bits of clothing. A former hot fudge warmer overflowed with her panties.

The other walls were bare brick, coated by layer after layer of her own extravagant spray-painted art-work. Wild depictions of flowers and bushes and sunsets, and in one corner a tall palm tree that spread its vibrant green fronds across the ceiling. Entwined throughout it all were the graffiti-style names of years' worth of friends and acquaintances, and even a couple of enemies.

The largest name written there was two letters— J.T. Her boyfriend. Okay, ex-boyfriend.

Marquez peeled off her clothes and let herself fall facedown on her bed. She felt a dampness on the edge of the cover, where, earlier, Diana had sat shivering and wet with rain.

"What a night," Marquez groaned aloud. Diana and Seth and Adam and Summer. Jeez. Way too much stuff going on. Too many complications. Too many consequences. Too many tears. Why couldn't people just deal with things and not let them get so complicated?

Summer had been pretty cool. She'd been upset, that was clear, but there was something strong and not easily shaken at her core. Maybe that was the way all the people were in whatever sleepy, boring, party-free Midwest town Summer was from. "They got nothing else to do there, probably, except grow character," Marquez muttered. Summer kept saying they had the largest mall in the world. "Sure," Marquez said, "no beaches. You got to have a mall when you have no beaches."

She moved back to the counter and shuffled through the messy pile of CDs, some in their boxes, some not, some in the wrong boxes. Death Cab for Cutie. Yeah, that was about right for her mood. Something mellow and nocturnal. She stuck in the CD and flopped back on her bed.

No, wait. Wrong song. This was all about not wanting to love someone but loving him just the same.

J.T. stood out on the wall, the letters drawn large, in relief, so they jumped out like a 3-D beacon. She should paint over it. A couple coats of white and it would be gone. *He* would be gone. Him *and* his problems. It would make him disappear from her life.

Except that in too few hours she had to go to work, where she couldn't avoid him. There he'd be with all his scrambled priorities, all his doubts. Another tortured, unhappy fool like Diana. What was it with people? It was easy enough to be happy. Just let the crap flow off you. Just don't let it reach you. What did it really matter if J.T.'s parents weren't his *real* parents? What did it matter if Summer had lost a brother long ago? A brother named Jonathan? Why should Marquez let the two facts coalesce in her mind and form this nagging core of doubt? It wasn't her problem. That's why she had broken it off with J.T.: Marquez didn't need a neurotic, messed-up boyfriend. It absolutely wasn't her problem. Any more than Diana's sick tangle with the Merricks was Marquez's problem. It didn't matter to her. Marquez had her own life and her own goals. She was going to college and law school and on to a life as a respected lawyer. Briefs and motions and hours in the law library.

Tomorrow she would paint over J.T.'s name. Two coats, maybe three coats of white.

She drifted into sleep and dreamed of J.T. wearing his white cook's uniform, emerging time and again from them, covered, then uncovered, flesh materializing, vibrant and real as each new coat of white failed to make him disappear.

Adam Merrick sat for a long time thinking of nothing, leaving his mind blank. His eyes focused without seeing on the huge stone mantel that dominated one end of the room. He didn't want to think. He didn't want to analyze the situation.

Instead his mind wandered back to the small stretch of private beach, where, earlier that same night, he and Summer had sat roasting marshmallows over a fire while the tide threatened to chase them away.

Roasting marshmallows. It was the kind of thing you did with Summer. A simple, unexciting thing. But it hadn't been boring. With her it had seemed transcendently sweet and perfect. It might have been the most perfect evening of his life.

Gone now. Never to be recaptured.

He had cared about two girls in his life. He had gone out with, what? Hundreds? Yes, at least a hundred: here, at the New Hampshire house, away at school, at the parties his father dragged him to. He'd even spent a week in Hollywood squiring a bimbo starlet from a sitcom.

But he'd cared only twice. Diana. And Summer.

And both had been ruined for him by Ross.

Adam slammed a fist down on the arm of the couch. Ross. Passed out in his room upstairs now, all the damage done.

How hard would it be to go into his room, take a pillow, and press it over Ross's face? People would say he'd suffocated accidentally, a result of too much booze.

Their father would make sure the coroner didn't report anything that would embarrass the family. After all, it was just a year to reelection.

The thought made Adam feel sick. Sick at his own hatred for his brother. His impotent, powerless, pointless rage.

He got up and paced rapidly to the stairs, then ran to the top. The hallway was lined with doors on each side. His own room. His brother's room. The many guest bedrooms.

Yes, Ross was passed out. Helpless. Defenseless. Enjoying a dreamless sleep. Adam knew he would do nothing to disturb his brother's peace. Ross was family. Family was everything.

Adam opened the door to the room Summer had slept in. Her overnight bag still lay on the dresser, open. He looked inside. Shampoo. Conditioner. A brush. A small assortment of makeup, toothbrush and toothpaste. A pair of panties. Socks. Allergy pills. He hadn't known she had hay fever.

Her clothes, the ones she had worn earlier, were draped over a chair. They smelled of smoke from the bonfire.

He would have to return all this tomorrow. He could drive over in the boat. Or maybe the next day.

It surprised Adam a bit to realize it. He'd reached a decision, without even really thinking about it. He was going to get her back. This time Ross would not win.

Adam sat on the edge of the bed. The pillow still showed a crumple where her head had lain.

He lifted the pillow to his face and smelled her lingering scent, a mix of coconut shampoo, vanilla, and smoke. He pressed the pillow against his face. Then he lay back and pulled the blankets over him.

No, this time he was not giving up. Ross was not going to win.

He would win Summer back.

Diana went to her private bathroom and undressed, leaving her rain-damp clothes lying on the tile floor. She adjusted the water to the highest temperature she could stand. Then she climbed in, wincing at the hot spray against her chilled flesh.

Diana slowly lowered herself until she was sitting on the floor of the shower, letting the spray hit her bowed head and wash down over her face.

It was just what she had done that night, a year earlier. She'd sat here, just like this, letting the water pour over her. She had felt powerless and betrayed. She had hated Ross and Adam. And she'd hated herself. The sight of her own naked limbs, tan against white porcelain, had filled her with revulsion.

Diana let the familiar emotions wash over her. It was a ritual by now, one she was familiar with—

the memories, and the many layers of "could have," "should have," "why didn't I" regrets.

A year of it. Hoping it would all go away. Realizing it never would. Falling again and again down the long, black hole of depression. Each time climbing slowly back out, only to fall farther the next time and emerge more slowly still. She was losing the battle.

Diana stood up and turned off the water. The mirrors were steamed so that her reflection was no more than a suggestion of pink flesh and dark hair. Good. She hated the sight of her body.

Downstairs, in her mother's medicine cabinet, was the brown bottle half-filled with the pills Diana had counted again and again and again—her security blanket. Her reassurance that there would, in the end, be a way out of the black hole.

But not tonight.

Tomorrow was her day to volunteer at the Dolphin Interactive Therapy Institute. A sad little girl named Lanessa would be expecting her.

So not tonight, though she could feel the black hole opening wide to welcome her in. Not tonight, but before her mother came home. Before then, Diana reassured herself. She would end the pain before then.

3

The Closeness of Stars

Summer lay on her second strange bed of the night, in her second strange bedroom, and listened to all the tiny night sounds that were different here. She wished desperately that she could be down in her own shabby little stilt house, hearing the reassuring sounds of the water as it lapped against the pilings. But the stilt house was a mess at the moment. Seth, who had been hired to fix it up, had gotten a bit overzealous, and for the moment, at least, the house was unlivable.

When Diana had first stuck Summer in the pelican-poop-covered stilt house, she'd been miserable. But since then she'd fallen in love with it. The stilt house was *hers,* after all, and it had the advantage of her mysterious housemate—an indescribably good-looking guy named Diver with no last name, and no place to live except the deck of Summer's little house.

Tonight she had taken the bedroom next to Diana's in the luxurious main house. Diana had refused all offers of conversation or company, and Summer hadn't had the will to push very hard. Earlier Summer had heard the shower running in the next room. Maybe now that Diana had told everyone her secret she would get better.

The pillow beneath Summer's head was firm. Her own pillow, down in the stilt house, was soft. Her pillow at home, a million miles away in Minnesota, was soft, too. There she had a stuffed pink and gold unicorn on the bed beside her pillow. She'd had it since she was four. It had only one eye.

For some reason, sleep didn't come. She had slept an hour or two at Adam's house. Maybe that was the problem. Or maybe it was what had happened after.

Summer jiggled her legs. They seemed to be energized. It happened sometimes when she would be bothered or just too awake to fall asleep. Her best friend from home, Jennifer, called it "wiggle-leg syndrome," as if it were a disease. She'd say, "I'm so tired because I couldn't sleep last night. I had dreaded wiggle-leg syndrome."

Summer threw back the thin covers and climbed out of her bed. Not *her* bed. Someone's bed.

She was still wearing the baby-tee and boxers she usually wore to sleep. The same thing she'd been wearing at Adam's house as she dreamed now-forgotten dreams.

Her robe was on a chair. She put it on.

The hallway was dark, lit only by a tiny cockleshell night-light stuck in one of the electrical sockets. The hallway was defined by a railing on one side, looking out over the foyer below with its twin curved stairways. The hall took a turn around a bathroom. The other bedrooms were out of sight.

Summer went down by the right-side stairs. Her plan was to go to the kitchen, find something containing lots of chocolate, and eat it until a sugar depression put her to sleep.

But once in the dark kitchen, she looked out at the backyard. It was a long, sloping lawn that fell away gradually till it touched the water.

Summer let herself out through the glass doors, out onto the patio. She pulled her robe tightly around her, but when she felt the night air, she laughed. Silly. She had to get used to the fact that "outside" here did not mean "cold." It was much warmer outside than in. The storm that had come through earlier in the night had blown away, leaving warm, moist air behind. She loosened the belt on her robe.

Summer stepped off the patio onto a lawn so lush and deep and springy it was like walking on a mattress. The grass pricked her bare feet, a wonderful feeling. A gentle breeze, smelling of salt and sweet hibiscus. She walked down to the water, stopping at the edge, a low concrete retaining wall just inches above the placid water.

From here, looking left, she could see the outline of the stilt house. It drew her with surprising force. It was amazing how quickly it had come to seem safe and familiar.

She walked a few steps closer, looking for . . . She wasn't sure what she was looking for.

Summer sat down quite suddenly on the grass just at the edge of the water, and lowered her face into her hands. She began to cry, silently at first, then sobbing.

She cried for herself. And for Diana. And even for Adam, so stiff and controlled at the end, looking so trapped, and yet so determined not to escape. She even cried for Seth, who loved her, so he said, and had been there for her when her relationship with Adam had crashed and burned.

At one point Summer wiped her eyes, using the sleeve of her robe. And when she glanced up she thought she saw movement, there on top of the stilt house. A shape silhouetted briefly, then gone.

She took a deep breath and tried to stifle her sobs. But her tears were not yet used up.

Then she heard the soft rustle of the grass very near, and, looking from beneath lowered brows, she saw two bare legs. She raised her sight, glad that in the darkness he couldn't see her red eyes.

"Hi," he said.

"Hi, Diver," Summer said.

For a while neither of them said anything. "I guess you were asleep up on the deck, huh?" Summer asked.

"Yeah."

"I woke you up?"

He shrugged uncomfortably.

"Sorry. It's been a bad night. A real bad night. And the worst thing is, it's just a part of all the bad things." She started crying again. She felt she was making a fool of herself, but that didn't help her stop.

Diver knelt down on the grass, still seeming skittish and bothered. But he didn't leave.

Summer managed a sobbing laugh. "I guess I'm disturbing your *wa,* huh?"

He shrugged again. He seemed about to say something, but remained silent.

"I thought this was all going to be this big party, you know?" she told him, not expecting an answer.

"I mean, summer vacation in the Keys, what could be better? Like nothing bad could ever happen here. Like it was all about sun and beaches and meeting guys. But then it turns out there's all this . . . this stuff going on." She wiped her eyes again. "God, Diver, I just feel so homesick now. I just keep thinking about my mom and dad and my room and—"

"Um, look . . ." he said, interrupting her.

"Yes?"

He fidgeted a bit, then stood up. "Look, come with me, okay?"

She looked up at him, standing over her, wearing his madras swimsuit. It was still, as far as Summer knew, his sole possession in the world. "Why?"

He held out his hand for her to take. She took it. He drew her to her feet and led her down along the shore.

"Where are we going?" Summer asked.

Diver just made a sighing, frustrated noise. "Just come, all right?"

So she did. They walked past the stilt house, down to where the retaining wall disappeared and a ramp had been cut, leading into the water.

"You'd better take that off," Diver said, pointing at her robe.

Summer did, letting the robe fall on the grass.

Diver led her to the water's edge. It was almost as warm as bathwater on her toes. The temperature of her own skin.

Diver took her hand again. "You *can* swim, right?"

"Of course I can swim. But it's dark."

"It's not dark," he said. "Look. The moon."

She looked, and the moon was riding low, three-quarters full, down over the Gulf.

Summer followed him into the water, feeling it climb up her body, soaking her boxers, creeping up to her T-shirt. At that point she let herself slip, raising her feet away from the sand and shells beneath.

The two of them swam in silence, the only sounds the water and their own breathing. Finally Diver stopped, well out into the water, out past the dark stilt house.

"Like this," he instructed. He lay back, floating with his beyond-handsome face turned up to the sky.

Summer let herself fall back. Water closed over her face, then receded. She spread her arms wide. She could feel her hair fanning out in a swirl.

She looked up and gasped. Stars. Stars like nothing she had ever seen beneath the obscuring lights of Bloomington, Minnesota.

Summer lay there, perfectly suspended. Black water beneath her, going down who knew how far. Black sky above, going on forever. Forever.

And stars. More and more appearing the longer she looked. Too many to count, or even think about counting. Bright, twinkling points of light.

"Do you know that the light of those stars began traveling toward us way back when there were dinosaurs?" she asked dreamily. "They're very far away."

"No, they're not," Diver said. "They're right here."

Summer smiled. Maybe he was right. Maybe it was just like the water. Maybe the water came from clear across the ocean but it was still right there, holding her, lifting her up to float high above the ocean floor, pressing her face up into space.

"Why did you bring me out here, Diver?" she asked. Her ears were under water, and her own voice sounded muffled and far away. Like his.

"You were sad," he said.

"And I can't be sad out here, floating in space and looking up at the stars?"

"No," he said simply.

"No," she agreed.

4

Video Blog

Jennifer, I don't even know where to begin. First I guess I should explain why I'm here and not down in my own house. I went down and got the video camera because I wanted to talk to someone, and, well, you're still my best friend.

What did I tell you the last time I recorded on this thing? That I was falling for Adam, right? Guess what? That isn't looking so great right now. I'm laughing, but only because it hurts. I mean, I was so, so into him, Jennifer. He's like . . . this perfect guy that every girl would like to fall in love with.

Only, I guess he wasn't.

Sorry. I drifted off there. Just fast-forward through

that part where I stared off into space like a moron.

Anyway . . . it turns out there was this whole thing between him and Diana and his brother, Ross. Ross tried to . . . I guess he tried to rape Diana, and they covered it up.

All I can say is I feel like a jerk for ever being annoyed by Diana. I didn't realize all the stuff she was going through. And I guess it makes my problems seem kind of unimportant. Which I suppose they are. Tomorrow I'll try to talk to her again, you know, try and get her to go see a counselor or something. But Diana is hard to get close to. She kind of shuts people out.

Seth was there tonight when this whole thing happened. You remember Seth. He's the guy from the airport. The guy I was kind of into before Adam? Of course you remember, I guess I probably talked about him enough on other tapes I've sent you. Anyway, Seth was there, too. He didn't do very much or say very much. He just was kind of . . . *there*.

You know, it's weird in a way, because Adam is a little taller than Seth, and maybe has bigger shoulders, but it was like Adam kept getting smaller, and Seth kept being Seth. I suddenly had this feeling that I'd been a complete moron and made this totally stupid decision.

I don't know. Forget it. Like I said, I'm tired and confused. It's not like I care about Seth. I would have to be the most superficial person on the planet to care about Seth when I haven't even had time to really cry over Adam.

Wouldn't I? I mean, it's wrong, right?

Except, you know, Seth was always kind of around, if you know what I mean. We did have that thing in the airport, and I know he likes me, or at least he *says* he likes me. Of course, he probably doesn't anymore because I blew him off to be with Adam.

You know what the problem is? I can't ever make a decision and stick with it. I'm indecisive, that's what it is. And you know whose fault it is? That stupid woman on the plane with her dumb tarot cards. She's the one who got me thinking about the *three* guys I would meet. You know, the right one, the mysterious one, and the dangerous one?

Well, not that I believe any of that stuff at all, because I don't—you know I'm not superstitious. I'm just saying it's like, okay, we now have a winner in the *dangerous* category, right? Adam was obviously the dangerous one. Only, it was his brother who was really dangerous. Which leaves the mysterious one and the *right* one. It doesn't take a genius to figure out that Diver is mysterious. There's nothing mysterious about Seth. Which means Seth is the *right* one.

I know, I said I don't believe any of that stuff, I'm just saying—what if?

I feel like I'm trapped in this big web of fate. Like I have no choices. Or else I have too many choices. And I don't know how to deal with it all.

The only good thing is that I never decided Adam was *the* one. What if I had decided that, and then this had happened? But I kept my options open, you know? And now I realize how smart that was, because it would be so incredibly sad to really love someone and then lose him. I mean, I learned that from Mom and Dad and all the years they've felt bad over losing Jonathan.

Yes, I know. That's different. Except not totally.

I want to really love someone and have him really love me. But I don't ever want to lose him. Just think how bad I'd feel if I had decided to be totally in love with Adam. As it is, I feel bad enough. The only reason I'm not boo-hooing right now is that I already cried.

Anyway, Jen, I've learned my little life lesson for the week: Don't get too far into things with guys until you really know them. You have to find some way to . . . I don't know, have some backup, or some insurance or something.

Otherwise, this whole falling in love thing is too dangerous. Remind me of that, okay? You know how I am with retaining deep philosophical insights. Especially when I'm sleepy.

5

Things Always Look Better in the Morning.

When Summer woke, she was surprised to find herself in the main house, surprised at all the things that weren't there—the smell of mildew, the lap, lap of water. Surprised at the firmness of a pillow that had given her a stiff neck.

Then she was surprised to discover she was wearing an oversize man's shirt. In a flash she recalled the night before, the terrible earlier parts, the sweet later parts. Her video camera was on the nightstand. Good grief, had she actually done a video blog entry for Jennifer? She'd probably babbled like an idiot. Her baby-tee and boxers were drying on the back of a chair, looking stiff from the salt water. She must have found the man's shirt in the closet. Had this room belonged to Diana's father, back before the divorce?

Summer got up, feeling strange and unsettled. She pulled on her robe, went to the window, and drew back the heavy shades.

"Whoa!" She staggered back, laughing and covering her eyes.

It was amazing. The sun! The sun of Florida, so much more intense than in her home state of Minnesota. The sun *there* was a light in the sky. The sun *here* seemed to penetrate everything, to be reflected back from every possible angle, to fill the world and everything in it with brilliant yellow light. The heat of it glowed from the window glass.

Outside the water sparkled, almost blinding in places. A sailboat was passing by on its way out to sea, big white triangular sails filled with morning breeze. It moved in slow motion, majestic and silent.

Summer slid the glass doors open and stepped out onto the balcony. The balcony was larger than the room, a vast wooden deck surrounded by white-painted rails. The chill of air-conditioning was just a memory in the heat that burned Summer's bare toes and baked her upturned face.

She went to the edge of the balcony and looked down toward the stilt house. It was mostly invisible from here, hidden by trees that ran down to the water's edge, but she could hear the sound of a hammer, pounding, stopping, then pounding again.

Seth. It could only be Seth.

It would be nice to go down and see Seth, she realized. And nice to go back to the stilt house. In fact, as long as the world was this gloriously bright, everything would have to be nice.

Summer went downstairs to make a pot of coffee. It was one advantage of being in the main house. Diana and her mother always bought great coffee. In the stilt house she had a jar of Folgers crystals. Even she could tell the difference.

Diana was already there in the kitchen, looking withdrawn and thoughtful. She was eating raisin toast and leafing indifferently through the newspaper.

"Hi," Summer said, trying to sound casual and normal and not as if she was talking to a delicate person.

"Hi," Diana said. "There's coffee there already. You have to work today?" she asked casually, making conversation.

"Yes, lunch shift. Unless, you know, you want me to stay around here?" Summer poured herself a cup of coffee. "Look, Diana, maybe we could talk."

"I don't think so," Diana said bluntly.

"Okay, then maybe you could talk to a counselor or something," Summer said. "I'd be glad to go with you if you're nervous about it."

Diana made a wry face. "Summer, whatever you do, don't start being sweet to me."

"I'm naturally sweet," Summer said with a trace of sarcasm. "I can't help myself."

"That's better," Diana said. "Listen, when you go down to the stilt house, I have something for you to give to Seth." She slid a manila envelope out from under her newspaper.

Summer had a pretty good idea what was in the envelope.

"Tell him for me that he is the original sweet, decent guy," Diana said softly. "I can't go on torturing a guy who'd let me blow my nose on his shirt."

Summer buttered her toast and sat down at the table. She waited for Diana to say more, but her cousin went back to gazing blankly at the paper, occasionally taking a quiet sip from her mug.

"Diana . . ." Summer began.

Diana sighed.

"Look, I really think we should talk about what happened last night."

"Not much to talk about," Diana said. "I put on a big dramatic scene. Now everyone knows just how messed up I am. I'm sure everyone is pleased—that cold witch Diana turns out to be nuts."

"That's not what anyone thinks," Summer said.

"Uh-huh." Diana tried a sneer that became a

quivering lip. She concentrated determinedly on the paper.

"Diana."

"Yeah? What?"

"I don't think that at all. I think you saved me."

Diana rolled her eyes. "That's me, a regular rescue 911."

Now it was Summer's turn to feel reluctant. For some reason she hadn't told anyone the details of the night before. It made her feel vulnerable or foolish.

Like Diana felt, Summer supposed.

"Diana, look. I didn't tell you," Summer began, "but Ross came to my room."

Diana looked up sharply.

"He was at my door, just when you and Marquez and Seth showed up," Summer said. "I thought he was Adam at first. He was drunk. I guess he'd been drinking for a while beforehand. I don't know what would have happened. Maybe you think you looked foolish or something, but that's not how it looked to me." Summer had blurted the story in a quick burst, trying to get rid of it. But the cold fear she'd experienced was not entirely gone. If Diana had not come to the Merrick mansion, Adam might not have awakened. No one might have heard Summer crying out. "Anyway, Diana, I owe you."

Diana was at a loss for words. She seemed to be

concentrating, trying to digest some unusual idea. Then, with a small, impatient shake of her head, she said, "Nice of you to say that." She stood up suddenly. "Well, I have to go take a shower."

Summer watched her go and felt frustrated. It was as if what she'd said just hadn't reached Diana. Like Diana had raised some wall of armor that kept out any expression of gratitude or friendship.

"Diana," Summer called.

Diana stopped and turned back, annoyance and impatience clear on her face. "What?"

"Thanks."

Summer poured coffee into two mugs and walked down to her stilt house with the manila envelope under her arm.

The stilt house sat out over the water of the bay, connected to land by a wooden catwalk. It was a modest little bungalow, even a bit shabby. When Summer had first learned that Diana had planned to stick her out here, rather than in the luxurious main house, she had been upset. But now it was home. Funny how quickly it had come to seem familiar.

A pelican sat on the railing, wearing an expression that seemed simultaneously dorky and scolding.

"Hi, Frank," Summer said to the pelican. "How's fishing?"

She knew the pelican's name because Diver had told her. How Diver knew that its name was Frank was a mystery. But then, everything about Diver was a mystery. Last night, as she had finally climbed out of the water, she had been talking to him and only then realized he was no longer there.

Probably he had gone back up to the deck of the stilt house. Probably. Or maybe he was just a figment of her imagination. She smiled at the thought. But no, Marquez had seen him once. So if Diver was a hallucination, he was one that others could see, too.

Summer hesitated at the door to her house. She could hear Seth still hammering away and pausing to sing, then hammering again. A lot was unsettled between her and Seth. An awful lot.

He had asked her to go out with him. He had asked her *after* he had kissed her in the airport minutes after they first met. But then it had turned out he had a girlfriend named Lianne. He'd said they had broken up, but then Summer had walked in on Lianne lying in Seth's bed.

After that, well, after that she no longer had any doubts about setting Seth Warner aside. It had seemed so obvious at the time. Seth was a two-timing jerk, while Adam . . .

Right, Summer. You have wonderful intuition about guys. You're the genius of love.

She remembered the manila envelope under her arm. Seth would be glad to get it. No doubt he'd immediately burn what was in it. Which would be a shame, because it really was a very artistic photograph. Diana had taken it the summer before, by accident of timing snapping the shutter at the moment when Seth was rudely pantsed by Adam and Ross and dived for cover off the end of a pier. Diana said she'd been trying to catch the sunset. She'd called the picture "The Sun and the Moon."

Summer put the mugs down on the rail. Yes, it *was* the photograph. *And* the negative. Yes, it was quite artistic. Nicely composed, all the elements balanced perfectly.

She put the picture back.

"That was wrong of me," she told Frank. "I'm ashamed."

Frank spread his wings and glided away, obviously shocked by her behavior.

Summer retrieved her mugs and went inside. An impressive amount of work had been done already. The kitchen floor gleamed, covered in shiny new linoleum. It was a real improvement over the dirty, stained, torn, ragged tile that had been there. The hammering continued in the bathroom. There was a smell of sawdust and glue.

Summer peeked around the corner. Seth was on his hands and knees, wearing jeans with no shirt. He had a very nice back. Muscular in a lanky sort of way, with a narrow waist and no fat. She contemplated the view for a moment.

Maybe the tarot lady had it right. Maybe Seth was the perfect guy all along.

Or else Diver was. Only . . . no, he wasn't, somehow.

Or maybe the *right* guy was someone else entirely.

She had to keep all her options open. No falling in love until she was absolutely, dead sure.

Seth had replaced a lot of the old rotting floor with fresh boards, all neatly nailed in place. He positioned a nail and raised his hammer back over his shoulder.

"Hi."

The hammer came down. "Aaaah, jeeeeeeez! Oh, man!" Seth jumped up, clutching his left thumb with his right hand and doing the dance of pain. "Mmm-mmaaaan, oh, man, man that hurt."

"Are you all right?" Summer asked, alarmed.

"Mmmph. Hhmmm. Oh, yeah, I'm swell. It's not the first time I've smashed my finger with a hammer. Which is not to say that I enjoy it." He inspected his thumb critically.

"Is it broken?"

"No, I don't think so." He wiggled it several times, wincing at the pain. He looked at her crossly. "Is that coffee for me?"

"Yes." Summer held out the cup. "Sorry if I surprised you."

He took the cup and tasted a sip. He shrugged. "No big deal. Just if you ever see me using a sledgehammer or an ax or anything, let alone a chain saw . . ." He worked his thumb back and forth.

Summer giggled. "You must have been down here working since the sun came up."

"It's better to start early," Seth said. "It's not as hot then. At least I should have the place ready to be lived in by tonight." He looked down, staring into his coffee cup. "I'm uh, really sorry about, you know, being a jerk."

"What are you talking about?" she asked.

"The way I tore this place up," he said. "I mean, I know it's my job and all, I know I had to do some of it, but I could have been more careful. I could have made sure you could still use the place. Then, you know—"

Summer sighed. "Look, Seth, what happened wasn't your fault. Besides, nothing did happen, so no biggie, right?"

"That's not the point. I can't just be a jerk because I feel like it." His face was stony. "I was mad at you."

Summer smiled ironically. "Yeah, I kind of figured that out, Seth."

"I know what happened with Lianne," he said. "I mean, I know what you think happened."

Now Summer began to feel uncomfortable. It was way too early to be talking to Seth as if maybe they were going to have some kind of relationship. She had just broken up with Adam—if you could call it breaking up. Summer wasn't sure. She'd never really had a serious boyfriend before. Was what had happened the night before an official breakup?

Maybe not official, but a breakup, definitely.

Seth seemed to sense that he had carried things too far, too fast. "Look, I'm sorry. I keep having to say that. I just meant that I know you're feeling bad, and I wanted to tell you that I still really care about you."

Summer made a frustrated noise. She couldn't deal with this, not yet. "Seth, I really don't think—"

He held up his hands. "Okay, I understand. You want time."

"That's right," Summer said, gratefully seizing on the opportunity, "I want time."

He pointed with his hammer at the floor. "I'll get the rest of the tile laid in here before noon. That way the adhesive can dry by this evening. I'll grout it tomorrow."

"Grout?" Summer grinned.

"Sure, grout. What? What's funny about grout?"

"I don't know, just the word. Grout. Grout. I've never known anyone who used the word *grout* in casual conversation before."

Seth smiled his reticent smile. "I'll try to watch my use of that word."

"No, I like it. It's so . . . you know, so *real*. It's a *guy* word, like *transmission* or *yo* or, I don't know, like *dude*."

"So if I go around saying 'Yo, dude, let's grout that transmission,' you'll know I'm a guy?" He made a face. "Of course, I'd have to be a stupid guy, to grout a transmission."

Summer laughed. "I guess I'd know you were a guy even if you didn't say that."

"I was beginning to wonder," he said.

"What?"

"If you knew I was a guy."

Summer shrugged, feeling embarrassed again. "I may have noticed. I mean, of course, duh." She pointed at his bare chest. "You're really flat chested. That was my first clue."

Now he was embarrassed, too.

"So, um, have you had breakfast or anything?" Summer said, heading briskly toward the kitchen.

"I had cereal when I got up, but that was hours ago," he said.

"I have some eggs and some bread, so I was going to maybe fry the eggs and make toast," Summer said. "Do you want some?"

Sure," Seth said gratefully. "You know how to cook?"

"Not really, but I'm trying to learn," Summer said. "I have to go to work in an hour, so I need to eat something first. Oh, by the way," she said with careful nonchalance, "Diana asked me to give you this envelope. I have no idea what it is."

Seth looked in the envelope and smiled. "She didn't have to do that," he said. "I'm extremely relieved that she did, but she didn't have to."

"I guess it was kind of embarrassing having that picture around," Summer agreed.

"Hah. You said you had no idea what was in the envelope," Seth said, smirking a little.

"I guessed," Summer said.

"You looked."

"No, I didn't."

"Uh-huh."

"Seth, I'm *trying* to cook. Could you not start arguments with me when I'm trying to cook?" Summer said severely.

Seth leaned against the wall while Summer began cooking. He winced a couple of times, at the way she cracked the eggs and the way she didn't butter the toast

all the way to the edges, and again at the way she tried
to turn the eggs over too early and broke the yolks, but
he stayed where he was.

"I broke only three out of the four eggs," Summer
said wryly. "I'm improving."

They sat at the simple round table. Summer gave
Seth the unbroken egg.

"Thanks. I was starving," he said, attacking the
food.

"Well, all that hard work," Summer said. "Hammering, grouting, and so on."

"Yeah. Plus it was a long night."

"Yes, it was," Summer agreed. He had a smear of
butter on his lower lip. It was hard not to stare at it.

"Thanks," Seth said. "You seem like you're okay.
You know, about last night."

Summer shrugged. "I *was* pretty upset."

"I wish I could have, I don't know, helped somehow."

"It wasn't your problem," Summer said.

"But maybe I could have helped you, you know?"
Seth looked embarrassed now, as if he'd said too
much.

Summer picked up the paper towel she was using
as a napkin and reached over to wipe the butter from
his lip.

"Thanks."

"You're welcome," she said.

He got up from the table, piled her dish together with his, and carried them to the kitchen. She followed him, intending to give the plates a quick rinse.

They collided. The collision lasted longer than it should have.

He put his arms around her. She pushed him, her palms flat against his lean, bare chest.

"I want to kiss you," Seth said.

"Well, you can't," Summer said. "This is just like in the airport. You think you can just go around kissing people when they don't even want you to?"

"I thought you wanted me to," he said. He was still very close. "Are you sure you don't?"

Summer hesitated. Seth took her in his arms again, and this time she didn't resist. He kissed her.

After several very pleasurable seconds, she pushed him away. "I'm sorry," she gasped. "I shouldn't have let you do that."

"You shouldn't have? Why?"

"Why? Why? How about because last night I was kissing Adam? I'm not some slut! That's why. Jeez, Seth, you of all people should know. You're the one who's always telling me how people come down here to the Keys and start acting strange and losing control of themselves and doing things they would never do in the *real* world."

"I said all that?" He looked disgruntled. "When am I going to learn to shut up?"

Summer twisted away from him and put some distance between them. What was it about Seth that he could get her to want to kiss him when she didn't really want to? "I have to get ready for work."

"Ready for work? La dee da?" He came close and took her hands in his. "Look, Summer, you can pretend you don't care," he said. "I don't know why you want to pretend you don't care, but that's okay. I *do* care. I'm in love with you. I keep thinking maybe I've lost you, first over Lianne, then over Adam. But you know what? I won't ever give up."

At that moment Summer wanted very much for him to kiss her again. And that realization made her queasy. How could she want Seth to kiss her? Hadn't she learned her lesson about leaping into relationships? She'd wanted Adam to kiss her, too, and look how that had turned out.

"You barely even know me," she said. "How can you say you're in love with me?"

"I don't know. I guess I can say it because it's the way I feel."

"Seth, what if it turns out that I don't feel the same way about you?"

He looked somber. "I don't know. That would be bad."

"Exactly. See? I don't want that," Summer said. "I mean, can't we just take everything slower until we're really, really sure?"

"Slower." He thought that over. "Yes, I guess I can do slower."

"That would be good," Summer said. She was glad he understood. She was not going to jump instantly from Adam to him. That would be wrong, even on Crab Claw Key.

He looked thoughtful, then brightened at some idea.

"So, how about tomorrow afternoon?"

"We could think about starting then," Summer said, actually a little disappointed that he was accepting it all so well. "We'll take everything slow, see if we get along, see if we have anything in common and all of that."

"After tomorrow we *will* have something in common," he said, grinning wolfishly. "Masks, rubber clothes, and great big feet."

6

Diana Figures It Out, and So Does Lianne

Thanks, Summer had said. Thanks. The word seemed not to mean anything to Diana. Why had Summer said it? It wasn't as if Diana had done much. On the contrary, she'd frozen up and babbled like an idiot, unable, without Marquez's goading, even to explain why she was there at the Merrick mansion in the middle of the night.

You didn't thank people for making asses of themselves. You didn't thank people for being weak and contemptible. That made no sense at all.

She climbed the stairs to her room. From far off she could hear the sound of hammering. Seth, out working on the stilt house.

Thanks. Like Diana had done something.

She stopped halfway up the stairs, descended, and went instead to her mother's vast bedroom suite. Mallory would be coming home soon. Any day now. Diana had to do what she'd been thinking of doing before then. Perhaps this afternoon, after she got back from volunteering at the institute.

She went into her mother's bathroom and opened the medicine cabinet. The bottle was there, as it had been on the countless occasions she'd looked. She twisted off the cap, feeling a strange satisfaction in the familiar feel of it. She spilled the pills out onto her palm and counted them carefully.

Yes, they were all still there. More than enough to do the job.

They would find her at the bottom of the circular stairs. She didn't know why she'd chosen that spot. Perhaps it was supposed to be symbolic—Diana, dead at the bottom of the twin staircases, unable to decide whether she should go left or right. It struck her as funny in an awful way.

It would be a small item in the local paper—daughter of famous romance novelist dies from a drug overdose. Dead from an overdose. It would be so common it wouldn't even make the big newspapers.

Although the Merrick family would certainly be relieved.

Relieved. Yes, that was the word. Relieved. Because . . . because they were afraid. Of her.

It was a new thought. A *new* thought, insinuated into the horribly familiar ritual thoughts of depression and self-loathing.

Was it true?

She replaced the pills in the bottle and put the bottle back precisely in its place on the shelf. She went upstairs to her own room.

She showered and was drying off when the thought poked up again into her brain.

The Merricks were afraid.

"So what?" she asked herself wearily. "So what?"

She shook her head impatiently and returned to more familiar thoughts. She wondered when her mother would come home. She wondered whether Adam had laughed at the way she'd stood there, trembling and incoherent. Probably. Why wouldn't he? It was funny, after all, the way she'd stood there unable to do or say anything. Funny.

And yet . . . Again the thought teased her. The Merricks were afraid of her.

"It's not like it matters," Diana said to her steamy reflection in the mirror. She began to dry her hair with a blow-dryer, fluffing it with her fingers. It wasn't as if she could actually do anything to change what had happened. She was who she was, and that was the important fact.

And yet . . . they feared her. Adam feared her. Ross. The senator, even . . .

But what could she do? What was she going to do? Get some kind of revenge on them?

She started to laugh.

Then she froze. She directed the blow-dryer at the mirror, burning a hole through the steam.

Revenge? Was that the point?

How would that change anything? No, wait, the word wasn't *revenge*.

"Justice," she said. That was the word.

Diana felt a chill that shivered her flesh and thrilled her mind.

Justice. Revenge. Call it whatever. They were afraid.

Her reflection became clear in the mirror, a face floating in a small circle made in the haze. Her dark, sad eyes stared back at her.

How many times had she looked into her own eyes, hoping to find something there? Something other than weakness and self-hatred. How many times had she looked and seen the eyes of a victim staring back at her, a contemptible, weak, disgusting . . .

They. Were. Afraid.

Her hand was clutching the handle of the dryer so tightly the plastic began to snap.

And then Diana did see something new in the eyes

that looked back at her. She had already done something to hurt Adam, hadn't she? She'd told Summer the truth, and look what had happened.

Diana laughed out loud, a strange, wild sound. Yes, she had already hurt one of the Merricks with a simple statement of truth.

That's what they were afraid of. They were afraid of the truth.

Maybe they should be.

"Marquez! Pick up! Now!"

J.T.'s voice could be heard clear from the kitchen, through the swinging doors, over the chattering sound of the precheck computer and above the clatter of the bartender rapidly restocking his glasses.

Marquez gritted her teeth. Oh, J.T. was in rare form today. She hefted a tray of dirty dishes and hitched it in one swift move high up over her head. She barreled toward the swinging doors, stuck out her foot and kicked it open. She slammed the dirty dishes down at the dish station.

"I heard you the first four times you screamed my name!" Marquez yelled.

"I shouldn't have to call you more than once, Marquez. If you weren't off flirting for tips, you'd be here to pick up your food."

J.T. was tall, a handsome, nineteen-year-old blond

with calm, mellow-looking blue eyes. Usually. The mellow look was not in evidence right now. His white cook's apron was stained green, red, and other colors that defied identification. He was sweating heavily and looked as if he might at any moment use the fourteen-inch chef's knife in his hand for some evil purpose.

Despite everything, Marquez felt a twinge of attraction to him. There was something cute about J.T. when he was in one of his towering cook's rages.

"You don't need to worry about my flirting." She glanced at her pad and at the dinner plates sitting up on the line. "Hah! The fries go on the pompano, the bake goes with the lobster. Hah. And you're screaming at me?" She added several words in Spanish that made the Guatemalan dishwasher grin. Then she added several more.

Summer, who was nearby ladling chowder into bowls, looked over discreetly. J.T. scared Summer, Marquez knew. At least a little. Summer didn't know him the way Marquez did.

"Don't curse at me in languages I don't understand," J.T. grumbled. He quickly shifted the potatoes.

"Hey, you must not even understand English or you would have gotten the order right in the first place."

"If you'd have picked up your order on time, you'd have spotted the problem earlier," J.T. said, shaking his finger at her.

"Don't you shake that at me," Marquez warned.

She tried to look fierce, but darn it, now he was smiling. "Jerk," she said, loading the plates onto her tray.

"Lianne, pick up!" J.T. yelled.

Naturally, Lianne appeared instantly, bustling her tiny, eternally thin, never-even-have-to-think-about-a-diet shape through the swinging door.

"It's so nice working with a real professional wait-ron," J.T. said, directing the sarcastic comment over Lianne's head at Marquez.

Marquez cursed at him under her breath. As she headed out to the dining room she heard a mock-angry J.T. say, "Lianne, did you hear that? I wish you'd have a talk with her about her attitude."

Suddenly, Marquez heard J.T. yelp in pain. She glanced back just in time to see that he had burned the palm of his left hand as he reached for a spatula and pressed the side of the oven instead.

At the same instant, Summer recoiled from the bowl she was handling. She raised her left hand and looked at the palm. "Ouch," she said. "I didn't think it was that hot."

Marquez shook her head. No. It was a simple coincidence. J.T. burned himself at least twice per shift, and Summer had been handling hot soup bowls.

But it had happened at the same instant. The same parts of the same hands.

Later, when the rush was over and Marquez could

take a break, she hooked up with Summer, who was looking a bit frazzled, leaning against the counter in the waitress station as she swallowed an aspirin with a big glass of water.

"Give me one of those," Marquez said wearily. "Is it your feet or your back that hurts?"

"Feet, back, and all parts in between," Summer muttered. She handed the bottle to Marquez. "And your boyfriend! I hate to say anything bad about anyone . . ."

Marquez smiled affectionately. Summer actually did hate to say anything bad about anyone. "He's my *ex*-boyfriend," Marquez said. "And yeah, he was raggin' big time today. It's because Skeet called in sick, so he's doing extra work."

"Oh. I didn't realize that. Now I feel bad. I shouldn't have gotten so mad."

"You got mad? What did you do, tell him to go to *heck*?" Marquez laughed.

Even Summer laughed. "You know, I have a lot of hostility down deep inside."

"Well, J.T. keeps his hostility right up front where he can reach it easily. It's funny, you two being so different." Marquez didn't realize what she was saying until she'd said it. She gulped hard. Probably Summer wouldn't even notice.

No, Summer might be a sweet blonde, but she was not a dumb one.

"What do you mean by that?" Summer asked.

"What?"

"Why would it be funny if J.T. and I were different?"

"Did I say that?" Marquez took a long swallow of iced tea.

"I thought you did," Summer said, tilting her head and giving Marquez a quizzical look.

"Why would I have said that? It wouldn't make any sense," Marquez pointed out.

"Oh."

"Exactly," Marquez said. Man, that had been close. Close and stupid, she realized as she poured three pitchers of iced tea. It was all a ridiculous idea, anyway. What were the odds that somehow J.T. was Summer's long-lost brother, Jonathan? About a million to one?

Of course, the age was right, so that lowered the odds a little, some relentlessly logical corner of Marquez's mind pointed out. And they were both white. Both blond. And in some ways they looked at least a little bit alike.

Marquez shook her head. This was nuts. It was beyond nuts.

"Guess what I'm doing tomorrow morning?" Summer said. "Scuba diving."

"Scuba diving?" Marquez said. "Cool. Everybody says the Keys are the place to scuba dive. Me, I like air. What are you doing, taking lessons?"

"Yes. From Seth."

Marquez's jaw dropped. "You sleazebag." She laughed. "Boom, out with the old, in with the new. That's my girl, Summer—don't waste any time. I mean, *any* time."

Summer made a face. "It's not what you think."

"No, of course not," Marquez said. "So, what's the deal? You talked to Seth this morning and he did an airport on you?" She leered. Then she realized Summer wasn't denying it. "You *slut*! You let him kiss you?"

"Shhh." Summer glanced around nervously. "He's broken up with Lianne, but there's no point in making her feel bad."

"Speaking of broken up . . ." Marquez grabbed the handles of two pitchers of iced tea in one hand. "The kitchen animals need their liquids." She shook her head. "Little Summer Smith from Horsepuckey, Iowa, can *move.*"

"Bloomington, Minnesota," Summer yelled as Marquez headed for the kitchen. "And it's not like I just met Seth."

Cooks were not allowed out of the kitchen, so waitresses generally brought them something cold to drink at the end of a shift. Generally, when J.T. was working everyone understood that Marquez took care of the duty. That, at least, had not changed since their breakup.

As she neared the kitchen she could hear the sound

of rock music. The Ramones were pounding out "Teenage Lobotomy" from the CD player. It was one of the throwbacks the cooks liked to play at the end of a tough shift, a sort of goof on the intensity of work, shouting out "lo-bo-to-my" with the chorus.

Marquez was dancing before she reached the door, using the iced tea pitchers as a partner.

She backed through the swinging doors, executed a neat spin, and set the teas on the counter. She had both hands over her head and was rocking out fairly fiercely before she spotted J.T drinking a large glass of tea.

A glass that had apparently been handed to him by Lianne, who was standing nearby, smiling up at him.

J.T. looked at Marquez. Marquez looked at Lianne. Lianne spared a brief glance at Marquez, then returned her full attention to J.T.

"Oh, hey, thanks, Marquez," J.T. said, seeming embarrassed.

"Yeah," Marquez said. "No problem."

She walked back out to the dining room. Lianne caught up with her.

"Hey, Marquez, I didn't know you were pouring drinks, too."

"I do that sometimes," Marquez said. She was steaming, but since she had no good reason to be angry she couldn't let Lianne see it. Let it go, Marquez told herself.

Lianne put her arm on Marquez's shoulder to stop her.

Not a good idea.

"You want something?" Marquez snapped.

"Look, it's not like I was doing anything sneaky."

Oh, no, no, Marquez thought. Like I don't recognize that whole tilted-head, smiling, laughing, admiring-look thing. Like I haven't used it on guys myself. "Oh, I know that," Marquez said poisonously. "I know you're still totally into Seth. Right? In fact, you guys are so tight you're not even worried that he's taking Summer scuba diving tomorrow."

Yeah, chew on that, Marquez thought. Hah. Yeah, hah! Summer told you that in confidence, Marquez, and you blurted it out just because you were angry at J.T.

But to Marquez's surprise, Lianne did not explode. Instead she just looked a little wistful. "Sethie and Summer." She sighed. "I guess . . . I guess I have no choice but to let that go. I was stupid to try so hard to hang on. I guess I'd gotten to the point of thinking Seth was the only guy in the world. And I was upset. But you know what?" She brightened. "Summer vacation will come to an end, and we'll both go back to Eau Claire. Maybe Seth needs his little summer fling. So to speak. And maybe I should follow his example. Why get so upset? This is Crab Claw Key, right? The land of total freedom. The place with no rules. So, yes, maybe I should let Seth go for now, and see what other fun things there are to do."

"Uh-huh. Maybe you could take up skydiving," Marquez said. "Maybe you could try it without the parachute."

"What a good idea," Lianne said, batting her eyes. "Or maybe I could just take up J.T. He's tall. I like tall guys. Do you think he likes petite, slender girls? Or is he just into . . . bigger girls, like you?"

Do not lose your temper, Marquez ordered herself. *Do not go off on her, she'd just enjoy it, the sneaky little . . .* She took a deep breath. It was all for the best. It was over between her and J.T. It was a time of change. Summer and Adam were finished; Seth and Lianne were finished; she and J.T. were finished.

Time to move on. Time to let it go.

"You want J.T?" Marquez said coolly. "He's all yours."

Very mature, she congratulated herself as she walked away. Very sensible. When a relationship came to an end it was only natural that people would move on.

Only, she hadn't expected J.T. to be able to move on quite this quickly. Fine. If that's the way he wanted to be, she'd show him some moving on.

7

Not for Sale at the Mall of America

"This will be the day when I finally cross over the line that separates the tan from the untan," Summer said. She lay back on the blanket and contemplated the red glow that came through her closed eyelids.

"This will be the day when I cross the line that separates the chubby thighs from the unchubby thighs," Marquez said, lying beside her, but on her stomach. She looked down the beach, eyes shielded by sunglasses and a green plastic visor. "Because, see, that guy down there with the totally ripped abs is not going to be interested in chubby thighs."

"Don't make me look at guys," Summer groaned. "If I have to roll over I'll get all sandy. Besides, what does lying in the sun have to do with chubby thighs?"

"Oh, fine, so you *do* think I have chubby thighs."

Summer sighed. "Marquez, you do not have chubby thighs. You have perfect thighs. If I were a guy, I'd go nuts for your thighs. No one in the entire history of the United States has ever had thighs to equal your thighs."

"So you're saying women in other countries have much better thighs?"

"I'm not talking to you anymore," Summer said.

"Not talking to me? Good. Then I guess I can tell you," Marquez said. "Because if you're not talking to me you can't yell at me. See, I may have kind of accidentally told Lianne you were going scuba diving with Seth."

"I am now officially talking to you again," Summer announced. "*Kind of* told Lianne?"

"As in I definitely told her. Look, I was mad," Marquez explained. "I thought she was coming on to J.T."

"The guy you don't care about," Summer said dryly.

"I don't."

"I see. You just get mad when some girl talks to him."

"Exactly. If I have to be broken up, I don't want him off having a good time somewhere," Marquez said. "So I told her about you and Seth because I just wanted to have something to rub her face in."

"Oh, great," Summer said. "I can't believe you let that slip."

"I know. I'm sorry. It was pretty low. But it was Lianne . . ."

Silence fell for a few minutes. "All right already, so tell me. What did she say?" Summer demanded.

"Basically that she was writing Seth off for the summer," Marquez said. "As in she's discovered the joys of summer vacation flings, so let *Sethie* play tag with Summer, Lianne will just play with her new toy, J.T."

"Ouch. Not that you care."

"Or you, for that matter. I think it's pretty clear that I don't care what J.T. does, and you don't really care about Seth."

"This is all well-established," Summer said.

"But I really am done with J.T.," Marquez said. "Whereas you are already lining up on Seth. Adam isn't even cold in his grave yet, and you're scoping Seth. Poor Adam, tossed aside like yesterday's trash. Good-bye, Mr. Merrick. Hello, Mr. Warner. Out with the charismatic boy billionaire, in with the sincere-yet-sexy carpenter."

"I told you, it's not like that," Summer said lamely. "You really think Seth is sexy?"

"Sure. Plus he's a nice guy."

"That's what I thought about Adam," Summer said.

"You think Seth is hiding some darker side? No way. Hey, what about that card-reading lady? Didn't she say one guy was going to be bad news? And wasn't that Adam? Duh? And isn't Diver the supposedly mysterious one? That leaves only Seth as the right one."

"The one who would *seem* right," Summer corrected. "Besides, I don't believe in all that stuff."

"Uh-huh."

"I *don't*. If I did, maybe I'd have figured out that Adam was trouble," Summer said.

"That makes no sense. Oh, my God."

"What?"

"You might want to dig a hole," Marquez said under her breath. "You know the aforementioned charismatic boy billionaire? He's about fifty feet away and closing in fast."

"What should I do?" Summer asked. She felt panicky, like she should try to avoid him. Yet that was pretty well impossible, given that they were on a public beach. Besides, it was silly.

"Hmm, too bad he's a dirtbag," Marquez said. "The boy does look fine in a bathing suit."

Summer decided against springing up and running like a scared rabbit. The only thing to do was be cool.

She'd spent most of her life trying to be cool. Now would be a nice time to actually succeed.

His shadow fell over her. "Hi, Summer," he said.

For once Marquez stayed quiet. For once Summer wished she wouldn't.

"Hi, Adam," Summer said in her squeaky fake-casual voice.

"Look, I . . . I kind of figured you might be here. I stopped by the Crab 'n' Conch and they said you two left right after lunch."

"Yes," Summer said. "Yes, we both left. Right after lunch. The two of us." She was half sitting, shading her eyes with her hand and squinting through one eye. Probably not an attractive look, she realized. Popeye in a two-piece.

"So, um, I was wondering if maybe we could talk," Adam said. "Maybe walk down the beach."

"I guess that means I'm not invited," Marquez said.

"I think we should talk," Adam said doggedly.

Summer hesitated only a moment. She let him take her hand and help her to her feet. They walked down to the water's edge, then along the beach, with just the tepid lip of the Gulf cooling her toes.

"So," he began. "What should we talk about? I wonder."

Summer couldn't think of anything to say.

"Not funny, I guess," he said. He ran his fingers back through his hair and looked past her out over the sparkling green sea. "First of all, I'm really sorry about last night. Everything was going so perfectly, and then it all went down the toilet. Not exactly a great end to our date."

"Adam, I don't think that's really the thing to worry about," Summer said. They were talking like strangers. Like people who had just met. And she did *not* want to do this. She had decided to move on. To get past it as quickly as she could.

"I'm just saying, I hope you remember that things were really great before the whole thing there at the end. I want you to know that I don't feel mad that you left or anything."

Summer almost laughed. "That's very generous of you." There was no sign that Adam heard the sarcasm.

"Since you mention generosity," he said. He reached into the pocket of his bathing suit and pulled out a small, gray, felt-covered jewelry box. It was oblong, with the name of a jeweler in gold letters. Adam opened the box, looked at what was inside, and handed the box to Summer. "Here. I hope this will help make it all up to you."

Summer looked at the box and caught her breath. Inside it was a necklace, gold with a pear-shaped diamond in a simple setting. It seemed unlikely that anyone in the Merrick family ever bought fake diamonds or less expensive gold plate. Which meant that the value of this necklace was probably greater than the sum total of everything Summer Smith owned.

"I know it was kind of an intense scene and all," Adam said, still holding the box out to her. "I just really hope we can go on, you know, get past it."

"Get *past* it?" She made no move to accept the gift. The more she looked at it, and the more the meaning of it became clear, the angrier she felt. Why was he doing this?

"Sure," Adam said. "I mean, there's no reason why this should affect us. You and me. You're not Diana."

"I can't believe you're saying this," Summer said. "I really can't. No reason why it should affect *us*?"

He moved closer now. His face was just inches from hers. A face that she had kissed many times and had wanted to kiss many, many more times. He still exerted an almost magnetic pull over her. She could still recall all too clearly the sensation as his lips trailed down her throat . . .

"Why should Diana's problems ruin what we have?" he pleaded earnestly.

"*Diana's* problems? You make it sound like it's no big deal."

He looked troubled at her reaction. His eyes darted

aside, then came back, renewing the link between them. "I don't mean that. I know Diana's been hurt. I wish I could do something to make her feel better, but I can't."

"Sure you can," Summer said. "You can tell her you'll back her up if she tries to do something about Ross."

"What, testify against my own brother?" He sounded incredulous. "Is that what you're saying I should do? I wouldn't even *have* a family anymore if I did that."

"Ross is messed up, Adam. I don't know if he's an alcoholic or what, but he's dangerous."

"He's family," Adam said, pleading. "Besides, give me a break. You think Diana's some kind of poster child for good mental health? She was depressed long before this."

"That doesn't justify anything," Summer said. Her voice was growing louder, to match his. "Ross tries to . . . he tries to rape Diana, and then you, her supposed boyfriend, help cover it all up?"

"My father is a rich and powerful man, Summer," Adam said, almost sadly. "It's the way the world is. I didn't make the rules. I have no choice. I have to stick with my family. No matter what. You understand that."

Summer bit her lip. "Yes," she said sadly. "Of course I do. And Diana's my cousin. *My* family."

At last understanding seemed to dawn in his eyes. Understanding, and pain. Slowly he closed the jewelry box.

"You know what, though, Adam? If someone in my family was like Ross, I'd have to do whatever I could to stop him, even if that did mean sending him to jail. Because sooner or later Ross is going to hurt someone worse, or even kill someone. For his own good—"

"I don't turn against my family," Adam repeated.

"Then I guess we don't have very much to say to each other." She was relieved that she kept the tears out of her voice. She was not going to cry. Not now.

A smile flickered at the corner of his mouth. "You can be pretty cold when you want to, can't you, Summer? Whatever happened to that golly, gee-whiz, Midwestern, Bloomington-Minnesota-home-of-the-Mall-of-America sweetness? Suddenly you're acting so tough."

Summer felt the tears welling up. Her throat was constricted and painful. Her voice was unnaturally low. "I guess you never really knew me all that well."

Adam made one last attempt. He reached for her. "Summer, don't just—"

Quite suddenly, without planning it or thinking about it, Summer slapped the jewelry box from his hand. It flew from his grasp and landed several feet away in the sand. "Whatever it is, I don't want to hear it, you *creep*," Summer yelled. "You jerk. You knew what Ross was capable of, and you put me right in the middle of it. And if he *had* tried to hurt me you'd have sold me out just like you did Diana. So don't go waving some necklace in my face like that means something. You never did care anything about me, Adam. Maybe that's why it's been so easy for me to move past you. And you know what? In Bloom-ington-Minnesota-home-of-the-Mall-of-America, as you so sarcastically put it, maybe we know what we're worth, and maybe we're worth more than even you can pay."

"Summer—"

"Oh, shut up," she said. She turned her back on him, hiding a face contorted by tears and burning anger and regret.

Diana arrived home from her stint at the Dolphin Interactive Therapy Institute in the early afternoon. She had worked mostly with Lanessa, a little girl whose personal history before coming to the security of the institute was so horrible that reading her case file made Diana cry.

But on this day Lanessa had performed the amaz-ing feat of actually talking to Jerry, one of the tame dolphins. Not just a whispered hello, but two long sentences. She'd told Jerry it was okay that he'd splashed her with water because she wasn't mad at him. It had been a big moment for Lanessa, and for Diana, and even, Diana would have sworn, for Jerry. There was, of course, no way that the dolphins could really understand what was happening—all the professionals at the institute agreed on that. And yet, among the volunteers there was agreement that somehow the big, powerful animals understood everything that happened on an emotional level.

Diana always felt an afterglow from her time at the institute, and today, as she drove the twenty miles down the highway, it lasted all the way home.

Diana parked her little Jetta and went to her mother's office. She sat down at the desk and filled in one of the presigned checks her mother had left her. She made it out to Seth Warner. He was almost done with the work on the stilt house, and Diana's mother had asked her to pay him when it was completed. On her own initiative, Diana added an extra hundred dollars. Her mother would never notice it, but it would mean a lot to Seth.

She headed down to the stilt house, intending to leave the check with Summer. Unless Summer wasn't home yet and Seth was still there.

Part of her hoped he was. He had been very kind. Her mind drifted back to disjointed memories of the night before. She had cried on his shoulder—literally.

And he had held her. Awkwardly, perhaps, maybe a little embarrassed, no doubt worried that she would misinterpret.

Diana hadn't misinterpreted. She knew he wasn't interested in her. Not in *that* way. How could he be? Seth was from that other world of normal, decent people. People of sun and laughter and easy happiness. People like Summer.

People not at all like Diana.

Diana walked out to the stilt house, holding the check in her hand, waving it like a big, visible excuse for intruding. She started to knock on the door, but it was ajar. She went in.

Seth was right there, his back to her, absorbed in something. A book.

Good grief, a school yearbook. Summer had brought her school yearbook with her. Diana almost laughed. Yes, Summer was a different variety of human being. And so was Seth, concentrating so closely on what was, undoubtedly, a grainy, badly done black-and-white picture of Summer.

Diana drew back outside. She sighed. She shouldn't feel disappointed. Of course Seth was in love with Summer. Of course he was. How could he not be?

A pelican (named Frank, Summer insisted) swept in, wings beating the air. He settled on the railing.

"True love," Diana whispered to Frank. She peeked

around the corner. Seth was seated at the table now, the better to admire the yearbook photo. He had a wistful half-smile on his lips and was running his finger over the image. It made Diana want to cry. It would be a wonderful thing to be loved that way. A really wonderful thing.

Had Diana ever been loved like that? Had Adam once longed for Diana the way Seth longed for Summer? Diana smiled ruefully. Hard to imagine anyone feeling that way about her.

She knocked on the doorjamb. Seth jumped, startled. He flushed, looking guilty, and snapped the book shut.

"Just me," Diana said. "You can continue drooling."

"I don't know what you're talking about," Seth said as though he actually expected her to believe him.

"Uh-huh. I have a check for you." She flourished it and put it on the table for him.

"Well, I still have a few things left to do around here," he said.

"Anything that will give you an excuse to be around Summer," Diana said.

He didn't answer. Instead he changed the subject. "It was nice of you to give me back the picture."

"Have you burned it yet?"

"No. I won't, either. It's a nice photograph—even

if it is the most embarrassing thing in my life. You were always talented with a camera."

"Thanks," she said.

"So, um, how are you doing?"

She shrugged. "It's all ancient history," she lied. "Old news. I don't even know why I was weeping last night. Probably just an excuse to get to slobber all over you and make Summer jealous."

"I don't think we're at the point where she'd be jealous of me," Seth said sheepishly.

"Well, you obviously are, even if she isn't," Diana said, pointing to the yearbook.

He had no answer, just looked even more sheepish. Diana started several times to say something. What she wanted to say was, *Seth, any girl who doesn't want you is a fool . . .* or, *Look, if it doesn't work out with Summer . . .* or just *It would be nice to think that your shoulder would be there for me again, the next time I need to cry. . . .*

But all of those things would be the wrong things to say.

Instead she said, "You realize, of course, that I kept one copy of the picture."

Seth laughed silently. "No, I don't think you did."

"No, I didn't," Diana admitted. "Seth, how come . . ."

"How come what?"

She'd been about to say, *How come we never went*

out? How come I never realized what a great guy you are? How come you never fell in love with me? But she knew the answer. Seth could not be the person he was and love a person like Diana.

"Never mind. Enjoy the check."

"Diana? I know this is none of my business, but are you thinking of doing anything about Ross? I hate to see him get away with what he did."

Diana smiled. "What should I do?"

"I don't know," Seth admitted. "I guess I'd like to see you get justice."

Diana nodded thoughtfully. "What's the difference between justice and revenge?"

Seth shrugged. "I'm not sure, Diana."

"Me neither," Diana said. "But I'm thinking about it."

8

Black Rubber and Blackmail

"Okay, now you see why you use powder on the inside, right? So it will slide on easier," Seth explained patiently. His upper torso was already encased in black and blue rubber. He stood with arms crossed over his chest, shaking his head critically.

Summer was making a spectacle of herself, trying to get her hand through the sleeve of the wet suit top. Her hand was stuck, and with every push or pull the rubber just stretched, with the result that she'd ended up turning in a circle trying to accomplish the simple act of getting dressed.

It would have been bad enough if only Seth had been there to watch her fight her idiot battle against the rubber, but they were at the end of the public beach, not far enough from afternoon sunbathers, several of whom were staring at her with frank amusement.

"Wasn't there somewhere more private we could have done this?" Summer demanded, grunting as she at last popped her hand through. "Finally. Of course, I'll never be able to get it off."

"The only other choice was in the bay, and that's no fun. Too much old crap, thrown-away tires, and old shoes and stuff in that water. Besides, over there you have all the tourists hot-rodding around in their rented motorboats."

"And on that side I might not have had to do this in front of a thousand people," Summer grumbled.

"Ignore them," Seth advised.

"Why is this even necessary? The water here is hot, and the suit makes me feel like I can't breathe."

"The water's not as warm deeper down," Seth advised. "Besides, it's just the top. Be grateful you aren't wearing the pants, too. Now, *those* are hard to put on." He smiled. "I think you look kind of sexy this way."

"Very funny. I'm burning up. Anyway, we're not going deep, are we?" She added the last part nervously. The fact that she was going to be breathing *under* the water was something she had avoided thinking about.

"No, not deep. I just want you to learn everything in the right order. Weight belt," he said. He lifted a heavy belt studded with lead weights and leaned close to wrap it around her waist. "Normally we'd use a buoyancy compensator—"

"Oh, I love those," Summer joked.

"Only, Trent didn't have any spare to lend out. Okay, now, the tanks. Turn around."

Seth hefted a single gray metal tank onto her back, helping her work her arms through the straps. It felt as if it weighed a hundred pounds. "I'm going to drown in all this."

"No, you won't drown. I won't let you drown. You have your mask? Put it on your head but don't pull it down yet."

"Yes, master," Summer grumbled. "At least that way no one will be able to recognize me. The whale girl. Free Willy. The newest attraction at Sea World."

"Snorkel?"

"No thanks, I don't snorkel. It's an unhealthy habit. I gave it up."

"Very funny," Seth said, smiling. "But not as funny as the next part. Go ahead and put on your fins."

"On my feet?"

"No, on your ears. Of course on your feet," Seth said. He handed the huge, triangular flippers to her.

"My feet are all the way down there," Summer

said, pointing. "I can't move, let alone bend over."

"I'll help you. This time."

He bent down and fitted the fins on her feet. Then he stood up.

"Why is it that you look like James Bond or something," Summer asked, "whereas I feel like Oprah *before* the diet?"

"You just have to get used to it. Besides, you look great."

"We're going to die, aren't we?" she asked.

"Eventually. Not today, though. Knock on wood."

"I don't have any wood."

"Oops."

"Oh, you're really funny," Summer said.

"Since we don't have any wood, how about a kiss for luck?" Seth said.

"In front of ten million people who are already trying not to laugh at me?" Not that she didn't want to kiss him. She'd been thinking about it much of the afternoon as he solemnly went through all the instructions she needed, being so serious that his very seriousness had started to seem funny.

"You want *bad* luck?" Seth asked.

"This is total blackmail," Summer grumbled. But she tilted back her head, lips parted, eyes drifting closed. The memory of their kiss over eggs had lingered. It had been an excellent kiss. And it wouldn't mean she was getting too deeply involved with him or anything. It was just for luck.

To her annoyance, Seth planted a brief, light kiss on her forehead.

"We don't need *that* much luck," he said, obviously hugely amused by himself. "Come on." He led the way the few feet to the water's edge. "Now, remember everything we talked about. All kidding aside, it's fairly easy to screw up, so do exactly what I tell you."

"You'd like that."

Flopping across the sand on her monstrous flippers, Summer made a face at Seth's back. Water washed over her toes, which just made walking in fins even more difficult.

"Okay. Time to get wet," he said after they had walked out a way. "Let's do it."

The first sensation was of drowning. Definite drowning. Summer sucked wet air through the snorkel in quick, panicky gasps. She couldn't see anything at all.

Of course, that was because her eyes were shut.

Summer opened her eyes and nearly screamed. Her head was definitely underwater. She was breathing, but her head was underwater.

Okay, it wasn't exactly deep water. Actually, the sandy floor of the Gulf of Mexico was only about two feet below her.

She sucked air through the snorkel again. A small wave broke over her and she caught a sickening mouthful of salty water. She swallowed it, and only then remembered that Seth had told her to spit it out and then clear her snorkel.

Great. Now she was going to die from drinking salt water. Everyone knew you couldn't drink salt water.

Summer felt something tapping her on the back of the head. She looked up, raising her mask out of the water.

Seth was standing in front of her, grinning. "Takes getting used to, huh? Breathing underwater and all?"

"Ung gwesh sho," Summer said. Then she spit out the snorkel mouthpiece. "I guess so."

"Okay, we're going to go out a little farther. You'll swallow less salt water that way. By the way, there's no shortage of oxygen on the planet. You don't need to try to breathe it all at once. Easy does it."

"We're not going out *too* far," Summer said anxiously.

"Summer, the water is so shallow here that if we swam out a quarter mile we'd barely be in ten feet."

"Oh."

"Follow me, now. I'll be just a little ahead of you, okay? And I won't let anything happen to you."

"Okay."

She stuck her mask under water again, this time

keeping her eyes open, and tried to breathe normally. It took a while till her breathing became anything like normal, but eventually it did. She learned to clear her snorkel when a gulp of seawater poured in. She learned to swim by moving her legs slowly, powerfully, letting her fins do part of the work.

Gradually, very, very gradually, the sandy floor of the Gulf fell away. Two feet. Three feet. Four feet. She glanced over at Seth, arms trailing casually at his side, legs working regularly. He looked at her every few seconds, checking to see that she was okay, his eyes looking overly intense behind the mask.

It wasn't the worst feeling in the world, the way he was so concerned. It did make her feel safe. And he was so obviously at home out here.

Kind of ironic, Summer thought. She'd gone floating at night with Diver, but she was diving with Seth. Somewhere in there was irony, she wasn't sure where.

Seth reached over and took her arm gently, signaling her to stop. They both came to rest, and Summer stood up.

Only, the Gulf floor wasn't four feet below her. It looked like four feet. But it was at least six, which was unfortunate, since that left all of Summer underwater.

She gasped and fought her way back to the surface. Seth put his arms around her. Summer spit salt water directly in his face.

"Oh, sorry! Oh, gross," she cried.

Seth laughed. "It's okay. I was already wet."

"Yeah, but I spit on you. I thought it was more shallow." She was chattering, not from cold, but from the shock of discovering she was so far out in the ocean. She twisted back and forth to try to find the land. It was harder treading water with tanks and a weight belt, though the wet suit top seemed to give her some buoyancy.

"We're only about a hundred yards out," Seth reassured her.

"How come I can't see the beach?"

"Because it's behind you." He turned her around, held her by the waist, and boosted her up to see over the crests of the tiny waves.

"Oh." Beach umbrellas could be seen very clearly. Parallel with her, a small boy rode an inflated air mattress. They had not exactly swum all the way to Bermuda.

"Okay, ready to try going on the regulator?"

"I guess so," Summer said gamely.

Seth went back over a list of all the things he'd told her on land, making sure she understood everything she had to do.

"By the way, *now* we need more luck," he said.

"I'll drown," she said.

"No, you won't." He put his arms around her, or at least as far as he could with the bulky tank on her back.

This time he really kissed her and she kissed him back, a salty, strange, intense kiss. He held her on the surface by powerful strokes of his fins, buoying her. She put her arms around his neck, feeling at once exposed and invisible in the trough between gentle swells.

"Now we'll have plenty of luck," he said.

"You're sure this is part of the training?" Summer asked, trying to sound flip, but with a slap of water in the face, gargling instead.

Finally, when she was ready, he helped fit the regulator mouthpiece in her mouth. It was a little like doing the kindergarten trick where you shove an orange peel over your teeth.

"Ung mung lnk hrnhy nhad," she said.

"Did you ask if you looked pretty silly with that thing in your mouth?"

Summer nodded.

"The answer is yes. Come on. See you below."

Summer tested the air coming through the regulator. It seemed like normal air.

She stuck her head under the water and let herself sink slowly down. Seth was already below her, looking up protectively. She began to swim, slowly descending toward him.

Now, this! This was cool, Summer thought. Okay, this was definitely cool. Much cooler than drifting around on the surface with the snorkel.

I am underwater!

She did a slow roll over onto her back and looked up at the surface of the water. The brilliant yellow sun was nearly blinding, even through the ripples of the sultry waves. She exhaled an explosive cloud of bubbles and watched them rise, circling and bobbing and sparkling in the sunlight.

Her mind went back to the night with Diver, watching the stars overhead, floating motionless between sea and space. And before that she had looked out over this same sea with Adam, skimming across it in his boat. Now here she was with Seth, encased in protective rubber armor, literally beneath the waves, invading an alien world, a vast new undiscovered universe.

She was sure there was some profound meaning there somewhere.

She touched the bottom and trailed her hand through the sand, stirring up a tiny whirlpool. Okay, Summer thought jubilantly, now summer vacation is back on track.

This would be fun with anyone, she told herself. It's not because I'm with Seth.

Seth floated by, paused, and waved his hand in a slow, beckoning gesture that meant "follow me."

He was leading her deeper. She hoped he wouldn't take her too deep.

"Look, you *have* to come," Summer insisted. "I want to get some stuff to go on my walls. I have brand-new linoleum and brand-new tile and even brand-new grout, and all I have on my walls is nothing. Besides, I need a book about fish."

Summer and Marquez were on the lawn with Diana, who wished they would go away. Marquez was just back from work, flush with tip money. Summer was back from scuba diving and had not shut up about it yet. They stood over Diana, who was lying on a beach chair under two layers of sunscreen, baking and thinking.

"Yeah, we really, really want you to come with us," Marquez said. "Really."

Diana shook her head wearily. "Let me guess. Marquez can't borrow her parents' car, and you both need a ride."

"You shouldn't be so cynical," Summer chided.

"Yeah. You're right, we do need you to drive, but still, cynicism isn't called for," Marquez said.

Diana nodded thoughtfully. "Summer, do you happen to have one of those little, tiny tape recorders?"

"What? Why?"

Diana looked bored. "I need one, okay?"

"I don't have one," Summer said.

Diana climbed to her feet. "Well, then I guess I'll just have to buy one. Which means I'll drive you to the mall. Give me a minute to change. If you want, we can take Mallory's Mercedes. The keys are on a hook in the pantry. Why don't you two get it out of the garage and put the top down."

"How does she manage to do that?" Marquez asked Summer. "Make us feel like we're her servants."

"Or you can walk to the mall," Diana said over her shoulder. "It's only like twenty miles."

Diana changed quickly into a patterned sarong skirt and a white top. She was on her way out of the house when the phone rang. She picked it up in her mother's office.

"Yes."

Her heart sank as she recognized her mother's voice. "Diana, I can't believe you're there. I expected to get the machine."

"Sorry to disappoint you. You're not back, are you?"

"No, honey, I'm in Sacramento. California. Don't even ask. They've extended the tour, and I have to go on talking about this silly book for another week."

Diana breathed a sigh of relief. It was a reprieve. So much had gotten tied up in her mind with the return of her mother. Another week to decide what to do. "Well, I guess I'll survive."

"I know *you'll* survive. How is Summer?"

Diana rolled her eyes. "She's fine. As a matter of

fact, I'm taking her shopping. The stilt house is almost all fixed up."

Diana heard the honking of the Mercedes's horn outside and the faint sound of Marquez shouting something impatient. "She's waiting. I better go."

"Okay. You still have my ATM card and the credit cards?"

"No, I've been supporting myself by picking up sailors."

Her mother made a phony laugh. "That would be unusually outgoing for you, Diana. It's nice to know you're meeting people."

"Uh-huh. Are we done?"

"Yes. Buy something nice for Summer, a gift from me. And get something for yourself, too."

Diana hung up the phone, seething as she did after almost any interaction with her mother. Her gaze fell on a small framed photograph on her mother's desk. It showed Mallory, back before she'd become a big success, back when her hair was still normal-size, before it had become romance-writer hair. She'd never noticed the picture before. In it, her mother seemed unusually frumpy. And it wasn't even a good picture, all fuzzy and off-center.

Then it occurred to Diana that the picture was there for a reason. This was Mallory's "before" picture. It was to remind her of what she had been and what she had become. On the wall, much larger, gilt-framed, was the publicity shot from her mother's first bestseller. A whole new Mallory Olan.

Before and after.

Diana could imagine her own "before" picture. It would be a picture of her now. Right now. *This* was the before.

Suddenly she took out her mother's address book. The number was bound to be there still. They'd done a little puff piece interview with Mallory . . . yes. There it was.

She could do it. She could do it right now. The idea excited her in a dark, unsettling way. Yes, why wait any longer?

It was all so new. The entire concept of doing anything at all was new. It had been so long. So much time had passed when all she had managed to do was wallow in depression and dream of how she would end her suffering.

Some new energy was inside her now. She could feel it. But it was fragile force, like a single candle in the darkness. She wanted to nurture that candle, keep it safe from blowing winds that might snuff it out.

Start it now.

The great dark hole of depression was still there, still tangible and real and oddly seductive. Against it just the one small light. She had to make it grow, give it air and fuel. To let the fire burn brighter and hotter, until it dispelled the last of the shadows.

Yes, start it *now*.

She checked the number again. But she didn't dial it. Instead she called a different number. Area code 202, Washington, D.C.

She took a deep breath. "Start it, Diana," she ordered herself sternly. "Do it now, or you'll find one excuse after another never to start."

She dialed the phone number. There was a delay, then it rang.

Click.

"Senator Merrick's office."

"I wan—" Diana's voice choked off. She almost crashed the receiver down in panic but stopped herself. She cleared her throat. "I want to speak to Senator Merrick."

"I'm sorry, but the senator cannot take calls. I'll be glad to take a message."

"No," Diana said sharply. "He will want to take this call himself. It's personal. It's about his son."

A long pause. "Who's calling?"

"My name is Diana Olan. Tell Senator Merrick to take this call. Or—" She hesitated. Her prepared speeches all sounded silly now. Like something a child would dream up. "Look, tell him if he doesn't want his son to go to jail, he'd better take this call."

An even longer pause. Then, "Please hold."

Outside, the car horn honked again, more insistent. Diana could picture Marquez and Summer out there, playing the stereo, talking away, getting annoyed that Diana was keeping them waiting.

And she could picture another scene, over a thousand miles away in Washington. She imagined a dark, paneled office. Maybe the Washington Monument was visible from the window. Maybe—

"Who is this?" A brusque, haughty voice, instantly recognizable.

"Senator Merrick?"

"Yes. Now, what do you have to say? I'm a busy man."

"Your son tried to rape me." The words came tumbling out, all of their own accord.

"Don't waste my time. I'm hanging up."

"I'll go to the police," Diana said.

"Do whatever you think you have to do, young lady," he said calmly. He even sounded a little bored.

But no, he wasn't bored, Diana knew. "Senator, your son Ross tried to rape me in your Crab Claw Key home last year. I know you heard about it. I know Adam told you what happened. That's why you put Ross through rehab."

"I know who you are, Diana. But I thought you were a smart girl," he said contemptuously. "I thought you knew better than to try to blackmail me."

"It isn't blackmail," Diana said. "I'm just . . . It's just that . . . I'm tired of being afraid."

"No one has tried to threaten you," he said. "You invent some incident and call me up—"

"I didn't invent anything and you know it!" Diana cried.

"So, you have witnesses? The police will want to know if you have witnesses."

"I realize that, Senator. I know the police will want witnesses. And I know Adam will lie to protect Ross. But you know what? I figured something out. The police may want witnesses, but there are other people who may not care all that much whether I have a witness or not."

"I think this conversation has gone on long enough."

"I have a number I want to give you. Write it down. And when you hang up, call them." Diana read off the phone number. At the other end she could hear a pen scratching on paper.

"Call that number, Senator Merrick. And then I want to meet with you, face-to-face, down here."

"What is this number supposed to be?" the senator demanded.

"It's the number for *Inside Edition*. You know, the tabloid show. The one that would be really interested in this kind of a story."

The only sound was that of a breath, sharply inhaled, then let out slowly, shakily.

"All right, young lady," the senator said at last. "You want a meeting? I'll be down on the island early next week. I'll have someone call you. But you want to be careful about trying to blackmail me."

"It isn't blackmail."

"Of course it is," he said, sounding weary and cynical.

"Call it whatever you want, then," Diana said. Slowly she replaced the receiver in its cradle. "I call it justice," she whispered to herself.

Outside, the horn now blared in one long sound. Diana grinned. Shopping. Why not? She did have certain purchases to make.

9

Video Blog

I'm sorry, I'm sorry, I'm sorry, I know it's been a long time since I posted anything for you. Like a week, I guess. No, wait, more than a week. But it's been kind of a busy week.

For one thing, this waitress at work quit, so I've picked up some of her shifts. I'm doing dinners now sometimes, which is good because the tips are a lot better. The other night I made eighty-two dollars. Of course, my feet were killing me afterward, and I pulled a muscle in my back lifting this one tray. But Seth gave me an excellent back rub after work. . . . Oh, wait. You don't know anything about all that, do you?

Seth and I are kind of going out sometimes. The thing is, we've both agreed that we can still see other people if we want, and we're not like capital "B" boyfriend and capital "G" girlfriend. We would be more lowercase boyfriend and girlfriend. We do things together, but I'm still very cool and in control about it.

Not that I'm seeing anyone else. It's just that I could if I wanted, and I probably will, because I have totally learned my lesson about falling in love with people too soon and getting hurt when it turns out they're dirtbags. I wouldn't mention any names. Especially any names that start with "Ad" and end with "am." Did I tell you he tried to give me this necklace? Like I would just forgive everything for gold and diamonds.

Okay, yes, I thought about it. But I said no. You'd probably agree with Marquez that I should have taken the necklace and *then* blown him off. Marquez got so mad at me she was yelling at me in Spanish. The only Spanish she ever speaks are four-letter words, or maybe they're five letters in Spanish. Of course, she wasn't serious. Maybe.

But speaking of Marquez, she's still broken up with J.T. Only, the other day she saw him making out with Lianne in the walk-in, and she was very upset over that, because that's where she and J.T. used to make out when they were at work. She tells me every day how she's totally over him, and then spends an hour muttering and grumbling under her breath about him and Lianne. Now she says she's going to get a new boyfriend. I'm not kidding—she's on the lookout for someone even better looking than J.T. so she can rub his nose in it. She painted out J.T.'s name on her wall, which is as serious as Marquez gets.

And as for Diana, I don't even know. I tried to talk to her a couple of times, but she's still as private as ever. Although, it's funny, because she *is* different. I mean, before you'd talk to her and there was always this feeling about her, like she was thinking about something else. Well, she still is that way, but it's as if what she's thinking about has changed. She has this look, like she's planning something. You know, like she's a secret agent or something. I don't know how to explain it any better than that.

Diana says Mallory, her mom, is coming home soon. Her book tour got extended, but she'll be back any day now. Maybe that will help.

Anyway, tomorrow I get certified.

Ha, ha, Jennifer, no, not certified insane. Very funny. Jennifer, I *so* know the way your mind works.

I'm getting certified as a scuba diver. Seth has been teaching me, and Jennifer, it is the most excellent, coolest thing on earth. You have *got* to learn, so we can go together when I get home. I'm serious—we can dive in lakes. Seth says lakes are boring, but you could learn there, and even when all you see is sand, which is all I've really seen, it's still way cool.

I'm feeling like things are going more normally now. Like all this stuff with Adam was just this unhappy phase. From now on, it's just happy happy, joy joy for the rest of the summer.

On the other hand, I have this other feeling that things never stay simple for very long. Like on *The Young and the Restless* or some other soap opera. Anytime everyone is happy, you just know that a murder or a divorce or a long-lost daughter is going to show up by the end of the show.

So tune in tomorrow, for more of *The Tan and the Clueless*.

10

All About Seeing and Not Seeing Guys

"Okay, now smile," Summer directed. She pointed the video camera at Seth, who was standing there, sullen, thumbs hooked in the waist of his jeans, refusing to cooperate.

Summer lowered the camera. "Would it kill you to smile?"

"I don't even know this Jennifer person," Seth grumbled.

"She's my best friend. And she just posted a video of *her* boyfriend. I mean, this guy she's sort of seeing, anyway," Summer amended quickly. "I don't know if he's actually a boyfriend."

"So now you want to be able to show her your *guy you're sort of seeing, anyway?*"

"Yes," Summer said. "I want her to see what you look like."

"Uh-huh. Have you taped Diver yet?"

"No. That's not the same," Summer said impatiently.

"Why not?"

"Because Diver is not a guy I'm sort of seeing. You are," Summer explained. Lately Seth had been trying to meet Diver. Like he was jealous of Diver, which made no sense at all. "See, Jennifer shows me the guy she's sort of seeing, and he's cute and all, so now I have to show her the guy I'm sort of seeing so she'll realize that the guy I'm sort of seeing is cuter . . . almost as cute . . . as the guy she's sort of seeing."

Seth just stared at her. "If two guys were doing this, you'd say it was sexist." Then, under his breath, but loud enough for Summer to hear, "*Almost* as cute." He shuddered. "*Cute* is such a girl word."

"Like *grout* is a boy word. You have *grout,* we have *cute.* Just like you boys have belching and grunting, and we have actual conversation."

"Ugh," Seth grunted. "Camera no good. Camera scare caveman." He took the camera from her hands. "Caveman need to be bribed." He wrapped his arms around her and kissed her.

Summer let him draw her down onto her bed. He lay on his back. She lay atop him, kissing his lips, enjoying the feel of his hard body. Then she noticed a familiar whirring noise.

She spun around and saw that Seth had raised the camera over them, pointed it down, and depressed the button. The little red light was on.

"Seth!" She slapped his chest.

"There! Do you see, Jennifer? Do you see how mean she is to me?"

"Seth, turn that thing off."

"Hi, Jennifer, I'm the guy Summer is sort of, kind of, maybe seeing, part of the time. But she has six other boyfriends, too, although none of them is as *cute* as me."

"They're all cuter," Summer said, laughing. "I'm kidding, Jen, obviously, duh."

"What?" Seth demanded. "Are you saying there are no other guys you're sort of maybe seeing?" He turned off the camera.

Summer started to climb off, but he wouldn't let her go.

"So how much longer do we have to go on avoiding the dreaded B-word?" Seth asked. "You know how I feel about you."

"Seth, we've been all over this at least six times," Summer said. "I just am not going to rush into some big commitment. I'm too young. Besides, what am I supposed to do when summer vacation is over?"

"I guess we'd have to figure that out when the end of summer comes around," Seth said seriously.

"Yeah. You'll be back in Wisconsin with Lianne."

"I'll be back in Wisconsin. Not with Lianne," he said.

Summer shrugged. She got up, crossed the room, and put the camera down on her dresser. "Can't we not put me under so much pressure?" Summer asked.

Seth sat up on the edge of the bed. "Sure. I'm sorry. I keep saying I won't press you, and then I do it anyway."

"It's not that I don't like you," Summer said. "I do. A lot. I just feel like I'm not ready to get as serious as you want to get."

"You mean, we're not getting married next week? Darn. I'll have to tell my mom the wedding's off."

"Very funny." Summer came back and sat beside him. She took his hand and held it on her lap. "It's . . . I know this is going to sound strange, but I've been thinking a lot lately. I keep having these dreams about my brother."

"Jonathan?"

"Yes. I mean, I think that's what it is. I see this little boy dressed in white. I know, it sounds nuts, I guess, because I never even saw Jonathan. He disappeared months before I was even born. But it's like the idea of him is coming back, and I think maybe it's sort of a warning to me."

"A warning?" Seth looked confused.

Not exactly surprising, Summer realized. This was the first time she'd articulated the feeling that had grown from the mess with Adam and the mess between Marquez and J.T., all combined with Jonathan.

"Look, I know this is silly, but it's like . . . like people forget that loving someone and committing to someone can sometimes be bad. I mean, I think about my parents and Jonathan. It's really messed up their lives in lots of ways, even though they try to not put it off on me."

"Oh." Seth nodded. "I get it."

"You do?"

"Sure," he said. "You think if you get totally into someone you might get hurt."

"Right, so the more slowly you take it and the more totally sure you feel, the less likely it is you'll get hurt."

"That's your theory?"

Summer nodded.

Seth tilted his head back and forth, as if he were holding an internal debate. "I guess I can live with that, for now. Actually, it's kind of nice, in a perverse way. You're saying if you admit you're in love with me and then you lose me, you'll be terribly unhappy."

"You make it sound kind of obvious," Summer said. "It seemed much more profound in my mind."

"The other side of what you're saying is that if we broke up right now, you'd just wash your hands of me, figure no big deal, bring on the next guy." Suddenly he pushed her onto her back and lowered his face to hers. "Too bad, it's not going to work. Because I'm not going to just go away."

He kissed her and for a while, at least, she forgot why it was that she'd ever even thought of losing him.

By the next morning, she had remembered.

"Because," she explained to Marquez, who was going through Summer's wardrobe making rude remarks, "the amount of possible pain is directly proportional to the degree of commitment."

"Uh-huh," Marquez said. "Is that geometry? Or algebra?" She held up a bulky sweater of Summer's. "Why is this here? Even in February it doesn't get that cold here. This is July. You have, like, one bathing suit and two sweaters."

"I am trying to discuss an important idea here," Summer said.

"You want an important idea? I'll give you an important idea—what are we doing today? We have the day off."

"I'm going diving with Seth this afternoon," Summer said.

"Okay, so we have the morning off. I repeat, what are we doing? I'm thinking shopping."

"I have nothing to shop for," Summer said.

"You are so wrong. You need so much stuff. And I know you made money Saturday night. You had that ten-top with all the champagne."

There was a knock on the door. "It's me." Diana's voice.

"Come in," Summer yelled.

"Diana," Marquez said. "Out walking in the sunlight? Isn't that dangerous for your species?"

"Ah, Marquez, as always, you're every bit as funny as your taste in outfits," Diana said as she walked to the center of the room.

"Ooh, right through the heart," Marquez said. "Diana's been drinking the caffeinated coffee again."

Marquez was right. There had been a noticeable change in Diana lately. She seemed preoccupied and yet jumpy with suppressed energy. Noticeably different from the depressed, sullen Diana Summer had gotten used to.

"I just came down to warn you," Diana said to Summer. "It's finally happening. Mallory is coming home tomorrow. It's definite."

"Oh no," Summer said. "I won't be here tomorrow.

I'm going on a diving trip with Seth. We won't get back until late."

"Lucky you," Diana said dryly. She noticed the video camera. "Wait, that's right. You have a video camera, don't you?"

"Yep. Why? Did you want to borrow it?"

"Maybe," Diana said thoughtfully. "Are you taking it on your trip?"

"No, I'd end up getting it wet," Summer said.

"Better and better," Diana said softly.

"What do you mean—" Summer fell silent. The hatchway in the floor had lifted two inches. She peered and saw a pair of eyes she recognized.

"You can come in, Diver. Diana knows about you. She's cool," Summer said. "And you've already met Marquez."

She's cool, Summer thought. Jeez, you sound like you're dealing drugs or something. But it reminded her of the fact that Mallory, Diana's mother, might *not* be so cool if she learned about Diver.

Diver raised the hatch a few inches higher. "Um, hi," he said to Diana. "Nice to meet you and all."

Diana bent over and looked down at him. "I don't know if this is exactly a meeting. But, you know, nice to . . . whatever."

"Come on in," Marquez said with sudden enthusiasm.

"Um, well . . ." Diver said.

He seemed even more at a loss for words than usual. Summer knelt down in front of him. "Is there something wrong?"

"Kind of," Diver said.

"What is it?"

"There was this nail, sticking out of this piling down by the marina, right?" he said.

"A nail. At the marina. Okay."

"See, I was doing this job."

"You work?" Marquez said, surprised. "I thought you just sort of absorbed nutrition from the environment, by osmosis or something."

Diver's eyes tracked left, puzzled. "Osmosis? I believe that's a feature of plants, not animals."

"Diver, what's the problem?" Summer asked impatiently. "Marquez, stop interrupting. Diver, come on in and tell us."

"Well, there was this nail. And I kind of caught my suit on it. And it kind of ripped."

"Ripped? As in—?"

"I was thinking I would just sew it up, right? Only, I don't have a needle or anything. So I was wondering if you had a needle and thread I could use."

"Of course she does," Marquez said enthusiastically. "Climb right on up and we'll fix it for you."

"It's kind of a big rip," Diver said. "I guess the

fabric was kind of old and rotten and it just pretty much fell apart."

"All the more reason to come right on up," Marquez said.

"I'll get you a towel to wrap around yourself," Summer said, with a scolding look at Marquez.

"A hand towel," Marquez called after her. "A washcloth."

Moments later Diver emerged into the living room, wearing a large beach towel wrapped around him. He wiggled and shifted until he could safely produce the bathing suit.

Summer held it up for all to see. The fabric was thoroughly rotted. If it hadn't torn, it would have soon disintegrated.

"That's a nasty rip," Marquez said. "All the way from the waistband down. What a shame. Lucky thing Summer gave you that towel." She shot Summer a dirty look.

"I'm glad to meet you, Diver," Diana said, smiling one of her rare smiles.

"Sure," Diver said, looking mightily uncomfortable. He glanced anxiously from Diana to Marquez. He seemed to have a hard time tearing his gaze away from Marquez, who was eyeing him like a hungry lioness sizing up a juicy lamb.

"So . . . where are the rest of your clothes?" Diana asked.

He shrugged. "I had this shirt," he said, looking around vaguely. "I don't remember where I put it, though."

Summer tossed the bathing suit to Diana. "*That* is his entire wardrobe. That and the beach towel he's wearing."

"Huh," Diana said.

"Hmm," Marquez said.

"You guys, try to be mature about this," Summer said. They were grinding her nerves now. The two of them leering and all but drooling. After all, Diver had a brain, and a heart, too. If either Marquez or Diana was interested in him they were going to have to recognize that and treat him with respect.

Good grief, Summer chided herself. *What am I, his mother, all of a sudden?*

"Mature, definitely. Gotta be mature," Marquez agreed.

"Diver, I think maybe you need some new clothes," Summer said.

"I guess so," he agreed. "But how am I going to go and buy them if I'm wearing a towel?"

"Ladies," Marquez announced, rubbing her hands gleefully, "I believe we have found something to do with the rest of the day. We have to buy this boy some clothes. You two get going, and I'll stay here."

"I can put it on Mallory's credit card," Diana offered. "Might as well do as much damage as I can before she gets back."

"I have money," Diver said.

"You do?" all three girls said at once.

"Sure. I do work, you know. I do stuff like clean boats down at the marina. I have it in a jar, up on the deck. Let me go get it."

He disappeared outside and they heard him climbing up onto the deck.

"Do you realize that he is the best-looking guy on planet earth?" Diana said under her breath. "I mean, I'm not alone in this, am I? He's like . . . He's prettier than any of the three of us. It's not natural."

"Like a perfect specimen," Marquez said dreamily. "This simple, beautiful child of nature, with this beautiful face, and this beautiful body, and just like . . . perfect. Uncomplicated and perfect."

Summer realized she was bridling at their reactions. Not that it would mean anything to Diver. "He isn't interested in girls," Summer whispered. "They disturb his *wa*."

"His *wa*?" Marquez said.

"His *wa*. His inner peace," Diana translated, much to Summer's surprise.

"See what I mean?" Marquez said. "Simple. Uncomplicated. No problems. The perfect guy. Of course, he's going to have to get over this thing about girls. Probably he just hasn't met the right one. What he needs is someone as calm and simple and accepting as he is. Like me."

Summer and Diana both laughed.

"So? I could change," Marquez said, laughing along.

"Oh. No. A terrible thought just occurred to me," Summer said.

"What?"

"We're going to leave Diver here, sitting around in nothing but a towel. Seth is coming over to pick me up. We have to be back before that meeting takes place."

"You had to trust Seth with Lianne, right?" Marquez suggested. "Maybe it's time to see how trusting Seth is. And if he can trust you with Diver . . ." She bit her lip and made a suggestive little movement. "I suppose you have dibs on him, right?" Marquez demanded.

"If she does, then I have dibs on Seth," Diana said. She laughed a little too loudly.

"Dibs?" Summer echoed.

"Dibs. You know, like he's yours or whatever."

"You mean like as a *guy*?" Summer said, incredulous. And what had Diana meant about Seth?

"No, as a pony," Marquez said. "What are you, getting stupid? Of course as a *guy*. I mean, are you going to scratch my eyes out if I happen to, you know, become Mrs. Diver?"

Summer realized she was surprised by the question. She had reacted to Diver a little that way, maybe, right at first. But since then, it hadn't occurred to her. She didn't really think of Diver as a *guy* in the way that Seth was a guy.

"You're taking an awful long time to answer a simple question," Marquez said. "I'm only asking because it would be really excellent to be able to accidentally run into J.T. and Lianne when I was with Diver."

"Sure," Summer said. "I mean, of course, I don't mind. But don't just treat Diver like he's some toy."

"Of course not," Marquez said. "Now, let's get him some clothes and dress him up like a Ken doll."

The girls bought Diver:
1 pair madras print trunks
1 Ralph Lauren blue work shirt
1 pair Levi's 501 jeans
3 pairs Calvin Klein underwear
3 pairs white socks
1 pair sneakers
1 Miami Dolphins jersey

In addition, Diana bought herself a large over-the-shoulder bag decorated with gaudy glass beads that everyone agreed was hideous and completely unlike anything Diana would ever be seen carrying in public.

Loaded down with their many gifts, they arrived back at the stilt house to find Seth calmly waiting for Summer. Diver was nowhere in sight. Seth explained that he had given Diver an old pair of extra trunks that he kept in his truck and Diver had taken off.

Marquez then threatened to hurt Seth very badly.

The Importance of Being Diver

The marina was downtown, not far from the Crab 'n' Conch. It was a small forest of masts: the tall, elegant masts of sailboats, the stubbier masts of powerboats. Several dozen white-and-blue-hulled boats were arrayed in tight little rows, connected by low wooden piers and adorned here and there with striped awnings, limp flags, flashes of chrome, and deeper tones of weathered teakwood.

The largest boats were out at the ends of the piers, huge wallowing palaces with uniformed crewmen performing maintenance while tanned women lounged in deck chairs drinking daiquiris. Marquez had stopped at her house to change clothes and try to think up some plausible excuse as to why she should be hanging around the marina. She never went to the marina. The marina was headquarters of the tourists she had to wait on at the restaurant.

She had not yet come up with an excuse. She'd tried out several, all starting with, "Why, Diver, what a surprise to run into *you* here. I was just on my way to . . ."

And that's as far as the excuses went. I was just on my way to . . .

Just on my way to see if you'd like to hang out with me or whatever, because basically I'm trying to get J.T. out of my mind permanently and you seem like just the guy who could make me forget that jerk forever.

"Excellent plan," Marquez muttered under her breath. "Just tell Diver all that and he'll run away, screaming for help."

As it turned out, she had a difficult time finding Diver in the cluttered maze of boats. She had no trouble attracting the attention of several other guys, since she had dressed in a way designed to get attention. But she breezed by them with an air of confident disdain, and they left her alone.

She had reached the end of the main pier and was enjoying a little shade cast by a monstrous cabin cruiser when she heard voices. Feminine voices. She shielded her eyes and saw two women, sun-glassed, tanned, liposuctioned, wearing gold-lace sandals and similar black one-piece bathing suits.

They didn't notice her. They were looking in the other direction and talking in low voices.

"Something's different about him," one said.

"Nothing's different. He's still adorable."

"I'm not saying he isn't. I'm just saying, something has changed. I think maybe it's the bathing suit."

"Maybe I'll call him over. We could get him to swab the decks or something."

Marquez had a pretty good idea who they were talking about. And when she went out to the end of the pier she could see Diver, standing up in a tiny dinghy, carefully applying paint to a beautiful, antique sailboat.

She was about to call to him, but then she had a better idea.

Marquez kicked off her sandals and dived into the water. She was halfway to him by the time she surfaced. She took a deep breath and went under again, swimming hard until she could see the little dinghy bobbing overhead.

She surfaced in the narrow space between the dinghy and the side of the sailboat. She spit out a mouthful of seawater, smoothed back her hair, and smiled. "Hi."

He stopped with his paintbrush in midair. "Oh. Hi."

It wasn't exactly giddy enthusiasm she saw on his face.

"I know you, right?" he said.

That nearly wiped the smile off Marquez's face. "Yes, I'm Marquez. You know, Summer's friend." Oh, great. She had to introduce herself as "Summer's friend." Obviously, she'd made a huge impression on him.

"Yeah," he said. He glanced around, looking a bit like a trapped animal.

"Give me a hand," Marquez ordered.

"A hand?"

"Help me up," she said. She stuck a hand up to him.

With reluctance he didn't even try to hide, he took her hand and helped heave her into the dinghy. "Careful, I have paint here. This man who owns the boat is in kind of a hurry."

Marquez sat in the stern of the dinghy and wondered if she wasn't totally wasting her time. She knew perfectly well that she was an attractive girl. An attractive girl wearing a small bathing suit *ought* to have gotten some reaction from Diver—other than the vaguely queasy look he had.

"You're painting the boat, huh?" she said.

"Just this part. See, where it got scraped against a piling."

"Maybe I could help," Marquez said with sudden inspiration. "You know, I paint a lot."

"You do?"

A faint flicker of interest.

"Yes. Some people think I'm a pretty good artist," Marquez said.

"Huh."

"Do you have an extra brush?"

"There." He pointed.

He still looked queasy and ill at ease, but he moved over a little to make room for her to take a brush, dip it, and begin to paint, feathering her edge into his.

"You know, we bought you some clothes. Summer and Diana and me."

"Thanks. This guy let me have this suit, though, so I'm set. This guy named Seth. He's Summer's boyfriend, right?"

What an interesting question, Marquez thought. Why exactly was he asking that? Was Diver interested in Summer? Oh, that would really be a major drag. "Yes, I guess so," Marquez said.

Well, it is the truth—kind of, she told herself. And if it wasn't the complete truth right now, it probably would be soon.

"Huh," Diver commented, a word that told Marquez nothing.

"No doubt you wish I was Summer," Marquez said snippily.

"Why should I? She doesn't paint, does she?"

"Maybe you prefer blondes," Marquez said.

"No, I like dark hair, too," he said.

Marquez told herself not to push it any further, but she never listened to her own advice. "Blue eyes? Is that it? Thighs? You like skinny thighs?"

Diver rested his brush on the lip of the paint can. "I like all kinds of girls," he said seriously. "I just don't do anything about it because they disturb my *wa*. I mean, I guess I'd rather just have a peaceful life."

"Uh-huh. So, do *I* disturb your *wa*?"

"Yes, very much," he said.

"Excellent," Marquez said, beaming with self-satisfaction. For the next thirty minutes, much to Marquez's frustration, Diver said not a word. She decided she should not force herself on him, so she remained silent, too. After all, she admired his strangeness, so she shouldn't be annoyed by it.

When they'd finished painting he looked at her, quickly looked away, and said, "Thanks. I can give you some of the money the guy is paying me."

"No, no," Marquez said with a laugh. "I didn't do it for money."

"Oh. Why did you do it?"

Good question, Marquez realized. Her bathing suit now had two speckles of white paint. And she had learned exactly nothing new about Diver.

"Like I said, I enjoy painting," she said.

"Cool."

"Um, in fact, I'd really . . . I mean, it would be cool if you would come over and take a look at my paintings. At my house, I mean." Marquez held her breath. This would be the point at which he would live out the meaning of his name and dive over the side of the boat, never to return.

"I guess I could," he said.

Marquez was delighted. And surprised. "Let's go, then," she said. Show him her paintings. Maybe they could share a little snack. Then, with any luck at all, she could begin to convince him that it wasn't such a bad thing to have your *wa* disturbed.

"This is my tree," Marquez said with a flourish of her hand. "See. The roots go out across the floor, then the trunk goes all the way up the wall, and the branches and leaves spread out across the ceiling."

Diver tilted back his head to take it all in. He nodded solemnly.

Marquez was a bit nonplussed by his reaction. The tree was her best thing. She pointed out several other features of her walls. "That's the moon, of course, and the sun." Yeah, like he wouldn't recognize the moon or the sun. "The moon and the stars are painted with fluorescent colors, so that way, when you turn off the lights at night, they keep glowing for a while. Want to see?"

She flipped off the lights, plunging the room into

almost total darkness. The sprinkling of stars on the ceiling glowed an eerie white. Then she turned the lights back on.

Diver seemed to guess that some response was being called for. "Cool," he said. He turned and focused on the graffiti names that intertwined with the many other small paintings. He pointed to a patch of pure white. "What's this?"

Marquez sighed. Perfect. He'd focused on the one thing she really did not want to discuss. "That's just something I wanted to cover over," she said.

"A name?"

"Yes, a name. Some guy's name." J.T., to be exact. She had covered it with three coats of white. And still she had the feeling she could make out the letters beneath.

"Did he die?"

"Die? No. Why would he be dead?"

"You erased him."

"Look, it's just some guy I didn't want to remember anymore."

Diver nodded. He remained focused with singular intensity on the painted-out J.T.

"I think it's good to remember things," Diver said softly.

"Some things yes, some things no," Marquez said impatiently.

"I don't think you can choose that way. I think you either remember stuff or you don't. It's not like you can just erase things. I mean, not deliberately, anyway."

Marquez had the distinct sense that Diver was telling her something important, but at the same time she was feeling harassed and annoyed. She had Diver right here in her room, and all they could talk about was J.T. Or the lack of J.T.

"Diver, J.T. is just my ex-boyfriend, okay? Things got strange between us, or at least *he* got strange, and now that's over."

He nodded. Then he smiled impishly. "I guess I should be careful not to get strange, huh?"

Now what exactly did that mean? "You want to listen to some music?" Marquez asked. No answer. He had moved on now, reading each name on her wall as if he was trying to memorize them.

Marquez chose a CD and hit Play. The music was danceable without being too loud. The plan was to see if Diver liked to dance. So far he had failed one of her tests of a worthy human being—he had not exactly been enthusiastic about her painting. But if he could dance, he might make up for that.

Marquez let the music seep through her, let it touch the control buttons in her mind that started her body swaying in time to the rhythm.

"I don't see Summer," Diver said.

"I'll put her up soon," Marquez said. "I haven't decided on the letters or the color yet. I'm thinking gold and blue."

Diver actually smiled. "Yes, gold and blue. Those are her colors."

"And what colors am I?" Marquez asked playfully.

Diver looked at her thoughtfully, concentrating, as if she had asked him a perfectly serious question. "You're like sunrise or sunset. Red and yellow and orange, fading into purple. Bright, intense colors. If they lasted too long they'd be overwhelming and make everything else look pale. So they just appear for a short time and then fade away, and you're wondering if they were even real. And then they reappear, but never for so long that you get tired of them. Just a short glimpse, and that's all you need."

Marquez swallowed hard. Okay, she was willing to forgive his lack of interest in her walls. She stepped closer. He did not run away.

He did not become any less attractive up close.

"Um, would you like to dance?" she asked him.

"I don't dance very much," he said.

That was it. He'd failed both her tests. Too bad she just didn't care.

"Can I ask you something, Diver?"

"If you want."

"Is Diver your real name?"

His crystal-clear eyes seemed to cloud over. "I don't think so," he said.

"What do you mean, you don't think so?" Marquez said, smiling.

"Never, mind. I guess either way, I'm me," he said simply. "I have to go."

"What are you talking about?" Marquez demanded. "You just got here. And don't start talking about your *wa* again."

He laughed self-deprecatingly. "Okay, I won't. But I still have to go."

Marquez threw up her hands. "What is it with me and guys? Do you know why I brought you here?"

"To show me your painting?"

"No, no, no. Because you were supposed to become interested in me. You were going to really like my paintings, and then we would maybe dance, and then, I figured unless I have totally lost it, you'd kiss me and I'd kiss you, and I'd tell you it was something I'd been wanting to do ever since I saw you."

"Oh."

Suddenly the telephone began to ring.

Diver stepped closer, and then, without warning, kissed Marquez lightly on the lips.

He drew back. "Did that make you happy?" he asked.

Marquez just groaned.

"I have to go now," Diver said for the third time.

The telephone rang again.

"Well, bye then," Marquez said.

He walked away, leaving her feeling as far from happy as she had felt in a long time.

The phone rang yet again.

Marquez snatched up the receiver. "YES, YES, YES, YES, what the hell is it and it had better be good!" She listened for a moment. "Sure," she said in a slightly more subdued voice. "Sure. I'd love to come to work. Why not? I obviously have no life!"

Shoot-out at the Cramp 'n' Croak

"What are you doing here?" Summer demanded.

"What do you mean, what am I doing here? They called me in to hostess," Marquez said. "What are you two doing here?"

The Crab 'n' Conch was half-full with early-dining families, old people just finishing up, and the first few later-dining couples being seated.

"We are celebrating," Seth said. He stood behind Summer, took her hands, and spread her arms out in a "ta-daa!" position. "You are looking at a certified scuba diver. As of about an hour ago. Take a bow, Summer."

Summer took a little bow, which Seth did along

with her. "Seth is buying me dinner, so we would like a window table."

"Oh, you'd like a window table, huh? You think you get special treatment?" Marquez asked.

"You know," Summer said, batting her eyes, "you look great in that dress. I mean it. Like a model. I wish I had your body and your hair."

Marquez laughed. "You're going to need your scuba gear to breathe in here if the crap gets piled any deeper. Okay, okay, I'll get you a window table." She grabbed a couple of menus. "At least *someone* thinks I look good, even if it is just another girl."

"What are you talking about, Marquez?" Summer asked.

Marquez stopped, handed the menus to Seth, and pointed to an empty table. "Here, take these and go seat yourself. I have to talk to Summer."

"Oh, fine," Seth grumbled. "Just dump the guy."

Marquez took Summer's arm and drew her away to a corner of the coatroom. "Don't get mad or any-thing, all right?" Marquez said. "I had Diver over at my house."

"Why would I be mad?" Summer said in a phony, shrill voice. "It's none of my business."

"Uh-huh. Anyway, it didn't work out all that great."

"Oh, really?"

"Don't gloat," Marquez said. "It just turned out . . .
I don't know. It's like there's more going on with him
than I thought. Also less. I mean, I think he may have
problems."

"Like what?"

"Like he doesn't *know* his own name. Either he
doesn't remember, like he has amnesia or something,
or else he was just blowing me off."

"Puh-leeze, he was just blowing you off. That's the
way he always is. You can never get a straight answer
out of Diver. Diver's . . . I don't know. He's just Diver.
But of course *you* had to cross-examine him."

"I asked a couple of simple questions," Marquez
said.

"And now you don't like the answers."

"I thought I would like the answers," Marquez said
crossly. "I guess."

"Maybe you shouldn't have asked questions. I
thought you liked him because he was so simple and
innocent and not at all like J.T. And then you start in
on him?"

"I didn't 'start in on him.' I was trying to get something going, that's all. Just because you treat him like
your platonic guy friend, doesn't mean *I* have to,"
Marquez grumbled. "Maybe *you* don't notice how he
looks anymore, but I do."

Summer felt troubled. "I'd hate to think he actually has amnesia or something. That means he's sick, kind of."

"Yeah. Besides, what happens if he regains his memory and it turns out he's really some kind of prep who buys all his clothes out of the J. Crew catalog? Then what?"

"Excuse me, *this* is from J. Crew," Summer said, pointing to her blouse.

The manager of the restaurant stuck his head around the corner. "Oh, *there* you are, Marquez. Maybe I should just tell the customers who are waiting at the hostess stand to come find you hack here."

"I'm on my way," Marquez promised. Then, to Summer in an undertone, "I volunteer to work an extra shift and he's ragging on me anyway."

"You'd better go," Summer said. "We'll talk later. Maybe we can figure out if Diver needs some kind of help. Maybe *we* could help him." She smiled wryly. "Help him turn into a prep."

Marquez rolled her eyes. "Oh, great. Look, if I wanted to be Mother Teresa and help screwed-up guys, I'd help J.T. He was first in line."

"You know, this really is a nice view," Summer said, gazing out through the floor-to-ceiling windows as she smoothed the cloth napkin on her lap. "I work here, but it's like I never have time to really notice it."

Outside was the dock, congested with evening strollers enjoying the early stages of sunset and the slight relief from the heat. It was the usual collection of humanity as it appeared on Crab Claw Key—too-fat people showing too much skin, too-fair tourists with bright red sunburns, too-rich people with too little taste.

But there were families as well, pushing baby strollers and trailing bright helium balloons; young married couples on their honeymoons, looking glazed and tired and ostentatiously sharing ice cream cones; then, like a time-lapse photograph, the older couples, gray men and bottle-blond women wearing gaudy matching outfits and sharing secret smiles and knowing winks with their partners as they watched their younger selves pass by.

"I should pay more attention to things," Summer said thoughtfully. "There's a lot going on."

Seth looked up from his menu and followed the direction of her gaze. "Kind of a good show, isn't it?" he said. "I mean, I don't know what Bloomington, Minnesota, is like, but where I'm from, in Eau Claire, you don't usually see this many different kinds of people."

"I suppose Eau Claire and Bloomington aren't very different," Summer said. "More like each other than either of them is like Crab Claw Key. Not that people there are boring or all the same—they aren't. But everything here is raised to a more extreme level."

"That's good *and* bad, I guess," Seth said.

"I know. You have to watch out or you lose yourself here, right?" She gave Seth an affectionate smile. "I remember you telling me that. What was it? 'Tropical rot'?"

Seth laughed. "Did I say that? Hmm, sounds like me, I have to admit." He grew more serious. "I think that at the time I just wanted to find some way to keep you from falling for Adam Merrick."

Summer's smile faded. "I guess I'd have been better off if I'd listened to you."

Seth kept his face immobile, but in his eyes there was a smug, satisfied look that annoyed Summer just a little.

"Go ahead. You want to say 'I told you so,'" Summer said.

"No, I don't," Seth said. "I don't want you to feel bad. I just want—"

"Yo, Summer, what are you doing in here? Trying to pretend you're a tourist?"

They both looked up and saw J.T., wearing his usual cook's whites. But there was something different, Summer realized—for once, his apron was clean.

J.T. noticed her dubious stare. "I can't come out into the dining room looking like my usual disaster area," he explained. "Seth, right?" He held out his hand to Seth.

Seth shook it. "Yeah, we met once, I guess, back last year when you and Marquez were . . . Um . . . Well, I stepped right in it, didn't I?"

J.T. waved it off. "Forget it, man. Ancient history. I just came out to see if I can cook up something special for my favorite waitress."

Just then Lianne walked up to the table, her order pad at the ready.

"I thought *I* was your favorite waitress, J.T," she said, looking up at him with a look of near-adoration.

J.T. returned the intimate smile. "Well . . ."

Lianne looked coolly down at Seth and deliberately put her arm around J.T.'s waist. J.T. put his arm around Lianne.

Seth looked at Lianne. Then he looked at J.T. He was clearly trying not to react, but Lianne had been his girlfriend for years.

Lianne shot a triumphant look at Summer. A look that said, "See, you may have Seth now, but I'm not exactly crying myself to sleep every night." Then Lianne turned a slow, cold smile on Seth.

J.T. glanced sheepishly at Summer, suffering the usual male embarrassment at any public display of affection. But he had forgotten the more important point— Seth was Lianne's former boyfriend. Then, seeming to make the connection in his mind, his eyes widened and he looked a bit nervously at Seth.

Just to complete the circle of discomfort, Marquez sauntered up.

Marquez instantly spotted Lianne's arm around J.T.'s waist. Her nostrils flared. Her lip tried to jerk itself into a sneer.

J.T. shifted uncomfortably, as though he suddenly wished Lianne's arm was somewhere else. Or at least wished *he* was somewhere else.

Seth took a deep breath and prudently buried his face in his menu.

Marquez sent Lianne a look that could have frozen the sun. But Lianne returned the look with one of defiant spite.

"So," Summer said brightly. "What's good on the menu tonight?" This was dangerous. Diver had just blown off Marquez. This was not the time for her to be around J.T. and Lianne acting lovey-dovey.

"Maybe you should get back in the kitchen," Marquez said to J.T. "Cooks aren't supposed to be out here making the place look bad."

"What are you, the manager now?" J.T. shot back.

"How about if *you* go back to the hostess stand," Lianne said to Marquez. "This is *my* table. I'm their waitress. It's my responsibility."

Summer saw the flame light up in Marquez's eyes. "Marquez, let's all just—" Summer began. Too late.

"Then why don't you *act* responsible instead of hanging all over the cook, practically feeling him up here in the middle of the restaurant. People are trying to eat."

Lianne sucked in her breath sharply. "How is this *any* of your business, Marquez? You and J.T. are not together anymore. So get lost."

"Only a sleazy lowlife would go after some guy who just broke up with his girlfriend," Marquez said in a voice that carried clearly to several adjoining tables. "I mean, are you so desperate you're going to jump all over J.T. when he and I just broke up a few weeks ago?"

Lianne lowered her voice to a silky, dangerous tone. "Is that so, Marquez? Then what about your friend Summer?"

Marquez looked blank. "What?"

"You may notice she's here with Seth, even though Seth and I just broke up. If I'm a sleazy lowlife, then so is Summer."

"That's different," Marquez said lamely. She sent Summer a quick shrug of apology.

"Lianne, why don't you just leave me and Summer out of this," Seth said quietly, emerging from his menu.

"Oh, perfect. Sethie doing his protective thing, as always," Lianne sneered. "Sethie is so protective. Like an extra father."

Summer glanced at Seth. He looked angry but calm. She felt embarrassed. It was pretty clear that J.T. felt the same way. Their eyes met. He shrugged helplessly.

"Look, how about if we—"

"Look, how about if we—"

Summer stopped and looked at J.T. in confusion. They had both said the same thing at the same moment.

"I was just going to say, how about if we all back off and start over again," J.T. said.

Summer nodded in agreement. "Yeah. Let's stop all this, okay, guys?" Her gaze met J.T.'s again. She saw her own troubled feelings reflected in his eyes.

To Summer's surprise, Marquez was suddenly reasonable. "Summer's right. Let's try and act our ages." To J.T. she added, "As opposed to our IQs." And to Lianne, "Or our bra size."

Well, as reasonable as Marquez ever was.

J.T. looked sheepish. "How about if I just go back to my kitchen and Marquez goes back to the hostess stand, and, um, maybe we'll just get someone else besides Lianne to wait on you."

"Whatever you say, sweetheart," Lianne said to

J.T., adding extra emphasis to the *sweetheart*. "I'll ask Tony to come over."

When they were all gone, Summer and Seth looked at each other for a few seconds in complete silence.

It was Summer who cracked first. She grinned. "See? This kind of stuff never used to happen back in Bloomington."

Seth chuckled. "Not in Eau Claire, either."

"It's that tropical rot," Summer said. She began to giggle. "I think we should run for it."

"Right behind you. I know a place where we can get some conch fritters. And then tomorrow we'll spend the whole day underwater with nice, sensible fish."

Marquez waited for an hour before she got the opportunity to corner J.T. She lurked around until she saw him go into the walk-in refrigerator. She glanced behind her, making sure that Lianne was nowhere in sight, then she swiftly followed him in. He had his back turned to her as he counted portions of fish in long steel trays.

She wasted no time on preliminaries. "I can't believe you would replace me with that skinny little witch Lianne. I thought you had better taste than that."

"Go away, Marquez. I have work to do."

"You totally made a fool of yourself out there," Marquez said. "I hope you're satisfied."

J.T. turned around. "I don't get it, Marquez. What do you want from me?"

"Nothing. I don't want anything from you," she said.

"Yeah? Then why are you here?"

"I just wanted to tell you I can't believe you're seeing Lianne."

"Why is it any of your business?"

"I have a right to have an opinion," Marquez said. "And that's my opinion. It's a free country."

J.T. sighed. "What is it with you? You dump me, but then you can't handle it when I start seeing someone else? What's that about?"

"Like I said, I can't believe you're going with Lianne, that's all. She's only the witch of the universe. You know what she did to try to hang on to Seth? Did you hear about that? How she tried to make Summer think she was sleeping with Seth? That's the kind of girl you want to go out with?"

To Marquez's surprise, J.T. nodded. "Yes," he said with perfect seriousness. "Maybe it is. So she went too far, trying to hold on to a relationship she cared about. At least she *did* care. At least she tried. Unlike some people who walk away as soon as things get a little difficult. Maybe that seems like a pretty good thing to me right now. I'd like to know what it's like to have a girlfriend who cares enough to fight for me."

The remark stung Marquez, and she struck back, harder than she'd intended. "Did you tell her all about your little fantasy that your parents aren't your real parents? Did you tell her all about how nuts you went?"

"Yes, I did," J.T. said softly. "I told her all of it. I told her it made me feel lost and confused. That I loved my parents, but I was worried about what it meant that I didn't have a birth certificate or adoption papers."

"You *told* her?"

"Yeah. And you know what? She didn't run for the nearest exit. Unlike certain people. She didn't just blow me off and tell me to get over it. Unlike certain people."

Marquez could tell him, tell him right now what she suspected about him and Summer and a lost boy named Jonathan. It would probably devastate him. He would be upset. He would feel hurt. Maybe it would serve him right. At this moment, she wanted to hurt him.

And then he would run straight to Lianne, and Lianne would comfort him.

"I'm sure it was a very sweet, tender scene," Marquez said, sneering as contemptuously as she could manage. But it wasn't very convincing. She suddenly realized she felt an ache inside her chest. She felt hollow. Empty. The cold of the walk-in seemed very noticeable.

J.T. wasn't just seeing Lianne to spite Marquez. That was a new and disturbing realization.

"It was something new for me," J.T. said. "I felt bad, and she made me feel better. And she told me how bad she felt over Seth, and I guess I made *her* feel better. I understand that's what relationships are like."

"But you're not . . . serious or anything," Marquez said. "Not about *Lianne*?"

He shook his head, almost pityingly. "I have work to do."

13

Video Blog

I don't really have much time to do this, Jen, but I wanted to get in one last message before I post this. I just played back the part of the video with Seth and me on it. He's usually more serious than he was being there.

Tomorrow morning Seth and I are going on a diving trip, now that I'm an official scuba diver, over to this island called Geiger Key. No one lives there, but the diving is supposed to be really cool. They have a sunken freighter and all these caves that are full of fish and stuff, and Seth says the tourists don't go there much.

Listen to me—like *I'm* some kind of local.

Anyway, it's going to be like an all-day thing. We won't get back until late. He kind of suggested we could just camp out overnight, but I gave that a big N-O. Last time I stayed overnight somewhere was at Adam's. Besides, if I said yes, Seth would just think it was a sign I was ready to make some big commitment, which I'm not.

I don't even know why, Jen, it's just this feeling I've had. I keep having the same dreams about Jonathan. I don't know why. I never, ever used to dream about him. I think maybe it's some kind of warning, you know, about losing someone you love. What else could it be?

Okay, yes, I know, it could be that I'm just having dreams and no big deal. Or else I'm eating pizza before I go to bed and it's giving me nightmares. Only they aren't nightmares. They're tied up somehow with being down here. I don't know, forget it, I'm babbling.

I have no time to babble. I have to get ready for this trip tomorrow. I'm really looking forward to it.

At least, I think I am. I really love diving now. And I really like spending time with Seth. Maybe that's the problem: I like spending time with him too much. Oh well, things could be worse.

And look, look at this—tan line. Definite tan line. That puts my Florida tan ahead of your California tan,

I believe. Anyway . . . I have to get to bed early, be rested and all. Long day tomorrow. And I'm really looking forward to it.

What I'm not looking forward to is falling asleep tonight and having that dream again.

14

Getting in Deeper and Deeper

It was a two-hour trip by boat, flying along over the light chop, skipping from wave to wave almost as fast as by car. Ten minutes into the trip Summer had felt a little seasick from the constant up-and-down movement, the series of small and large shocks, but then, after a while, her body adjusted. She managed not to hurl, which she considered a major accomplishment.

Seth had borrowed the boat from a friend. It was not as sleek as Adam's boat, but it felt safe enough and was as fast as Summer could stand.

The morning had started gray and overcast with fog that had hidden the sun and turned the water dark and threatening. But by nine in the morning the fog had burned away, and soon after, the clouds blew away to the west. Now, as they neared the small, low island, the sun was at full midmorning intensity, climbing the blue sky, turning the water green and translucent, like an antique glass bottle.

"There it is, Geiger Key," Seth yelled over the roar of the engines. "Either that or I've gone too far and it's Cuba. In which case we can go visit Marquez's relatives." He throttled down, reducing speed.

"I don't see any other boats," Summer said, scanning with a hand over her eyes to block the sun. The island was little more than a stretch of beach some quarter-mile long, a boomerang-shaped sandbar with a decorative fringe of palm trees and some low bushes clumped around incongruous outcroppings of rock. It looked as if a few good waves could wash it away permanently. "Not much to it, is there?" Summer said. "I mean, somehow you expect to see some waterfront condos or a Marriott."

"It's not what's above the water that counts, it's what's down below," Seth said. He reduced speed still further, letting the boat creep along the shoreline, close enough to the beach so that Summer could have easily swum ashore. The sand was pure white and smooth— no human footprints, no tire tracks, just the tiny three-toed prints of shore birds.

A dozen or so tiny sanderlings scurried busily along

the wet sand, evading the lapping edge of the surf. A snow-white egret stood nearby, looking superior and a little stupid on its tall, toothpick legs.

"How do you know when we're in the right spot?" Summer wondered.

"See that big palm there? And that rocky outcropping there? I just line them up. Nothing to it, once you know where to look."

Seth looked confident, but the isolation of the little island, in the middle of what looked like a million square miles of trackless Gulf water, was a little intimidating to Summer. They hadn't seen another boat in the last half hour. And with the constant roar of the boat's engines suddenly gone, it seemed to Summer that the world was vast and empty around them. Endless blue sky above, broken only by a few cotton ball clouds far off, the endless blue-green sea around them, and nothing to cling to in all that emptiness but this minuscule boat and a scarcely larger island.

"Quiet, isn't it?" Seth whispered, grinning, as if he'd read her mind.

"It does kind of make you want to whisper, like being in a huge museum or church or something."

"So, ready to suit up?" He climbed up onto the bow, freed the anchor, and threw it over the side.

"I guess so," Summer said, still oppressed by the isolation.

"Okay, we have to pace ourselves, stay down a little while, then take a break before we go down again. I thought maybe we'd have a picnic lunch on the beach after we work up an appetite. Eat those sandwiches you made."

"Cool," Summer said, trying to sound as nonchalant as he.

Since her first dive, Summer had grown competent at the ritual of suiting up—sliding into the tight rubber jacket, adjusting it to eliminate uncomfortable binding, carefully seating the straps of her tank, automatically checking her air hose and regulator, even spitting into her face mask like a professional.

Seth double-checked every step, watching over her protectively.

"Ready?" he asked.

"Ready."

"Okay, now remember, keep clear of any sharp edges. There's rusted steel down there, and you don't want to slice your air hose. If you do and I'm right there, we'll buddy breathe, right? Otherwise, make an ascent with the air you have. Just remember—"

"Never rise faster than the smallest bubble," Summer said. "I'll be good."

"And of course, look out for old Stinker," Seth said.

"Who—what—?"

"Oh, he's the great white shark who hangs around

here. Huge." Seth spread his hands as far as they would go. "He's got a mouth wider than this. They say he got fat on the bodies of all the guys who went down with the freighter, and he's never lost his taste for human flesh."

Summer turned pale.

"I'm kidding," Seth said, terribly amused by his joke. "Kidding. Just a little diving humor."

To show him he hadn't scared her, Summer calmly sat down on the side of the boat, pulled down her mask, and rolled backward into the sea. Once under, she took a quick survey, just in case Seth hadn't really been joking. There were no sharks, as far as she could see.

There was a depth-charge explosion as Seth dropped into the water above her. He paddled down and took a slow inspection tour around her, checking her gear one more time. Then, with a "follow me" wave, he was off.

Summer twisted to point in the same direction, then gave several hard kicks to catch up.

Suddenly, out of nowhere, a blizzard swirled around her, a tornado of tiny silver-and-black fish that sparkled like diamonds in the flickering shafts of sunlight and blocked her view of Seth. In her various practice dives, Summer had never seen more than a few distant fish and, once, a graceful stingray. Now it was if she had been invited to join the school of fish as it darted left and right, seemingly all of one mind, then shot forward, following some unknowable logic.

Just as suddenly as it had come, the blizzard of fish blew away and there was Seth, wiggling his eyebrows, an expression that Summer translated as "wasn't that cool?" She nodded.

The wreck of the freighter was scarcely recognizable at first. It looked more like a natural phenomenon, a rusted, shell-encrusted, half-buried reef shaggily adorned with waving seaweed.

But as they got closer, Summer could see the distinctive outlines of a large ship lying on its side, the superstructure mostly buried, the hull still rising from the sea bed.

It was this strange, out-of-place work of man that made Summer feel most alien. She was flying far above it, hovering over it like an ungainly, slow-motion bird. She felt a passing moment of giddiness, a fear of heights, as if she might at any moment lose the buoyancy of the water and fall the twenty or thirty feet to the dead ship.

Seth led the way down, gliding through the separate beams of milky sunlight, one moment dark, the next bright. Summer kept close to him, oppressed by the sense of distant tragedy. Had people died here, going down with this ship?

Summer and Seth skimmed above the ship's crusty flank, inches above the hull, like airplanes buzzing a landing field. She touched the ship, surprised at the sensation—it was hard and real and substantial. She glanced ahead and saw that Seth was standing upright, using his hands to keep his balance. He waved for her to come.

He was standing beside a huge, jagged tear in the ship's side. The death wound, Summer had no doubt. She looked down into the darkness of the ship. And then, from the dark gash a pop-eyed face appeared, a large fish that looked for all the world like a grumpy old man who'd been awakened from his nap. It floated out and past them, nearly three feet long and in no hurry at all.

Summer gazed around more closely, looking less at the wreck of the ship and more at all the living things on or around or within it. Tiny shells clustered on the hull, each a living creature; the octopus that scuttled along, a liquid flurry of graceful motion; the amazing snail that crept toward her foot. There were small forests of soft, willowy plants that made a home for crabs and squid and rays. Fish, big and small, alone or in schools, darted in and out, up and down, crossing between her and the sun above like flights of birds.

In a single moment of awareness she realized that the dead ship was no longer dead. The machine that had failed to protect its human cargo now protected an entire universe of colorful, indescribably strange, stunningly creative, incredible life.

A moment ago she had been sad, seeing only a wreck. Now she smiled—as well as she could with a regulator in her mouth—and felt a surge of happiness. It was a new, unexpected sort of happiness, a satisfied feeling that had nothing directly to do with her own wants and desires. It was funny, really, Summer thought, the way she got caught up in her own minuscule fears and worries, her own tiny plans, as if she were the star in the big story of the universe.

Just like the people on this ship who had probably seen nothing but tragedy when it sank, perhaps the confirmation of their own minuscule fears and the end of their own tiny plans. Those people had not been the whole story, either. A much bigger story was being told.

Summer laughed an explosion of bubbles. And then, for some reason that she could not possibly have explained in words, she swam over to Seth. She caught his hands in hers and drew him into a swirling, giddy dance that went round and round and round, a slow tornado of bubbles and limbs caught in a shaft of sunlight.

"So, aren't you going to ask me about the trip?" Mallory Olan demanded. She was in the passenger seat of the Mercedes, having said she was just too exhausted to drive after the overnight flight in from the West Coast.

Mallory looked almost nothing like her daughter. She was expensively, if loudly, dressed. Her hair was big and out of a bottle. It was flattened a little in back from leaning against the airline seat.

Diana hated to drive with her mother in the car. It wasn't that her mother criticized her driving; she rarely did. Rather it was that Diana had to cope with morbid fantasies of running the car into a concrete abutment and killing her mother. It wasn't exactly a wish, and it wasn't exactly a fear. But it was distracting.

"How was your trip?" Diana asked.

Mallory began to tell her, in great detail, and after a few minutes Diana forgot her mother was talking. This day was not even supposed to come. At one point Diana had nearly decided that she would be dead on the day her mother returned. She'd played that scene so many times in her mind that it seemed unreal that her mother should now be here, right beside her, chattering away and complaining, and Diana, far from being dead, was being forced to interject semi-interested "uh-huhs" and "hmms."

Well, maybe that wasn't *so* far from being dead.

Diana popped in a CD. Saves the Day. She didn't especially like them. She only had the CD in the car to annoy her mother.

"I can't wait to see Summer," Mallory said, shouting over the anarchic music. "I feel bad that I haven't even seen her for more than a minute since she's been here. What *is* this music? They're just screaming."

"It's a tender love song," Diana said, straight-faced.

"Why didn't Summer come with you to pick me up?"

Diana enjoyed the moment. "Summer is off with a boy she met. I guess they're going to spend the day scuba diving and nude sunbathing on an uninhabited island. Don't worry, though. I made sure they packed plenty of sunblock."

Okay, so the part about nude sunbathing had been a slight embellishment. And who cared about the sunblock?

Unfortunately, Mallory didn't fall for it. "I'm glad she's meeting people," she said.

They arrived at the house, and the housekeeper came out to help with the bags. The phone was ringing as they went inside.

Her mother grabbed it in the hallway, assuming of course it was for her. And it almost certainly was, Diana thought. She was dragging one bag down the hall when she heard her mother say, "Adam! How nice to hear from you. It's been a long time."

Diana dropped the bag.

"Yes, I had a fine trip," Mallory said. "Me, too. Yes, here's Diana now." She put her hand over the receiver and in a loud stage whisper called Diana over. "It's Adam Merrick." Then she wiggled her eyebrows suggestively.

Diana took the receiver. Her heart rate had shot up as soon as she'd heard the name Adam.

"Yes?"

His voice was curt, cold, formal. "You wanted a meeting. My father is in town today. Four o'clock this afternoon, at the estate. That is, if you're still sure you want this."

He sounded as if he expected her to argue or perhaps to have changed her mind.

"You and Ross, too," she said. She glanced at her mother, who was looking expectant, as if somehow Diana might be discussing marriage plans with Adam.

"Oh, we'll be there," Adam sneered.

Diana hung up the phone.

"So? So, has something been happening while I was away?" Mallory asked.

To Diana's own amazement, she laughed. Well, it *was* funny. "All sorts of things have happened while you were away," Diana said.

15

Seth Crosses the Line, and Adam Crosses Back Over It

"If it wasn't for that beer can, you would almost think no other person had ever been here before," Summer said, gazing down the beach.

The boat bobbed contentedly just offshore, pulling at its anchor rope. They had brought their blanket and picnic supplies ashore in a tiny inflatable dinghy, after exhaling themselves into a giddy high inflating it. The dinghy was just large enough for their things, with the two of them swimming alongside. Now it sat on the sand, limp and partly deflated.

They had laid out their blanket under the shade of a stand of palms, enjoying their peanut butter and jelly and sliced turkey sandwiches while they watched pelicans dive-bombing the water.

For the most part, they'd been silent. It didn't bother Summer. She'd noticed that this easy silence often fell over them after they went for a dive. As if they were reluctant to reintegrate into the normal world of conversations that were carried on in words rather than gestures.

Summer stood up, brushing sand off the seat of her bathing suit, and walked up the beach to pry the can out of the wet sand. When she looked back she saw that Seth was bent over, collecting the debris of their picnic and putting it all in a plastic bag. She started back, then paused for a moment, unnoticed by Seth, enjoying the scene. Seth had the gift of seeming perfectly at home in every environment—when he was hammering and sawing and covered with sweat and sawdust; when he was sitting down to a dinner in a nice restaurant wearing the infrequent shirt; when he was underwater in a wet suit or just a bathing suit. She supposed it was something that came from inside him, this easiness in his own skin, the understated confidence. Not showy or charismatic like Adam, just centered and calm and sure of himself.

Even when he was holding her in his arms, looking solemn and serious, even as he . . .

Especially then, Summer realized with a pleasurable twinge. She walked back to him, and he held the bag open for her can. She bent to pick up a sandy crust of peanut butter and jelly sandwich that had fallen.

Summer wiped her sticky fingers on Seth's bare, smooth chest.

"Hey," he protested.

"Sorry, I forgot to bring paper towels," she said.

"And that's all I am to you—a paper towel." He grabbed her and swung her to the ground. In contrast to the roughness with which he'd grabbed her, he kissed her with supreme gentleness, on her forehead, on her closed eyelids, on her throat, on her left ear . . . on her lips.

His lips were salty, as Summer supposed she was, herself. Salty and no longer so gentle. He kissed her deeply. Summer wrapped her arms around his neck and pulled him closer still, suddenly possessed by a hunger that the peanut butter and jelly sandwiches hadn't exactly addressed. Summer smoothed her own hands down his sun-warmed back, savoring the heat of his skin. Seth pulled his lips away, but only to kiss her neck, and then to move in slow, ever-so-slow increments toward the first swell of her breast.

"Um, wait," Summer said, quite suddenly.

Seth raised his head and smiled. "Did I cross the 'line of death'?"

Summer laughed and kissed him again, but in a way that signaled that they were done—for now. "I don't know if it's exactly a 'line of death.'"

"But there *is* a line," he said.

"Um, yes. I don't exactly know where it's located," she said, "but I'll know when you've reached it."

"Is it"—he touched the swell of her breast where it met the edge of her bathing suit—"there?"

"Mmm, could be," she said. "But it's more like in my head."

"Oh, *that* line," he said thoughtfully. "You mean the line where you suddenly realize you aren't exactly thinking clearly anymore and something *else* is taking over?"

"So you know that line?" Summer said, trying to make a joke out of it.

He nodded. "I go there every time I'm with you," he said seriously. "I've been living right on that line since the first time I kissed you in the airport."

Summer unintentionally made a little whimpering noise deep in her throat. "Sure. Right. You probably went to the line with lots of girls. Like you never did with Lianne?"

"Did you with Adam?"

Yes, she had, Summer realized. On a night that had a certain similarity with this day. There had been a beach. There had been a picnic. It had seemed a perfect day up to that point. And then . . .

"I think we should go back in the water," Summer said, pushing him back, but not urgently.

"She says, avoiding the question."

"I just think we both might cool off a little in the water," Summer said. She got to her feet and helped drag a reluctant Seth to his.

"The water's warm. We'd have to go deep to cool off," he said. "And you are trying so hard to stay shallow." He paused for a beat, then grinned unexpectedly.

Summer began to giggle.

"Okay, that did sound a little pretentious and serious, even for me," Seth said. "Come on, let's get wet."

Diana dressed carefully, almost as if she were performing a ritual. She combed her hair. She brushed her teeth. She checked the tape recorder batteries and the tape itself. She slipped the tape recorder into the waistband of her loose-fitting silk slacks and carefully fluffed the tail of her blouse, checking the result in her mirror.

She had checked it all a dozen times, hundreds, if you counted just running the plan over and over in her mind. The small tape recorder could not be seen or heard. She had taped over the little red indicator light after an early experiment had revealed that it shined through.

Diana picked up the bag she'd bought. It was a hideous thing. Fortunately, neither Adam nor Ross had ever had much fashion sense when it came to female styles.

Diana went downstairs, sidling past the kitchen where her mother was talking to the housekeeper.

She went down to the stilt house and let herself in. It felt odd being there when Summer was away—sneaky, dishonest, like she'd have a hard time explaining herself if anyone discovered her. But Summer was far away, and Diana was confident that Diver would not be around. Summer said he only appeared late at night and early in the morning.

She got what she needed and left, feeling the weight of the bag on her shoulder.

She took her own car and drove to the Merrick estate, all the while going over and over what she had to say, how she had to act, the things she had to be careful *not* to say.

The Merrick mansion loomed huge and intimidating as she parked her tiny Jetta between a silver-and-black Rolls Royce and a mean, low-slung red Viper.

I should be afraid, Diana realized. *I should be shaking, trembling, the way I was the last time I was here.* But as she took internal inventory, she knew she wasn't afraid. Or if fear was present, it had been transformed somehow, had assumed a new and utterly different shape.

She took a deep, calming breath and got out. At the door she pressed the buzzer. Then she slipped her hand under the tail of her blouse. And, finally, she squeezed her bag.

"Do it, Diana," she muttered under her breath. "Do it."

The door opened. She'd expected Manolo, the butler. It was Ross. He leered cockily at her, and she took a step back, shocked.

Of course. They had deliberately sent Ross, thinking it would unsettle her. She reminded herself of what she had told herself a thousand times already—these were the Merricks. They were experts at using power and intimidation.

"Hello, Ross," she said.

"Why, it's Diana," he said. "What a surprise." He leaned close, to whispering distance. "Come back to get more of what I started to give you?"

"I'm here to see your father," Diana said, fighting down the feeling of loathing. The burning anger deep inside her flared. Good. Anger was her friend.

She followed Ross down the hall, past the gloomy portraits of Merricks past. He led her to a room she'd never been in before, a huge, dark, walnut-paneled library with stacks of leather-bound books. More clever intimidation, she noted, another attempt to make her feel ill at ease.

She felt like laughing. The Merricks didn't realize that they were not dealing with the same Diana they'd known. Not anymore.

Ross pointed to a single chair positioned before a massive desk. Diana sat stiffly, legs crossed. She rested her bag on her leg, holding it tight.

Adam entered the room, dressed in well-weathered but still spotless jeans, and a pale yellow shirt. She recognized the shirt. She had given it to him, part of an attempt to broaden his preppy clothing choices.

"Hi, Diana," he said quietly. "It's good to see you again."

For a split second Diana almost believed the warmth in his voice. Almost.

"I'm sure you're thrilled that I'm here," Diana said dryly.

Then the senator came in. He was a big, impressive man, wearing an expensively tailored suit that did not conceal his beefy shoulders or his spreading waistline. But the good looks he'd passed on to his sons were still in evidence.

He took a long look at her as he stood behind his desk, surveying her with open disdain.

It would have worked, Diana realized. Even two weeks ago, a week ago, she would have collapsed. His look, loaded with contempt, would have found resonance in her own mind. Even now she could feel that dark, twisted part of her endorsing his contempt, knowing, as he knew, that she was unworthy to be sitting here.

But Diana reached out for the new feeling she had allowed to grow. Anger. She let it flare and grow hot, and felt the power of it.

The senator sat down. His sons arranged themselves on either side of him. He waved a hand toward her. "You had something to say?"

"Yes, I did," Diana said.

"Well, let's hear it," the senator said. He glanced at his watch. "What's this about?"

"This is about rape."

"*Attempted* rape," Ross broke in. His father silenced him with a cold glare. The look surprised Diana. She'd thought the senator had treated *her* with contempt. But the frozen look he'd sent his son showed he was capable of much greater scorn.

Diana reminded herself to stay steady. She had a game plan worked out. So far it was still on track.

"Maybe it was just *attempted* rape," Diana said. "But maybe it would make a much more interesting story if I left out the word *attempted*."

"You lying bitch!" Ross exploded.

"Diana," Adam said much more calmly, cutting his

brother off, "you know that's not true. I was there. I know that didn't happen. There is no point in trying to pretend that more happened than actually did."

"Sure, there's a point, all right," Ross sneered. "She's thinking she can squeeze us for more money if she makes it look worse than it was."

"Shut up, Ross." The senator's voice was like a knife. He breathed deeply and ran his tongue over his teeth while he favored Diana with a new look— amusement. "Yes, I suppose you *are* right," he said, chuckling softly. "It would make a better story that way. I guess for once I should actually be glad that Ross failed to follow through on what he started. He's had so many failures."

"What is it you want, Diana?" Adam asked.

"They always want the same thing," the senator said dryly. "You'll learn that eventually, Adam. When you are rich, all anyone ever wants from you is money. Did you have a dollar amount in mind, Diana?"

"Did *you*, Senator?" Diana shot back.

The man laughed out loud. "Oh, Adam, you really should have found a way to hold on to this one," he said. "What a perfect political wife she would have made. It's a useful thing to have a smart, ruthless, and, may I say, beautiful wife at your side." But Adam looked troubled. He was gazing narrowly at Diana, sensing that something was wrong. He had known her too long and too well. "She doesn't want money," he said.

"Then, what?" Ross demanded.

"You, Ross," Diana said through gritted teeth. "I want you. In prison."

Ross barked a wild laugh. "You *are* crazy. You think you're going to put a Merrick in prison?" Unable to control himself any longer, he jumped around the corner of the desk, lunging toward Diana. "You want to mess with me?" he shouted. "I'll finish what I started with you last year! I'll finish it right now."

Diana jumped up from her chair, just as Ross thrust out a hand to grab her. Suddenly everything was in motion.

Adam came around the desk from his side. But the senator, old as he was, was closer, and surprisingly fast. He reached Ross first. He swung his fist and buried it in Ross's stomach.

Ross fell to the floor, gasping for breath and clutching his stomach. He looked stunned and horrified. But no more horrified than Adam.

"Dad, Dad!" Adam took his father by his shoulders, restraining him and comforting him, too.

"Now do you see?" Diana screamed, shaking with rage and fresh terror. "Do you see what he is? Do you see what your son is, Senator?"

"Yes, damn it, I know what he is," the senator

bellowed, in a voice that seemed to make the room vibrate. "Do you think I've lived this long and still don't recognize garbage when I see it?" Diana could only stand there, unable to think of anything to say. This was not in the plan. Ross was gagging and gasping on the floor, still doubled over.

The senator yanked at his cuffs and straightened his jacket. Then, more quietly, "I know what Ross is. Yes. I know."

"Dad, come on," Adam said, now near tears. He guided his father back to his chair. "Come on, Dad, don't do this to yourself."

Ross crawled away, then carefully, still clutching his stomach, slowly rose far enough to slide into a chair.

For a while no one said anything. Diana sat back down in her seat. She clutched the bag again on her knee.

"Here it is, young lady," the senator said. His voice was flat now, empty of any emotion. "If you try to charge my son with any crime or accuse him publicly of any crime, I will use every bit of my power and influence to destroy you. I'll have every minute of your life investigated. I'll investigate your family, your friends. Maybe I'll find something incriminating, maybe not—it doesn't matter. Because one way or another, I'll destroy you. I *own* the prosecutor here, she was elected with my support, and she'll do what I say. The same with the local police. Chief Dorman is a personal friend of mine. You won't find anyone who will believe you or support you. And in the end you'll be made to look like a hysterical, pathetic figure."

As this speech went on, Diana noticed Adam's face growing sadder. He looked steadily down at the floor. She thought he might be close to crying. Ross just sat silently. At last, it seemed, it had penetrated his mind that he was in trouble, and being rescued by a father who was sickened by the necessity of saving him.

"On the other hand," the senator said, "we can forget all of this. And you can have a check for enough money to pay your way through any college in the country, and have a nicely furnished apartment off-campus, and a nice little sports car to drive back and forth to classes. Those are your choices—walk away with a fat check, or get a lesson in the influence of a senior senator with a great deal of money."

He pushed back from the desk and stood up. "Think about it for twenty-four hours. Let me know what you decide. Adam, see her to the door."

Adam walked with her down the long hallway. They walked in silence. Diana just felt numb. It had worked. She had not failed. She had not broken down. She had not succumbed to fear but had let her anger guide her.

But it was a strange feeling, winning. More melancholy than happy.

Adam walked with her out onto the front steps and stopped. It was hot and bright and there was a soft breeze blowing from the water.

"Diana," Adam said.

"Yes?"

He moved with sudden speed, grabbed one arm, and, with his free hand, fumbled for the tape player in her belt. He yanked it out. He looked at it and nodded, as if he'd expected it all along.

Diana froze.

"My dad said you'd try something like this," Adam said. "He told me to be sure to get it away from you."

He pushed the Rewind button, then Play. Ross's voice.

". . . to mess with me? I'll finish what I started with you last year!"

Adam clicked it off. Then he held it out to her.

Diana took the tape player from him. She searched his face for some explanation, but he would not meet her gaze.

"Adam, tell your father I have made up my mind," Diana said.

"I know," he said.

16

Black Holes

Down, down they went, deeper than they had ever gone before. Sunlight, so brilliant above on the surface, was filtered and pale at this depth, like a light from another world.

They played a slow-motion game of tag, Summer following Seth through forests of seaweed, around miniature mountain ranges of tumbled rock and fabulous extrusions of coral, pausing to watch an eel warily poking its nose out of its lair, sharing a moment of pretended terror at the appearance of a small, harmless baby lemon shark. Seth had brought his speargun and looked unusually fierce, prowling the ocean floor with it held casually in his left hand.

He was determined, he said, to spear their dinner.

Summer watched a huge crab, or what looked like a crab to her, shoot backward, stirring up a little whirlpool of sand in its wake. She grabbed Seth's leg and pointed. Better than spearing some poor helpless fish, she decided. Somehow that would have felt wrong.

Seth nodded. Crabmeat would be fine by him. He went off in pursuit.

The crab went straight into a fissure in the rocks. The fissure was large, and Seth cautiously stuck his head in, probing the darkness with the tip of his speargun.

He motioned for Summer to shine the underwater flashlight inside. She floated alongside him and aimed the beam inside. The light played around crusted walls and caught the retreating crab.

Seth turned to face her and made a wide, encompassing gesture with his arms. She took it that he was telling her the cave was big. Then he shrugged, not dismissively, but more in a "how about it?" way.

Summer automatically checked her watch. She still had thirty minutes of air. More than enough. But the idea of swimming into the cave scared her. She made a back-and-forth gesture with her head—"not sure."

He held up a finger—"look." He unwrapped a length of yellow nylon rope and fastened one end around a large bulb of coral. Then, with hand gestures, Seth explained that they would go in only as far as the rope would go. That way, there would be no danger of becoming lost inside.

Summer nodded. Yes. She was up for it.

Seth winked and led the way through the fissure. It was narrow enough that they could go through only one at a time. Summer kept the flashlight trained on Seth, spotlighting his dull-gray tank, a flash of flipper, a tan, muscular leg.

She realized she was breathing too fast, unnerved by the suddenly confined space. She bumped against the wall and heard a scraping sound.

Then it leapt at her, a lightning-quick strike that was just a blur in the water. She screamed into her regulator. The eel slapped hard against the side of her face, dislodging her mask. Water rushed in, blinding her.

She recoiled, paddling back in panic. Her tank slammed hard into the low roof of the cave.

She had the sense of an arm, feeling for her, missing. Then the eel whipped across her stomach.

The light fell away, turning down through the water, a strange slow-motion firework. It came to rest in the sand, pointing uselessly at the wall of the cave.

She tried to calm herself, but now something else had brushed against her leg. Blind and in terror she twisted hard, slamming her tank again against the low roof.

There was a muffled cracking sound, like splintering wood or distant thunder.

Something heavy dropped on the back of her legs. She kicked and moved out of its way. She had lost one of her fins. Something else struck her arm. Another sharp, hard object grazed her left thigh.

She swam forward with all her strength and plowed directly into something soft and yielding. Seth! His arms found her in the darkness and held her close, gripping her like a vise, forcing her to stop moving.

For a while she just waited, listening to the scraping, sliding sounds behind her, trying to slow the panicked beat of her heart, trying to gain control over the panting that seemed to bring less and less air from the regulator.

Seth tapped gently on her face mask. He was telling her to clear her mask, to blow out the water so that she would be able to see. She did, and realized it was not completely black in the cave. A few feet below was the flashlight. Seth dived to get it. But there was some other light, too, very faint but definite.

Seth aimed the flashlight back at the entrance to the cave. It was gone.

The yellow nylon rope went to, and then through, a jumbled wall of fallen rock.

They were trapped. Summer felt the panic beginning to rise in her chest again. Seth came over and patted her on the shoulder. He handed her the light, and she directed it as he worked to dislodge the fallen rocks.

He was able to toss aside a dozen small stones. But one huge slab of rock lay unmovable.

Seth tried by himself, and with Summer's desperate help, but the slab would not budge.

Finally, Seth pointed to her gauge. Ten minutes of air left. He looked at his own watch and held up seven fingers. In about seven minutes he would be out of air. Three minutes later her own air would be gone.

The thought of those three minutes shook Summer Smith like nothing she had ever felt before.

Diana arrived back at her house feeling weird and disconnected from everything that had just happened. It was as if she were watching herself park the car, watching herself go inside, watching herself watching herself from a long way off.

What had it all meant? On one level it was easy to understand—she had succeeded in getting hard proof of what Ross had done a year earlier. For a year she'd felt beaten and defeated. She'd lived without hope, spiraling down and down, into "the hole," as she'd called it, the deep, black hole of depression.

And then, almost at the last minute, she'd seen the way out of the hole. She'd seen that the Merricks were afraid, and that had allowed her anger, for so long turned inward, to explode outward, directed at a better target.

She should feel wonderful. She felt nothing at all.

Her mother was in the living room and called to her as she passed by.

"You're back early," Mallory said. She sounded tense.

"It didn't take long," Diana said absently.

"What didn't take long?" her mother asked, speaking in clipped, angry cadences. "It didn't take long for you to try to blackmail Senator Merrick?"

Diana literally staggered. She looked at her mother with pure, undisguised horror. "How—"

"The senator called me, how do you think? I just hung up the phone with him." Mallory stood up and marched over to Diana. She grabbed her arm hard and dragged her to the couch. She practically flung her daughter into it.

"Do you want to tell me what in hell you think you're up to?" Mallory demanded.

"Didn't Merrick already tell you?"

"I want to hear it from *you*, Diana. Because I'm hoping that you have some good explanation for the fact that you are trying to blackmail a United States senator, for God's sake!"

Her mother was screaming at her. Literally screaming, in a voice Diana hadn't heard her use since the divorce. A wild, bitter, sarcastic voice.

"I'm not blackmailing anyone," Diana said weakly.

She felt as if the air were being crushed out of her, as if she couldn't breathe. All she wanted to do was run away.

"Don't lie to me," Mallory exploded. "I'm not that stupid, Diana. I know when I'm being lied to. Senator Merrick himself called me and told me what you were up to. Are you trying to tell me that *he* is making this up?"

Diana wanted to speak, but her throat was one big lump. Tears were filling her eyes, threatening to spill over. She was determined not to cry in front of her mother.

"Diana," Mallory said in a slightly less hostile tone, "I know you're young, but this is still inexcusable. Do you have any idea what that old man can do to me? To us?"

"He can't do anything to *me*," Diana said, forcing the words out through gritted teeth. She needed to find her own anger again. Needed to hold on to it.

"Oh, can't he?" her mother sneered. "You pathetic little creature, don't you know? Don't you know anything? Are you that ignorant? Who do you think pays for this house and your clothes and your cute little car? I do. *I* do."

Diana shook her head in puzzlement. What was her mother ranting about?

"Oh, I see—you don't get the connection?" Mallory

said with savage sarcasm. "Well, here's the connection. My publisher is owned twenty-five percent by a company called M.H.G. You know what M.H.G. is? The Merrick Holdings Group. You know how much influence a twenty-five percent share buys? Plenty. More than enough to cut my throat professionally."

Diana felt sick. She feared she might throw up from the churning in her stomach. Her head was spinning. She'd thought she'd won. She'd thought she had outsmarted the Merricks. Now they were showing her that the battle had only begun. They had reached right into her home, threatening the one thing her mother really cared about—her career.

Mallory laughed derisively. "You thought you could blackmail someone like Senator Merrick? Do you need money that badly? I'd have given you money. Rather than have you making up ridiculous stories . . ."

Diana felt her lip quivering. Tears were spilling now, and she was past worrying about them. "It isn't a story," she said. She pulled the tape recorder out of her waistband. She pushed the button, and sat the recorder on the seat beside her.

The voices were hollow-sounding but clear. The entire conversation had recorded plainly, except for a few scratching noises.

Mallory turned away, listening, hiding her face.

Diana sat very still, saying nothing, vaguely interested

in the words, feeling as if she were listening to a conversation that had taken place somewhere else, involving people she didn't know.

The tape came to an end.

Mallory walked the few steps to her daughter. With one hand she picked up the tape recorder. With the other she absently stroked her daughter's head.

Then she went to the coffee table and sat down. Methodically she pulled the tape from the cartridge, piling the loops in a crystal ashtray.

Diana watched her mother in horror, unable to move. *You can't do this!* she wanted to scream, but no words came out.

Mallory picked up a matching crystal cigarette lighter and touched the flame to the tape. "I'm doing this for your own good," she said.

Diana sat passively. Her anger was gone. She felt nothing. Nothing at all.

The black hole opened beneath her, welcoming her back.

17

Running Out of Time

Ten minutes of air. Ten minutes. Not a long time for Summer to think about all the things she would never know in her life. Her short life, down suddenly to ten minutes.

Seth patted her shoulder. She held his hand and squeezed it tight.

Once more Summer swept the beam around them. Walls of stone and crusted shellfish surrounded them, except in one direction where the cave went down deeper still. The huge crab they had chased was nowhere to be seen. The yellow nylon rope disappeared into the crush of fallen rocks, as if it had gone off into another dimension entirely.

Summer wondered if the flashlight battery would last as long as their air. Probably. Ten minutes—no, nine—was not a long time.

Then she remembered it. The light. The *other* light.

She turned off the flashlight. Seth shook her, telling her to turn it back on, but she squeezed his hand again to signal that she had a reason. Slowly her eyes adjusted to the darkness. Once again, she was able to make out dim shapes.

Now Seth had noticed it, too. There should be no light at all.

She snapped the flashlight on again, pointing it at Seth, then directing the beam along the cave floor. Seth nodded. His eyes were worried but determined. He set off at a moderate speed with Summer close behind. They followed the sandy cave floor down several more feet, reaching a point where the cave roof almost closed off further progress.

The end of the rope was played out now. Seth used a loose bit of rock to anchor it to the cave floor. Then he went through the narrow opening. Summer followed, careful not to scrape the rock.

They were in a larger cavern, how large it was impossible to say. But the cave roof was too far overhead even to be seen in the flashlight beam. Summer turned the flashlight off again.

Hope! The emotion surged in her heart. There was light overhead. Filtered, dim as earliest gray dawn, but definite light. She started up. Seth restrained her, shaking his head slowly.

Summer understood. They could not shoot suddenly upward. The decompression would cause the bends, a very painful form of death. Even now, they had to be careful.

They rose slowly, slowly, fighting the panicky urge to hurry.

Suddenly, Summer realized, her head was out of the water. It seemed unbelievable. But when she raised her mask cautiously, it was true. Air. Genuine, breathable air.

"Thank God," she gasped. "There's air."

There was air but no sunlight. Where *were* they?

Seth surfaced beside her and tore off his own mask. He swiftly shut the valves on their tanks. "We're in some kind of air pocket," he said.

Summer trained the flashlight around. They were in a huge, vaulted cavern, with sheer rock walls on three sides. On the other side the rock rose more gradually, creating a low, jumbled, dry shelf before it continued up and up.

At the very apex of the cavern was a tiny window of brilliant blue. The sky.

Seeing it brought tears to Summer's eyes. The sky.

Seth was laughing, a relieved, tired, half-hysterical laugh. Summer realized she was laughing, too, even as tears blurred her vision.

Seth looked at his gauge. "Three minutes," he said. "I was on fumes."

Summer swam to the shelf and pulled herself heavily out of the water. "Air," she said. "Boy, do I love air."

Seth slumped exhausted beside her. "Air is excellent," he agreed. He sat up and looked around. "Of course, stairs or a ladder would be nice, too. We're beneath the island now. I guess this is basically an underground lake."

"There has to be some way to get up there," Summer said. But as she surveyed the cave her confidence faded quickly. The patch of sky was high, very high overhead. The cave was like an overturned bowl, sides sloping upward, utterly impossible to climb unless you were a spider.

"Someone will come," Seth said, trying to sound confident. "You know, other divers. They'll see the boat, and then if they go down, they'll see the rope. They'll figure out about the cave-in."

Summer nodded in agreement. "You're probably right."

They both stared up at the patch of blue.

"We won't freeze or anything," Seth said. "I mean, it's a little chilly here, but with the wet suit tops . . ."

"And we have air," Summer said. "A few minutes ago I thought I would gladly sell my soul for fresh air. Or stale air. Or for a chance to suck on bus exhaust. I've never been so terrified."

"Yeah," he agreed. "Look, I'm sorry about getting you into this."

"You? Jeez, I'm the one who panicked and caused an avalanche or whatever it was."

"A cave-in," he said glumly. "Cave. Cave-in."

"That makes sense," she said, echoing his grim tone.

"It's *my* fault, not yours," he said.

"Let's not argue about it," Summer said. The adrenaline was wearing off now, and lassitude was setting in. She wanted to savor the sense of relief a little longer before having to move on to recognizing that they were still in serious trouble.

"Why not argue about it?" Seth said. "We have plenty of time."

They fell silent and stared up at the patch of blue. Already it seemed the light was fading, the blue growing darker, shading toward violet.

The dinner shift had been busy. Marquez had more than a hundred dollars in tips weighing down the pocket of her apron. And she still had a twenty sitting out in the dining room as she began her side work, cleaning the salad and soup area in the kitchen. The job involved emptying the sloppy, destroyed containers of salad dressing they'd used all night into new containers and topping them off from the big bins in the walk-in.

In the old days she'd liked this job. It gave her an opportunity to be in the kitchen and make frequent trips to the walk-in, where J.T. would manage to be at the same time. It was a little game they played, meeting, kissing, then going back out to work to start the cycle over again. It had been strangely exciting.

Now she minimized her opportunities to run into J.T. He did the same, steering clear of her.

He had come over at one point to apologize for the scene in the dining room the night before. She'd apologized, too. Yes, they had both agreed, they were acting immature.

She'd told him that she was glad if Lianne was good for him. He'd asked her if she had found anyone, and she'd lied and said that she was seeing someone. She stopped short of telling him it was Diver. That lie was too easy to check out, and then she would just look pathetic.

Despite the hundred and two dollars she had after paying out the bartender and the busboys, she felt low when she left the Crab 'n' Conch. Low and restless. She went home and called Summer. No answer. Too bad. Summer would have picked up her spirits.

She showered and called Summer again. Still no answer. If the girl was in the bathroom or something, she was certainly taking her time. Marquez glanced at the clock. Almost a quarter after eleven. Summer had to be back from her trip by now.

Maybe she had disconnected her phone. Maybe she didn't want to be disturbed. Maybe she and Seth were . . .

"That's right, Marquez," she muttered, "torture yourself. Everyone is having a great time but you."

But no, Summer wouldn't have Seth still over at the house. Diver would be there by now, and Summer wasn't the kind of girl who would feel comfortable making out while someone was snoozing on her roof. Marquez considered calling Diana, but her mom was back and might pick up the phone. The last thing Summer needed was Mallory Olan bursting into the stilt house looking for her.

Marquez decided to go by and check for herself. There was probably nothing to worry about. And maybe she would run into Diver. They had gotten off to a bad start the other day. Marquez had been too aggressive. She'd forgotten that Diver was different from most guys.

"Different from most humans, for that matter," Marquez said. Of course, right now J.T. was probably baring his soul and whatever else he could get away with baring to Lianne. Maybe Marquez should give Diver another chance.

She looked at the white patch on her wall. The white paint covering the letters J.T. "Jerk," she said to the patch. And yet, she wished she hadn't painted his name out. It was easier to be mad at a name than a blank patch.

She drove her parents' car to the Olan house, parking down the street rather than in the driveway. She walked quietly past the main house, feeling relieved when she reached the stilt house unchallenged.

The stilt house was dark and silent, the only sounds the slap of water against the pilings and the slow, mournful creak of the pier.

She considered turning back. Obviously Summer was just asleep, exhausted from the long day. "Well, tough," Marquez muttered. "She'll just have to wake her little self up."

Marquez knocked on the door.

She was startled by a voice from above.

"She's not here." Diver, a dark shape, standing on the deck, looking down.

Even now Marquez remembered his brief kiss, just a brush of his perfect lips against hers. Maybe they just needed to try that a second time. Or . . . maybe not.

"She went out?"

"I don't think so," Diver said. His voice sounded troubled.

"You mean she never came home?" Marquez opened the door, reached in, and flipped on a light. The bed was made, a surprising sight to Marquez, who never actually made her own bed.

"Summer? You home?" She looked into the bathroom, the only separate room.

Diver dropped down behind her and followed Marquez inside.

"I don't think she's been back," Marquez said. She felt out of place, as if the familiar surroundings had become different somehow.

"She hasn't been back," Diver said. "I'm sure."

"Diver, you're worrying me," Marquez said.

"I'm worried," he said. "I—I feel she may be in trouble."

"It's almost midnight. She should have gotten back hours ago. She went scuba diving with Seth. You don't think anything could have happened, do you?"

"Yes," he said. "I do think something happened."

"Oh my God. What should we do?" Marquez wondered. "Should I tell Mrs. Olan? Or call the Coast Guard?"

"What can Mrs. Olan do?" Diver asked. "Maybe the Coast Guard."

"Yeah, you're right. She'd just get all upset and it's

probably nothing. But we could call the Coast Guard and, you know, find out if . . . if they've picked up any boats out of gas or whatever."

Diver nodded solemnly. He seemed to have withdrawn even further inside himself than usual.

Suddenly the atmosphere in the room seemed frightening to Marquez. As if the temperature had dropped. "I'll call the Coast Guard," she said briskly, anxious to be doing something.

"I guess that's all we *can* do," Diver said.

But another possibility had occurred to Marquez. A possibility that had to do with burned hands and two people talking at the very same moment. "There's another person who might be able to help, too," Marquez said.

Diana lay in her bed, uncovered, wearing a simple, white gauze shift, watching the numbers on the clock change. Eleven thirty-eight to eleven thirty-nine. She was waiting for midnight. Midnight seemed right. She didn't know why. It was just that she had to pick some time, some definite time, when she would do it. Midnight was definite.

She tightened her grip on the small brown bottle. Her palm was dry, not sweating with nerves. She didn't feel nervous. Hadn't felt nervous when she took the bottle from her mother's bathroom. Her mother had not noticed it missing from her medicine cabinet.

Or perhaps she had noticed it and just didn't care.

Mallory had burned the tape, saying it was for Diana's own good. Maybe she even halfway believed it. But Diana knew that her own good was no longer an issue. There would be no good for Diana. She was no longer part of the world that others inhabited. The world that Summer—and Seth—lived in.

She had been lying here forever, it seemed, indifferent to the failing light, indifferent to falling night. Thinking of nothing. Feeling nothing but the presence of the hole as she fell and fell and fell into it, deeper and deeper, like Alice in Wonderland. Too far even to hope for a way back out.

She had fallen all the way down the hole. And she had found no last-minute salvation. At the end of it all, she was alone. Alone with herself.

"Just me," Diana whispered. "Just me."

Eleven-forty. Twenty minutes to go.

18

Late News and News Too Late

J.T.'s apartment was a tiny, unexceptional place, with two windows over the main drag, upstairs from a kite store. He had a small balcony off to one side, and the people who owned the store had him hang brightly colored kites from it. He had moved in at the beginning of the summer, wanting to have more independence and freedom than he had in his parents' home. The thought had also been that he and Marquez could enjoy some privacy there.

A set of exterior wooden steps led up to the apartment. Marquez climbed them quietly, not wanting to wake J.T. prematurely. She was still undecided about whether to wake him up at all. It was a fairly amazing thing she would have to lay on him, if she decided to go ahead. Her natural reluctance to get further into other people's problems inclined her to walk away. But it was after midnight, and Summer still wasn't home.

She knocked on the door and only then considered the possibility that Lianne might be inside with J.T.

"That would certainly be embarrassing," she said under her breath. But then, one way or the other, this was not going to be an easy visit to J.T.

She had to knock three different times, louder each time, before she saw a light go on inside. The ratty little curtain in the door window moved slightly. J.T. appeared, squinting out of one eye, the other scrunched closed. When he saw her, he opened the other eye as well. Then he opened the door.

"I suppose you're wondering why I'm here in the middle of the night?" Marquez said brightly. J.T. was wearing pajama bottoms and no shirt.

"It crossed my mind, yeah," he said. He scratched his hair, which just made a bigger mess of it. He seemed to be tasting something he didn't like.

"It's about Summer," she said.

He thought about this for a moment. "The waitress or the season?"

"Summer Smith. She's not at home."

He nodded. "Summer's not at home. Okay. Thanks for coming by and telling me. I'd been tossing and turning in bed, asking myself: do you think Summer is at home or not? You've cleared that up for me."

"Can I come in?" Marquez asked, letting his sarcasm flow past without a response.

He shrugged and led the way inside. The apartment was a typical "guy" apartment—a few sticks of furniture, a large quantity of dirty clothing, posters sagging on the walls, a stone-dead potted plant.

J.T. went to the kitchen, reappearing with a carton of orange juice from which he took several long swallows.

Marquez took the one chair. J.T. sat on the edge of the bed and scratched himself indiscreetly.

"Sorry," he mumbled, when he saw her disapproving look. "So, Summer isn't home. What's the rest of the secret message?"

"She went out early this morning with Seth Warner. They were going to some island to do some diving. They were supposed to be home this evening. They aren't home yet."

This penetrated. J.T. was a diver himself. He nodded seriously. "Could be engine problems with the boat," he said. "That's most likely. Or maybe they lost track of time and decided to sleep over on the island. It isn't necessarily something . . . bad."

"I called the Coast Guard. They said the same

things, but they also said they'd put out an alert." Marquez hesitated. So far she hadn't told J.T. anything troubling. She hadn't passed the point of no return.

"Why did you come here?" J.T. asked. "Getting my expert opinion as a diver? I'm not exactly a professional. You've already called the C.G. It's probably like they said."

Oh, well, Marquez realized, there was probably no avoiding it. "But what do *you* think it is?" Marquez asked, leaning forward in her chair.

"I have no idea," J.T. said.

Marquez took a deep breath. Then another. This was going to be strange. "Um, J.T., I don't know how much you've ever talked to Summer . . ."

"Not much. You know, just work gossip."

"So I guess she never told you about . . . about Jonathan." Okay, *now* she was past the point of no return.

J.T. looked impatient. "You know, Marquez, I was thinking sleep might not be a bad thing."

"He was her brother. Jonathan. He disappeared when he was two years old. Before Summer was even born. They never found out what happened to him."

Suddenly J.T. was sitting very still. His eyes were narrowly focused on Marquez's face.

Marquez plunged ahead. "The other day at work, I noticed that you burned yourself, and at the exact same moment, Summer burned herself in the same place. I know this seems crazy, just let me finish. There was another time when Summer was complaining she had a headache and you had a headache, too. And then the other day, when you both said exactly the same thing at exactly the same time—"

"How old is Summer?" he asked in a quiet voice.

"She's seventeen, I guess. She said her brother disappeared just a couple of months before she was born."

"Which would mean, if he's alive today, he would be about eighteen, maybe just turned nineteen," J.T. said.

"Yeah," Marquez confirmed.

"My age."

"Your age."

"How long have you suspected this?" he asked.

"I don't know, a week, I guess," Marquez said. "It seemed totally insane. But tonight I got to thinking, you know, about the burning and the headache and all. You know, people talk about brothers and sisters having these . . . these connections, you know?"

J.T.'s calm facade began to break down. He looked overwhelmed, like he wanted to hide somewhere. He rubbed his face with his palms.

"I thought, I don't know, you might have some idea, some feeling about whether she's in trouble."

Marquez threw up her hands. "Sorry. This is insane. I can't believe I even said anything. This is nuts."

"Do you know what this would mean?" J.T. asked, his face stricken. "Do you know what it would mean for my parents? I mean, are they some kind of kidnappers? Is that what I'm supposed to believe?"

"I don't know," Marquez said. She fidgeted in her seat for a minute, trying to decide what to do.

J.T. kept rubbing his face. It was becoming a compulsive movement now, one he couldn't seem to stop.

Marquez got up and went to sit beside him. She carefully did not touch him and kept her hands folded in her lap. "Look, J.T., I know this is a lot to even think about. I wouldn't have said anything, except I'm worried about Summer. The girl seems to have a talent for getting herself into one kind of mess or another."

"I don't have any idea where she is," J.T. said distractedly. "How would I know? This is nuts. You're right, this is insane. I mean, I'm not having some kind of psychic connection, if that's what you think."

"But could you maybe *think* about it?" Marquez pleaded.

J.T. made an effort to focus. "Look, as a diver I can tell you that there are only a couple of good diving places where they could have gone in an open boat from here and gotten back in the same day."

"That's something, at least," Marquez said.

He laughed bitterly. "Marquez, if they're in serious trouble, that information is worth nothing. They probably went down with about an hour of air. An hour."

"I know," Marquez said, "but I have to try, right?" She jumped up to try to find a shirt and pants for him to put on.

J.T. managed a small, wistful smile. "You getting in the middle of other people's problems, Marquez?"

Marquez concentrated on digging through a pile of dirty clothes. "I guess staying *out* of other people's problems doesn't always work out that great, either."

The patch of blue was no more than a distant memory. Now only two faint stars were visible through the hole above. Summer was hungry and thirsty, despite the fact that Seth had showed her how to lick condensation from the rocks.

Worse than hungry or thirsty, she was afraid.

It was dark in the cave. Totally dark, since they were conserving their precious flashlight. So dark that Summer could literally not see her hand in front of her face.

There was no way out. They had spent hours trying to think of a way to escape. But there was no escape. None. And it was too easy to conjure up images of two rubber-clad skeletons being found down here someday.

"I wonder which stars those are," Seth said.

He was just a voice, nearby in the total darkness. Not a happy voice.

"Someone told me once that stars weren't really far away," Summer said. "That they were right here."

"I guess that's true of the starlight," Seth said. "It's right here."

Summer smiled sadly in the darkness. Poor Diver. He'd wonder what happened to her. Or would he? He'd have the stilt house all to himself again.

"This summer vacation is not turning out quite the way I had planned," Summer said. There was a plopping sound in the water. Summer was used to it now. A fish, coming by to take a look at the odd phenomenon of two humans trapped like goldfish in a tank. "I kind of had this image of it just being sun and surf and parties."

"Sorry," Seth said softly.

"Sorry? Why are *you* sorry?" she said crossly.

"I got you into this," Seth said. "I helped get you into the mess with Ross and Adam. I've single-handedly ruined your life."

Summer thought for a while. "No, you didn't ruin anything. You've been the best part of this whole thing so far. Marquez and Diver, too, but mostly you."

"Don't be sweet to me," Seth said grimly. "I swear if you're nice to me I'll start crying."

"Crying wouldn't be so bad," Summer said. "I

won't tell anyone. Ever," she added with deliberate dark humor.

"So much for my big theory that you and I were . . ." He sighed, an audible sound in the profound silence.

"That we were what?" Summer asked.

"You know," he said. "I told you already."

"Tell me again," she whispered.

"I had this feeling," he began. "It was so strong I was sure it had to be real. It was like I could see the future, and I knew, totally, beyond any doubt, that you and I were going to be together."

"We *are* together," Summer said, trying to interject a weak note of levity.

"I had us going to college together and traveling around the world together, and I don't know, it sounds pretty idiotic now."

"No, it doesn't," Summer said.

"I even had us married someday, with kids and all that. A dog. I was thinking a Labrador. Maybe a mutt. It seemed so real. That first time, when we kissed, it was like 'Wake up, Seth, this is *her*. This is your one great love.'"

Summer stretched out her hand, searching for him. She touched his leg and from there found his hand. They linked their fingers together.

"You kind of scared me when you talked that way before," Summer confessed.

"It doesn't scare you now?"

"I have better things to be scared of," Summer pointed out. "But at the time I thought, you know, that if I got too involved . . . Jeez, I don't even know *what* I was thinking. That all seems like it was a completely different world. I was worried, you know, about committing. I thought if I didn't watch out I would fall totally in love with you, and then naturally it would end up in some kind of mess. That's how it always works."

"How it always works? What do you mean, like no one ever gets to be happy?"

"Not on TV," Summer said. "Anytime a couple is happy it just means something terrible is coming. I mean, my parents were happy. They had my brother. And me on the way. And then suddenly it was time for something terrible to happen, and so it did."

"But, Summer, that doesn't mean it's a law of nature or something," Seth argued.

"Maybe not for everyone," Summer allowed.

"Not for you, either."

Summer hesitated before telling him any more. Wouldn't it just hurt him? Then again, they were probably going to die down here. If this wasn't a time for honesty, when was?

"See, it *did* happen," Summer said. "I was kind of falling for Adam. And look what happened."

There was a long silence. She wondered what his face would show, if she could see it.

"Yeah, but nothing happened to *you*," Seth said. "I mean, it might have, but it didn't. Whereas *this* is a real mess." Again he was quiet for a while. "So if your idea is that being happy and in love is what leads to terrible things happening—"

"Then that would mean that I *was* in love and happy before this happened," Summer completed the thought. "See? Proof."

"Are you saying that—What are you saying?" he asked.

Summer sighed profoundly. "I tried not to let it happen," she said. "But it did. I fell in love with you, anyway. And then, boom, total disaster."

"You love me?" he asked, his voice soft and hopeful.

"Yes," Summer said. Then she raised his unseen hand to her lips, kissed it, and pressed it against her heart.

Seth shifted closer and put his arm around her shoulders. "Excellent timing, Summer," he said. "You couldn't fall in love with me *after* we went cave diving?"

"Sorry," she said, turning to him.

"Are you really sorry?" he asked, his lips close to hers.

And for a long time, no more words were spoken.

19

I Believe the Point Here Is . . . Never Give Up.

In her dream, Summer sat beside the tarot lady again. The tarot lady seemed not to want to meet her gaze, so in her dream, Summer was annoyed.

"So," she said accusingly, "you tell me all this stuff about these guys I'll meet, and you can't mention that maybe I should avoid small, damp, confined spaces?"

The tarot lady shuffled her cards. "Who knew?"

"Not you. Duh."

"The future is always shifting."

"Oh, that's perfect," Summer said. "Nice way to weasel out of it. You know what? No one can tell the future. All this stuff is just baloney. A big baloney sand-wich. With cheese and mayonnaise and mustard and lettuce. And maybe it's a sub, one of those big Subway subs, what are they called . . . B.M.T.'s, yeah, all this different meat and you can have it with everything, even hot peppers—"

"You're hungry, aren't you?" the woman asked.

"I guess you can tell that from the cards," Summer said. "Let's see them. Turn them over. Stop keeping secrets from me."

The woman turned over a single card. It was the figure of a small boy, dressed all in white. He was holding something in his hand. A red ball.

"That card scares me," Summer said.

"Why?"

"You *know* why," she said. "Death. That's why, because he's dead. You're showing him to me because you think I'm going to die."

Suddenly Summer awoke. Her hair was standing on end.

She was in the cave still, she could tell from the sound of the water. She was in Seth's arms. The taste of his lips was still in her mouth. There was no light but for two stars far overhead, peeking through the hole in the roof.

Then she saw him—the boy in white. He was standing a little way off.

"Who are you?" Summer asked him in a whisper.

"I don't know," the little boy said. "I've been look-ing for you. For a long time."

Then the little boy threw a red ball, high, straight up. The ball flew up through the hole in the roof of the cave.

To her great surprise, Diana awoke.

She had not closed the curtains the night before because she had not expected to be worrying about being awakened by sunlight. But now the early-morning light was beaming directly into her eyes.

Diana blinked and squinted and looked around, confused. Why was she still here? Impossible. She'd decided to kill herself. She'd made up her mind to do it, at long last.

Diana realized she was holding something, clutched in her right hand. The brown pill bottle, the cap still securely in place. She opened her cramped, aching fin-gers, and the bottle rolled off onto the sheet.

She'd failed. She'd meant to kill herself, and instead she'd fallen asleep before she could take the pills. Fallen asleep before she could take the sleeping pills.

It was almost funny, she thought bitterly.

In fact, it *was* funny. She tried not to grin but couldn't help herself. She'd fallen asleep before she could take the fatal dose of sleeping pills.

"See, the thing is, I was *going* to kill myself," she said aloud, "but I was just too sleepy." Diana laughed. "If only I'd had another cup of coffee, I could be dead now."

Now what? Should she go back to sleep? Get up and take a shower? Kill herself?

She laughed some more. Shower or suicide? Hmm, there was a choice. And it brought up the question of whether, even if she *was* going to kill herself, she shouldn't take a shower first. "Who wants to die with morning breath and that grubby, unwashed feeling?"

She jumped out of bed and went to her porch door. She opened it and went outside. A slight morning breeze ruffled her sheer nightgown. It was almost cool out, not too humid, and the sun was still so low that it had not become the terror it would be by noon.

The water looked good. Maybe she should go for a swim.

"Then I can kill myself," she said, and immediately began laughing again.

"What is the matter with me?" she wondered aloud. Yesterday she'd been beaten down, falling back into the hole of depression. It was just too clichéd to think that because it was a nice day out she didn't want to kill herself. It was a nice day *every* day.

But it was too simplistic to think that she had just fallen asleep before she could carry out her plans. No.

Something had to have changed her mind. Something had to have let her slip safely away into normal slumber.

The truth was, right now, with the warm deck under her feet and the sun on her face, she just didn't feel like killing herself.

"There. I admit it," she said to no one but herself.

She tried to think back to the night before, to lying in her bed, the bottle of pills in her hand, dark, dramatic images playing in her mind. The depression had been all around her then, had swallowed her whole. She remembered thinking that she couldn't ever trust her mother again. That she couldn't count on anyone or anything. That she had no one to turn to. That she was alone. Totally alone.

"That's right," she murmured, smiling sadly at the realization. She *was* totally alone. Maybe everyone was alone. Maybe that was the point. Maybe that's what she'd had to learn, that in the darkest times there wasn't anyone to turn to but yourself.

"What a sad thought," Diana whispered.

Let's face it, Diana, what are you? she asked herself. A sad, weak, screwed-up, inadequate person. No great genius. No great beauty. No perfect specimen of kindness or decency or morality. Sometimes a fool. Sometimes a jerk. Sometimes humiliated and pathetic.

All of it was true.

KATHERINE APPLEGATE

And yet, down at the bottom of that deep hole of depression, at the very end, whom had she found but herself? All alone. All alone with a messed-up person named Diana.

You're the only person I have, Diana told herself. The only person I am.

I guess you'll have to do.

She went back inside and retrieved the bottle of pills and carried it to the bathroom. She emptied the contents into the toilet bowl. "Bye," she said, and flushed.

She caught sight of herself in the mirror. The same reflection she'd looked at with loathing so many times. The memory brought tears to her eyes. She pointed a finger at herself. "You and me, kid."

For a long time she stood there, watching herself watching herself. Not bad-looking. Good hair. Not a complete idiot. Weak? Yes, she had been, for a long, long time. The reasons why she'd felt that way were tedious and obvious and probably unimportant—her absent, half-forgotten father, her unfortunately not absent mother . . . Ross. And Adam, the one guy she'd ever loved. Even more recently, the reproach represented by Summer and Seth—people she would never be, or have.

A long list of reasons to feel bad.

Her mouth twitched into a smile. Time to shorten up that long list.

In her bedroom she found the hideous shoulder bag. She poked her finger through the hole she'd cut into the fabric, the hole that was concealed by the awful pattern of the fabric.

She opened the bag. Yes, it was still there. Summer's video camera. The lens was duct-taped up against the hole.

She popped out the videotape. Now to figure out how to make a copy. She wanted to keep the original.

Summer woke hungry. She woke hungry with her head resting on Seth's bare chest. She could tell from his breathing that he was already awake.

"Good morning," he said.

She slid up his body to give him a kiss. "Good morning," she said, several seconds later.

"I don't know how good a morning it's going to be," he said regretfully. "The night was good, though."

"Mmm," Summer said. "I'm starving."

"Well, there is the sushi option," Seth said. "We have the speargun, and we know we have fish trapped in here with us."

Summer shuddered. "I guess they eat sushi in Japan, right? And they seem to be doing okay."

"They eat it in Los Angeles and New York, too," Seth said. "Not so much in Eau Claire, Wisconsin."

"Or Bloomington, Minnesota," Summer said.

"What? Not even in the home of the Mall of America?" Seth joked.

"I wish I were there," Summer said. "They have all these fast-food places overlooking the amusement park. Hamburgers. Stuffed potatoes. Pizza. Mrs. Fields cookies. Fried chicken."

"Don't even say fried chicken," Seth groaned.

Summer forced herself to look around their hard, stony prison. It hadn't changed. It hadn't become any more comfortable. It was still a trap, and there was still no way out.

At the top of the dome, the same irregular patch of blue, lighter and brighter now than it had been yesterday. Outside in the world it was morning. Only this one small slice of morning made it inside of this cave, but it was still morning, and it was hard not to feel a little surge of hope.

"Okay," Summer said, "sushi it is."

Seth held her in his arms. "Do you still love me?" he asked.

"Still," Summer said.

"It isn't just because we're trapped and there's almost no hope of escape?"

Summer sighed. "That's how it's been since that first kiss in the airport, Seth. I've been trapped, and there was almost no hope of escape."

Seth grinned. So did Summer.

"Was that the corniest thing anyone's ever said to you?" Summer asked him.

"I believe it was," he said. "Now I'll tell you something even cornier—all this is worth it, because it brought us together, and that's worth anything."

"Even eating raw fish?"

He made a back-and-forth gesture with his hand.

It took an hour for Seth, wearing a wet suit and with just a snorkel, to spear a fish. He filleted it with his knife, laying out small bites of glistening white flesh on a clean rock.

The two of them stared at it.

"The Japanese love this stuff," Seth said.

"That's what I hear," Summer said.

The warm afterglow of early morning had worn off. Now Summer was facing a breakfast of raw fish, washed down with trickling condensation licked from the smooth rock walls of the cave.

"Seth, are we ever going to get out of here?"

"Sure," he said with hearty and phony enthusiasm. "Someone will see the boat, then they'll see the rope and dive down and realize that . . ." His optimism collapsed. "They'll figure even if we were diving here that we're dead by now. That's what they'll figure."

"Or the boat could have slipped its anchor and could be drifting on the current a hundred miles from here," Summer said.

For a while neither of them spoke. At last Seth picked up a piece of the fish. "I hear it's best when it's fresh," he said. He screwed up his face and popped it into his mouth. Slowly his expression changed. "Hey, this isn't bad."

"Yeah, right," Summer said.

"Seriously. It's no cheeseburger, but it's not gross, either."

Summer picked up a piece. "I guess I don't have much choice." She swallowed the piece whole without chewing. It wasn't awful. As long as she didn't think about it.

"Well, I guess we can survive awhile down here," Summer said grimly. "Licking the walls and eating raw fish. That's exactly what I had in mind for my summer vacation."

"Arrrrrggghhhh!" Seth suddenly exploded.

"What's the matter?" Summer cried.

Seth was pointing up at the patch of blue overhead. "What am I? An idiot? A moron?"

"Seth, what is it?"

"The speargun," he said. "The speargun. Jeez, am I slow sometimes. There's about twenty feet of rope on our side of the cave-in. We cut it, tie it around the spear shaft, and fire the spear up through the hole. If we're lucky it will wedge in the hole and we can climb up."

Summer stared at him. "That hole is too small for us to fit through."

"I know." He bit his lip. "But it's something. It's better than doing nothing."

Ten feverish minutes later, they were ready. Seth had used the last few minutes of air in his tank to retrieve the available rope. The yellow nylon cord was now tied firmly to the spear.

"Here goes nothing," Seth said. He took careful aim and fired the spear. On the first two attempts it missed and clattered futilely off the rock.

On the third try it sailed up, straight through the patch of sky.

Like the red ball, Summer realized. Like the little boy's red ball.

Marquez leaned over the side of the boat and plunged her face into the water. She kept her entire head under for a few seconds, letting the warm salt water soak her hair. Then she pulled back. The water had done nothing to wake her up. Maybe if it had been cold water . . .

She was bleary and exhausted. J.T. was no better. The two of them were depressed and miserable and stunned into stupidity. For most of the long, long night they had bickered and snapped at each other. But now they were both too tired for that.

"I don't see anything here," J.T. said. He was on the bow of the boat they'd borrowed from J.T.'s father, surveying the island through binoculars. "No boat. Nothing on the beach. There's what may be some footprints in the sand, but that isn't going to help us."

"Just like the others," Marquez said grimly. They had spent the night racing from one far-flung islet to the next. The more J.T. thought about it, the more plausible places he'd come up with where Seth and Summer might have gone. They had covered miles of black water under a starry sky. Miles without sleep and with less hope.

"Let's call the Coast Guard again," Marquez said. "Maybe they've found something."

"Go ahead," J.T. said.

Marquez keyed the radio handset and called the now-familiar signal for the Coast Guard station on Key West. "Hi, it's me again," she said without preliminary. They knew her by now.

The answer came, scratchy and metallic. "Ma'am, I do now have some data. We just got a message from the cutter. They've found a boat answering the description you gave."

Marquez's heart leapt. J.T. came running back to her. "They did?" Marquez asked shakily.

"Yes, ma'am. It was capsized out in the channel,

about nine miles southeast of Geiger Key. It looks like it may have been struck by a passing ship."

"Oh, my God," Marquez said.

"We're conducting an air and sea search in that area, looking for survivors."

"Oh, no," Marquez whispered. She handed the handset to J.T., who thanked the Coast Guardsman and signed off. Marquez collapsed on the vinyl-padded bench.

"It doesn't mean they're dead," J.T. said. "They could still be alive."

"Can you—" she pleaded. "Can you feel anything? I mean, do you have a sense that, one way or the other . . . ?"

J.T. looked sad. "Marquez, I told you. I don't really think I have some kind of psychic connection with Summer. Maybe she *is* my sister. But I can't do what you think I can." He sat beside her, miserable. "I wish I could."

Marquez patted his leg. "I don't even believe in stuff like that. Superstition and all."

He put his arm around her.

"This is bad," Marquez said.

"Yeah. This is bad," he agreed.

"You know, I don't like getting into other people's messes," she said.

"I may have known that about you," J.T. said ironically.

Marquez managed a slight smile. "Yes, I guess you did know that about me. And now, look. It's me who's dragged you into this mess. I could have kept my mouth shut. You'd have been sad, I mean, you knew Summer from work. But now it's like, you kind of find this sister, and then—"

"Don't give up yet," J.T. said.

"No, I won't give—Wait a second. Did you see that?"

"What?"

Marquez frowned and shook her head. No, she was just sleepy. Sleepy and seeing things that weren't there.

20

All Together Now: Hmm . . .

Summer climbed the rope. She was lighter than Seth, and smaller. She was more likely to fit through the tiny hole.

She used the gloves from her wet suit to help her grip with her hands. The hard part was gripping the slippery rope with her bare legs. The climb was difficult—nearly twenty feet straight up, though Seth was able to help lift her the first few feet.

Her arms were burning by the time she reached the top. The patch of blue grew larger, closer. Soon she would reach it, and then—

The spear bent in two. The rope collapsed. Summer fell, screaming in surprise and anger.

Seth caught most of her weight, and both of them fell to the floor of the cave. The bent spear clattered down and fell beside them. The coil of rope looped over them.

"Oh, God, can't anything work out?" Summer cried. She buried her face in her hands and began sobbing.

Seth seemed crushed. He said nothing, just hung his head.

A long time passed with no sound but Summer's soft sobbing and the plop of curious fish in the water.

"There's still hope . . ." Seth began to say, but then he seemed unable to carry the thought any further.

"Hey. Anyone down there?"

For a moment Summer did not believe she'd heard it.

She looked up. The patch of blue was dark.

"Hey! Yes! We're down here!" Summer yelled.

"Is that you, Summer?"

"Marquez?" Summer said incredulously. "Marquez? Is that you?"

"Like I'm going to leave you here and end up having to work all your shifts? What the hell are you guys doing down there?"

"Eating sushi," Summer yelled back, convulsing with relieved laughter. Seth swept her up in his arms and spun her around again and again.

"*Eating sushi?* Is that supposed to mean something?" Marquez asked J.T.

It took only twenty minutes for the Coast Guard helicopter to arrive. The Guardsmen used picks and shovels to widen the hole in the top of the cave. Then they lowered a harness on the end of a winch.

The light in the real world was blinding after the cave. Summer could not open her eyes at all for several minutes while Marquez hugged her and J.T. hugged her and various unknown Coast Guard guys hugged her.

Finally she scrunched open one eye and saw Marquez, looking ratty but beautiful. J.T. was standing there, looking unusually shy.

"How are you guys?" Marquez asked.

"Great," Seth said. "Excellent fun. We'll really have to do this again someday, like when hell freezes over. By the way, did you guys see the boat?"

"No. The boat got loose. I hope it's insured," J.T. explained. "I guess it got in the way of a tanker."

"So how did you find us? I mean, how did you even know we were here?" Seth asked.

"Marquez saw something come flying up out of the ground, right here," J.T. said. "She said it looked like an arrow with a yellow snake attached. We were just getting ready to give up."

"As for how we picked this island . . ." Marquez

said. She looked at J.T. He nodded, giving her his permission.

"What?" Summer asked.

"I thought maybe J.T. might have some instinct about the right place," Marquez said.

"Actually, it turned out I didn't," J.T. said, grinning crookedly.

"But . . ." Marquez took a deep breath. "Look, I don't know if this is the right time to lay this on you, Summer, but I have an idea that . . . I mean, there's all these reasons to think that . . ." She looked to J.T. again.

J.T. looked down at the ground. "Summer, I think it's possible that I am . . . your brother. I think I may be Jonathan."

Diana whistled as she poured herself a cup of coffee in a travel mug.

Her mother came into the kitchen looking early-morning grumpy. "Oh, good, you made coffee."

"Yes. I did," Diana said.

Her mother eyed her suspiciously. "You're awfully cheerful."

"Am I? Well, I'm anticipating an excellent day."

"Uh-huh. Not still angry with me?" her mother asked.

Diana smiled coolly and walked away.

"Diana, what *are* you doing?" Mallory demanded, sounding alarmed.

Diane left her behind, still yapping, and went out to her car. She drove through town and onto the highway, heading south to Key West. It really was a stunningly beautiful day, she realized. Just because almost every day was beautiful was no reason not to appreciate this one.

She pulled off the highway and into the parking lot of the state police barracks. Senator Merrick might think he owned the local police. He didn't own the *state* police.

At the front desk a sharply uniformed officer smiled at her, not quite flirting, but definitely friendly. Diana smiled back.

"What can I do for you, miss?"

"Beautiful out, isn't it?" Diana said.

"Yes, miss, it certainly is. Can I help you?"

"I'm here to report a crime," Diana said.

"Oh. What crime?"

Diana considered. "I think it's called attempted rape. Also, hitting. What's that? Like assault and battery? That, too."

The trooper's eyes grew serious. The smile was gone. "You're charging someone with attempted rape?"

"Not just someone," Diana corrected. "Ross Merrick."

"Merrick, as in—"

"Yes. *That* Merrick." Diana opened her purse and handed the trooper the videocassette. "And the really cool thing is, I have a full confession right here."

Diver sat in Summer's empty house, feeling like an intruder. It was odd how much this place seemed to belong to her now. It had been all his for a long time, till she had come.

He'd felt even stranger standing here the other day with all three girls—Summer, Marquez, Diana. He hadn't felt right ever since. Not since he had seen *her*. She had popped up again and again in his thoughts since then, adding her own subtle influences to the troubled, uneasy feeling he now had over Summer.

He looked around. He had to admit, she'd fixed it up. There were curtains now. The smell of mildew was mostly gone. She'd put up posters and things.

He looked at the picture by her bed. He'd looked at the picture before—Summer's parents. It was an interesting picture. It showed her life when she was back in her home, what it was like there.

He hoped Summer was okay. It would be terribly sad for the people in the picture if something had happened to her. But though he had been worried all night, troubled by strange, frightening, incomprehensible dreams, he felt better now, as if somehow the light of day had chased away all fear.

The people in the picture seemed all right to him. Like Summer herself. The house in the background looked pleasant, as well. A yard. A badminton net. A barbecue grill. Grass. A nice place to play.

A place where a kid could play ball.

With a red ball.

august

All You Need Is Air, Water, Food, and . . . a Little Revenge.

When Summer woke up, she was in a large helicopter, strapped onto a stretcher, surrounded by a gallery of concerned faces.

"What?" Summer said, frowning.

"I said, you're awake!" Marquez yelled, making herself heard over the vibrating, thumping roar of the helicopter's engines.

"I know," Summer said. "I know when I'm awake. Why wouldn't I be?"

"Because you passed out," Marquez said.

"No way." Summer tried to sit up, couldn't, and looked down at the red webbing strap that went across her chest like a seat belt. "Oh. What happened?"

"It was very *Gone with the Wind*!" Marquez said, shouting to be heard. "You zoned. You went out."

"Here," Seth said. He was holding a canteen to her lips. "Water."

Summer took it in greedy mouthfuls, not an easy thing to manage since she was lying on her back. When she was done she smiled at Seth. "Excellent. Much better than trying to lick condensation."

"They have food too," Seth said, saying the word *food* the way very hungry people say it.

"Can I get unstrapped?" Summer asked the nearest Guardsman.

"Um, sure, I guess," he said. He unfastened the strap, and she sat up, gazing around the inside of the helicopter. It was very spare, just bare aluminum and big yellow-and-black warning signs advertising various dangerous things.

The door was partly open, letting in damp, super-heated air, and through the opening she could look down and see the perfect blue-green waters of the Gulf of Mexico zipping by a hundred feet down. The sun blazed, as it usually did in these islands beyond the southernmost tip of Florida. It would have been a beautiful sight at any time, but at the moment it was even more moving, and almost as beautiful as the ham and cheese sandwich Seth handed her.

"Don't scarf it too fast," Seth advised, putting his

lips to her ear so she could hear him. He wanted to be close to her, and she wanted him to be close too.

"Food," Summer said reverently between bites. "Food. Food is so good. Air and water and food, that's all that matters. If you have air and water and food, you should just shut up and be happy."

"They'll have us back on Crab Claw Key in just a few minutes," Seth said. He leaned close again and stroked Summer's blond hair, now matted with dried salt and somewhat less than Herbal Essence clean.

Summer leaned into him, pressed her cheek against his warm, bare chest, and circled him with her free arm. She continued eating. "We made it," she said.

"Yeah. Thanks to Marquez and J.T. and the Coast Guard," Seth said, carefully including everyone.

Summer gave him a kiss that was partly flavored with mustard. He looked as if he wanted to continue the kiss, but Summer had her priorities, and priority number one was finishing the sandwich and moving on to the package of Hostess cream-filled cupcakes she'd spotted in the plastic bag the Coast Guard had provided.

And then it came back to her: J.T.

He was sitting a little back from the knot of bodies, leaning forward in a red webbing seat, watching her with an intense, prying, skeptical expression. He was looking past her, in a way, or through her.

Their eyes met. Summer's eyes were blue. So were J.T.'s. His hair, like hers, was blond. They certainly looked as if they could be brother and sister. But there were a lot of blue-eyed blonds in the world. They weren't all part of the Smith family of Bloomington, Minnesota.

And if he really was Jonathan . . . She felt as if she might faint again. Fainting might be easier than coming to grips with reality . . . if J.T. was Jonathan. If Jonathan was *alive*.

If J.T. really *was* Jonathan . . . The incredible hugeness of the idea hit her with sudden force. No wonder she'd fainted. It would mean so much. To her parents, and to his parents, who now would not really be his parents anymore, who might in fact be kidnappers.

"Mom and Dad," Summer whispered, lost in her own careening thoughts. How could she tell them? What could she tell them? This was impossible. She stared hard at J.T. Was this some kind of a joke? Was this his idea of funny?

Summer reached for the cupcakes and tore open the plastic. She was still hungry. But she got no pleasure from the food. Monumental, endless, unpredictable repercussions . . . Some people would come out feeling that their lives had suddenly changed for the better, and others might be destroyed.

J.T. must have been thinking much the same thing.

He shrugged and made a worried who-knows face.

Summer met his gaze and tried for a reassuring smile that never formed. Are you my brother? she wondered. Are you Jonathan?

And in J.T.'s eyes, so like her own, she saw the same question: Am I Jonathan? Am I your brother?

"What are we going to do?" Summer asked him.

" I don't know," J.T. admitted.

"My parents . . ." Summer let the thought hang there. J.T. understood.

"Yeah. Mine too. I mean, my folks, my . . . I think of them as my parents, you know?"

Seth cleared his throat tentatively. "Um, look, this is none of my business, but Summer has had a really bad time here. And so have I. And I think maybe this whole thing should be put on hold for a while. You know, let everyone get some sleep? You don't have to make any decisions right this minute."

Summer felt deep relief. Too much relief. She should not *want* to avoid reality. But she saw the same relief reflected in J.T.'s eyes.

"Maybe, yes," J.T. said, "maybe we'd better chill for a while. See what's what before we jump to any big conclusions."

"Yeah," Summer said. She still felt a little guilty. But the relief outweighed the guilt. There was plenty of time to examine this explosive possibility. Plenty of time.

Seth stroked her hair. Summer smiled at him. For many hours in the dark she had been unable to see his face clearly. It was a wonderful face.

She pulled him close till his ear was next to her lips. "I love you," she said.

"It wasn't just the cave?" he asked, serious as usual. "Maybe you just wanted me to die happy."

Summer started to kiss him. She didn't care if the Coast Guard guys grinned and Marquez rolled her eyes. But J.T. was still watching her, dissecting her with his eyes. So she gave Seth a brief kiss on his cheek and tried to remind herself that all she needed to be happy was air and water and food.

"Don't expect great photography," Diana Olan said self-consciously. "I'm not exactly Steven Spielberg."

Two Florida Department of Law Enforcement special agents were in the small, stuffy room with her. The one named Reynoso seemed to be in charge. He was a small, dark man with a close-trimmed mustache and hair that had retreated back from most of his forehead. Diana had forgotten the other agent's name.

"This isn't film school," Reynoso said gloomily. "Go ahead and hit it, Pete," he said to the other detective.

Now the name came back to her—Pete Wallace.

Alan Reynoso and Pete Wallace. She should probably try to remember those names.

Wallace aimed a remote control at the television. The TV sat on an industrial-looking steel stand with a VCR underneath. Diana sat at a painted metal table between the two detectives, feeling totally out of place in her wraparound skirt and halter top. The cops were wearing what might have been the only two business suits within fifty miles of Crab Claw Key.

"I'm hoping for an Oscar nomination," Diana said.

The special agents said nothing. The tape started.

The picture on the TV screen was jerky, making sudden sharp lurches to the left and right. The color was poor, giving the tape a washed-out, faded look, like a colorized black-and-white movie.

"This is the front door of the Merricks' mansion," Diana narrated.

On the screen the door opened.

"That's Ross Merrick," Diana said, trying not to sound as hostile as she felt.

"I'm familiar with him," Wallace said dryly. "Most cops in the area are."

"Turn up the volume," Reynoso directed.

Wallace pressed a button on the remote, and Ross's leering tones filled the room. "Why, it's Diana. What a surprise. Come back to get more of what I started to give you?"

Diana intercepted a glance that went from Reynoso to Wallace. Reynoso cocked an eyebrow.

"This is the main entrance hall at the Merrick estate," Diana said. "It's very impressive."

"I could put my whole house in that hallway," Wallace said glumly.

The picture followed Ross, swinging back and forth as Diana walked. The camera had been concealed in a shoulder bag. She'd done what she could to keep it stable, but she hadn't wanted to alert anyone to what she was doing.

The next shot was of an unoccupied desk with bookshelves behind it. At this point the picture grew less jerky, since she'd sat down and the camera was positioned on her knee.

"You could probably fast-forward through this part," Diana suggested.

Wallace did, stopping at the sudden arrival of another person in the room, a handsome, athletic, dark-haired young man with a very somber expression on his face.

"That's Adam," Diana said. "He's Ross's younger brother. He . . . he used to be my boyfriend."

Senator Merrick walked into the picture. Diana heard both cops shift in their seats. Wallace leaned forward, focusing intently.

"Well, let's hear it," the senator said. He glanced at his watch. "What's this about?"

"This is about rape." Diana heard the tremor in her own voice. At the time she had felt bold and fearless, but there had been fear in her tone. Maybe it was just distortion from the video camera.

"*Attempted* rape," Ross said.

Diana saw a slight, predatory smile on Wallace's face, quickly erased.

The conversation played as she remembered it, as she had seen it already on this same videotape. Ross, furious and contemptuous; Adam, sad and disturbed; the senator, barely containing his fury at his own son and the mess he'd created.

"This is the good part," Diana announced in a low voice.

On the TV screen Ross lost control and lunged at her. The picture went crazy, jerking wildly, focusing on the ceiling, on the floor, on the arm of the chair.

A crazy, sideways view of the senator came into focus. He swung hard and buried his fist in Ross's stomach. Ross collapsed on the floor.

Wallace whistled softly. "That had to hurt."

Even Reynoso seemed mildly impressed. "Huh," he said.

Diana's voice came next, a shrieking, enraged cry. "Now do you see? Do you see what he is? Do you see what your son is, Senator?"

The scene calmed somewhat. The picture showed Ross, only partly in the frame, crawling to a chair. It showed Adam comforting his father.

And then the senator delivered his ultimatum—if Diana ever accused Ross of anything, the senator would ruin her. He owned the prosecutor, he said. He controlled the local police. He would find a way to destroy Diana. Or . . . she could keep quiet and walk away with a large check.

"Oh, man," Wallace said, awestruck.

Diana realized that he and Reynoso were more stunned by this portion of the tape than by what had gone before.

The tape went on. The senator left. Adam walked her out to the front steps of the Merrick estate.

And then had come the strangest moment of all for Diana.

She'd been carrying a small tape recorder as well as the video camera, wanting some backup, knowing she'd never get a second chance to do this.

Adam had spotted the tape recorder in the waistband of her slacks and had yanked it out. He'd listened to the recording and then, to Diana's amazement, he'd handed the tape back to her.

The picture on the TV screen went to gray fuzz. Wallace turned it off.

"I guess they aren't *all* rotten, huh?" Wallace said. "The kid, Adam, he seems all right."

"That did surprise me," Diana said softly. "He swore he'd never go against his family."

"Hell of a piece of work," Reynoso said, eyeing Diana with open respect.

"Can you . . . can you arrest Ross?" Diana asked.

Reynoso looked thoughtful. "There's nothing on there that is a straight confession. He never says, 'Look, I tried to rape you.'"

Diana felt panicky. "But . . . but isn't it obvious?"

"Obvious, yes. But is it evidence? That's another question. We can arrest Ross Merrick, but can we get to court? Can we convict? That's the next question. We have the tape, and we have your testimony."

Diana felt confused. She'd been certain that the tape was more than enough proof.

"Of course, Ross Merrick may choose to work out an arrangement for the sake of his father," Reynoso said.

Wallace nodded. "Yeah, I guess we'll see if the family loyalty goes both ways. See whether he's going to leave his old man hanging out to dry."

"His old man? What? You mean the senator?" Diana asked. "Why would this involve him?"

Reynoso shook his head in amusement. "Don't you know what you have with this tape? It isn't a confession from Ross Merrick, but it *is* stone-cold proof that the senator threatened you and offered you a bribe to keep you from reporting a crime."

"Ms. Olan, you have one of the richest and most powerful men in America by the . . . Well, let's just say you have him," Wallace said. "You have him good."

2

Home, Strange Home

The stilt house seemed almost unbearably pretty. It brought tears to Summer's eyes. She had thought many times over the past day that she would never see it again.

It didn't look like much, perhaps. It was a shabby, wooden-sided bungalow built out over the water, raised on tall pilings and connected to the shore by a walkway. Frank the pelican was sitting on the railing, and as they approached he deposited a glob of bird poop on the wood.

"Home, sweet home," Summer said, laughing. She and Seth were finally alone after a Coast Guard doctor had pronounced them both fit to be released.

They had slipped around the side of the Olan house, hoping to avoid Diana and her mother, Mallory. As far as Summer knew, neither her cousin nor her aunt had heard anything about her misadventure, and she wanted to keep it that way. Aunt Mallory would almost certainly have told Summer's parents, and they would have yanked her back to Minnesota faster than the speed of light.

Summer didn't want to leave Crab Claw Key, not yet. Not anytime soon. In fact, she wondered if she'd ever want to leave. Seth was there for the rest of the summer, and J.T. lived there year-round. Two very powerful reasons for her to want to stay.

She had to figure out the truth about J.T. And Seth . . . She didn't even want to think about having to leave him when summer ended. She wasn't going to do anything to hurry that moment.

She squeezed his hand tightly.

They reached the door. Summer went inside. All was how she'd left it. Nothing had changed. The very normalcy of it all seemed odd. It *had* been only a little more than a day, but it felt as if days and weeks and lifetimes had passed. How could her bed still be made? How could there still be the odor of adhesive and paint from the work Seth had done fixing up the house? How could the same posters be on the walls, the same picture of her parents be sitting on the table beside her bed?

"Seems kind of alien, doesn't it?" Seth said, echoing her thoughts as he joined her.

"A bed. With actual sheets," Summer said. She went over to it and sat down. It seemed very soft. She stroked her pillowcase.

"You okay?" Seth asked.

Summer thought about the question before answering. "I guess so. I'm weirded out over this whole thing with J.T. You know?"

"I can kind of guess," Seth said. He sat beside her.

"Plus, I halfway feel like I'm still in that cave," Summer said. "Although the part that really sticks with me is the part *before* we found the cave. When we were down to just a few minutes of air . . ."

Summer took a very deep breath, filling her lungs to capacity. Seth did the same. Neither of them thought it was funny.

"Yeah. I don't think I'll forget that myself," Seth said grimly. "Later, though—" He brightened a little. "Well, that had its nice parts."

"Yes, it did." Summer took his hand and raised it to her lips, kissing the bruised knuckles and pressing the palm against her face. "I guess it shouldn't have taken that to get me to admit how much I love you. I mean, maybe actually being on the edge of death was not necessary."

Seth laughed. "In the future let's agree to avoid

situations that involve dying. I'm totally opposed to dying."

"It's going to seem almost strange sleeping alone tonight," Summer said.

"I could—" Seth began.

Summer shoved him playfully. "No, you couldn't."

He made a face. "Anyway, I have to go tell Trent what happened to his boat. The Coast Guard towed it back in, but it's going to take some major work to repair."

"You'll fix it," Summer said. "You're good with your hands." She kissed him deeply. "And you're not so bad with your lips, either. Now go away. I need to brush my teeth six or eight times and take a hot bath and eat every single thing in the refrigerator. And then I'm just going to sleep."

Seth stood. "Okay, I'll go," he said reluctantly. "Do what you said—sleep. Try not to think about all this with J.T.," he advised. "You'll think better when you're rested and everything is back to normal again."

Summer nodded agreement. "The question is, can I go back to normal again?"

"I know it will work out," Seth said.

"Yeah?" Summer asked, unconvinced. "Suddenly my brother reappears in my life—maybe. I don't know how it can work out. Not for everyone. Not for J.T.'s parents." She started to say something else, then stopped herself.

"What?" Seth asked.

"Nothing, I guess. It's just . . . last night, when we were in the cave, I saw something. Some*one*. I know this is going to sound totally insane, but it was this little boy, dressed all in white. And I've seen this boy in my dreams lately. Only, this wasn't a dream. He was there, in the cave. I mean, *really* there."

Seth looked worried for her. "Do you think it means something?"

"I don't know," Summer admitted. "He was in my dreams, and then he appeared in the cave." She shrugged and shook her head dismissively. "I probably was dreaming."

"What did this little boy do?"

"I asked him who he was, and he said he didn't know. And then he took a little red ball he was holding and threw it up through the hole. The hole we escaped through."

"Summer?" Seth said. "You are creeping me out."

Summer laughed. "Okay, okay. It was just a dream. Forget about it."

Seth kissed her on the forehead. "Get some sleep. And no dreams, unless they're about me."

Marquez slept too. She and J.T. had been up all night searching for Summer and Seth, and she was exhausted. But after only four hours of slumber she woke, fully alert.

She looked at her clock. It said 10:47. But whether that was A.M. or P.M., she wasn't sure at first. She looked at the curtain drawn across the storefront window that was one wall of her room. No sunlight peeked around the edges. It was P.M.

She snapped on the lights, a series of shaded lamps positioned around her cavernous room. Over the years Marquez had covered the walls from floor to ceiling with a huge, brilliant, confused, intricate mural of pictures and graffiti. A spray-painted palm tree filled one corner, roots spread across the cement floor, branches fanned across the ceiling. A stylized mural showed her own family's arrival in Florida in a fugitive rowboat from Cuba, complete with an infant Maria Esmeralda Marquez. A stunning sunset sprayed red and gold covered a field of graffitied names—from Orlando Bloom to Hillary Clinton; from Ms. Palmer, her eighth-grade history teacher, to Lloyd Cutler, the lawyer Marquez wanted to be like someday; from Kurt Cobain to Bob Marley. And then there were the other names: former boyfriends, school friends, family friends, her brothers, her parents—even the old man who thought he was Ernest Hemingway and swept the downtown sidewalks with an imaginary broom.

In the middle of the maze of names and images was a rough white rectangle—the place where she had painted over J.T.'s name.

Marquez knew she should go back to sleep. But she felt restless and agitated, as she sometimes did in the wake of disturbing dreams. She didn't remember anything specific from her dreams, just a feeling of certain vivid colors and shapes.

Marquez knew that if she was going to be awake she ought to go upstairs and take a shower, wash her hair, watch some TV with her mom and dad and brothers. Or at least put on some clothes. But she didn't feel like performing familiar rituals. She was fired up. She was jumpy. Her skin was crawling with electricity.

Marquez snapped her fingers and tossed her head in short, quick jerks. Music. That was the first thing.

Keane? No, too mellow. The Shins? No, way too mellow. No, something harder, something to fit her dangerous mood. Old Nirvana, maybe. She slid *Nevermind* into the CD player and hit Play.

She swept all the paint cans together and dumped them next to the wall, just below the blank white square. She realized she was breathing heavily, as if excited or exhausted, or maybe both. She was. Both. It happened sometimes, for no apparent reason, this sudden need to paint.

She snatched up a spray can and began shaking

it, the rattling little ball a perfect counterpoint to the music pounding from the CD.

With quick strokes she directed the crimson spray against the white. As she did something came over Marquez, as it did from time to time. Her thinking, rationalizing mind simply went away for a while. Her brain became as blank as the patch of white. Her hands grabbed at paints, then threw them impatiently away and reached for some new color. The sweat began to run down her forehead, and her hair flew with each angry toss of her head. Fumes filled the room, barely controlled by the big exhaust fan that had been painted to look like a sunflower. Her eyes stung, the music pounded, her bare feet slipped on the concrete floor, and her hair and body were highlighted with careless reds and blues and golds. She dragged her ladder over, and her brushes and rags and sponges and every tool she had.

The music had long since stopped, the CD played out, when at last she was done. Hours had passed unnoticed. She stepped back to look at it—J.T. reborn. Huge letters, shaded for a 3-D effect so that they leaped out from the wall and picked up the glint of the mural sunset, each line woven through the entire tapestry of her walls by connections of color that insinuated themselves around each name, each picture.

The real J.T., as he was in her life: too much a part

of the whole ever to be completely painted out again.

Marquez sat down on one of the red vinyl stools and hung her head. She cried, and in wiping away tears smeared new colors over her face—the same colors that made J.T.'s name. She had tried to paint him out. He was confusion and trouble, now more than ever.

When they'd started going out, he'd just been the cute cook at work. Then the simple, fun-loving guy had grown complicated. He'd learned he was not the biological son of his parents, though they had never told him directly. And he'd begun to wonder who he was and where he fit in. In the midst of it all, he'd grown angry and depressed. Who knew how he would respond to all this about being Summer's brother Jonathan? Knowing J.T., it would not be a peaceful adjustment.

It had all been too much for Marquez. She wasn't interested in complications and emotional problems. She was determined to keep her life orderly. She had her plan—one more year of high school, and sure, during that time she could be free and have fun and party. But then, she had determined, a different life would begin—college, law school, then a brilliant career in law. It was laid out. She already had the grades and the SAT scores.

Sixteen years ago her family had landed penniless in the United States, and the USA had taken them in, given them a chance and a hope they'd never had in Cuba. The family was dedicated to making good on that hope. Marquez was not going to be the weak link. She was not going to be the flake, the failure.

She looked around the room. The clock showed it was after two in the morning. The room reeked of fresh paint. She herself smelled of paint and sweat.

She saw herself reflected in the mirrors behind the counter—her hair and face and arms covered with paint, so that she seemed just another wild image, a part of the incredible wall behind her, like one of those 3-D hologram pictures you could stare at and then, whoa, a girl appeared.

"Very nice, Marquez," she said aloud to her reflection. She was exhausted and angry with herself, as she usually was after working on the wall. "Just be sure when you go to Harvard you get a room with wallpaper."

3

You Meet the Most Interesting People When You Should Be Sleeping.

Lying back asleep, his chest and legs bare, his blond hair fanned out, his eyes closed but fluttering behind his eyelids, he swirled down and down, falling in a way that had once scared him but now seemed familiar. He was falling down that same whirlpool, landing in that same dusty corridor, sticky with cobwebs, dimly lit. He followed it, the way he always did, back through time, back and back, brushing the cobwebs aside.

He emerged in the grassy field again, smaller, as he always was in the dream. A tiny little boy, struck by how close the grass seemed, how near he was to the ground.

And there it was. The red ball.

And there she was. The sun. The bright ball of light that had begun to appear in his dream.

As he bent to pick up the ball, he noticed for the first time that he was wearing shorts. White shorts. And a white shirt.

Summer lay on her side, a sheet pulled up to her neck, one foot sticking out, her blond hair fanned across the pillow. Her breathing grew thready and uncertain, as it did when she dreamed.

For a while she was on the plane, listening yet again to the woman tell her tale of the tarot cards.

"But look," Summer said to the woman, "I didn't meet *three* guys. It was four."

"No, no, no," the woman said, shaking her head. "Just three. The other one isn't yours. Pay attention."

And then Summer was no longer on the airplane. She was no longer anyplace she knew. She was standing in a field, beside a swing set, only not standing. She was floating.

And there before her was the little boy in white. He was just picking up a red ball.

"I know you," she said to the little boy.

It was then that for the first time in his dreams, the sun spoke to him. "I know you," the sun said.

He held the ball in his hand. "I don't know *you*," he said. "I can't. You aren't here yet."

"Oh," the sun said. "I don't like that ball."

He nodded. "I know. It's not the ball's fault, though."

"I guess not," the sun said. "But . . . don't throw it."

He knew the sun was right. He knew what followed from throwing the ball. "I've tried not to," he said. "But what *was* has to *be*."

Summer wanted to reach out and stop him somehow, but she seemed not to have a body. She was just a warm circle of light.

The little boy threw the ball. It flew through the air and landed. It rolled and came to a stop by a fence.

"Don't chase it," she pleaded. She didn't know why, but she felt dread filling her up, dimming the golden light she cast, chilling the warmth.

"I have to. I always have to," the little boy said. "It's the way it happened. . . ."

". . . I have to chase it. Maybe then I can find the truth," he said. He smiled at the sun. The sun was worried, but she couldn't help. She wasn't really there. That much he knew. That she wasn't real . . . not yet.

"Who are you?" the sun asked.

"I don't know," he said. "That's why I have to chase the ball."

Summer watched, helpless, as he chased the ball to the fence. Beyond the low fence, on the other side, was a car. The car door was open, and sitting there, sad beyond endurance, was a woman. A man stood by the fence.

The little boy in white stopped at the fence. He picked up the ball.

"No," Summer whispered.

The man reached over the fence and lifted the boy up high over the fence.

In her mind, she heard the boy cry out in fear. And all the light was gone. She was no longer the sun, though she was still warm, a glowing circle of warmth, safe and secure. But she heard that echoing cry deep in her heart even as she emerged from darkness into a harsh light and heard for the first time her own shrill, tiny, newborn voice repeating her brother's wail.

Summer cried out.

Her cry woke her. Her pillow was soaked with tears.

"Oh, jeez," she moaned. "Stop eating before you go to bed, Summer."

That was how it had happened, Summer realized. Sixteen years ago. Jonathan had been in the playground at the day care center, playing with his favorite chewed-up red ball. Then he had simply disappeared.

Witnesses said they might have noticed a car parked by the fence. There might have been a man standing there. But no one could be sure.

Jonathan. J.T.? Had she really met him in her dream? Had any of it been real?

What kind of reality could you expect in a dream?

The night before, she'd been in the cave, with Seth sleeping beside her. She'd slept with her head resting on his chest, listening to the sound of his breathing. Now she felt so alone.

She hugged her pillow close. It just wasn't the same. She felt abandoned, which she knew was dumb. She hated feeling abandoned. Hated it.

"I wish you were here, Seth," she whispered.

Diana had often had difficulty sleeping, especially during the past year—the year that had come to be defined by the incident with Ross. She'd often lain awake, thinking of death. It had become a ritual—recalling the attempted rape; recalling in excruciating detail the moment when she'd realized that Adam was betraying her to protect his brother; remembering the feelings of self-loathing that had eaten at her, driving her again and again into the deep hole she thought would one day become her final experience of life.

But on this night she was not lying awake for

those reasons. Not that depression was so far away—she could still feel its evil, seductive contours close by, calling softly to her. Depression had lured her often, even before the incident with Ross. That had merely lowered her defenses, made her vulnerable. And even now Diana was not on the verge of becoming a giddy optimist. She was not, she thought wryly, about to be reborn as Summer. But she *had* flushed the carefully hoarded pills down the toilet, flushed away her safety net of suicide.

She was restless. At first she'd fallen asleep easily, but she'd awakened an hour later, alert. Since then she'd lain there, tossing the covers on or off, fluffing pillows, trying every sleeping position—her back, her side, her other side, facedown. None with any success.

She replayed the events of the day till they became as familiar as old *Simpsons* reruns. The trip to the police. Showing the video. The statement she'd dictated and signed. The realization that her actions had sent a weird thrill through everyone in the FDLE office, part awe, part anticipation. They'd asked her to speak to no one, to let them decide when to take action. But she had come away certain that they would take action. By the time she'd left, the number of FDLE personnel had tripled—men staring at her, not in the usual way at all, but as if she were some rare, dangerous animal.

It was interesting, being dangerous. It made her

smile in the darkness. But at the same time she felt uneasy. Not afraid so much as vaguely nauseated.

"I'm not going to get any sleep, am I?" she muttered.

She answered her own question by climbing out of bed. She retrieved the gauzy white robe she'd left on her chair, slipped it on, and went to the sliding glass door that opened onto her private balcony.

The night air was warmer than the air-conditioning by at least ten degrees. It had to be close to eighty, with humidity so thick it sparkled in the air like steam.

She went to the railing and rested both her hands on the wood. The moon peeked around a drifting cumulus. Most of the sky was clear, starlight twinkling through the damp air. The water of the bay was calm, as it almost always was, just tiny ripples to reflect the moonlight. Across the bay was the other side of Crab Claw Key—a few porch lights shining here and there; someone who insisted on shining spotlights on a tall palm; and down near the point, the green light that marked the end of the Merricks' dock.

Suddenly Diana felt uncomfortable. She felt as if . . . as if she were being watched. She glanced toward the Merrick estate. Surely there was no way they could see her from that distance—

She heard a slight rustling in the bushes below. Diana peered through the gloom. "Hey, who's there?"

No answer for a moment. Then a less surreptitious movement, someone stepping back from the bushes, stepping into the moonlight on the lawn.

"Don't be scared, it's just me."

It took Diana a moment to place the voice. She'd only heard it once before. One meeting, every single detail of which had stayed fresh in her mind. "Diver?"

"Yeah. Sorry. I wasn't sneaking around or anything."

Diana considered this. If he wasn't sneaking around, what exactly was he doing? Her heart was pounding. Her throat was tight. If she didn't know better, if Diana had not known herself to be cool and removed and not even slightly interested in a flake like Diver . . . well, if she hadn't known all those things, she'd have thought she was excited to see him.

"Wait there, I'll come down," Diana said. "I don't want Mallory—my mother—to wake up."

"I could come up there," Diver said. His voice sounded strange, almost shaky. Probably just the strain of whispering.

"The door's locked downstairs," Diana said. "I'd have to come down to let you in, anyway."

"No problem," Diver said.

To Diana's amazement, he planted a foot on the trellis that covered the outside wall of the family room, climbed to the top, levered himself up onto the roof of the family room, and walked across the sloping Spanish tiles to a point just above her balcony.

He stood there above her, wearing, as always, nothing but a pair of trunks. Summer had told her Diver never wore anything more. When his original trunks had been ripped, Diana, Summer, and Marquez had gone shopping to buy him a more complete wardrobe, but by the time they'd returned, he'd bummed an old pair of Seth's trunks and now seemed to think all his needs were met.

And, in fact, looking at him now, arm and shoulder and chest outlined in moonlight, Diana could see no good reason why he should be wearing anything more than he was.

"Come on down," Diana said.

He squatted at the edge of the roof and jumped lightly down beside her.

Diana was suddenly very aware of the sheerness of her robe, and the way the humidity had made it cling here and there. She backed away a few feet, making it look like a natural desire to gaze off toward the open water at the bay's mouth.

Diver seemed content to let the silence stretch. Diana considered going inside, finding some less flagrant thing to wear. But then, Diver always said he wasn't interested in girls. That's what Summer reported, anyway. He said that girls would disturb his inner peace, his *wa*.

It would serve him right if she did disturb his *wa*. Having him this close by seemed to be disturbing *hers*.

"Summer's okay," Diver said after a while. "I thought I should tell you."

"What do you mean?"

"They found her."

"What do you mean? Was she lost?"

"Yes," he said.

Diana shook her head. Clearly this was supposed to mean something, but she didn't have the slightest idea what. And she was a little annoyed to be standing there discussing Summer.

"Then I'm glad they found her," Diana said, making a mental note to ask Summer what had been going on.

Silence fell again. But now Diana realized she'd moved closer to Diver, and the obscure agitation she'd felt lying in bed was worse. She felt irritated. She plucked at the front of her robe to keep it from clinging.

"You know, I think Summer is kind of into Seth," Diana said. The words were out of her mouth several seconds before she began to think about them. "I mean . . ." Okay, now what *did* she mean?

"I like Seth," Diver said. "He's the one who gave me these." He pointed at his trunks.

"So you're not jealous?" Diana said, digging the hole deeper.

He looked at her blankly. Then a slow, dawning smile.

He was beautiful, Diana realized, feeling inexplicably demoralized by the realization.

"It's not that way with Summer," Diver said shyly.

"Yeah, I know," Diana said dismissively. "Girls disturb your *wa*." Beautiful eyes. Beautiful lips. Even his hands . . . She wouldn't mind holding his hand. The thought shocked her. Because it wasn't as if she was thinking with her usual casual detachment that she would like to hold his hand—no, it was as if she was suddenly entirely focused, with absolute intensity, on the single idea of touching him.

"Some more than others," Diver said.

"What?" Diana managed to ask.

"Some girls disturb me more than others," he clarified.

Diana struggled for just the right thing to say. Something clever but not too coy. Something normal-sounding, even though she was feeling distinctly abnormal. What she wanted to say was, What girl? Summer? Marquez? Me? Hillary Clinton? Did I mention me? What she did say was, "Uh-huh. Yeah. I guess that would be true. So I guess you'd just want to stay away from that type of girl."

He nodded solemnly. "Yes." Then he grinned impishly. "I suppose you think I'm crazy, right?"

Diana started to mouth the properly polite response, but then she laughed. "Diver, I can't call anyone crazy. When it comes to crazy, I don't think you're even in my league."

He said nothing, just waited.

"You know what I used to do? Every night?" Diana asked. "Right inside there, in my bed?"

"No."

"I used to lie there and think about killing myself," she said. "So how's that for crazy?" She began tapping her fingers on the wooden railing. "I had these pills. I used to enjoy counting them, you know? As long as I had them, I felt safe, like in a way I could deal with everything because in the end—well, in the end, there was always the end."

She waited for him to say something. And when he remained silent, she sighed. Brilliant, Diana. Wonderful. By all means, spill your guts to this near stranger. Right now he's wondering how he got himself into this. Right now he's hoping you don't have a weapon.

"Maybe you'd better take off," Diana said bitterly. Why had she done this? Why had she dragged her problems out for display?

"I don't think that would be an end," Diver said, surprising her.

"What?"

"I think that killing yourself isn't a real end to whatever pain you have. I think . . . I guess I think you can't look at life as having a neat beginning and middle and end, like a book. If you felt bad and killed yourself, those bad feelings would just go on to someone else—your mother, your friends. That's not right. You have to take the bad things that happen to you and . . . I don't know, change them. Turn them into something else."

"How about turning them into revenge?" Diana asked. "That's my present plan. Do to them what they did to you."

Diver shrugged. "I don't know about that. I guess I never got that chance."

Diana looked at him closely. He was telling her something important about himself. She started to ask him, but stopped herself. "You know, if you ever wanted to tell anyone . . . talk to anyone . . . I mean, like I said, I'm not someone who can ever call anyone else crazy."

Diver nodded.

"I wouldn't disturb your *wa* or anything," Diana said, trying to lighten the mood.

Diver bit his lip and looked away. "Yes, you would." He faced her, solemn, even sad. He raised his hand and, with only the lightest touch, stroked her cheek.

"The other day, when I saw you . . . Afterward I went to Marquez's house with her," he said. "I thought maybe she would make me forget. She kissed me. But I didn't forget. I was waiting for you tonight. Down in the bushes. Hoping you'd come out on the balcony. I was wishing you could just *know* that I was there. That I was calling you."

Diana took his hand and held it pressed against her cheek. "I couldn't sleep. I guess I heard you." She closed her eyes and savored the touch of his hand.

"I have to go," Diver said.

"Yes. Me too. Thanks for coming by."

Diana let him leave, though breaking the contact caused an almost physical sensation of pain and loss. He'd revealed all he could for one night, Diana knew. And so had she.

4

Unknowns, Uncertains, and Unstables

"Hi, Mom, it's me, Summer. Look, I have something very serious to tell you. Maybe you should sit down. This is going to be the biggest thing I have ever told you."

Summer wiped the steam off the bathroom mirror and looked at her reflection. Her reflection made a dissatisfied face at her and slowly shook her head.

"If I tell Mom she should sit down, she'll think I got pregnant or something," she told her reflection. "She'll reach through the phone and strangle me."

Summer flipped on the blow-dryer, used it to evaporate the rest of the steam, and then started on her hair.

"Mom! Hey, guess what! You are never going to believe this. Jonathan isn't dead or anything. He may be right here. He's a cook."

She rolled her eyes. "*He's a cook?* Any other irrelevant information you'd like to include?"

She hung the dryer on the hook and went into the main room. Her gaze fell on the framed picture of her parents that she kept on her nightstand. She sat on the edge of her unmade bed and held the picture in her hands. "Mom, I have to tell you something, and it's kind of major, so I'm just going to say it—Jonathan is alive, and I think I've found him." She sighed. "At least, *maybe* I have. So *maybe* you should be happy. *Maybe* you should get all excited and call Daddy and tell him that sixteen years of being sad are over. Maybe."

She replaced the picture on the nightstand.

"Yeah, right, Summer," she muttered. "Why not also tell them that *maybe* they won the lottery so they should both quit their jobs? Maybe they should think Jonathan is alive and then find out he isn't, so they can go through all that pain again."

There was a discreet knock at the door. Quiet as it was, it made Summer jump.

"Yes?"

"It's me." Diver's voice.

"Come in," she said, relieved.

He stuck his head in. "I thought I heard you talking

to someone. I was just going to make some breakfast."

"No, I wasn't talking to anyone," Summer said. "Go ahead. Hey, I have some excellent juice in the fridge if you'd like some."

"Cool." He looked at her quizzically. "Talking to yourself, huh?"

"Yeah. I guess so." She smiled at him. "I'm going to lie out on the beach with Marquez, so take your time here."

"You're okay, right?" Diver asked. He was searching for the juice in the refrigerator.

"Mmm. Yes, *I'm* okay," she said thoughtfully. "I'm sort of like Typhoid Mary. You know, someone who has a disease, only it doesn't affect them but they give it to whoever they touch? And then whoever they give it to is sick?"

Diver had found the juice. Now he withdrew his hand gingerly. "Um, what disease? You didn't drink out of this bottle, right?"

Summer laughed softly. "Don't worry, Diver. This disease won't affect *you*. J.T., sure. And his parents, and my parents . . ."

She was silent for a moment while Diver poured and drank a glass of juice. She could just tell her parents what she knew, let them do all the checking. After all, they were parental units, and she was slightly too young to be taking on all the burdens of the world.

Only, it would devastate her parents. It would raise their hopes, and then, if it turned out not to be true, it would leave them feeling worse than ever.

Suddenly she jumped up. "No," she said decisively. "As a matter of fact, it isn't going to be *anyone's* problem. Not until I'm completely sure. Thanks for working it through with me, Diver."

"No problem," he said.

It was a bright, sunny day. It almost always was in the Florida Keys. Which did not change the fact that bright was still bright, and sunny was still sunny, and the heat was just as real for being almost constant.

Summer and Marquez were heading for the beach, wearing sandals and sunglasses and bathing suits—as common an outfit on Crab Claw Key as a business suit was in Manhattan or a down parka in Minnesota. It was strange, Summer reflected, how quickly she had become inured to the idea of walking around in public half naked all the time. The other day she'd gone into Burger King dressed in a bathing suit—not a thing one did back where she was from.

"I have a question," Summer said.

"What?"

"Is your butt painted green?"

Marquez stopped and twisted around to look. "Huh. Yes, it is."

"Any particular reason?" Summer asked.

"I was painting. I guess when I cleaned up I missed a spot." She resumed walking, but shot Summer a wicked grin. "Maybe later I'll ask Diver if he can come over and help me clean it off."

Summer wasn't buying it. Marquez was just trying to distract her. "What were you painting?"

"Stuff," Marquez said.

"Stuff like . . . *J.T.*?"

"Big deal. That doesn't mean anything," Marquez said unconvincingly. "I was just tired of that big, blank white spot on the wall."

"Right. I completely and totally believe you, Marquez."

"Oh, shut up," Marquez grumbled. "Besides, he's still seeing Lianne. It's not as if we're back together. And I need *someone* to go with me to the Bacch. J.T.'s with Lianne. Diver is with whatever weird, invisible spirit he's with."

"The what?"

"The Bacch. The McSween Bacchanal," Marquez explained to Summer. "What, you don't know about it? The party to end all parties? It's in five days. Jeez, do you live in a cave? It's this big street thing, like Mardi Gras, only no one speaks French. Lots of food, lots of drinks, lots of everything else you can think of. Music. Dancing. Vandalism. Guys peeing in alleyways. You know, pretty much the kind of good time you're used to back home in Blimpyburg, Iowasota."

"When are you going to stop making fun of Bloomington?" Summer asked grumpily. She hadn't slept all that well, and now, out in the heat, she felt groggy. First had come the strange, disturbing dream. And Diver had kept her awake, which was unusual. He slept on her roof deck, unless it was raining. Most nights she never even knew he was there. But the previous night he'd been humming some song for an hour. Very un-Diver-like. And then she'd spent the morning deciding just how many lives she should throw into turmoil. "So what are you saying? This is like some kind of local Mardi Gras?"

"Yeah, it's to celebrate the day when the guy who founded Crab Claw Key was hanged."

"Excuse me?"

"This guy named John Bonner McSween was some kind of pirate, and he used to have his boat here. But then the British Navy caught up with him and hanged him. So I guess before they finished him off he made some big speech about how he hoped they'd all have themselves a big party celebrating the fact that they'd got him at last. Anyway, that's the story. Every year it's a big thing."

"Like costumes and all?" Summer asked. They turned left, and the beach came into view at the end of a blessedly tree-shaded road. The trees framed a nice view at the far end of the street—a perfect, three-layered slice of crystal white sand, blue-green water, and pure, unclouded blue sky.

"It's not quite that organized," Marquez said. "Costumes would require actual planning. Mostly we're talking bathing suits."

"That's all people ever wear around here. This has to be the only place on earth where people wear shorts and halter tops to church."

"The important thing is, don't let them make you work that night," Marquez said. "They're going to try to get you to. But only total losers and married people work the night of the McSween Bacchanal."

"I guess I'll ask Seth what he's going to do," Summer said.

Marquez rolled her eyes. "Oh, so now you need his permission?"

They had reached the beach and were hotfooting around, looking for the perfect spot to spread their blanket. For Marquez, a perfect spot was usually defined as one with an easy view of good-looking guys playing volleyball.

"I don't need Seth's permission, but he and I are kind of boyfriend and girlfriend now," Summer said. "I mean, that's sort of official. Look, just put the blanket down already."

Marquez looked at her curiously as she unfolded the blanket. "What exactly went on between you two in that cave?"

Summer lay back and began spreading sunblock on her stomach. She had achieved a good tan and now didn't want to carry it too far. On Crab Claw Key the sun was out almost every day, and if she wasn't careful, she'd be a piece of leather by the time summer came to an end. Plus she didn't have Marquez's naturally dark skin.

"Nothing," Summer said. "I just kind of realized that I was being silly, keeping Seth at a distance."

"Uh-huh. So did you guys do it?"

"No!" Summer said, flustered, as she often was, by her friend's directness.

"You didn't?" Marquez seemed surprised. "You're stuck in a cave with a cute guy and only a few hours to live and you didn't even think to yourself, whoa, I don't want to die a virgin?"

"It didn't really come up," Summer said, tossing a handful of sugar white sand on Marquez's oiled back.

"Hey, stop that. Look, all I'm saying is that it would have been a pretty good excuse. Who's going to say you shouldn't just go for it under those circumstances?"

"The circumstances were that we were both scared and I hadn't brushed my teeth since that morning."

Marquez sighed. "Wait a minute. You're on death's

doorstep, you're trapped with a very cute guy—even if he is a little too wholesome for me—and you don't do it because you think you might have bad breath?" She sighed again. "On second thought, maybe you *should* work the night of the Bacch."

"You're saying you would have done it?" Summer asked.

"Absolutely."

"Have you ever done it? Or are you just talking big, as usual?" Summer asked. She felt a little forward asking the question, but Marquez had goaded her.

"I've never been trapped in a cave," Marquez said defensively.

"Hah," Summer said.

"Oh, shut up. So if you didn't do it, why all this stuff about having to ask Seth's permission to go to the Bacchanal?"

"Did I say I had to ask his permission? No."

"But it's the big *L,* huh?" Marquez asked. "I mean, the *L* word was spoken out loud by both parties?"

Summer laughed. "The *L* word may have been spoken." She closed her eyes for a moment, savoring the memory. Yes, the *L* word had definitely been mentioned.

Marquez gave an exaggerated shudder. "That's too bad. Once the *L* word is out there, it's hard to ever take it back. Believe me, I know."

"Speaking of which . . ." Summer began.

"Let's not change the subject. We're discussing your messed-up love life, not mine," Marquez said. "All I'm saying is this whole love thing is like . . . what's that disease? The one you get from mosquitoes, and it keeps coming back?"

"Encephalitis?"

"No. The other one."

"Malaria."

"Like malaria, right. Once you have the fever it can just come back all of a sudden, making you hot and feverish and delirious." Marquez panted theatrically. "Anyway, I'm just telling you, once you start saying the *L* word, it isn't easy to take it back."

"Maybe I don't want to take it back," Summer said. Everything was bright red beneath her closed eyes. She scrunched her eyelids tighter and got nice dark blue explosions. "I do love him."

"Yeah? That's what you think now," Marquez said. "But I have one word for you. One very important word."

Summer waited, but naturally Marquez outwaited her. "All right, what word?" Summer demanded, opening her eyes. "Jeez, make me beg already."

"The word is . . . *August.*"

"August. Okay. That clears everything up," Summer said dryly.

"Laugh all you want. People always forget August when they come down here for the summer. And you may have noticed that as of today, it's August. And after August?"

"Call me crazy, but I have to say . . . September?"

"Exactly. June is fine. July is fine. But August is upon us, and you're on the downside of summer, Summer. At the end of the month all you tourists fly off in different directions. You go back to Billybobtown, and Seth goes off to whatever pathetic, repressed Midwestern cemetery he's from."

"Eau Claire, Wisconsin," Summer said automatically.

"Exactly. Ear Clean, Wisconosa. I knew that." Marquez grinned, hugely amused by herself.

But Summer wasn't. Billybobtown and Ear Clean were not a million miles apart. But they were not the same place, either. Not the same schools. Not the same lives.

And another thought had just appeared in Summer's mind—Marquez was still in love with J.T. That wasn't news. Summer had realized that long ago. But if J.T. really was Jonathan . . .

"Marquez?" she said. "Are you going to try to get back together with J.T.?"

"No. Absolutely not. But I think maybe I am going to let him get back together with me," Marquez said.

"And I hope it's before the Bacch, unless I can get Diver to go with me, which seems unlikely."

When Summer didn't laugh, Marquez turned to peer at her from beneath shaded brows. "What?" she demanded. "What's the serious look all about?"

Summer shrugged. "It's just—What if J.T. really is my brother?"

"I give up. What if?"

"Nothing, I guess," Summer said. "Only, I was wondering whether he would stay here, or maybe go to Minnesota."

Marquez's smile disappeared. "I guess he would want to meet your—his—parents," she said slowly. "But that doesn't mean he'd live there."

"I guess you're right," Summer said."

"Of course I am," Marquez said confidently. "What kind of an idiot would deliberately choose Bloomington, Minnesota, over Crab Claw Key, Florida?"

Summer laughed along in agreement, and would almost have believed Marquez felt as sure as she sounded. Only, Marquez had never before actually said "Bloomington, Minnesota," without making a joke.

When Summer got home from the beach, the phone was ringing. To her surprise, it was Marquez. Summer had left her only twenty minutes earlier.

"Hey, Summer. Babe. What's been going on in

your life since we got together last?" Marquez asked.

"I walked home. Then I picked up the phone. There, now you're up to date," Summer said. She squeezed the phone against her ear with her shoulder and glanced around the room. The stilt house wasn't always perfectly private—Diver occasionally appeared with very little announcement through the hatch in the floor.

"I got a call from work. They have a catering thing on board some big boat that just pulled in. They need a couple of waitresses who aren't doing anything tonight."

"But I *am* doing something tonight," Summer said. "I'm going out with Seth."

"You can go out with Seth any night," Marquez argued. "We'd split fifteen percent of the total food bill, so right there we'll probably make fifty each. Last summer when I did things like this, the boat guys always tipped extra. Last time the guy gave each waitress a hundred-dollar bill."

"Whoa."

"Yeah, whoa."

"Okay, I'm there. I'll just call and tell Seth."

Summer hung up the phone. She dialed Seth's number. He wasn't home, so she left a message on his answering machine. "Hi, it's me. Listen, I have to work tonight, but maybe we could get together afterward, if you still feel like it." She almost hung up the phone, but then remembered that Seth lived with his grandfather. "I'll miss you, little fuzzy wuzzy bunny," Summer said, choking down her own laughter. "Wittle Summer wuvs you." She hung up the phone, well satisfied by the image of Seth playing the message back with his grandfather listening.

"Jeez, I'm spending too much time with Marquez," Summer muttered.

At seven o'clock Summer arrived at the Crab 'n' Conch, wearing a pair of white shorts and a matching white halter top. Uniforms were not required on jobs outside the restaurant, and she knew that it would be hot work, at least until the sun set.

Marquez was already there, folding linen napkins in a corner of the kitchen. She was wearing a pair of shorts too, though hers were several degrees less modest than Summer's, and a brightly patterned bikini top. The usual evening rush was going on around them, waitresses hurrying in and out shouting orders, dishwashers clattering plates, cooks cursing and sweating in the intense heat.

J.T. was down on one end of the line, assembling the food for the private party. He was preoccupied and busy, but when Summer arrived he glanced up and sent her a smile.

"Hi," Summer said.

"Hi. You look great. In fact, normally I'd make some clever, flirtatious remark." He shook his head in bemusement. "I guess that would be in pretty bad taste now."

"I don't know," Summer admitted. "I guess so."

J.T. returned to arranging little finger foods on a long steel tray. "I don't exactly know what to do now, about all that stuff."

"Me neither," Summer said. "I mean, we should try to figure out whether it's true or not."

"I thought the same thing. First of all, what are the odds? We can't just screw up everyone's lives without being sure. But how do we be sure, exactly?" he asked. "I mean, what are we going to do? Compare blood tests?"

Summer shook her head. "I don't know. I just know I don't want to get my parents all excited and then find out it isn't true."

"I agree," he said solemnly. "And there's something else too. Whatever the truth is, I can't get my folks in trouble."

"Trouble? Why would they be in trouble?" Summer asked.

J.T. met her gaze with eyes so like her own. "Look, someone is going to want some explanation for how I came to be J.T. instead of Jonathan."

"Wow, I hadn't even really thought about that," Summer lied, suddenly feeling overwhelmed.

"I have," J.T. said solemnly. "It's about all I can think of." Summer saw his gaze dart toward Marquez. She was flirting ostentatiously with Alec, the bartender, who was by the sink cutting lemons.

"Are you going with us to this thing?" Summer asked.

"Yep. I'm handling the food. So you're stuck with me tonight." J.T. grinned. "And we're both stuck with her." He jerked his head at Marquez.

"We'll figure everything out, J.T.," Summer said reassuringly. She took his hand, which was greasy with crabmeat stuffing. For some reason she felt like crying. What if? The question never seemed to be far away from her thoughts. What if?

"Yeah, of course we will," J.T. said.

"Honestly, J.T., I can't leave you alone for five minutes." It was Lianne, bustling back into the kitchen with a full tray of dirty dishes. She set the tray down and took J.T.'s hand from Summer. "Summer, I'm disappointed in you. I expect Marquez to be trying to steal other people's boyfriends."

Lianne's voice was only mock angry, but in the reference to Marquez there was genuine resentment. Lianne stretched up on her toes to kiss J.T. on the lips. Summer found the moment strangely embarrassing. Marquez obviously wasn't pleased either.

"Lianne," Marquez said, leaving the bartender's side, "I'm surprised to see you here. I heard that you joined the circus as the two-faced woman."

"That's funny," Lianne shot back. "I heard the same thing about you, only it was as part of the elephant act."

"I guess everything looks big when you're a midget," Marquez said.

"Excuse me," J.T. interrupted, "but we all have work to do, right?"

"Well, I'd love to go on trading insults with you, Marquez, you're such an easy target," Lianne said, "but I have to get changed."

"Finally getting that plastic surgery?" Marquez said gleefully.

"No. I'm going with all of you. They just called in to say they're adding guests, which means an extra waitress."

5

Revenge in Different Degrees of Purity

The cabin cruiser was long, and not a particularly elegant-looking boat, but definitely large. Larger than a Greyhound bus, and brightly lit with red Japanese lanterns hung on lines that drooped from the mast to the bow and from the radar dish to the stern.

Summer, Marquez, Lianne, J.T., and Alec the bartender all arrived on time, just as the sun was dipping toward the cooling waters of the Gulf of Mexico.

"Nice little raft, isn't it?" Marquez remarked dryly. "Someday I'm going to own one of these, only not so tiny and cramped." Marquez and Summer helped set up the buffet inside the carpeted and wood-paneled main cabin, which opened out onto the broad stern deck, where most of the party was to take place.

J.T. was nearby, lighting little cans of Sterno under the steel chafing dishes on a side table and shuttling back and forth to the galley, which was down a short set of three steps.

"Has anyone seen the guy who owns the boat?" Lianne asked, coming up with a box of paper napkins.

"No," Summer said. "Why?"

Lianne shrugged. "Nice to know who we're working for."

"Some fat, rich old guy with a hairy back, little stick legs, and pinkie rings," Marquez muttered under her breath. "That's what they always are. He'll drink Crown Royal, and after he's had two or three he'll start asking me if I like older men."

J.T. laughed. "The world according to Marquez."

"Marquez, why are you so cynical?" Lianne asked petulantly, seemingly annoyed that J.T. had laughed.

"Why am I cynical?" Marquez asked. "Because it works. Anytime you want to try to figure out why someone is doing something, just apply the most cynical interpretation you can come up with, and you'll be right about ninety percent of the time."

Lianne shook her head in disgust. "You should

be a politician or a lawyer when you grow up. *If* you grow up."

Marquez laughed delightedly. "Exactly! That's just what I plan to be—a lawyer."

J.T. snorted derisively. He winked at Summer, who was drinking a glass of soda and trying to stay out of what looked like a brewing fight. "Marquez a lawyer. And I might become a transvestite pygmy rabbit jockey," J.T. said.

This struck Summer as so funny that she choked on her soda. But Marquez didn't think it was at all funny. "See, that's why you and me are no longer you and me, J.T.," she said. "You have no faith in me."

J.T.'s eyes flashed. "Bull, Marquez. You're the one who doesn't have faith. Lawyer. Jeez, give me a break. You're the only person who knows you who is dumb enough to believe that."

"Now you're calling me stupid?" Marquez demanded.

Summer noticed that Lianne was content to stand by and watch, smugly pleased at this new evidence of the permanent rift between her new boyfriend and his old girlfriend.

"No, I'm not calling you stupid," J.T. said angrily. Then, much more softly, "I'm calling you an artist."

Marquez started to say something angry, but hesitated, looking confused.

Lianne seemed to realize that the conversation had

taken a dangerous turn. "I think Marquez should be whatever she wants to be," she said, suddenly Marquez's defender.

"It isn't a question of what she should be someday." J.T.'s look was just for Marquez. "It's a case of what she is right now. She's an artist. She'll always be an artist. Send her to Harvard, or put her in a little gray business outfit and stick a briefcase in her hand, and she'll still be an artist." He returned his attention to a Sterno pot that would not catch fire.

Marquez busied herself with her work, viciously slicing limes into little wedges. Summer watched her, recalling the awed, overwhelmed feeling she'd experienced when she first went into Marquez's room. J.T. was right—Marquez was an artist. It bothered Summer a little that she hadn't seen it clearly before. It made her a little jealous of Marquez. It would be nice to *be* something, to be so precisely identified. Although evidently Marquez didn't think it was so great.

Then Summer shifted her gaze to J.T., and once again she experienced the queasy feeling that he represented change on a scale so massive it was impossible to grasp. What would her parents think of him? Would her mother—*their* mother, perhaps—be proud of the way he had grown up?

Summer saw Marquez jerk her head toward the

gangway, a warning. Someone was coming aboard from the pier.

It was a man in his sixties, carrying a cocktail glass. He was fat, with a huge stomach hanging over his shorts. From the bottom of the shorts extended two narrow stick legs. His bare chest and back were matted with white and gray hair. Summer peered closely at his hands. Yes, there was a pinkie ring.

Marquez arched an eyebrow and grinned cockily.

Summer looked at J.T. "Just like she described," she said under her breath.

"Oh, yeah?" Lianne said. "Well, she didn't predict *him*."

Summer looked back, and there, emerging from behind the wide, waddling form of the man, was a tall, muscular, darkly handsome young guy. He looked as if he might be anywhere from eighteen to twenty-five years old. But, as it happened, Summer knew for a fact that he was only seventeen.

She knew for a fact how old he was because, as impossible as it seemed to her as she stood gaping with open mouth, her forgotten knife falling from her hand, he was none other than Sean Valletti.

Sean Valletti, the crush of her life. The guy she'd drooled over since freshman year. The guy who'd broken her heart a thousand times without even noticing it.

"Ah, good, good, you're here already," the man with the pinkie ring said.

"All set up," J.T. affirmed. "Are you Mr. Holland?"

"Dex Holland," the man said, extending a chubby hand to J.T. "And this here is my nephew. Just came down from Minnesota."

"Minnesota?" Marquez said. She gave Sean a good, long look in her inevitably provocative way, being even more blatant than usual in hopes of annoying J.T. She turned to Summer. "I didn't know they grew them this cute in Minnesota. Why did you ever leave?"

Summer could feel the blush crawling up her neck. It would have been nice if Marquez had just, for once, kept her mouth shut.

"Are you from . . ." Sean began, looking at Summer in confusion. He paused and tilted his head. "You remind me of someone."

Someone you managed to look right through for the last three years, Summer thought. *The invisible girl.* "Yes. I, uh, I mean, you do know me. I guess. Or not. I mean, I know you, anyway."

"You two actually know each other?" Marquez said.

"I don't think I do," Sean said.

"I'm Summer Smith," Summer said miserably. "You know, I sit behind you in—"

"Summer Smith?" Sean said incredulously. "No

way." He looked her up and down with no attempt to be subtle. He smiled. "You've been sitting behind me all year? Wow, I must have been blind."

"Diana, someone is here to see you."

Her mother's voice rose up the stairs, a too-coy tone that affected Diana like fingernails on a chalkboard. But then a thought occurred to her. Diver? Could it be Diver?

No, that was ridiculous. Diver wouldn't just come up, knock on the front door, and announce himself to her mother. Diana smiled. No, that wasn't Diver's style.

"*Diana.* Do you hear me?"

"Unfortunately, yes," Diana muttered. She turned off the TV. She had been reorganizing her room, moving things here and there, piling up clothing and possessions she no longer wanted. Too much of it held memories of sadder times.

She sighed and got to her feet. "Coming!" she yelled. But by the time she had risen completely and turned, he was standing there in the doorway.

"Adam!" she said, surprised and even a little frightened. "What are you doing here?"

Adam Merrick had always seemed to be surrounded by some kind of magnetic field that created in other guys a desire to like him and in girls a desire, period. He was tall and powerfully built without seeming at all ungainly. His dark hair was expensively cut, designed to look ever so casual. In all the time she had gone out with him, Diana had seldom seen him emotional or out of control. So it was a particular shock to see that his eyes were red, as if he had been crying. There was an odd, ashen color beneath the perpetual tan.

"Damn you, Diana," he said.

Diana recoiled. Before she could form a coherent response, he was in her room, closing the door behind him with a slam.

"I understood your going after Ross," he said. He was pointing his finger at her, trembling with barely controlled rage. "I understood that. Ross is dangerous. He's out of control. But my father? What's my father ever done to hurt you?"

"Get out of here, Adam," Diana said. Her voice sounded firm enough, but she was quivering inside. Not so much from fear—Adam was not the type to become violent—but from the realization that it had all truly begun.

"No way, Diana. I want an answer. I *let* you keep that tape recorder, you know I did. I could have stopped you, but I let it go because I know Ross needs help, and I know he won't get it until someone shakes him up real badly. But my dad wasn't part of the deal."

"What's happened?" Diana asked, taking a deep breath to steady herself.

Adam snorted. "Like you don't know."

"They never told me what they were going to do," Diana said.

"No, you just put the knife in their hands, and however they decide to stick it in, well, that's not your problem, right?" The muscles in his jaw were in spasm. "They were just at the house, questioning him. Questioning my father. They told him to get a lawyer. I was there. He was . . . He couldn't look at me. My dad, he couldn't even look at me, and those idiots in their cheap suits smirking the whole time, pretending to be so respectful but practically drooling like a pack of hungry dogs."

Diana felt a knot tightening in her stomach. "And where was Ross?" she asked.

The question seemed to stun Adam momentarily. "Ross?"

"Yes. Where was Ross during all this?"

Adam looked away. His brow was furrowed. "He wasn't there."

"Hiding like the gutless little worm he is," Diana snapped.

But Adam wasn't really listening. "My dad sitting there having to listen to . . . these creeps, these Kmart cops cross-examining him. 'No, sir, we are not prepared to make an arrest at this time. But you need to get in touch with your lawyer, Senator. And don't leave the state of Florida, see, or otherwise it could be a matter for the FBI.'"

"I didn't want this to come down on your father," Diana said honestly. "It's Ross I want to see behind bars."

"Well, your little revenge is really all that counts," Adam sneered. "It doesn't matter to you that you're ruining a great man's life. Do you know what the media will do with this? Do you have any clue as to the kind of—You have to stop this," he said. He looked at her, threatening, blaming, pleading all at once. "You have to put an end to this."

"It's too late," Diana said. She felt her fear receding. Anger was returning, clean, strengthening anger. "You could have dealt with it a year ago, but the mighty Merricks always protect their own."

"That's something you'd better remember," Adam snapped. "We *do* protect our own."

There was scorn in Diana's laugh. "Really? How well did you and Ross protect your father?"

The shot went straight home. Adam seemed to crumple. Diana pressed on, noticing Adam's stricken look and not caring one bit. No more than Ross had cared for her that night when he'd slapped her and torn at her clothing and laughed at her cries for help. No more than Adam had really cared when he'd made his choice between his girlfriend and his brother.

"So the senator is in trouble?" Diana demanded. "Tough luck. I don't care. I don't give a damn. He threatened to ruin me if I charged Ross, right? Now look who's ruined. He threatened to make me look pathetic? Now who looks pathetic? You do, Adam, that's who."

"It's my fault," Adam said. "I should never have let you keep that tape. I was weak. I looked at you and remembered the way it was when we were together. I was stupid."

Diana shook her head. "It wasn't the tape recorder, Adam. It wouldn't have mattered if you had kept it. See, I had Summer's video camera in my bag. I figured you might find one or the other, but not both. Besides, my sweet mother burned the little tape. She's against me in this, but I don't even care."

Adam stared at her in amazement. "Well, you cold, calculating little witch." He laughed bitterly. "Don't count us out just yet," he said, but without much conviction.

"I know. You're very rich and very powerful, blah, blah, and you always protect your own, blah, blah, blah. But you know what? Pretty soon everyone in the country is going to know that Ross Merrick is a rapist, and law-and-order Senator Merrick covered up his crimes."

Adam was silent, staring at her with a weird, sideways look. Disbelief. Shock. "I don't even know you anymore, Diana," he said. "I don't even know what you've become."

"I guess you're right, Adam," Diana agreed. "You don't know me anymore. See, you used to recognize me better when I had the word *victim* tattooed on my forehead. You liked me that way. Diana the victim. Diana the depressed. Poor, screwed-up Diana. Go ahead, dump on Diana, she won't even know the difference."

Diana nodded thoughtfully, and even smiled. "That's okay. I understand why you treated me like crap, Adam. I treated myself like crap. I blamed myself. I turned it all inward. And to be honest, I got off on it in a way. In some sick way I enjoyed it, all the thoughts of suicide, all the drama of being the poor little victim. See, that's the beauty of depression, that's why it works. Because it seduces you. You start by *being* a victim, and then you begin *thinking* of yourself as a victim, *defining* yourself as a victim, and pretty soon you're a double victim, because now you're a victim of the feeling of being a victim. It's a spiral that sucks you further and further down."

"That's a great little speech," Adam said derisively. "Very Oprah. But now it's just about revenge."

"Justice," Diana said.

"Revenge. You just want to hurt the people who you think hurt you. Don't dress it up, Diana, it's just revenge."

Diana laughed, surprising both of them. "You're right, Adam. It is just revenge. And you know what? It's just like they say. Revenge really *is* sweet."

"I won't let this destroy my father," Adam said.

"I don't think that's up to you," Diana said. "It's up to Ross. All he has to do is confess. After that, no one will go after your father anymore."

Adam fell silent again. He nodded, a slight, unconscious movement. He knew she was right. If Ross confessed, that would probably be the end of it. "You have a videotape?" Adam said.

"The police have it now, at least one copy of it," Diana said.

"I—I know I don't have any right to ask you anything," he said. "It's just that if you give that tape to the media or anything, my dad . . . He's a proud guy, you know. Proud. To be on TV, with that tape making him look like a fool . . . I mean, okay, I know Ross has to be stopped. I'm just asking—I'm *begging* you. He's a great man. He has a position in the world. . . ."

"I'm not going to give the tape to anyone," Diana said, annoyed at herself for being moved by Adam's plea. But then, whatever else might be wrong with the Merrick family, there was genuine love between

Adam and his father. Love and admiration of a degree that had always made Diana a little jealous. "I'm not going to give the tape to some sleazy tabloid show or anything," she promised. "I don't want to humiliate anyone. I just want Ross not to be able to hurt anyone else."

"Thanks for that," Adam said, sagging with relief. "Thanks."

"Adam, we both know Ross is dangerous," Diana said. "I have to stop him. Call it revenge if you want. You know it has to be done. Your problem isn't with me. It's with your brother."

6

Summer Is a Very Bad Girl but a Good Sister.

The party lasted the better part of five hours. Five hours of serving food and emptying ashtrays, and, as Marquez had predicted, dodging a few drunken come-ons. But through it all, Summer focused on one overarching fact—Sean Valletti was there. He was there on Crab Claw Key, and he had not missed a single opportunity all night to talk to her, to compliment her, even to help her carry more ice aboard from the pier. When she had spilled a drink and one of the old ladies had started giving her a hard time, Sean had intervened, forcefully defending Summer. And it seemed, though she might just be imagining it, that his gaze was never far from her.

Summer suspected he was interested in her.

This suspicion was heightened when Marquez said, "Jeez, he's panting around after you."

"Who?" Summer asked innocently. They were taking a brief coffee break, hiding in the dark on the seaward side of the boat, letting Lianne do all the work for a while.

"Oh, please. Even *you* aren't that much of a little Sunday school girl, Summer," Marquez said. "I'm talking about Mr. Complexion over there. Mr. Legs. Mr. Upper-Body Strength. Sean what's-his-name."

"Valletti. Sean Valletti." Summer grinned coyly. "He does have nice legs, doesn't he?"

"He has better legs than I have," Marquez said, "which I wouldn't mind, if he at least had the good taste to be interested in me, but apparently he is attracted only to his own kind—milk-fed Midwestern virginal types."

"Well, I'm not interested in *him*," Summer said, a little too strongly.

"Nooooo, of course not. Although I did see your jaw drop when you first saw him."

"I was surprised. I mean, I know him. I was surprised that he would be here, of all places."

"You two have anything going on back in Cheeseville?" Marquez asked.

"Not really," Summer said. "Although, to tell you

the truth, I did always kind of think he was cute. For a while I had sort of a crush on him." She forced a laugh. "It was nothing. I get crushes on lots of guys. For a while I had this weird crush on the Vulcan guy on reruns of *Star Trek Voyager,* and I don't even watch the show."

"So, cutting through the crap, you were basically slobbering after this Sean guy, writing his name and your name together in hearts, trying out the sound of the name *Summer Valletti*—or maybe, being a good feminist, it was *Summer Smith-Valletti*—and kissing your pillow at night, wishing it were him."

"You know, Marquez, sometimes you get on my nerves," Summer said, annoyed at the total accuracy of Marquez's guesses.

"Oh, hi, there you are."

It was him. He had sneaked up from the far side, coming around from the bow. Summer jumped and blushed furiously, hoping and praying that he hadn't heard the last few seconds of their conversation.

"Guess I'd better go help Lianne clean up," Marquez said, batting her eyelashes at Summer and making a suggestive little kissy-kissy mouth that made Summer want to push her over the side of the boat.

"I should probably go too," Summer said, making no move to follow Marquez.

"Don't go," Sean said quickly. "You've been busy

all night. The other two can handle it. Just about everyone's gone, anyway."

He was standing unnaturally close, and Summer
held her Pepsi in front of her like a shield. "Did everything go okay?" she asked, at a loss for any more substantial conversation. "I mean, was the service all right?
Did everyone get enough crab puffs?"

Did everyone get enough crab puffs? Yes, this was what
she had waited three years to ask Sean Valletti.

"Who cares?" he asked, laughing.

"Well, it's my job," Summer said lamely.

"Don't worry. I told my uncle to be sure to give
you a really big tip." He winked at her.

"Oh, that's okay," Summer said. "I mean, that's
good, because the others like tips, but I don't really,
you know . . . I mean, it's okay. You don't have to
have him give us anything special."

Shut up now, Summer ordered herself. If she managed to babble until Marquez and Lianne missed out
on a nice tip, they would take turns killing her.

"Can you believe this? Your running into me
here?" Sean said.

"What are the odds?" Summer agreed.

"You know, I just can't believe we never went
out," he said.

"We didn't," Summer said. "I'm pretty sure I'd
remember."

"I know you would," he said. "Me too. I'd remember. You always just seemed like . . . like this girl, you know?"

"Uh-huh," she said, nodding agreement although she was entirely perplexed.

"Just this girl who was there and all," Sean clarified. "Then, when I saw you here, you were this *girl*." He looked at her appreciatively. "You're a babe. I hope you don't mind my saying that."

A babe. Sean Valletti had just called her a babe. "I guess I don't mind," Summer said, gulping her drink and coming up with nothing but ice cubes. On the one hand, the phrase "a babe" was like some throwback. On the other hand, what did it matter what words he used? The point was, he had suddenly, amazingly, noticed her.

It could only be her carefully nurtured tan.

"So, when can we get together?" he asked. "You're staying here, right? I mean, all summer? All summer, Summer," he added, delighted by his wit.

"Um, sure, I'm here all summer," she said.

"Where are you staying?" he asked.

"I have this . . . this house. It's hard to describe."

"A house? By yourself? You have your own place?" he asked eagerly.

"Kind of." If you didn't count the guy who lived on her roof and used her bathroom and kitchen.

Sean grinned, showing a perfect smile. "Cool. So, how about this big festival thing they do here, this Botchanail?"

"The Bacchanal?"

"Yeah. I hear it's a major party. You and me? Are we there?" he asked.

"I, I, I, um, I, I, uh, see, I have this . . . I have to see if I can get off work," Summer babbled.

"Try real hard," Sean said. He took Summer's drink from her hand and tossed it into the water. He leaned close, too close by far, and before Summer could object, and before she could decide if she was even considering objecting, he kissed her lightly on the mouth.

Summer practically ran below deck, her head spinning. Standing there waiting for her was Marquez, a giant smirk on her face. Somehow Marquez had managed to help Lianne with the cleanup and still witness everything.

"Boy, Summer," Marquez said. "I mention the problem of the end of summer, and darned if you don't go right out and solve it."

It was a long walk home from the marina, and Summer was not looking forward to the trip in the dark. Marquez had walked from her own home, which was much closer. Summer had planned to go over to see

Seth after work, since he lived just down the block from Marquez. But now she felt too tired.

Too tired and too guilty. When Sean had asked her to go to the Bacchanal with him, she *should* have told him no, sorry, I have a boyfriend. Instead she had babbled and evaded until he'd kissed her. She was a thoroughly rotten person. The first thing she would do the next day was see Sean Valletti and blow him off. Great, one more thing to worry about.

Even though she wasn't interested in walking a mile or more through the dark with nothing for accompaniment but a guilty conscience, Summer was not entirely grateful when J.T. pulled over and offered to drive her home. She had the feeling that he would use the opportunity for a talk. And she wasn't sure she was up for it.

"So, did they take care of you waitresses?" J.T. asked as she climbed into his car, a wonderfully decrepit old Dodge Dart.

"A hundred-dollar bill, over and above the fifteen percent," Summer said.

"Hmm. Lianne and Marquez and I only got fifties," J.T. said, giving Summer a dubious look. "Must be they didn't like my legs as much as yours."

Summer shook her head in real annoyance. "I told him not to do that," she said. "See, I know that one guy, the young one, from back home. But I'll split the extra with you guys so that everything's fair."

J.T. laughed. "No, no, keep it. I was just giving you a hard time."

"Yeah, well, Marquez won't take that same attitude," Summer said.

"Marquez," he said, without elaborating.

She waited to see if he would add anything, but all he did was shake his head a couple of times, obviously lost in some internal dialogue.

"You really think Marquez is an artist?" Summer asked.

"You've seen her room, right?"

"But she says that's just a hobby," Summer said.

"Does it look like it's just a hobby? Ever seen her actually working on it?" He smiled fondly. "It's a real sight. I went over there once, banged on her door for about twenty minutes. She wouldn't answer, so I went in, right? Marquez is wearing this dress, a very expensive dress, something you'd wear out to someplace nice. Only, she's past caring about the dress, because it's totally destroyed with paint. She was like . . . like I don't know what. It's probably a bad analogy, but she reminded me of a punker guitar player, just spazzing out, lost to all contact with the regular world. In a frenzy, that's the word. I stood there for twenty minutes watching her, and I swear she never even noticed I was there. After a while I left quietly because I realized she was in a place that was just for her. I don't know. Maybe she let me watch so I would understand something about her. Or maybe she wasn't even able to see me."

Summer thought about this for a moment. At one level it made her terribly jealous. It would be wonderful to be that driven by something . . . anything. "The other day she had paint on her . . . on her body."

"I'm not surprised. Our little rescue mission to find you and Seth probably got her fired up."

"See, it's hard for me to see Marquez as being that way. She's always in such control. Except when she's dancing."

"Marquez thinks she's in control," J.T. said. "She actually believes this junk about living some straight, normal life. Why do you think we broke up?"

"I don't know. All she ever says is that you started getting weird when . . . when you realized you and your parents weren't—"

"Related?" J.T. offered. "Yeah, I know Marquez's *story*. She doesn't want to deal with other people's problems. She wants to be around nice, normal, sensible people. Everything cool and ironic and detached."

Summer nodded, understanding suddenly. "She can't be around complicated emotional situations or people who are out of control. She's afraid that she'll lose control."

"Yeah. She's afraid she'll suddenly be what she really

is. Because, you see, when she loses that control she becomes this out-there creature who doesn't care about anything but putting an image down on a wall."

They had arrived at their destination, but now Summer felt reluctant to break the contact with J.T.

"Hey, you've never seen my house, have you?" she said lightly.

"The stilt house, right? Only from the water, passing by. When I was a kid we used to think it was inhabited by trolls and orcs." He laughed in embarrassment. "Too much Tolkien, I think."

"I haven't seen any trolls," Summer said. "The occasional cockroach, maybe."

She led him down the pathway that passed the Olan house. She felt vaguely guilty that she hadn't spoken to Diana in a while.

Maybe I'm becoming like Marquez, Summer thought. *Maybe I'm avoiding Diana because she's complicated.*

They crossed the dark lawn, which sloped gently down toward the bay. The stilt house came into view as they turned left along the retaining wall. It was a black silhouette against a star-bright sky. Summer wondered if Diver was up top on his deck. She saw nothing, but that didn't prove he wasn't there. When in doubt, Diver's instinct seemed to be to remain invisible.

She gave J.T. the tour of the house, a tour that took

all of twenty seconds as she pointed out the obvious—kitchen, bathroom, everything else.

J.T. stopped beside her bed, staring at something.

The framed picture of her family.

He picked it up gently, holding it closer for examination. Summer felt a chill tingle up her spine.

"Are these—" he asked.

"My parents," Summer acknowledged. *And maybe yours,* she added silently.

J.T. nodded solemnly. "They're a good-looking couple." He turned to face her and held the picture up next to his face. "See any family resemblance?"

He no doubt intended it as a funny question, but it came out wrong. He could not hide the pleading element in his voice.

When Summer said nothing, his self-mocking expression crumbled. Carefully, he put the picture back on the nightstand. Then, with one finger, he touched the face of Summer's mother. His brow was furrowed in concentration.

"I don't know these people," he said at last.

"You wouldn't, I guess," Summer said. "You were just two years old at the time. I mean, if it's true."

"Still," he said. "Two years old . . . Shouldn't I remember something? I remember things from when I was little, but it's all disconnected stuff, just images, bits and pieces, like anyone has. Toys. Going to get a shot at the doctor. Laughing really hard when someone was tickling me. This cool little car I had. A pair of pants that were too scratchy. There's nothing there. I don't even have any way of knowing how old I was, and those memories aren't *important* because little kids don't know what's important. I mean, when I was two I don't exactly remember who was president or what was going on in the Middle East. Kids remember dumb stuff. Falling off a swing, that's a big event."

"I'm sorry." It was all Summer could think of to say. "I don't know how we're ever going to figure this out. You and I do look alike, but you look a little like Brad Pitt too, so I don't know."

"Yeah, I've been over and over all this in my mind," J.T. said. "What do we have? I know that I'm not biologically related to my parents. I know that I couldn't find a birth certificate for myself, and I had to use a baptism certificate to get my driver's license. Why? I don't know. Then Marquez tells me that you lost a brother who would be just my age. And she says she's seen us do things or say things at the same time, as if there's some kind of psychic link."

Summer started to say something, then hesitated. What was she going to say? Are you the boy in white who keeps appearing in my dreams? That would sound slightly insane.

"What?" J.T. asked. Then he wiggled his eyebrows.

"See? I *knew* you were about to say something. Proof!"

They both laughed, the mood momentarily a little lighter.

"I was just going to ask you . . . do you ever have dreams about the past?"

He shrugged. "I don't have many dreams, I guess. Or at least when I do, I usually forget them within a minute or two of waking up."

"Oh."

"Why do you ask?" He looked at her closely.

"I don't know. They say dreams tell you things sometimes."

"If they do, then they aren't speaking very clearly to me," J.T. said.

"This is going to sound like a strange question," Summer said. "But when you were saying you remembered things from your childhood—you know, like toys and all—was one of them a red ball?"

He smiled. "A red ball? Was that what Jonathan . . . I . . . had when he, or I, disappeared?"

"No one really knows. Forget it," she said.

Silence fell between them, and J.T. returned his gaze to the picture. Summer could see he was trying to find something in it that would open up his dark past. Some explanation.

"I'm going to have to ask them, aren't I?" J.T. said softly.

There was no doubt in Summer's mind whom J.T. meant by *them*. His parents. The people he had always believed were his mother and father.

"The only problem is, do I really want to know the truth?"

Then, surprisingly, his usual devil-may-care smile was back, like the sun poking unexpectedly through storm clouds. He took Summer's hand and met her gaze. "I know one thing. I'd be proud to be your big brother."

Summer looked past him at the picture of her parents. If it was true . . .

Sixteen years of grieving would be ended. A miracle would have occurred.

"I'd be proud to be your little sister, too," Summer said.

7

Jonathan Leaves Footprints, and Diana Swings the Pendulum Just a Wee Bit Too Hard

Summer went to sleep worried that she would be haunted by some nightmare from hell involving not only small boys dressed all in white, but also Seth Warner and Sean Valletti. The idea of all those elements coming together—especially Seth and Sean—was almost enough to keep her awake.

But when she woke she remembered no dreams at all. She did, however, notice a pounding noise like the worst headache on earth. It took several seconds of blank, stupid staring before she realized it actually was pounding and not a headache.

"Who is it?" she yelled, sounding cranky.

"Are you decent?" It was Seth's voice.

"Oh. Seth? Come in!" she yelled. She did not stir from the bed, but pulled the covers higher. She was wearing her usual sleep attire—a baby-tee and boxers. She quickly turned over her pillow after noticing a drool spot. Seth might be grossed out.

The door opened and he came in, looking like a parody of a blue-collar romance hero—tool belt, tight-fitting T-shirt, well-worn and paint-splattered Levi's, clunky brown work boots.

"What, you're still in bed?" he asked incredulously.

"I couldn't get to sleep last night," Summer muttered. *Mostly because I was racked with guilt over having let Sean Valletti kiss me.*

Seth came over to the bed and sat on the edge of it. He bent down and kissed her lightly on the lips.

"I probably have morning breath," Summer said. "And speaking of morning, why are you here? Not that I'm not glad to see you."

"I told you I was coming to put molding in your bathroom and lay in a line for cable," he said. "All part of the original work order from your aunt."

"She actually said I should have cable TV down here?" Summer asked skeptically.

"Well . . . she said I should fix whatever needed fixing and do whatever needed to be done to make this place livable. And how am I going to hang out with you down here if you don't get ESPN? Don't make me choose between you and the Milwaukee Brewers."

Summer wrapped her arms around his neck and with sudden force pulled him onto the bed beside her. "If you have to choose, I'd better win." She kissed him deeply, with intensity spurred at least in part by the guilty memory of Sean.

"Why, Ms. Smith," Seth protested, "I'm only here to install your cable. What kind of guy do you think I am?"

"I don't know," Summer said in as sultry a voice as she could manage at that hour of the morning. "Are you the kind of guy who would do something really wonderful and exciting for me?"

"Yes, I am," Seth said, not fooled.

Summer collapsed onto his chest and closed her eyes. "Then make me some coffee, because I'm sleepy."

She managed to stumble to the bathroom and subject her body to toothpaste, soap, and deodorant by the time Seth had coffee ready.

She had also managed to run every possible scenario regarding the question of Sean Valletti through her head. They boiled down to two simple options: tell Seth, or don't tell Seth. If she told Seth, he might blow it all out of proportion. If she didn't tell Seth and he later found out, he was certain to blow it all out of proportion.

The unanswered question was, what was the *right* proportion?

"Thanks," she said, accepting a cup from him.

They decided to go outside. They circled the walkway that formed a narrow deck all the way around the stilt house, leaning against the railing and sipping coffee in silence for a while as they watched boat traffic move in and out of the bay. Little boats, big boats, sailboats, Jet Skis, windsurfers. It was a beautiful day, not too horribly humid, with the heat still many hours away from its afternoon peak. The sky was a perfect cornflower blue, with all the clouds gathered neatly together, far off to the east.

Frank the pelican was away from his usual perch, off for a day of dive-bombing fish. Diver was missing from his perch, too. Off early, as usual, to a day of doing whatever it was Diver did.

"So what happened to you last night?" Seth asked, yanking Summer away from her contemplation of the sky.

"What do you mean?" Summer demanded in a too-loud voice. She could feel herself blushing.

"I mean, we were going to get together after you finished working that boat party," he said. No sign that he was suspicious.

"Oh, right," Summer said. "Well, it was J.T. After we got done, which was later than we expected, he wanted to talk. You know, about all that stuff."

Seth nodded sympathetically. "How is he doing? How are *you* doing?"

"I think it's harder for him," Summer said. "Much harder. If it turns out to be true, if he is Jonathan, I gain a brother, and my parents find their long-lost son. But J.T. suddenly has to find a new place in the world. He has a new name, a new history, a new family."

Seth whistled sympathetically. "What are you guys going to do?"

"I don't know," Summer admitted. "None of this has really penetrated. I mean, it all still seems so unreal. I guess I'm just lying back and waiting to see what *he* does. I sure can't tell my parents about it. Not until it's definite."

"How about footprints?"

"Huh? Footprints?"

"Yeah. Most hospitals take a footprint when a baby is born. You know, it's like a fingerprint, except I guess with babies the fingers are too tiny to use. If you know which hospital Jonathan was born at, maybe you can send away for the records."

Summer just stared at him.

"I mean, it would tell you for sure, one way or the other. You would know once and for all whether Jonathan is alive and living right here on Crab Claw

Key. Get them to FedEx the stuff and you could have proof within a couple of days."

The first call, the first of what would be many calls, came in at ten-thirty in the morning, just after Diana had finished working out to a TV fitness show. Diana hadn't performed anything like real exercise in at least a year, perhaps more, and she found she was easily exhausted. Long before the half-hour show was over, Diana had grown sullen, spending more and more time coming up with imaginative insults to throw at the insanely perky exer-witch.

Still, she told herself, it was exercise, of a sort. A small step of progress away from lying around in bed most of the day. There were actual beads of sweat on her forehead. That had to count for something.

Her mother appeared in the doorway. She had "home" hair at the moment, which was to say hair of a normal human size, not the bouffant monstrosity she wore out in public because she thought that was what her fans expected of a successful romance novelist.

Mallory looked suspicious. "There's someone on the phone for you," she said, eyeing her daughter closely.

"Uh-huh. So?" Diana wondered if it was one of the agents from the FDLE. She hadn't told her mother about going to the police. Mallory had tried to stop her from pursuing an action against the Merricks. Partly out of justifiable fear of the Merrick millions, partly out of self-interest—the Merrick family owned a piece of Mallory's publisher.

"So he says his name is Mark DeWayne," Mallory said. "Do you know someone named Mark DeWayne?"

That wasn't the name of any of the cops Diana had met. "Never heard of him."

She levered herself up off the floor, where she had been stretching out, and went to the phone in the kitchen. Her mother followed close behind.

"Yes?"

"Is this Diana Olan?" a voice asked.

"Yes, that's me. Who is this?"

He identified himself as Mark DeWayne, a producer for *The Last Word*.

Diana met her mother's anxious gaze. *"The Last Word?"* she said clearly, enjoying the dawning look of dark worry on her mother's face. *The Last Word* was the new challenger to the more established TV tabloid shows such as *Hard Copy* and *Inside Edition.*

"Yes," Diana said in response to the next question, still holding her mother's gaze. "Yes, I *did* level certain charges, as you say. I spoke with the Florida Department of Law Enforcement the day before yesterday."

Mallory's eyes flew open wide. Her lip was trembling with suppressed rage. She seemed poised to rush forward, perhaps hang up the phone.

"And you are the daughter of Mallory Olan, the writer?"

"Yes, my mother is the famous writer," Diana said, enjoying the moment. "You're probably curious about how she's reacting to this too, right?"

Mallory froze.

"Well," Diana said, "of course my mother's been very supportive. What kind of mother would be anything but supportive?" She sent her mother a look of cold triumph. From this moment on, Diana was in charge. What could Mallory possibly do, now that everything was going public? If she failed to support her daughter, she would look like an unfeeling monster.

"I haven't decided whether I want to do any interviews," Diana said. "I mean, the FDLE guys advised me not to talk to people like you, no offense. So I'm going to have to think about it."

She listened a moment longer. One more surprise for Mallory. "Yes, there is a tape," Diana said.

Her mother rocked back, pressing her palm against the counter for support.

"A videotape," Diana said. "Sure, I can confirm that. The FDLE has a copy and I have a copy. What does it show? It shows Ross Merrick confessing, and it shows the senator trying to intimidate me."

To Diana's surprise, her mother did not faint. On the contrary, she laughed, a dry, amused, perhaps amazed sound.

A few minutes later, after repeated and increasingly annoyed refusals to sit for an interview, Diana hung up the phone.

Mallory began clapping her hands, slow, ironic applause. "You're a piece of work, aren't you?" she asked.

"Am I?"

"Oh, yes," Mallory said. "You have one of the richest, most powerful families in America shaking in its boots."

"I guess I do. Plus the other thing."

"Which is?"

"I also have one of the biggest romance writers in the country shaking in *her* boots."

Mallory bit her lip and said nothing. Diana moved close, close enough for her harsh whisper to be heard clearly. "You had your chance to decide who to support, *Mother*."

"I was only trying to protect you," Mallory protested.

Diana laughed derisively. "Sure you were. You were trying to protect me. All you cared about was the well-being of your daughter. And that's the story I'll keep telling everyone . . . which is a good thing, because if I didn't, if I told people you tried to destroy evidence because you wanted to protect your career . . . I guess after that got out, you wouldn't *have* much of a career."

Mallory took a deep, steadying breath. "Diana, whatever you think, I do love you."

"I love me too," Diana said. "Now."

Just then Summer opened the kitchen door and came in. Reading the mood, her face went from sunny to guarded in an instant.

"Is this a bad time?" Summer asked.

"No, not at all," Diana said brightly. "This is a great time."

"Hi, Aunt Mallory," Summer said.

"Summer. Well, I've barely had a chance to see you since you got here," Mallory said. "We'll have to remedy that. But right now I have a little headache."

Summer started to answer, but her aunt was already on her way out of the room.

"Sense a certain tension in the air?" Diana asked gleefully.

"Kind of," Summer answered neutrally. "Were you guys planning World War Three or something?"

Diana laughed, saw that her laughter had startled Summer, and laughed all the harder.

"I, um, just was wondering if you'd seen my video

camera," Summer said, looking mightily uncomfortable. "I couldn't find it. I use it to post a video blog."

Diana just laughed harder. "I have a very interesting story to tell you about your video camera," she said. "Come on, we'll get it, and then you and I—and why not, we'll even pick up Marquez—we'll all go shopping or something."

"Are you all right?" Summer asked skeptically.

"I'm the greatest I've ever been," Diana said. "And you know what, Summer? You helped start it all."

"Me? What did I help start?"

"Everything. You know what you said to me the day after the whole big thing at the Merrick estate? You remember, the next day? You told me thanks. For coming to make sure you were okay, and for telling you everything. *Thanks.* That's what started it."

Diana realized she was babbling, but she didn't care. Summer looked as if she was measuring the distance to the nearest exit, but that just made Diana want to laugh again.

"See, you said thanks, and I started thinking, thanks for what?"

"Because you had taken a risk to protect me," Summer said.

"Exactly. You said I was brave. And I thought about it, and after a while I started to wonder if maybe you weren't right. And then I started thinking, you know, Diana, maybe if you were brave for Summer, you could be brave for yourself, because what it all comes down to in the end is that you have absolutely no one in the world but yourself. And from that the whole answer became clear."

"What answer?"

"The answer to why I should live rather than die," Diana said simply.

"So . . ."

"The answer is revenge. Hurt everyone who ever hurt you. Hurt them worse than they hurt you. Hurt them until they never want to hurt you again."

It was obvious, really, now that she understood it.

And yet Summer was looking at her with pain in her eyes. Pain and concern.

"Come on," Diana said, "let's go do something."

"Okay," Summer said reluctantly. "Just remind me not to make you mad."

8

Hairy Chests, Tape, and Doing the Right Thing with Each

It was an unusual get-together, to say the least.

Summer, Diana, and Marquez, sunglassed, sandaled, and bare-midriffed, occupied an outdoor table on the deck of the appropriately named Marina Deck restaurant. They had before them various extravagant, rapidly wilting salads and sweating cold beverages. The sun was high in the sky, but only their bare legs stuck out from beneath the shade of the umbrella.

One of the unusual parts was the conversation, which had started with Diana's incredible tale of the video camera and moved to Summer's even more incredible tale of the underwater cave and her long-lost brother.

The other unusual part was that while Summer was behaving like herself, Diana and Marquez seemed to have switched personalities. Marquez was acting just short of sullen, while Diana, of all people, was the life of their little party, giddy, witty, flirting with the waiter, and admiring the parade of passing men in shorts and trunks and Speedos.

They were down just a little from the Crab 'n' Conch, overlooking the marina. The large boat—Sean Valletti's uncle's boat—was still parked at the far end of the pier.

"Footprints," Diana said, nodding her head sagely. "Sounds like a good idea to send for them. Seth is always very practical that way. The kind of guy who's good with his hands, if you know what I mean, and, Summer, I'm sure you know what I mean." Diana wiggled her eyebrows suggestively.

Summer exchanged a look with Marquez. Yes, Diana was definitely acting strangely.

"You know, Summer, I thought for a while there that I might take a quick pass at Seth myself," Diana chatted away. "I mean, he is cute, isn't he?"

"I think so," Summer said darkly.

"He has a better behind than anything I've seen here on the boardwalk." Diana laughed. "Don't worry, just kidding, Summer. I've decided against that." She took a long sip of her virgin strawberry daiquiri. "But now that I'm back, well, I'm *back*. Just because Adam was a disaster doesn't mean I should become a nun."

"I'm sure the sisters at the convent will breathe a sigh of relief," Marquez muttered. "Do you have a guy in mind? Or will this be someone you call from the fiery pits with a pentagram and a Black Mass?"

"That's better, *Maria*," Diana said patronizingly, patting Marquez's knee. "See, Summer? *Maria's* finally waking up."

Marquez made a halfhearted attempt to stab Diana's hand with a straw.

"Actually, there is a guy—" Diana began.

Summer cut her off with a karate chop in the air. "Shh. Turn around. Don't look!" She turned away from the boardwalk, rested her elbows on the table, and cradled her head in her hands.

"Where? What are we looking at?" Diana demanded, rising from her chair to look around.

"I said, *don't* look!" Summer hissed.

"Oh, I know what she's hiding from," Marquez said, with a glint of her usual mischief. But to Summer's relief, Marquez too shielded her face from view.

"Now, *there* is a specimen," Diana said. "Great shoulders."

"Diana. Will. You. Sit. Down?" Summer said through gritted teeth.

Diana sat down abruptly. But it was too late. Sean

had spotted her, and from spotting her, had spotted Summer.

"Summer!" he yelled, plowing through a passing flock of in-line skaters.

"What am I going to say?" Summer asked Marquez. "He's going to ask me out."

Marquez shrugged.

"Pretty sure of yourself, aren't you?" Diana asked grumpily. "What am I? Skank woman?"

"No, you're just schizo," Marquez said. "Look, Summer knows this guy from back in Mootown."

"Hey, Summer, I almost didn't see you," Sean said as he arrived. Instantly he bent over and placed a quick kiss on her cheek. Then he grabbed a vacant chair and pulled it over to the table, sitting between Summer and Diana.

He was wearing trunks and no shirt, still Minnesota pale but reddening. Summer noticed that he had actual chest hair. She had not encountered much chest hair before, and it disturbed her a little. Seth was completely smooth. Boyish. Sean managed to look as if he was ten years older somehow.

"Sean Valletti, this is Marquez, and Diana Olan. Diana is my cousin."

"You're one of the waitresses from last night, right?" Sean asked Marquez. "What kind of a name is Marquez?"

"Japanese," Marquez said.

"Oh, I get it," Sean said after a moment's hesitation. He turned his attention to Diana. "You two are cousins, huh? You don't look at all alike."

"Well, we're not biologically related," Diana explained. "I mean, Summer's father is my mother's brother, but my mother was adopted, so, see, no actual blood relation."

Sean looked doubtful. "Are you pulling my leg? Some kind of a joke, right?"

"No, it's true," Summer said. She was shifting away from him slightly and glancing over her shoulder every few seconds, hoping that Seth was not done with his work, and that if he *was* done, he had not decided to go for a walk by the marina.

"I didn't know that," Marquez said. She made a gesture of relief. "Thank God. I couldn't figure out how good and evil could come from the same family tree like that."

"So, Summer," Sean said, "we on for the Bacchanal?"

"Um . . ." Summer began.

Marquez and Diana both waited attentively. Sean smiled his toothy smile and unconsciously rippled the muscles of his chest as he leaned close.

"Um, I may have to work that night. I'll have to see," Summer temporized.

Sean surprised her by taking her hand between both of his. "Try hard, okay? I feel like I had to come all the way here to realize what I was missing back home, you know? But now that we're both here, why not?"

"I thought you were seeing Liz Block," Summer said, trying again to find a graceful way to resolve everything without having to tell him no. Actually having to tell Sean Valletti no was not something she had ever expected to do. She wasn't any more prepared for it than she was for blowing off Zac Efron.

Sean waved his hand dismissively. "History. I had to end that. I mean, she's sweet and all, but she's not very interesting. To be honest, it was because she was great-looking, you know?" He smiled a dazzling smile. "But you . . . you have the looks and the brains."

"Thanks," Summer said, blushing in a way she hoped was invisible in the shade of the umbrella.

"So make it happen, all right?" Sean said. He got to his feet. "Gotta go now. Nice to meet everyone." He pointed an index finger at Summer. "You and me at the big party."

And then he was gone.

Marquez and Diana both sipped their drinks and said nothing.

"All right, *what*?" Summer demanded angrily.

"I didn't say anything," Diana protested. "Did you say anything, Marquez?"

"Not me."

"Look, what was I supposed to do?" Summer

pleaded. "He's *Sean Valletti*. He's the cutest guy in my school. Every girl in school dreams about him. I had a crush on him for years."

"I can see why," Diana admitted. "Great body. Great hair. Great face. I'm undecided on the chest hair."

"I kind of like the chest hair," Marquez said. "I mean, the way he has it—mostly on his chest, not on his stomach or on his shoulders or anything gross."

"He's not exactly a genius," Diana said.

"But that's good, not bad," Marquez said. "You don't want a guy who's too smart. J.T. is too smart for his own good. Always analyzing everything and getting all confused. What you want is a guy who's just good-looking and basically sweet."

"Like Diver," Marquez and Diana said at exactly the same moment.

"I mean, *like* Diver, as one possible example," Diana said quickly, blushing furiously. "Not necessarily Diver himself. He was just the first example that came to mind."

"Uh-huh," Marquez said. She smiled and shook her head. "I'd forget about Mr. Diver. Getting through to the mysterious Mr. Diver is like nailing Jell-O to the wall. Whenever you think maybe something is going on, he's out of there."

"You're probably right," Diana said neutrally.

"Whereas, say, Sean Valletti is right out front, hairy chest and all," Marquez said.

"I'm going to tell him no," Summer said defensively. "I'm *not* going out with Sean. I am totally committed to Seth. I'm going out with him tonight. It's just . . ."

"The end-of-August thing?" Marquez suggested. "Maybe you should think about it. I mean, pretty soon Seth goes one way and you . . . *and* Sean . . . go another way."

"Ah." Diana nodded, understanding. "I get it. Either the summer ends with tearful farewells and broken hearts, or it ends with Summer arriving back home with the coolest guy in her school. Wow."

"Both of you shut up. I'm not even thinking about that," Summer said, annoyed and impatient, as she often was when she was lying.

Diana felt strangely exhausted by the day spent with Summer and Marquez. She had the feeling she might have talked too much, revealed too much of herself, and that kind of thing always gave her the willies. Sometimes, like the song said, she gave herself the creeps.

There was a surprise waiting for her when she got back home. A very large white van was parked just down the street. As she drove past it and pulled into her driveway, two people literally leaped from the back, followed by a third a few seconds later.

By the time she had turned off the ignition and opened the door of her little Jetta, a camera was in her face, a light brighter than the sun was in her eyes, and a woman seemed to be trying to force-feed her a microphone.

"Diana! Diana!" the woman shouted. "Are you Diana Olan? I'm Wendy Rackman, *The Last Word*. You are Diana Olan, right?"

Diana squinted into the light and said, "No, I'm Maria Marquez. I'm just a friend of Diana's."

The reporter sagged a little. "Oh. Okay, what do you know about this situation between Diana Olan and Senator Merrick?"

Diana shrugged. "Look, I told your producer on the phone I wasn't sure if I was going to talk to reporters," she said, abandoning the lame pretense.

"So you *are* Diana Olan?" The reporter came alive again.

"Yes. Now would you go away?" Diana turned to go inside.

"Diana, Ross Merrick says you're just an embittered former girlfriend of his brother, Adam, and that you tried to extort money from them with a made-up story about an attempted rape."

Diana stopped with her hand on the doorknob.

Obviously the reporter was simply trying to goad her. And just as obviously it had worked.

"If you don't talk to us, Diana, we have to go with Ross's version of events. We'll have no other choice," the reporter said.

Diana shrugged. "There's Ross's version and there's my version, and then there's the videotape. So I guess when the cops release the videotape, the truth will be obvious to everyone."

"Diana, the Merrick family's lawyers say they can keep that videotape out of court, if this case even goes to trial."

"What do you mean?" Diana asked sharply.

"Diana," the reporter said, affecting a sincere tone, "evidence can be suppressed by smart lawyers sometimes. But no one can stop the free press from showing the world the truth. If you give us a copy of the tape, we can have it on the air by tonight. After that, no one will ever be able to suppress the truth."

"I'm *not* going to let you have the tape," Diana said firmly. "I told the police I wouldn't." She had also promised Adam.

Just then the door opened. Mallory came out, hurriedly made up but camera-ready. "Diana, why don't you come inside?"

"Ms. Olan, your daughter's story needs to be told," the reporter said.

"I'll handle this," Diana told her mother, making no attempt to hide her annoyance at the intrusion.

"I think you should talk to me first," Mallory said.

Diana looked uncertainly from the predatory reporter to her mother. "What, you're offering to help me? Why?"

"Excuse us a moment," Mallory told the reporter. She pulled Diana inside and closed the door.

"You don't really understand what you've unleashed, do you?" Mallory asked. "All you're thinking about now is lashing out. You want to hurt the Merricks, fine, but they won't just lie down and play dead."

"What can they do to me?" Diana asked.

"There's an old saying, Diana, something like, 'If you strike at a king, make sure you kill him.' The point being, make sure you don't leave him a chance to hit back."

"Are you telling me I *should* let them see the videotape?" Diana asked, incredulous.

Mallory nodded, her face grim. "It's about who gets to write the story, Diana. The Merricks know how to use the media. They are professionals. Either the Merricks write the story, or *you* write the story. The tape will destroy them."

"I don't get this. Why are you suddenly on my side?"

"I've always been on your side," her mother said wearily. "Whatever you may think about me. I was—I am—afraid of the Merricks. Afraid for me, true, but also for you." She smiled crookedly. "I'm sorry if that isn't pure enough for you. I know a perfect mother would never think of herself at all, but I'm not a perfect mother. I had to think of what this could do to my career. And I also had to think about what all this could mean for you. Wanting to hurt people, even those who hurt you, is a bad thing."

"How else can you keep them from hurting someone else?" Diana demanded.

Her mother shook her head. "I don't know. It's just that when I saw my only daughter about to get into a fight, I wanted to stop it. But now it's too late. It's already begun, so now you have no choice but to try your best to win."

Diana hesitated. "I . . . Adam. You remember when he came to see me? I promised him I wouldn't give the tape to the media."

"Look, it's your choice, Diana," her mother said. She smiled ruefully. "This is a bad time for me to suddenly realize that you're an adult, but this is an adult choice. The tape will hurt them very badly."

Diana considered this for a moment. The image that came to mind was of the pills she had, again and again, counted out into her hand. The pills she had planned to take to end her life.

"I want to hurt them," she said at last.

9

Video Blog

So in any case, Jennifer, now you can see why I haven't posted a video lately. Like I said, this whole summer vacation keeps going off in one unusual direction after another. I thought I'd be down here all summer and have nothing to tell you except how my tan was doing. It's good, by the way. I have achieved major, definite tan lines.

But, see, I figured that would be all I'd have to tell you about. That, and maybe I'd meet a guy or something. Instead, I keep meeting additional guys, which brings me to the one thing I haven't told you yet. Guess who is down here on Crab Claw Key? If I gave you a week to guess, you'd never get it right.

Sean Valletti. Yes, *the* Sean Valletti. He's down here with his uncle, who has this huge boat. But the amazing thing is that he asked me out.

Yes, Sean Valletti asked me out, and he even kissed me.

I will pause for a moment while you pick yourself back up off the floor, since I bet you fainted.

He wants me to go to this big festival of a dead pirate called the Bacchanal. They say it's like Mardi Gras, kind of. Anyway, Sean actually asked me to go to it with him.

Not that I'm going, of course. I mean, I am totally and completely in love with Seth. Really.

The only reason I didn't tell Sean no right away is because . . . well, he *is* Sean Valletti, right? Liz Block and Annie Bashears and that Elise girl, all those supposedly popular girls, all those cheerleader creatures, would totally have to *die* if I showed up back in Bloomington with Sean. Summer Smith and Sean Valletti? No one would even believe it if they didn't see it.

It would be like, "Hah, so there!" Like I was magically transported from the level of "Oh, she's not bad, but she's kind of into getting good grades" to "Whoa, she's going with Sean Valletti."

Actually, though, I'm not sure I like Sean that much. He's cute, but that's about all he is. So even if we broke up after we got back to Bloomington, it would be okay.

Seth is a whole different story, Jen. I mean, Seth makes me sick. No, wait, that came out wrong. What I meant was, sometimes I'm lying in bed at night and I can't go right to sleep and I start thinking about Seth . . . and I just really wish he were there. I mean, in this powerful way. Like if I think about him ever breaking up with me, I get a sick feeling.

That's what I meant by making me sick. I feel that way right now, talking to you about it, even thinking about it. Kind of like really bad cramps combined with running too much in gym.

Marquez . . . I've told you how Marquez isn't exactly subtle . . . anyway, she keeps reminding me about the end of summer, when I have to go home. What am I supposed to do then? Seth and I are going to be at the airport, right where we met and where he first kissed me, and I'm going to get on one plane, and he's going to get on another, and it's going to be the worst day of my life.

See? I'm starting to get all weepy just thinking about it.

I should have just stayed home for the summer. I would have been miserable, but not *that* miserable. Not to be all psychological or anything, but maybe that's why I haven't told Sean to go away. I mean, maybe part of me *wants* to keep Seth at arm's length. It's just so totally superficial with Sean it's almost a relief. . . . I don't know. It's stupid. Because in the end I'm in love with Seth, and summer's almost over, and I am going to be totally destroyed.

Still, the thing I keep thinking is, how can I really be sure what's going to happen in the future? I mean, did I think I was suddenly going to run into Jonathan? A guy who might be my own brother reappears from nowhere. That's practically a miracle. So who knows, right? Who knows what could happen by the end of summer? Maybe it will be something I haven't even thought about.

10

A Little Night Music

Toward the end of the shift, when the orders from the waitresses had slowed to a trickle and the cleaning up of the kitchen had begun, J.T. picked a CD and slipped it into the CD player the cooks kept on top of a reach-in refrigerator.

He cranked the volume to seven and hit Play. Offspring doing "Bad Habit." It was one of the kitchen staff's standards. They favored seriously hard-edged rock at the end of a tough night. The worse the night, the wilder the music.

Skeet, one of the other cooks, heard the opening bars and gave J.T. a wink. "It wasn't *that* bad a night," she said.

"Oh, Skeet, you think every night is a Melissa Etheridge night," J.T. teased. He waltzed over, took Skeet by the waist, and drew her into a completely incongruous dance, as if they were keeping time to a different piece of music. "First time you've danced with a guy, Skeet?"

"No, only I prefer guys with some idea of rhythm," Skeet said.

J.T. released her, laughing. "Come on, Tom," he said, inviting the fry cook to dance. "Let's go."

"Yeah, when pigs fly," Tom said.

"No one wants to dance," J.T. complained. Then he spotted Lianne coming through the swinging doors. "Lianne! Dance with me." He snapped his fingers. "I got dancin' feet."

"Dance to this?" Lianne said, turning up her nose.

"Skeet! Stick in Rihanna," J.T. ordered. Seconds later Rihanna came on. But still Lianne refused.

"J.T., we're at work," she said. She gave him a peck on the cheek and went back to the dining room just as Marquez passed through the door.

J.T. retreated a bit, stepping back behind the line and pretending to go back to work. Marquez started to do side work, dipping tartar sauce into little plastic cups, but J.T. knew her too well to think she could ignore the music. Within seconds he could see the effect—a motion beginning with her head, swaying just slightly at first, translated down her neck to her shoulders, her bottom, her legs, topped off by a little twirl with the tartar sauce spoon still in her hand.

J.T. smiled ruefully. The future Harvard girl. The future corporate lawyer.

There wasn't anything wrong in dancing with his former girlfriend, was there? After all, a moment earlier he'd been dancing with Skeet. He'd even asked Tom, although the fry cook was unlikely to be seen as a threat by Lianne. No, he should stick to his work.

Marquez was now dancing far more than she was filling cups of tartar sauce.

J.T. whipped off his apron. Screw it. He had dancin' feet. What was he supposed to do?

He took the spoon from Marquez and set it down.

"Crank it, Skeet," he said.

By the time Lianne reappeared in the kitchen, Marquez was up on the stainless steel counter, hands in the air over her head, hips thrusting, hair loose and flying, doing death-defying moves. J.T. was dancing more sedately below her, choosing to keep his feet on the ground.

"Is this really—" Lianne began, but the music drowned her out.

She caught J.T.'s eye. He gave her a wan grin and tried to draw her into the moment. But Lianne just looked angry and hurt.

Skeet, sensing the mood, turned the music down. Marquez opened her eyes, annoyed. "What are you— Oh," she said, spotting Lianne. She hopped down from the counter, flushed and perspiring. "Why, Lianne. Thank goodness you got here in time. We were all in danger of having fun."

"Well, that's so *you*, isn't it?" Lianne said. "Always there for the fun, and out the door anytime things get serious."

"Oh, shut up, Lianne," Marquez said dismissively.

"Hey, that's not called for, Marquez," J.T. said, quietly but firmly.

"What? You're defending little Miss Mood-killer?" Marquez demanded.

J.T. told himself just to let it go. Marquez could be volatile when embarrassed, and she had quite a mean tongue when she was mad. But by the same token, he couldn't stand by and let her dump on Lianne.

"Marquez, look, we had some fun, let's not start something," J.T. said.

"I'm not starting anything," Marquez fired back. "It's this life-size Barbie here—"

"Come on, Marquez," J.T. began.

Lianne put a hand on his arm. "Let her say whatever she wants," she said, looking at Marquez with contempt. "It's all she can do—flirt and party and be a witch. It doesn't bother me. I feel sorry for her. She has to put on a big show for everyone to distract them from the fact that she's a cold, selfish person with nothing inside."

"You know nothing about me, Lianne," Marquez said scornfully.

"I know one thing. J.T. is with *me* now because you couldn't be bothered to be there for him."

"I think everyone has said enough," J.T. said.

"Everyone but you, J.T.," Lianne said, suddenly turning on him.

He realized with a shock that there were tears in her eyes. It had never occurred to him that Lianne *could* cry. A quiver had appeared in her voice. "You haven't said the thing you need to say, J.T. You need to tell Marquez it's over, for good, forever. You need to give her up."

J.T. felt stunned. The entire room was quiet. Even the dishwasher was between cycles. "Marquez knows I'm with you, Lianne," he said.

"Yeah. That's why I come in and find you dancing with her," Lianne sneered. "And when you see me you get this bad-little-boy look on your face, like I'm the teacher who caught you throwing spit wads."

"That's not it at all," J.T. protested.

"Then tell her it's over, J.T., because she knows she still has a hold on you," Lianne said sadly. "Marquez isn't stupid. But neither am I."

"I think it's pretty clear, given everything," J.T. tried again.

"I'm out of here," Lianne said suddenly. She bit her lip. "I'll get someone to do my side work for me. I'll be at home, J.T. I guess you'll either come over or you won't."

"Oh, I don't even believe that," Seth said, disgusted. "That's pathetic. They call him out? That was out? He was so safe." He pointed the remote control and clicked off the TV.

"We lost, right?" Summer said, playing dumb. Seth was sitting on her bed. Summer was lying back, her head in his lap.

"Only by three runs," Seth said glumly.

"And we care deeply about this because . . ."

"Because Milwaukee is my team," Seth said.

"But you live in Eau Claire, and isn't Eau Claire actually closer to Minneapolis than Milwaukee?"

"Yes," he agreed patiently. "But that's in Minnesota, not Wisconsin. Besides, the Brewers are so pathetic they need every fan they can get. The Twins have plenty of fans. They don't need me the way the Brewers do. Especially this season, because they really, truly suck."

"Isn't there anything I can do to make you feel better?" Summer said, wiggling her eyebrows suggestively.

"Hmm, I don't know. You don't happen to know any great unemployed pitchers, do you?"

"Fine, you had your chance." She started to get up, but Seth caught her arm and pulled her back.

He put his arms around her, drawing her close, then closer, till her lips touched his. As always, his kisses started sweet and gentle. But each new contact was more intense, more urgent, until soon she was gasping for air, feeling that she wanted to devour him, to go beyond anything their lips could accomplish, to enter his soul and make one person out of two.

She withdrew, holding him away with a hand pressed against his mouth. Her breath was shuddery, her face burning hot. Her mind was a confusion of thoughts and images—none of which her mother would have approved of.

"I wish I had a couch," she muttered.

"What's wrong with the bed?" Seth said in a low voice.

"It's a *bed*, that's what's wrong with it," Summer said.

"You know I'd never ask you to do anything you don't want to do," he said, even sounding sincere. "It doesn't matter if it's a couch or a bed. All you have to do is say no."

She buried her face in the hollow of his neck.

"I know. That's not the problem. Saying no is the problem."

He lifted her head and kissed her again. His hand touched her chin, her throat. He moved it down a little farther and—

"No!" Summer said, pushing him away.

"Now, see? That wasn't so hard," he said, grinning. "You say no just fine. Unfortunately."

"It's so easy for guys," Summer complained. "With you it's like an on-off switch. You go till someone stops you, but it always ends up being the girl's decision. We're always the ones who have to have self-control."

"That's not true," Seth protested. "I have to have self-control too. I mean, I wanted to start making out with you an hour ago, but no, I knew I wanted to see the game, so I controlled myself until it was over."

Summer smiled at him affectionately. Then she hit him over the head with a pillow.

She got up and went to her tiny kitchen. On the way she turned on her radio. "You want something to eat?" she called over her shoulder.

"What do you have?"

"Um . . ." She opened her refrigerator. "Milk, yogurt, and wilted lettuce." She checked her cupboard. "Cheerios. Instant grits. Sorry—I figured that since this is technically the South, I should try grits. Ah-hah! Pop-Tarts."

"Pop-Tarts! All right," he said enthusiastically. He came to join her as she loaded the toaster. "Life. It just doesn't get any better than this. You and Pop-Tarts."

"While they last," Summer said. Instantly she regretted it, but the thought had popped into her head and straight out through her mouth.

"What do you mean?" he asked. "We're low on Pop-Tarts?"

"Nothing," she said. But suddenly she felt terribly sad. Probably just the result of coming down off the intense high of making out.

But Seth wasn't going to let it go. "Summer, what's the matter?"

"I really . . . really like this. Being with you. Being here. Being here with you," she said. Tears were filling her eyes, and that annoyed her because she was ruining a perfectly good night.

The Pop-Tarts popped up from the toaster, but before she could grab them, Seth turned her around to face him. "Summer, talk to me. Look at you, you're crying."

"No, I'm not," she said, wiping at her tears. "It's just . . . the end of the summer."

"What about the end of the summer?"

"It's going to come soon, isn't it? Then no more—" She swept her hand around the room. "No more any of this. I'll be in school. In Bloomington. You'll be in school in Eau Claire. I don't even have a car," she said.

"What does a car—"

"In case we ever wanted to see each other, duh. Or did you not even think about that? Are you just assuming we'll never ever be able to see each other again, because I—" She began sobbing, and her words were swallowed up.

"What are you talking about?" he said. "Why are you worrying about the end of August? We have four weeks till then."

"So I shouldn't worry about what will happen because it's a long way off?" she demanded, having brought her vocal cords under some control.

"We could . . . I don't know, we could die tomorrow," he said, looking beleaguered. "I could get crushed by a meteor or something. You could get run over by a bus."

"A meteor?"

"Jeez, Summer, I'm just saying we've barely gotten together, so don't start trying to figure out the whole future." He was compulsively running his hand through his hair and shrugging, both of which were things he did when he was confused.

It wasn't the answer she had been looking for. He sounded almost indifferent. No, that wasn't fair—not indifferent, just puzzled, as if the problem had never occurred to him. He looked as if he'd just been asked to define the entire nature of the universe.

Summer took the Pop-Tarts out of the toaster and handed one to him. "Careful, they're a little hot."

"Summer, you know I love you," he said.

"I love you, too," she said in a voice choked by surging tears.

"So everything will work out." He took a bite of his pastry.

But at that moment Summer had the clearest mental image, almost a vision—Seth kissing her one last time in the airport, with tears and promises to get together every chance they had. Slowly he would walk away. He would pause at the gate, turn, and mouth the words *I love you,* and she would mouth the same words back.

And the terrible thing would be that they would both mean them.

Marquez told herself at least a million times that she didn't care. That the last thing she wanted was for J.T. to show up. He was with Lianne, and that was fine with her. He was trouble. Nothing but trouble and heartbreak.

He didn't even respect her. Trying to tell her how she should live her life. Trying to tell her what she was and what she wasn't.

Basically, he was a jerk. Basically, he could drop dead. Basically, he could disappear without a trace and she wouldn't care, because there was absolutely no way that he could ever, conceivably, by the strangest fate she could imagine, ever, ever fit into the life she saw for herself.

Although she hated to think that Lianne was with him at that moment. Not that it was about Marquez wanting *him*. That wasn't it. She just didn't want Lianne to have the satisfaction. Calling Marquez a cold, selfish person with nothing inside—for that, Lianne deserved to be lying alone in her room thinking J.T. really had dumped her to be with Marquez.

Hah. That would show her.

Marquez fell asleep after a while, listening to a Damien Rice CD—haunting, wispy songs that were like some halfway station between waking and sleep.

She woke suddenly, eyes wide, with the realization that someone had just come into her room. "Who's there?" she demanded of the darkness.

"Me," he said.

She relaxed, sagging back against her pillows. "How did you get in?"

"Key. I remembered where you guys keep the esstra key."

"I'll have to remember to hide it somewhere new."

His speech was slurred. Not extremely, but noticeably. He had been drinking. Marquez heard him fumbling around in the dark. Probably looking for the light switch.

"Don't turn on the lights, I'm in bed," she said.

"'Fraid I'll see your jammies?"

"I don't wear jammies," she said coolly. She felt around in the pile of clothes near her bed for an oversize T-shirt and pulled it over her head. "J.T., why are you here?" She could barely make out the hint of his shape, still beside the door, probably leaning against the wall. Half ready to topple over and pass out. Wonderful.

"I wanted to see it," he answered.

"See what?"

"The place where you painted out my name, erased me," he said. "You tole me it was erased."

"J.T., just go away," Marquez said, alarmed now. She *had* told him she'd taken his name off the wall. Unfortunately she had, for reasons that escaped her now, painted him in again. If he saw that, he would get the wrong idea.

Suddenly the overhead lights snapped on. Marquez snatched at her sheets. J.T. was definitely drunk. He was swaying like a tree in a gale. He had on shorts and a T-shirt and, for some reason, a gray raincoat. His hair was a mess. He blinked like a mole in the light, shading his eyes with his hand.

"Jeez, that's bright," he said.

"It just seems that way because your pupils are probably twice their normal size," Marquez said.

"I've been drinking. Beer. Also, I've been doing sad things. So don't be all cranky with me, Marquez," he said.

He pried himself away from the wall and walked to the middle of the room. For a long time he just stared. Stared and swayed. He swayed far enough that Marquez leaped out of bed to grab his arm and keep him from falling over.

"You said you painted over me," he said.

"I did," Marquez said. "But it was just this big, empty hole, so I had to put your name back in. Temporarily. Until I can think of something else."

J.T. snorted. "You're such a liar. You lie about everything. You lie about that." He pointed to his name on the wall, huge, 3-D letters that made it the single biggest feature of the mural, bigger by far than it had originally been. "Plus, you lie about . . . everything."

Marquez was tempted to let him go and watch him fall on his face. Instead she walked him over to the bed, lined him up, and with no unnecessary gentleness, pushed him straight back. He fell spread-eagled, faceup.

"I broke up with Lianne," he said to the ceiling.

"Why did you do that?" Marquez demanded, There was a small refrigerator under the Formica and chrome counter. She retrieved a Coke and popped the top.

"She cried," J.T. said, ignoring Marquez's question. "Also cursed."

"Well, you probably shouldn't have broken up with her," Marquez said, feeling guilty and vaguely triumphant, and then feeling guilty that she felt triumphant.

"Had to," J.T. said. "She wanned to know if I was over you. Guess what the answer was?"

"Drink some of this," Marquez said, sitting beside him and pressing the Coke into his hand. "A little caffeine. Sorry, I don't have a coffee machine here."

He sat up partway and took a long swig.

"I'm messed up," he said sadly. "I don't know what to do anymore. One minute all happy. The next . . . messed up."

Marquez could not think of anything to say.

"I . . . I mean, I don't even know *who* I am anymore. J.T.? Jonathan? I don't know."

"You're whoever you always were," Marquez said impatiently. "But you know, maybe you should see a shrink or something. Get some help."

He nodded and smiled to himself over some secret joke. "Yeah, I need help. I need help. I need someone."

"J.T., look, you know I'm not good at—"

"Not *you*," J.T. sneered. "I don't need you."

"Then what the—"

"Her," J.T. said. He swept the room with his hand, then pointed at the painted walls. "Her, that's who I need. I need the girl who painted all this. Not you."

Marquez swallowed hard. Typical J.T. He just *had* to make everything complicated when it could be so simple. He just *had* to pick at everything.

"Look, J.T., once and for all, I'm me, that's me too, but I have a right to be whatever I choose. I'm not going to be some loser artsy-fartsy type selling crappy paintings to tourists on the boardwalk. So get off it."

But he was looking at the wall, smiling and nodding, ignoring her. "That girl, she's the one I love. She's the one I can't forget. I saw her once, dressed in this gown, this fancy dress, painting and . . . just gone, just not even part of the world anymore. Did you know that?" He focused his bleary gaze on her. His breath reeked of beer. "Did you know I was there and saw you that one time?"

"No," Marquez lied. Why *had* she let him watch her?

To her amazement, since she would not have thought he could walk, he got up and went to the door. But he didn't leave. He switched off the light.

"There. Now I don't have to see *her*. I better go."

"J.T., you're too drunk to make it home. You'll fall in front of a truck and get run over."

"I'll bounce right off," he said, giggling incongruously.

Marquez grabbed him rudely by the lapels of his raincoat and marched him back to the bed. She pulled the coat off and pushed him onto the bed.

Under the cover of darkness she unwrapped her sheet partway and spread it over both of them.

For a while she thought he might just have fallen asleep. But then he rolled closer and laid his arm across her stomach. And then, quite naturally, he kissed her.

It was not a great kiss. He was sloppy and smelly.

"I love you," he said.

"Sleep it off," she said roughly. "You'll feel better in the morning."

He held her. "I feel better now," he said.

"J.T., let me just make this clear. I'm not going to make love to you," she whispered.

"I don't need you to *make* love," he said. "Just love me."

Marquez sighed. "Like I have a choice," she said. "Jerk."

He buried his face in her soft explosion of curls and whispered in her ear, "You're not so tough. Just say it."

"J.T., just go to sleep. You're drunk, and you're getting on my nerves," Marquez said irascibly. She closed her eyes. "Okay. So I love you. Big deal. You make one wrong move, and I break your arm."

Summer Lies to Herself, While Dolphins Tell the Truth

The woman on TV was telling a talk show host a complicated story having to do with marrying her husband's best friend while she was still married to her husband. But it was okay, she said, because she'd only done it to get close to the live-in girlfriend of the second husband, because they shared an interest in alien abductions. Both of them had at one time been abducted love slaves of the Venusians, who, according to the woman, were really pretty nice people, once you got past the extra eye.

Summer was ironing her work uniform, messing up the annoying pleats because she was paying too much attention to the show. There were footsteps on the deck outside, and Summer found herself hoping it wasn't Seth. Her hair was half done, she was wearing a ratty robe over a ratty T-shirt (having fallen behind on laundry), and besides, she wanted to learn more about the Venusians.

"Who is it?"

"Diana."

"Diana?" Summer said under her breath. "Come in!" she yelled.

Diana was elegant, as always, dressed in a sarong skirt that seemed to be wrapped over a one-piece bathing suit. The striking thing, though, was the big blond wig. She looked like a cool *Glamour* model wearing Dolly Parton's hair.

"Can I come in?" she asked.

"Sure. What's up?" Summer asked, looking pointedly at the hair.

"What do you mean, what's up? Don't you watch TV?" Diana asked.

"We watched baseball last night."

"Too bad. Should have watched *The Last Word*. Suddenly I'm famous, or infamous, or something." She took off the wig and looked at it with amusement. "Nice, huh? It's Mallory's. There are six TV trucks parked out in the driveway. I thought they might spot me coming down here." She tossed the wig on Summer's bed.

"Yeah, I noticed something going on out there. They must have run that tape you gave them, huh?" Summer said.

"Good guess," Diana said dryly. "Now it's like a sleaze convention in our driveway, and I have someplace I have to go—without them following me."

"You think they'd actually follow you?"

"Mallory says I should count on it. I'm refusing to say anything more to anyone. She says that otherwise it will look as if I'm trying to exploit the situation." Diana rolled her eyes expressively. "It turns out Mallory is pretty smart about this kind of stuff. I should have known."

"Jeez, Diana," Summer said, "isn't this kind of weirding you out?"

Diana shrugged. "A little, I guess. But it's been a weird year for me. It is gross, yes. Like now the entire country knows who I am, and that Ross tried to rape me. They disguised my face, you know, with one of those fuzzy spots, but that just increases the desire of these other creeps to get a picture."

Summer felt a little overwhelmed. She pulled back her curtain and looked in the direction of the house. Of course, all she could see were the trees that always blocked the land view. Diana seemed cool and in control, but then, Diana had seemed perfectly cool and in control at a time when, Summer now knew, she was actively planning to commit suicide. Cool and in control didn't necessarily mean anything.

"Jeez, Diana," Summer said again, having thought of nothing better to say. This was a situation completely outside her experience.

Diana began unwrapping her skirt. "Anyway, look, I've got places to go, people to see. I want to use one of the Jet Skis under the house."

"Well, they are yours," Summer pointed out.

"As a matter of fact, I was going to say you'd better come with me. That is, if you're going into work. Those guys will jump any warm body that appears, and you'd have to walk right through them. I mean, unless you want to get famous too."

"No," Summer said quickly, alarmed by the idea. She hadn't told her parents about her own near run-in with Ross Merrick. It was just the first of an ever-expanding list of things she hadn't told her parents in their weekly phone calls. She could only hope they hadn't somehow accidentally watched any of the tabloid shows the night before.

"The last time I rode that stupid Jet Ski I was with Marquez, and we ran out of gas," Summer said.

"Come on," Diana said, ignoring her protest. "If you're coming with me, I've got to go." She checked her watch. "I'm going to go to the marina and borrow a car."

Summer began folding her uniform neatly. She wrapped it in a plastic trash bag. "What is this place you have to go to?"

"None of your business," Diana said, softening the harsh statement with a reluctant smile.

They descended through the trapdoor in the floor, and minutes later were skimming across the choppy little waves at what seemed like a hundred miles an hour. It was only her second time, but Summer felt like an old pro on the machine now, flexing her knees to absorb each new shock as the Jet Ski went airborne and crashed, sending up a white plume of warm salty spray. It meant arriving at work wearing a bathing suit, with her hair tangled and salty, but that was nothing very unusual at the Crab 'n' Conch.

And there was such sheer pleasure in flying along under the bright yellow sun, her legs stinging from the force of the water, hot wind whipping her hair, that she wondered why she didn't get to work this way every day.

Diana rode just ahead, her own hair a dark tornado, pushing the speed ever upward, past the point where Summer cared to keep up.

They arrived too soon at the marina, both slowing to meld with the busy to-ing and fro-ing of other craft: white-winged sailboats, colorful windsurfers, and needle-sharp cigarette boats.

Summer glanced over at Mr. Holland's boat. Sean was not on deck, and she felt vaguely relieved. Diana had disappeared, going her own way in the small maze of floating docks.

Summer parked just below the Crab 'n' Conch, tying up the little Jet Ski with what she hoped was professional-looking confidence.

She climbed the ladder, carrying her bag, and went in the back door of the restaurant, where she was promptly informed that she was not on the schedule to work that day. She protested that she was, but a check of the schedule showed that she was not.

Back outside, feeling a little lost since Marquez *did* have to work and Summer had no plans for the day, she felt a shadow fall over her, blocking the sun.

"Hi," Sean said. "Going in to work?"

"Yes," Summer said quickly. She was proud of herself. She was blowing him off. She was blowing off Sean Valletti.

"Cool, then you can wait on me," he said.

"Well, actually . . ." she said, shifting gears, trying again to get rid of him, "I *was* going into work, but I got my schedule screwed up."

"Better yet." He grinned. "In fact, perfect. I have one of my uncle's cars and I was thinking of driving down to Key West, maybe shop for something for my mom. Her birthday's coming up, and it would be cool to have a girl's advice on what to get."

"I guess I could do that," Summer said.

It sounded perfectly innocent, and she *had* tried twice to get rid of him. She was just going to help Sean shop for a present for his mom. No one could possibly imply that it meant anything. Some article of clothing, Summer thought, yes, that would be best. That way Mrs. Valletti would wear it when she went to PTA stuff, and Summer would be able to point it out to everyone as the thing she had helped Sean pick out when they were in Florida together.

Oh, come on, Summer, she told herself, angrily trying to suppress the guilt, *it's just a harmless little way to annoy whichever girl will probably be going with Sean by then, because you certainly won't be.*

Harmless. As in no problem. As in no big deal.

Unless they ran into Seth.

Diana tied her Jet Ski up in a far corner of the marina. She unpacked her skirt, watch, and purse from the little compartment under the seat, wrapped the skirt around her waist, and jumped two feet straight up when someone said, "Diana!"

But then she recognized the voice, and a wave of pleasure, a very unfamiliar feeling for her, swept over her. Diver. He was standing on the deck of a sailboat a few feet away, wearing his inevitable bathing suit. He jumped down to the dock, causing it to rock sluggishly back and forth.

"Hi, Diver," she said, feeling a little shy.

"Hi, Diana," he said, looking almost as uncomfortable as she felt.

She hadn't seen him since the amazing moment they'd shared on her balcony. He had not grown less attractive. His eyes were no less deep. His lips were still . . .

"Did you come to see me?" he asked.

"To tell you the truth, no," she admitted. "I, um, I wasn't sure if I was ready for that yet. The last time—" She lowered her eyes and stared at the boards, and, incidentally, at his legs. "I wasn't sure if you wanted to see me," she said.

"I thought about it," he said solemnly.

Diana couldn't help but smile. There was something irresistibly sweet about his sincerity. "And what did you decide, Diver?"

"I decided yes."

Diana nodded, satisfied. "Hey, I guess you wouldn't want to go with me, would you?"

"I wouldn't?" He seemed confused.

"What I meant was, maybe you're busy."

"No. I'm not."

"Okay. Then how do you feel about little kids? And dolphins?"

She picked up the car she'd arranged to borrow and drove calmly past yet another TV truck that seemed to be heading out toward the Merrick estate. She sped along the highway, island hopping, feeling wonderfully free at being off Crab Claw Key, and nervous and excited, and incredulous that Diver was sitting beside her.

On the way she told him a little about the Dolphin Interactive Therapy Institute and her work there over the past year.

Diana checked in with her supervisor and introduced Diver to the mostly female staff and volunteers, who, Diana noticed, had the usual response to Diver—overly long handshakes and sappy smiles.

When the introductions were over, Diana went to get her most special charge. "Diver, this is Lanessa," she said as they walked out to the dolphin pool. It was a huge crystal-blue tank filled by the waters of the Gulf. There was a covered area, an awning that stretched out over the last few feet of the tank, but beyond it the sun beat down, and the very faint breeze did little to cool the air. "Lanessa, this is my friend Diver."

Diana had expected something like instantaneous rapport between the little girl and Diver. But the first contact was disappointing.

"Hi," Diver said.

Lanessa just looked up at him and sidled behind Diana.

Just then Jerry, Lanessa's favorite dolphin, burst from the water in a high, flying jump with a midair turn.

"He learned that himself," Diana said apologetically. "We don't train them to do any dumb Sea World tricks."

"You wouldn't have to train Jerry," Diver said.

"No, he's always—" Diana stopped. Had she told Diver the dolphin's name? She couldn't remember telling him. But obviously she must have.

Jerry swam to them under the water, surfaced, and began chattering away, bobbing his head at Lanessa as he usually did. Lanessa smiled at the dolphin, as she had for the past couple of weeks. It had taken her more than a month to learn that smile.

"Shall we go in and swim with Jerry today?" Diana asked Lanessa. Sometimes the answer was yes, and then they would stay in the water for a few minutes while Jerry waited patiently for Lanessa to pat his head. Other times, for reasons Diana could not decipher, the answer was no, and they merely watched Jerry.

Today Lanessa just shook her head.

"I don't understand why," Diana said to Diver.

Then, to the little girl, "Should we just watch Jerry play today?"

Lanessa nodded.

It had been a mistake bringing Diver, Diana realized. His presence had upset the equilibrium, had made

Lanessa withdraw again. Given her history, she had never been comfortable with any of the male staff or volunteers. Diver was male.

But then Diver leaned over to the little girl. He seemed to be whispering in her ear.

Lanessa nodded. She turned and looked straight at Diana. There was something in that look that sent chills up Diana's spine.

Lanessa pointed at Jerry and tugged weakly at Diana's hand.

"You *do* want to go in?" Diana asked.

"Yes," Lanessa said.

"Should Diver come with us, do you think?"

Lanessa exhibited one of her rare smiles. "Yes."

For an hour they played in the warm water—more real play than Lanessa had ever managed before. She even went for a brief ride on Jerry's back, with Diver holding on to her.

By the time their hour was up, half the staff of the institute was standing by the edge of the pool, watching. They had all seen breakthroughs with the children, but no one had expected to see so rapid a change in Lanessa. Either that, Diana thought, just a bit annoyed, or they were ogling Diver.

She was still a little annoyed on the drive back to Crab Claw Key. On the one hand, she'd had the feeling Diver might make some special contact with the little girl. In a lot of ways Diver was just a big child himself. On the other hand, she hadn't expected it to work as well as it had. On the way out, everyone had made a point of suggesting she bring Diver with her next time she came. It was enough to make her feel a little inferior.

"Jerry is amazing with Lanessa," she said to Diver. "It's too bad, really. He's due to be released in a couple of weeks. We don't want to keep the dolphins prisoner, so we let them go after a while."

Diver nodded. "Yeah, but he doesn't want to go yet. He wants to make sure Lanessa is okay."

Oka-a-a-a-y, Diana thought, glancing at Diver to see if he was joking. "What makes you think he wants to stay on?"

Diver shrugged. Then he smiled ruefully. "I don't want you to think I'm crazy. Summer's not totally sure I'm not crazy, and that Marquez girl, she *is* sure. That I'm crazy."

"I won't think you're crazy," Diana said.

"Well . . . Jerry told me."

Deep breath. "Jerry *told* you?"

"Yes, he wants to make sure Lanessa is okay, but then he does have to go. He has things he wants to do."

"What does he want to do?" Diana asked, curiosity getting the better of her.

Diver looked at her solemnly. "He wants to mate. You know, if he can meet the right female."

Diana giggled, then stopped herself. "Sometimes I can't always tell when you're kidding," she said.

Diver just looked at her. If he was kidding, he was keeping a very straight face.

"Just out of curiosity," Diana said, "what did you tell Lanessa that got her into the pool?"

Now Diver looked uncomfortable. He stared out of the window, seemingly absorbed by the sight of a beautiful gold and blue windsurfer scooting beneath the causeway.

"What is it, a secret?" Diana asked. "One minute she didn't want to play, the next minute she did. It would be nice to know what you told her. Did you tell her not to be afraid of Jerry? What?"

"She's not afraid of Jerry," Diver said. "She was afraid of you."

Diana stared, dumbstruck. Then she was angry. "Afraid of *me*? What do you mean? She loves me."

"She does. But sometimes you scare her. She can tell when you're angry, even deep down. I don't know what happened to her," he said grimly, "but she knows all about anger. She can feel it, like knowing when a storm is coming. She learned to sense it."

"I am not angry," Diana said angrily. "At least, I wasn't then."

Diver shrugged. "I guess she thought you were. Deep down, maybe. I don't know."

"Yeah, right," Diana snapped. "So what did you tell her? What did you whisper in her ear?"

"I told her not to be afraid, because you were hurt too, just like her."

Diana felt her stomach lurch. Tears sprang to her eyes, blurring her vision. That was the look Lanessa had given her. Pity. Shared sadness.

"Oh, God," Diana said, brushing furiously at her tears. "Don't ever . . . That's not right. I don't deserve . . ." She took a deep, steadying breath. "Diver, I've read that girl's file. Whatever I've gone through is nothing. It's nothing. Not compared to her. Besides, look, I've hit back. I've gotten revenge, and that has . . . has cured me, made me strong again."

They had arrived back on the key. Diana pulled the car to a stop in the marina parking lot.

"Lanessa can't get revenge," Diver said. "So how will she get strong again?"

"I don't know," Diana admitted. Then she put her hand on Diver's arm. She and Lanessa weren't the only ones with secrets. "Did you, Diver? Did you ever get revenge?"

"No," he said simply.

He got out of the car, but then leaned down to look in the window. "By the way, Jerry says you're the most beautiful human female he's ever seen. He thinks it doesn't matter if you disturb my *wa*. He says it's worth it."

"*Jerry* said that?"

Diver smiled. "Okay, maybe I made up that part."

12

When Fantasies and Enemies Die

Summer's day with Sean Valletti turned out not to be entirely innocent.

They drove to Key West, listening to loud music on the way. This was the most innocent part of the day, since conversation was pretty much impossible as long as Sean had the stereo cranked.

But when they reached Key West and got out to wander the streets in a search for the perfect birthday gift for Mrs. Valletti, conversation became almost unavoidable.

"What kind of things does she like?" Summer asked. She had stashed her uniform back on the Jet Ski and had borrowed a T-shirt from Sean to go over her bathing suit. It turned out to be one of his football jerseys. She was walking around with *Valletti* on her back, above the number twenty-two.

"She likes the usual kind of stuff, I guess," he answered, sounding puzzled by the question. "You know, mom stuff."

"Does she have any hobbies or anything? Does she like to cook? Does she garden? Does she read books?"

He shrugged. "How about some kind of clothing?

"Do you know what size she is?" Summer asked.

"About like this." He held his hand up beside Summer, indicating his mother's height. "Somewhere around there."

They shopped without much direction, wandering from shop to shop as Summer became increasingly desperate to get some clue as to what would make Mrs. Valletti happy. The wrong choice could make Summer a laughingstock. She could become the girl who had bought a pair of sandals for Mrs. Valletti, only to discover that she was an amputee.

It wouldn't be *that* bad, she reassured herself. Surely Sean would mention it if his mother was missing a leg.

But just as bad, from Summer's point of view, was the way Sean insisted on touching her—a little pressure in the small of her back when she went in front of him through a door, a little shoulder-to-shoulder hug, a chin chuck when she said something dumb about football. All of this while she was walking around wearing his shirt, his number and name plastered on her as if she were his private property.

They stopped for lunch at a waterfront restaurant where they ordered fried conch and grouper fingers and ate them on paper plates out in the sun. It could not have been a more conspicuous place.

"How's yours?" he asked.

"Good," she said, her mouth full of food. She was trying to keep her face lowered, avoiding eye contact with passersby while at the same time trying to check each face.

"I like you," Sean said suddenly. "You're different."

"I am?" Summer said, hating herself for the giddy little-girl tone that crept into her voice.

"Yeah. I mean, you're, like, normal and all."

Summer felt a little deflated.

"What I mean is, you're easy to hang out with," he clarified. "You know, like I don't have to be . . . whatever. There's all this pressure sometimes. Being the big football player and driving a cool car and so on. Girls always expect so much out of me."

"I guess that would be true," Summer said.

"Totally. I mean, Liz? Liz Block? She told me she was surprised when I didn't try to do her on the first date. Like she just assumed I was this animal."

Summer choked violently on a piece of fried grouper. She ran to a nearby trash can and hacked it up with a seriously disgusting noise. When she returned to the table, between the gagging and the humiliation, she could tell her face was a brilliant shade of red.

"Sorry," she said.

"No prob," he said. "You didn't get anything on my shirt, right?"

Summer checked. "No, I don't think so."

"It would be okay even if you did," Sean said generously. "I've had blood all over it, anyway. Football gets kind of violent."

Summer tried out a nonchalant smile. Nonchalant, as if she weren't replaying every second of her gagging-and-choking routine. As if she weren't replaying what Sean had said that had led to her gagging and choking. She had the definite feeling that she was out of her usual milieu, that Sean Valletti, while he might be no older than she, was moving in a completely different circle.

"See? That's what I mean by your being cool," Sean said. "You didn't get all grossed out when I was talking about blood."

"I guess we're even, then," Summer said. "You didn't get all grossed out when I blew fish out of my nose."

He stared at her, and the furious blush that had just begun to recede came back like a flood tide.

Blew fish out of my nose? Blew fish out of my nose?

Then he smiled. "Yep, I like you. I can't wait till we get back to school in the fall. It'll be like, 'What? You're going with Summer Smith?' And then you'll come in, only you'll look totally different. You know, the way you look now."

This was confusing. He liked the way she looked now. But he didn't like the way she usually looked. Not that she cared, she reminded herself, suddenly remembering with a flash of intense guilt that the only guy whose opinion she cared about was Seth.

"Do I look different than I usually do?" Well, it couldn't hurt to ask.

"Duh," he said. "Back home you're always wearing all these big, floppy things, and scarves and coats and all, and glasses."

"I don't wear glasses," she said.

"Really? Huh. I thought you wore glasses."

"No."

"Anyway, you just need to dress more like this," he said.

"I can't exactly wear a bathing suit and a football jersey to class," Summer pointed out.

Sean smiled. "It would be kind of cold. All I know is, I saw you here, and you were this totally different girl. You're all tan and you look really hot. You don't mind if I say that, do you? I mean, about looking hot. Because you do."

"Thanks. Probably deep down inside I'm still the same humble, average girl, though," she said, with the first sarcasm she had shown toward him. He did not notice.

Sean laughed. "Who cares? You and I will be the coolest-looking couple at this big party, this Bachelorama."

"The Bacchanal." Okay, so Diana was right. He was not a genius.

"Bacchanal. Party. Whatever, right?"

Summer tapped her foot against her chair distractedly. "Actually, Sean, I'm not sure about that. I—I kind of already told this other guy I'd go with him."

Sean didn't try to hide his surprise. "What guy?"

"This guy I met down here," Summer said, gazing at her plate of fish.

"Can you call it off?" Sean asked. It sounded more like an order than a question. "I mean, seriously. What's the point of a little summer fling, when you and I have something that could last?"

Summer couldn't even respond. Sean didn't strike her as the most astute guy in the world, but it was almost as if he'd read her mind.

He reached across the table and took her hand. "Please? This whole summer has changed for me since I found you—"

He pulled her around the table and onto his lap. Summer resisted, but not with any sincerity.

He kissed her.

He was not a bad kisser.

"Because I feel like a total creep. I feel like something that would get stuck on the bottom of your shoe if you walked through a gas station bathroom. I feel like a criminal. Like someone should track me down and arrest me and throw me into jail and beat me with sticks." Summer made a face that expressed total self-loathing, absolute disgust with herself.

Diana just grinned. "Arrest you? Who would that be? The Love Police?" She laughed her dry, not-quite-sincere laugh.

"It isn't funny." Summer threw herself on Diana's bed and curled up in a ball. "I have to hide somewhere. I can't let Seth find me yet. I would just blurt out everything. I can't believe I let him kiss me. I am such scum."

"Ah, self-loathing," Diana said brightly. "You've come to the right place. I know all about feeling like scum. But you chose the wrong place to hide out. I mean, there's still one TV truck camped out in the driveway."

"I thought there were six," Summer said.

Diana shrugged. "I guess the others went off after

some other story. I heard some supermodel freaked out and shot her husband. Anyway, I guess that's a bigger deal than poor little Ross Merrick, who couldn't quite . . . anyway."

The phone rang. Summer jumped.

"If that's Seth, I'm not here!"

Diana picked it up, listened, arched an eyebrow. "Diana. Who else would it be?" She listened some more. "Yeah, Summer is here. . . . Uh-huh. Yeah, she's all upset because she let that guy with the hairy chest kiss her."

Summer leaped up off the bed and menaced Diana with her fist. "If that's Seth . . ."

"Relax. It's Marquez." Into the phone she said, "Come on over, then. Just tell the TV guy you're our maid."

Marquez arrived twenty minutes later, looking disgruntled and cranky. Once again Summer wondered if Diana and Marquez had somehow switched personalities.

"The TV guy isn't there anymore," Marquez told Diana.

"No one?" Diana seemed surprised.

"He was driving off just as I came up," Marquez said, "tearing out of here so fast I thought maybe he found out about, you know, how you feed on human souls."

"Maybe he just got a look at that blouse," Diana said, sneering at Marquez's outfit.

"So," Marquez said to Summer. "Tonsil hockey with the big dumb guy from Bonzoburg."

"Bloomington," Summer corrected automatically. "And it was mostly him doing it."

Marquez winked at Diana. "Mostly," she repeated.

"I just keep thinking, what if Seth had walked by right then?" Summer said.

"Yes, that would have been bad," Marquez agreed. "Although maybe it would do him good. You know, guys get so arrogant when they think you like them. It never hurts to put them in their place a little."

"I don't *want* to put Seth in his place," Summer wailed.

"So then what's the deal?" Diana asked. "Why are you going out with Sean and *mostly* letting him kiss you?"

Summer shrugged. "You guys wouldn't understand."

Marquez clapped her hands together briskly. "Yeah, you're right. So now what should we talk about?"

Summer ignored her. "Look, Sean Valletti is *the* cool guy at our school."

"It's a sad little school, isn't it?" Marquez said.

"You don't think he's cute?" Summer demanded.

"Cute? Sure, he's cute," Marquez said. "Big deal. Cute is fine. But look, even I don't think cute is everything. I mean, if cute was all anyone cared about, we'd all three be going after Diver, since he is undeniably the cutest guy on planet earth." She paused and in a deeper voice added, "Totally cute." Then, as if snapping out of a momentary trance, "But look, as cute as he is, there was nothing there. You know."

"Just because when *you* kissed him he ran screaming for the nearest exit," Diana said.

"That's not exactly how it happened," Marquez said sharply. "Although . . . close enough," she admitted.

Diana just smiled, a smug, faraway expression that intrigued Summer.

"My point is," Marquez continued, "that just being cute or popular is not everything. And I'm shocked that you, Summer, of all people, would be affected by such superficial considerations."

Diana agreed. "Yes, I always thought of you as deep and sort of moral, you know?"

Marquez put her arm around Diana's shoulders, and the two of them slowly shook their heads at Summer. "Your mother and I are very disappointed in you, Summer," Marquez said solemnly.

"Yeah, right," Summer said. "You can't say anything, Marquez. You're the one who taught me that relationships shouldn't mess up your life. That's why you were chasing Diver, because you kept saying how nice and low-stress it would be, no heavy emotional stuff like with J.T. Plus you were the one telling me about the end of summer, how Seth would go off one way and I'd go off the other, and I'd be devastated."

"You took romantic advice from Marquez?" Diana asked, rolling her eyes.

Marquez winced. "Look, forget all that. Okay? Do you like this Sean guy?"

Summer sighed. "Actually, it was kind of a surprise. He's this major cute guy, and every girl is all hot for him. But it turns out he's kind of a jerk."

"Kind of a jerk?" Diana said.

"Kind of a jerk in the way that Bloomington is kind of cold in January," Summer clarified.

"And how do you feel about Seth?" Marquez asked.

"I'm totally in love. Like I get these warm flashes every time I think about kissing him. Like when I think about *not* seeing him, I feel sick to my stomach."

Marquez actually smiled. "Well, then, duh. Even you can figure this out."

"But summer's going to end. How can I stay with him when I know that it's going to be really painful?"

"I guess if you love someone that much, you have to accept the fact that it can end up being painful," Marquez said solemnly.

"I do *not* believe I'm hearing that come out of your mouth, Marquez," Diana said. "If that's true, then why aren't you going with J.T. anymore?"

Marquez looked mightily uncomfortable. "Oh, that. Did I mention that we're back together?"

Summer and Diana just stared at her.

"It's no big deal," Marquez said. "It's not like it's happily-ever-after time."

Suddenly there was a light tapping sound at the glass door of Diana's balcony.

Summer jumped. Marquez cursed. Diana smiled.

"Call the cops," Marquez hissed. "This is the second floor!"

But Diana opened the door. The shock when Diver stepped inside was total. At least it was for Summer and Marquez.

"I didn't want to ring the doorbell," he offered by way of explanation.

"That's okay," Diana said. "You don't have to worry about my mom."

Diver looked down at the ground. He usually seemed rather serious, but now he seemed several stages past serious. His mouth was grim, his eyes uncharacteristically evasive.

"I, um, thought I'd better come tell you, before someone else told you," he said to Diana.

"What?" she asked sharply.

"Out in the bay. The harbor patrol is out there. They're fishing out a body."

"Someone drowned?" Marquez asked.

Diver nodded. He kept his attention focused on Diana. "I was out there, and a guy I know came by in his boat. He told me who it was. I didn't want you to hear about it on TV or something. It's Ross Merrick. The harbor patrol say it was an accident. Ross is dead."

They watched from Summer's deck, the deck where Diver spent most nights sleeping. The sky was clear and the stars were out, blazing gloriously overhead.

Brighter, though, was the searchlight of the harbor patrol boat, making an artificial noon out of a few square meters of black water. Other small craft had clustered around—the curious, anxious to find out what was going on. And on one of those boats Diana watched a second bright light appear—the light of a television camera.

The body of Ross Merrick had already been dragged aboard the harbor patrol launch, but they weren't leaving yet. Everyone was hanging around in hopes of being on TV, Diana thought cynically. Or, to be grim, they were looking for some kind of evidence associated with Ross's death.

Diana, Summer, Marquez, and Diver watched as a

boat left from the dock of the Merrick estate. It sped toward the scene, slowing as it neared. Two silhouettes were visible. Diana had little doubt who they were: Adam and his father. Adam, going to identify his dead brother. The senator, going to view the remains of his eldest son.

Diana turned away, unnoticed by the others. She sat on the far edge of the deck, looking back toward her own home, so reassuringly bright in the night. Her own bedroom window, glittering through the branches of the trees.

It was odd, she thought, watching the way emotions boiled up within her, watching herself as if she were really up there on her balcony looking down at this sad little spectacle.

It was hard to sort out any one single emotion. The first, instant reaction had been pity. For Adam, mostly. She had loved Adam once. And Adam had never been all bad. Not even mostly bad. He was just loyal to his brother and, more important, loyal to his father.

She even felt a small share of pity for Ross. Nothing he had done—not even what he had tried to do—deserved death. She supposed he had been drunk, as he usually was. Probably while out in the Merrick boat, recklessly high, he'd fallen overboard.

However he had died, it was a shame. Ross had deserved to go to jail. He had needed to get some help.

He had not deserved to end up facedown in the bay with his lungs full of warm salt water.

Diana shuddered at the image. These gentle, familiar waters would never again seem so benign.

There was another emotion too. It struggled with the decent emotions of pity and concern. It was dark and evil, and yet it pushed its way to the surface of her mind repeatedly. Triumph. Not joy exactly, but a cruel, animalistic sense of triumph. Ross had been made to pay for his assault on her. He had paid. He would never again threaten her or any other woman.

Diana noticed that her leg was pressed against a small, metal box with a hinged lid. It was battered and rusty, and had been shoved under an overhang of the eaves.

She opened it, idly curious. Inside were things she recognized—the clothing that she and Summer and Marquez had bought for Diver. It brought a faint smile to her lips. The store tags were still on every item.

She lifted the clothing, and underneath saw more things, junk mostly. A key chain in the shape of a tiny buoy; a cheap disposable razor; a bar of soap; a small, tattered book of poetry; bits of string; Band-Aids; and a chewed-up ball.

"Diana?"

Summer's voice. Diana quickly dropped the lid on the box.

"Diana? Are you okay?" Summer came and sat beside her.

Diana tried to still her emotions. She didn't want to betray anything to the others. They would understand pity. They would never understand, or forgive, those darker feelings.

"Sure," Diana said. "I just didn't want to watch anymore."

"I understand," Summer said. "This wasn't your fault. You know that, right?"

"Yeah, it was probably because Ross got drunk," she said. "He drank a lot, even before all this."

"Exactly."

"I didn't want this to happen," Diana said.

"Of course you didn't," Summer agreed.

"I mean, no, *really,*" Diana insisted, as if Summer had argued. "No way did I want this to happen. I was mad, sure. I did try to get him to . . . to deal with what he'd done. I mean, I'm sorry. I even said I was sorry that his father got dragged into it and that it had to become this whole scandal, with TV and everything."

"Diana, listen to me," Summer said. "This is *not* your fault."

Why did Summer keep saying that? Diana wondered angrily. Of course it wasn't her fault. She didn't kill Ross, for heaven's sake. She had just been trying to get him to admit . . . to deal . . . to . . .

"I wanted to hurt him," Diana whispered.

Summer said nothing. Behind her, Diana could feel Marquez and Diver watching her silently.

"I wanted revenge," Diana said softly. "I wanted him to suffer. I wanted them all to suffer. That's what I wanted. I . . . I guess . . ." She couldn't talk anymore. Her throat had closed up, and her stomach felt as if it might heave at any moment.

"Got to go," she said through gritted teeth. She slithered and scraped her way down to the walkway and ran blindly toward the house.

"I have to go after her," Summer said.

"No, leave her alone," Diver said.

"But she's hurting, Diver," Summer protested. "I know what she's thinking, I know what she's feeling."

Diver smiled crookedly. "No, you don't, Summer," he said gently. "I do. Let her be alone."

13

Video Blog

Anyway, Jennifer, those are all the exciting times here on beautiful Crab Claw Key. Diana has turned back into Diana—withdrawn and snippy and antisocial. I've tried to talk to her a couple of times over the last few days, but as usual, she isn't easy to get close to. Diver just says to leave her alone. For some reason he's now the expert on Diana. The cops have dropped the whole thing because no one really sees any point in investigating. The senator says he's going to resign. I guess you saw that on TV. He looked sad.

Marquez and J.T. are back together, which means they're always either having these screaming fights or else they're making out.

The four of us, me and Seth and J.T. and Marquez, went out as a group the other night. It was kind of cool, because obviously I love Seth, and I really like hanging out with Marquez, and J.T. and I have this relationship . . . I don't know, it's kind of hard to define, really. I guess it's a little like brother and sister. He teases me and I tease him back, but we also feel kind of close. Maybe I'm starting to get adjusted to the fact that he really might be related to me. I guess now I kind of hope he is, because despite the fact that he's temperamental and can get into these really deep low points, he's mostly funny and sweet.

Maybe you'll get to meet him. You know, if. And if, and if, and if. And if! My entire life is one big if. I wish I could be sure of just one thing. Is J.T. Jonathan? Are Seth and I going to stay together? What about the fact that I can practically see the end of summer coming?

Fortunately Sean Valletti has been off on his uncle's boat. They went up to Miami for some stupid reason, and I think by the time he gets back he will have totally forgotten I even exist.

I know, that *does* sound strange, doesn't it? It used to be I thought it would be the greatest thing in the world if Sean even noticed me. Now I hope he gets over me.

But you *know* how I drive all the men wild with desire.

I really hope Seth never finds out. It was just this stupid flirtation because I used to have a crush on Sean. Really immature of me, I know.

Anyway, tomorrow is the Bacchanal, the big street party. Marquez totally *lives* for this thing. I got the night off, so I'm going. Seth, naturally, hates the whole thing. Seth isn't exactly Mr. Wild-Dance-in-the-Streets, but he says he'll meet me there, for part of the time at least.

I wish you could be there, Jen. I miss you. Things get so weird around here sometimes. It would be nice to have someone around who knows me the way I really am. For some reason I've been thinking a lot about home lately. I'm not exactly homesick, but it's as if this vacation has gotten bigger and more important than I ever thought it would be. It was supposed to just be . . . like punctuation. A period at the end of the sentence. Then on to the next sentence.

But somehow it has changed everything. What if J.T. really *is* Jonathan? My life back home won't be my old life back home anymore. And then there's Seth. Like I said, it's all ifs.

I would really like at least one thing to be for sure. It's eating at me, grinding my nerves, wearing me down. I wish J.T. would just *do* something to get an answer. Anything. And as for Seth and me . . .

When I left home to come here I was this person

who'd never had a serious boyfriend. I'd had crushes on guys—duh, Sean Valletti for one—but actually being in love is a whole new level. A crush . . . well, there's no pain in a crush. But if you really love someone, there's always the possibility of getting hurt, this feeling like you have no defenses.

I'm scared of summer ending, Jen. Every time I kiss Seth, every time he kisses me, every time I even just look at him, I get this little jab, this little voice saying, "It won't last, Summer. It's almost over." I feel as if I've gotten so much older in just the short time I've been here. My dad used to lecture me to think about consequences, right? "Actions have consequences, young lady." Well, I guess Daddy would be happy now, because all I think about is consequences. All I think about is, how many more times will I be with Seth? How many more times will he kiss me before the last time?

Somehow this is all Marquez's fault. I haven't figured out how or why, but I have to blame someone.

Or else it's the fault of that tarot card lady. She told me I would meet three guys. Why didn't she tell me I wouldn't get to keep even one?

14

The Idyllic Interlude Seems to Be Coming to an End.

Summer walked to work. It wasn't as dramatic as going by Jet Ski, but this way she arrived dry and with her uniform unwrinkled. And now that the TV truck had disappeared from Diana's driveway, there was no reason not to walk. Aside from the fact that at ten A.M. it was already blisteringly hot.

Heat waves shimmered up from the pavement. The sun aimed a laser beam right at her head, completely unobstructed by any cloud. Even for Florida in midsummer it was hot. Back in Minnesota, people baked cookies in ovens that weren't this hot.

The sight of Seth's battered, sagging pickup truck,

rattling and shimmying down the road, was welcome. He stopped and leaned out of the window.

"So. Looking for a ride, young lady?"

"No, I like to be at least medium rare by the time I get to work," Summer said. She walked around the truck and climbed in.

"Mmm," Seth said, leering outrageously. "I like a woman in uniform."

"Seth, I am really hot and sweaty," Summer said.

Just the same he leaned across and kissed her. And just the same she let him. Again. And again. And despite the heat they were soon completely lost to the normal world.

"I have to get to work," Summer gasped.

"Me too," Seth said. "I have to meet my grandfather on the job site."

"Marquez will cover for me if I'm a little late," Summer said.

"My grandfather's always late," Seth said.

They kissed again. Summer slipped her hand under his shirt, enjoying the warm, taut feel of his stomach and chest, the smooth skin, the way she could feel his heart beat. It was one of her favorite things, touching him that way. It had replaced Oreos on her list of favorite things.

A horn blared loudly and continuously.

They separated. Summer looked out of the back window. Diana in her little Jetta.

Diana pulled around to Summer's side and rolled down her window. "You do know this is a road, right?" Diana asked. "Like people might want to drive on it?"

"Sorry," Seth said. "We were stalled. Couldn't get into third gear."

Diana rolled her eyes and drove away. Seth started down the road after her.

"Third gear, huh?" Summer said.

"That's not to say I wasn't enjoying second gear an awful lot," he said.

They arrived quickly at the restaurant. Summer straightened her uniform and checked her hair in the mirror. "Now my lips are swollen."

"You look perfect," Seth said.

"I look like a girl who's been making out in an un-air-conditioned truck."

"I love you," he said. He said it at least once a day, but suddenly it made Summer angry.

"Do you?" she asked bitterly. "For how much longer?"

Seth looked at her warily. He seemed unsure whether this sudden mood change was serious or some kind of unfathomable joke. "Look, Seth, I love you, too," Summer said miserably, her anger already evaporated. "But it's like I'm living in fear. I know that sounds dramatic and all, but I can't help this feeling. It's . . . dread. That's the word. Between J.T. and you, I don't feel sure of anything anymore."

He put his arm around her, and for a moment she enjoyed his embrace, but then she pushed him away. "See? That's it, right there, the way I feel. Like I love it every time you touch me, and right behind that comes this fear, and I think no, push him away, keep him away, because the closer he gets the more it will hurt later."

"Look, Summer, somehow we're going to work everything out," Seth said.

"Really?"

"Yes. Absolutely."

"How?"

He stared at her, and then looked down at the floor.

Summer sighed. "I have to get to work," she said heavily.

"Summer, I love you," he said again, "and the end of summer vacation won't change that."

"I love you, too," she said, touching his cheek. "But I have to go."

"Look, um, this is probably not the time to mention this, but I may not make it to the Bacch." He seemed to flinch in anticipation. "My grandfather has this rush job, and we may end up working late tomorrow night."

"Oh," Summer said. She bit her lip. Then she smiled crookedly. "Kind of a preview of the end of summer, huh?"

He looked miserable. "We're still on for diving this afternoon, right?"

She wanted to say no, just to give him a taste of his own medicine. But she could not deliberately push him away. At least not yet. "Yes, of course," she said. "Gotta go."

She climbed out of the truck, went around to the back door of the restaurant, and ran smack into Marquez and J.T. They were making out, leaning against the whitewashed back wall of the restaurant.

"I can't believe you two," Summer said with mock disgust. "Making out in this heat?" She was doing her best to shake off the tears of frustration that threatened to fill her eyes.

"Oh, Summer," J.T. said, seeming flustered. A meaningful look went between him and Marquez.

"J.T. wants to ask you something," Marquez said.

He smiled ruefully. "Yeah, I kind of do," he said.

"So?" Summer said.

"Look," J.T. began, "it's this whole thing. I realized that it's just kind of eating away at me. Not knowing."

"Yeah, not knowing does kind of chew on your

nerves," Summer agreed, way too strongly. Should she tell him about her call to the hospital in Minnesota? No. They hadn't promised to send her the footprint, and even if they did, would it really prove anything?

"Anyway, what I was thinking was, maybe I should just ask my parents outright, you know?" J.T. said.

Summer nodded. She felt a wave of relief. Yes, he should just ask his parents. That was the answer. Then at least she'd have one answer. "If you feel you can do that, J.T., I think it would be a good idea.

"Now you're getting to the fun part," Marquez warned under her breath.

"I can't just blurt it out," J.T. said. "I mean, you can see that, right? It's like accusing them of . . . I don't even know. If I'm Jonathan, then they could be kidnappers or something." He shook his head in bewilderment. "It sounds insane even to say it."

"Yeah, so J.T.'s concept of a sane way to handle it is for all of us to go over to his house together," Marquez explained, "and we'll do a little barbecue—"

"I'll cook and everything," J.T. said.

"—and we'll tell them the story about Jonathan," Marquez said, watching Summer for a reaction. "And see if they totally lose it."

"Oh," Summer said. She took several deep breaths. She liked the idea of J.T. finding out. The idea that she had to be involved too . . . she liked that idea a lot less.

"Like Hamlet," J.T. offered helpfully. "You know, where he tricks his stepfather by reenacting the—"

"No," Summer interrupted. "You two are crazy."

"It could be a little intense," Marquez said.

But J.T. wasn't laughing. "Summer, I have to know. Sooner or later."

"I understand," she said.

"I tried to convince him later was a better way to go," Marquez interjected.

"And you would go along with this?" Summer asked Marquez. "You? What happened to avoiding other people's potentially horrible personal messes?"

"I'm still hoping to break a leg before then," Marquez said. "I don't even like barbecue."

"Will you do it?" J.T. asked Summer, pleading with his eyes.

"Well, you may be my brother," Summer said, trying to make a joke of it. "So I guess I have to. But even if you weren't, you'd still be my friend. I guess the answer is yes. When?"

"Tomorrow. Right before the Bacchanal gets going. A little backyard barbecue," J.T. said.

"Barbecue and intense family psychodrama," Marquez said. "Please, someone kill me before then."

Several hours later, Summer was underwater. The last time she had gone scuba diving with Seth, things hadn't worked out so well. But they had made a solemn vow since then to leave cave diving off the agenda.

They glided over the coral, careful not to break any of the fragile protrusions. The sun was still high in the sky at four in the afternoon, and it sent down rays that were like individual searchlights, each seemingly adjusted to highlight a particularly beautiful bit of coral or brighten a passing fish. Summer passed her hand through a beam, actually feeling the warmth of it though they were twenty feet down. She exhaled and watched the turmoil of bubbles roil up through the light, diamonds floating toward the surface.

It was an incredible place, as alien as anything could be while still being part of planet earth. A hundred species of fish darted by, alone or in schools, some on urgent errands, some just floating along, droopy-lipped and sad-eyed like the grouper that seemed to be watching them. Maybe he was bummed that Summer had eaten one of his relatives with Sean.

The coral was mostly white, but with fantastic extrusions in pink and blue. It served as home to crabs and snails and eels and things whose names she didn't know. Unfortunately, it was also home to more divers than Summer could keep track of—some with tanks, some snorkeling, dropping down for as long as their air lasted, then kicking hard for the surface.

Oh, well, their last dive had been private. Far too private. She would try not to resent the fact that the reef was as crowded as a supermarket at rush hour.

Seth tapped her shoulder and pointed up. They began their slow ascent, never rising faster than the tiniest of their bubbles.

They broke the surface. It was always a sort of mystical experience for Summer as she passed through the barrier between one world and another. She pulled off her face mask.

"Hey, what are all those great big fish that look exactly like us?" she asked Seth.

"It is kind of crowded down there, isn't it?" he said.

"But totally beautiful," Summer said. "Thanks for bringing me."

They swam to their small motorboat and climbed in heavily. Summer lay sideways on the bottom of the boat, exhausted. Seth slithered in beside her. They both laughed.

"I'm much, much heavier up here in the air," Summer said. She shrugged out of her tank, grateful for the freedom of movement. "I have regulator lips," she said, laughing some more. Her lips often felt a little numb and rubbery after being wrapped for an hour around the regulator mouthpiece.

"I can fix that," Seth said. He kissed her. His lips were as cold as hers.

After a while they separated and lay side by side, Seth's chest cushioning Summer's head. The sun had slipped toward the horizon, but although it was low enough not to be in their eyes, the sky was still a bright blue, with only a solitary cotton puff of cloud.

"Now I'm hot again," Summer said.

"You're always hot," Seth said.

"Oh, don't you sound like—" She stopped herself just in time. She had been about to say Sean Valletti.

"Sound like who?" he asked.

"Um, like this guy on TV whose name I can't remember," she temporized. Another opportunity to tell Seth about Sean. Another chance to confess her relatively minor sin. But she said nothing. And Seth—trusting Seth—let it go.

"This is nice, huh?" he said. He stroked her hair, which was already drying in the blow-dryer-hot breeze.

"This is perfect," she agreed. And it was—the boat rocking gently on the water, the cries of gulls, the sight of a pelican, that prehistoric relic, swooping majestically overhead. "The sky is never this blue back home."

"No. I guess it has to do with how far south you are. It's a paler blue up there."

"And cold," she said.

"Definitely colder," he said.

"I don't want this to end," Summer said. "This

summer, I mean. Marquez, Diana, Diver, J.T . . . you. It's like the sky. Like everything in my old life will be paler and colder than here. There's no one like Marquez in Bloomington."

"There's no one like Marquez anywhere," Seth said, chuckling.

Summer was annoyed. Obviously she was trying to bring up the subject of her and Seth, not Marquez. "I just don't want it to end," she repeated.

He shrugged. "Everything ends eventually. I guess that's what makes summer so intense, this feeling that it lasts for only a short while and then it's back to reality."

"So you're saying things that are cool for summer vacation wouldn't be so good the rest of the time?"

"Maybe so," he said.

Summer sat up abruptly, breaking the physical contact.

"What's the matter?" Seth asked.

"Nothing," Summer said sullenly. "We should get back."

Seth looked mystified, but he started the outboard engine and aimed the boat back toward Crab Claw Key. It was a thirty-minute trip, and the first half of it passed in silence.

"Hey, is this about the end of summer again?" Seth asked, sounding as if it were a crazy question.

"I'll take 'Doctor Duh' for two hundred dollars, please," Summer said sarcastically.

"I thought we already talked about it this morning," Seth pointed out.

"Yes, but we didn't decide anything."

"Summer, what can we decide? You know how I feel about you. What can I say?"

Summer glared at him. "So you don't even think about it? You don't even care that when summer does end, you go one way, and I go another way, and that's it?"

"What do you mean, that's it?" Seth was beginning to look troubled.

It was a small victory, but Summer was relieved to see that he wasn't totally obtuse. Could it really be that he was just now getting it?

"I mean, I'm in Bloomington, you're in Eau Claire. Me in one place, you in another place. As opposed to now, when we're together in the same place."

"Well, jeez, it's not even a hundred miles, and it's highway the whole way," Seth said.

"Oh, right. So in January when it's two degrees and the snow is falling, you'll be driving over from Eau Claire a hundred miles to take me to the homecoming dance?" Her sudden outburst of sarcasm shocked them both.

"I . . . I, uh, don't have a car," Seth admitted. "Yet."

"You don't have a car? Neither do I. Then how—"

They stared at each other until Seth looked away to steer the boat toward Crab Claw Key.

Summer felt deflated. Somehow, despite her worrying, she'd believed that Seth would have some ready answer to give her. Some reassurance, if only she continued to press him. But he had nothing. He was just denying the problem existed.

"Look, all we can do is try to work it out," Seth said, kicking at a life jacket that was in his way.

Summer turned away and looked at the island. She could just make out the silhouette of the stilt house, dark against the bright water and the pastel waterfront homes. Her home—for now.

Somehow it will work out, she told herself. She couldn't see how, but it would. It was not possible to believe that fate had brought her here to find Jonathan, only to make her lose her love. Somehow it would all work out.

15

Little Boys, Big Boys, and Brothers

Much later that night, late enough that it was really the next day, Summer found herself in a different boat, alone, it seemed. Sails billowed overhead, red from the setting sun. The sun was already low, bisected by the horizon, and Summer willed the boat onward, chasing the sun as it set in the south.

The sun doesn't set in the south, she told herself. It's a dream. Oh.

Pale blue storm clouds chased her, scudding across the water with frightening speed, as in a time-lapse film, racing clouds like horses galloping down from the north.

A new boat was there, pushed along by the clouds,

skimming toward her. Standing in the bow was a small boy dressed all in white.

The little boy's boat was fast. And then he was with her, on her boat, or she was on his, and he was standing, his bare feet—had his feet always been bare?—not quite touching the deck, as if he were floating there.

"Where's the ball? The red ball?" Summer asked.

"I still have it," he said.

"Are you a ghost? You must be dead if you're a ghost."

He smiled. "I'm a memory."

"But I don't remember you," Summer said. "You were already gone when I was born."

Then they were no longer on the boat. They were in the living room of Summer's home in Bloomington, and her mother, her belly hugely swollen, was lying back on the couch (the awful old couch they'd had back then) while the little boy sat beside her and solemnly placed his hands on her stomach, feeling the movements of the baby inside.

A chill went through Summer. This was the closest she and Jonathan had ever come to each other.

"Are you dead, Jonathan?" Summer asked. Now he was standing in the grassy field, preparing to throw the red ball.

He threw it. It landed, bounced sluggishly, and rolled to the fence. The unseen man waited there.

"Jonathan?" Summer said. "Are you Jonathan?"

And then they were back on the boat, racing toward a dwindling sun, the clouds over them turning the sails dark gray.

"Who are you?" Summer demanded, her voice rising to a scream. "Who are you?"

But the little boy in white floated upward, arms outstretched, till he was as high as the top of the mast. Then, with a cry of perfect joy, he plummeted, sliced into the water like an arrow, and disappeared.

In the instant before he struck the water and disappeared, Summer had seen him change. His body was no longer the body of a small child, but of a young man.

She woke crying, sobbing uncontrollably. It had been a dream full of loss and sorrow, and her sleeping mind was unprepared for the onslaught of emotion. None of her defenses had been up.

She had lost Jonathan. She had never even known him, but he had dominated so much of her life with her parents—all the times she had come upon her mother crying silently in some darkened room; all the times she had found her father staring blankly into space, eyes filled with tears of guilt and sorrow. Grief for the loss of Jonathan had always been there, hidden by her parents to the best of their ability, but there all the more for being unspoken.

Summer had grown up dreading that grief, and yet never really feeling that it would touch her. Now grief came in a new guise—Seth. And she was walking toward it, unable to stop herself, heading toward loss and sadness.

Her parents had not known they would lose Jonathan. She knew she would lose Seth. Was it inevitable? Was there some quota of sadness that had to be dealt to every person? Was that just the way love worked? Because that was the underlying problem—without love, there could be no real pain. Love contained within it the seeds of loss and bitterness and grief.

She had known that. She'd known it, and had always kept her distance, but, trapped in the cave with Seth, when it had seemed the future was not going to be much of a problem, she had forgotten. She had let herself say the words to Seth. Let herself feel the words.

And now she was trapped. She loved someone she would lose.

Summer got out of bed and dried her tears, feeling cried out for the moment. She twisted her baby-tee around the right way and went to the door. She opened it silently, anxious to see a world outside of her dreams.

The sky was already gray in the east, and the stars had already retreated toward the west. She stepped out onto the deck. It was no more than eighty degrees, practically cold, with humidity like steam.

"Hi," Diver said.

Summer was not surprised by his voice. He was above her on his deck, sitting in a lotus position, facing the east. She had long since accepted the strangeness of his sleeping out here, alone, uncovered.

"I hope I didn't wake Frank up," Summer said, nodding toward the pelican, who sat perched with his ridiculous beak tucked down low.

"No. He woke up earlier," Diver said. "We heard you crying. In your sleep."

"Oh. Sorry. I guess I was having bad dreams."

"Come on," he said. He gave her a hand up the ladder. She sat beside him. The horizon was showing just the first trace of pink.

"You know this *wa* thing you talk about?" Summer said. "This inner peace?"

"Yes."

"Mine is shot totally. Blown up. Destroyed. I have no inner peace," Summer said. "I have no balance."

Diver nodded. "Me neither."

"You too?" Summer asked, surprised.

"Yes. For the same reason." He watched the horizon glumly.

"Love?"

"Yes."

"Diana?"

He sighed. "Yes."

"So how is she? Diana?"

He shrugged. "I hope she'll be okay," he said uncertainly.

"She feels bad, doesn't she? Like she was to blame for Ross?"

"It's complicated," he said cryptically.

"Everything is," Summer agreed. She smiled sadly. "It's a bad idea, this whole love thing. Totally disturbs your *wa*."

"Yep."

The sun appeared, a fiery yellow eye peeking over the rim of the earth. "I usually love sunrise," Summer said. Maybe it was just the lingering sadness of the dream, but the rising sun seemed more ominous than welcome. "The start of a new day and all."

Diver nodded. He seemed to be in tune with her mood. "Not every new day is good."

"I have to do this thing today," Summer said, thinking of her promise to go to J.T.'s. "It's something I want and don't want at the same time. Like hope and fear all in one."

Diver nodded. "Well, I guess every day is like that. Hope and fear."

Summer smiled. He was only pretending to pay attention. His thoughts were somewhere else entirely.

With Diana, Summer supposed. At one time she would have been almost jealous. Now she was actually pleased.

"Every day may be like that," she said, "but somehow I think this one is going to be a little more intense than usual."

Across the bay, on the balcony of his downtown apartment, J.T. sat watching the same sunrise, having spent a nearly sleepless night. He had fallen asleep for an hour, perhaps a little longer, but then had been awakened by odd, disturbing dreams.

"Jeez, no wonder," he muttered, taking a swig from a stale beer. He never remembered his dreams, but it was not surprising that he would have them, not with the day he was anticipating. It wouldn't have been surprising if he'd had screaming nightmares.

He tilted the bottle up and drained it. He made a face and shook his head. "Yuck."

He went back inside, grimly sure that he would never get back to sleep. If he got back into bed, it would just mean more of the same—playing scenes over and over in his head. Scenes he'd already played a million times.

He remembered the day he'd cut himself at work and had been taken to the emergency room. He'd been bleeding pretty dramatically, and the doctor had thought he might need a transfusion. He was blood-typed. A passably rare type. Fortunately his parents had been in the waiting room by then. The doctor had pulled their medical records, which were on file.

J.T. remembered the look on the doctor's face. "Oh, you're adopted," he'd said. Why had he said that? Because the blood types didn't make any sense otherwise.

Only, J.T. had never been told he was adopted.

He had tried to get a birth certificate. He had tried to find an adoption certificate. Neither existed.

J.T. got a new beer from his little refrigerator. And then Marquez had told him Summer's story. About the brother who had disappeared sixteen years ago, just when Summer herself was being born. Jonathan, who would be the same age as J.T.

Blue-eyed, blond-haired Summer. Blue-eyed, blond-haired J.T. And, Marquez had said, she'd noticed times when J.T. and Summer seemed to feel the same thing at the same time, to say the same thing at precisely the same moment.

Probably just a coincidence.

Or else some strange fate.

He should try to sleep. He really should. In just a few hours, too few hours, he would try to learn the truth once and forever.

Who was he? Who were his parents?

No, sleep wasn't likely.

࿐

J.T.'s parents' home was over on the "new side" of the key, just a few blocks from the gate of the Merrick estate, on one of the canal-front blocks of nearly identical pastel tract homes. It was the sort of place where backyard barbecues were to be found almost any evening.

Summer arrived with Marquez in tow. And "in tow" was the right phrase. At the last minute, Marquez had tried to weasel out of it, coming up with a series of increasingly desperate excuses, including a sudden conversion to Judaism or Islam or any other religion that would forbid her to eat barbecued ribs.

"You're going," Summer had said firmly. "You promised J.T. Besides, you've been to his folks' house before, so you know the way. It'll be fun."

"I could draw you a map," Marquez offered.

But in the end, they had shown up in Marquez's parents' big old sedan.

The first introduction to J.T.'s mother was a shock. Summer took one look at her and wondered how J.T. could have failed to suspect long ago that this woman was not his natural mother. She was short, with dark salt-and-pepper hair drawn back in a bun. She was cheerful and greeted Marquez with a big hug. Summer shook her hand.

"Call me Janet, okay?"

She didn't look like some horrible kidnapper, Summer thought. If she was the sort of person who would steal someone else's child, she hid it well under a disguise of middle-aged normalcy.

J.T. was in the backyard with his father, already tending a pile of glowing coals. J.T. waved as the two girls arrived. He managed a smile, but it was a sickly, nervous grimace.

His father was a second surprise for Summer. He looked so much like his son, they could almost be . . . well, father and son. The same tall, thin body, the same blue eyes, so much like Summer's own. Only, J.T.'s father had brown hair.

Summer tried to remember her genetics lessons from school. Was it possible for two parents with brown hair to have a child with blond hair like J.T.'s? It had something to do with dominants and recessives, but how that applied in this case, she couldn't recall.

"This is my dad," J.T. said, accenting the word *dad*.

"Everyone calls me Chess," he said.

Janet and Chess, Summer noted. Not exactly the textbook picture of deranged kidnappers. Suddenly the whole thing seemed utterly preposterous. What in the world was she doing there? Marquez was absolutely right. This was beyond nuts. This was a whole new level of bizarre.

Why had it not penetrated her mind what this

might involve? So, Janet, Chess, are you kidnappers? Did you steal my brother?

She felt an edge of panic, which was not helped much by the fact that J.T. was grinning like a skull and giggling half hysterically at anything that even sounded as if it might be a joke.

"Oh, yeah," Marquez said under her breath, "this will be fun. How did I let you two talk me into this?"

"My son the cook is handling the barbecue duties tonight," Chess said. "Can I get you girls a drink? Iced tea? Soda?"

"Soda would be fine," Summer said.

"Me too," Marquez agreed. Then, after J.T.'s father had ambled off in search of beverages, she added, "Also perhaps some Valium, you know, just to make this evening at all tolerable."

"Thanks for coming," J.T. said, sounding way too sincere. "I wasn't sure you'd make it, Marquez."

"Summer said it would be fun," Marquez said, giving J.T. a discreet kiss.

J.T. just looked grimmer still. "I don't know about fun. I'm . . . I don't know, I'm feeling like this is insane. Do you think this is just nuts?" He directed the question at Summer.

"No, J.T.," she assured him. "I mean, look, you want to know. I want to know, too."

"One way or the other," J.T. said, "I'm not letting

anything bad happen to my folks. I don't care what they did sixteen years ago. They're my folks. They'll always be my folks. There are lots of reasons—I mean, maybe it wasn't like that at all. Maybe it was someone else who took me, and they just adopted me, not knowing."

"They seem awfully nice," Summer said.

"They *are* nice," J.T. said, too fiercely. "Sorry. I'm kind of jumpy. I'm a wreck. I barely got any sleep at all."

"I understand," Summer said. J.T.'s nervousness was definitely catching. Was that a sign of some kind of brother-sister psychic link between them? If so, then Marquez must be related too, because she looked ready to crawl out of her skin.

"I'm not going to wait," J.T. said suddenly. "Everyone's here. I can't stand here cooking ribs as if nothing is going on."

Marquez muttered a woeful curse.

J.T.'s parents were heading back toward them. Chess carried two sweating glasses of soda. Janet had a plate of what looked like some kind of finger food.

"Mom. Dad," J.T. said. He looked as if he were about to go into shock.

"What?" Janet said. She peered at him in concern.

"We have to talk. All of us."

"I . . . I can't do this," Marquez said suddenly. "I . . .

look, I just remembered, I have to be at this place. This, um, place where I have to go."

She turned and almost ran from the yard.

Summer had to fight an urge to go after her. J.T. looked stricken but determined. "That's okay," he said stiffly.

"J.T., what is going on?" his father asked. "Are you and Maria having some kind of a fight?"

"Maybe we should sit," J.T. said, still rigid as a board. He marched over to the picnic table and sat. After a moment's hesitation and an exchange of worried looks, his parents went over too.

I'm going to kill Marquez, Summer decided. But the truth was, this really wasn't about Marquez. With a horrible, sinking feeling, she sat down with the others.

"Mom, Dad," J.T. began again. "I'm eighteen years old. I have a job. I have my own place." It was a prepared speech, and it sounded like one. "I'm an adult. And I think I have a right to know the truth. About me. About who I am."

Summer expected them to act shocked or puzzled or to ask him what he was talking about. Instead Janet just seemed to crumple a little. Her husband slowly lowered his face into his hands.

For a while no one spoke. Then J.T.'s father said, "Summer, I think this is sort of one of those family-only moments—"

"Summer *is* family," J.T. said.

His father raised an eyebrow and looked troubled.

"Tell them, Summer," J.T. commanded, still stiff and formal.

"I don't think—" Summer began.

"Summer is my sister," J.T. said.

"She's what?" Janet said.

"My sister. She . . ." J.T. took a deep breath. "She had a brother named Jonathan. I think . . . we both think . . . that I *am* Jonathan."

"Jonathan disappeared sixteen years ago," Summer said. "We never . . . no one ever found . . ."

Summer waited for Janet to cry out her confession. But to her surprise, J.T.'s mother just reached over and put her hand gently on Summer's arm.

"I'm terribly sorry for you," she said. "I can only imagine what your parents must have gone through all these years." She turned to J.T. "But sweetheart, you are not Summer's brother."

16

Diana Turns a Corner, but Summer Falls Off the Edge

Diana stood under the eaves of Summer's stilt house and called his name. No answer. She hadn't really expected Diver to be there. It was early yet, though darkness had fallen. From downtown the music and mayhem of the Bacchanal drifted across the water.

"Diver!" she yelled one last time. No answer. He wasn't there.

Diana couldn't wait any longer. She ran up the lawn and around the side of the main house, then tumbled into her car and started the engine.

Maybe he was downtown. At the Bacch. Or else at the marina, where he did odd jobs. But did she have time to try to find him in the crowds? No. The call from the institute had been for her, anyway, not Diver. It was her fault, all her fault, not Diver's.

Still, as the headlights pierced the darkness of the road, she wished he were with her.

She soon encountered the outer edge of the Bacchanal, parked cars lining the road on both sides, reducing it to a single lane. People were everywhere, streaming toward downtown, laughing, playing, some in fantastic homemade costumes, many already half drunk.

Diana honked the horn, but the people blocking her way took it as a joke. They raised a bottle of champagne in her direction, a toast.

Then he was there. Standing just to the side, as if he'd been waiting for her. Like a commuter, waiting for his ride to work.

Diana pulled up next to him. "I need you," she said.

Diver climbed in beside her.

"It's Lanessa," Diana said tersely. "They called from the institute. She's having some kind of breakdown. She won't stop crying. I have to go there."

"I'll go with you," Diver said.

"It's my fault," Diana said. They were deep in the revelers now, crawling along at a frustrating pace through a sprawling party. Masked faces peered into the car. Crude, good-natured invitations were shouted.

"It isn't your fault," Diver said.

"It is," Diana insisted. "I've never missed a day when I was supposed to go. I didn't go today, and Lanessa expected me. I didn't go." She chewed her thumbnail viciously and beat on the steering wheel. "This stupid party!"

"Diana—"

"Get out of my way, or I swear I'll run you down!" Diana yelled out of her window.

The crowd parted enough to let the car through. Diver fell silent. Diana sped toward the highway on-ramp.

The highway was an eerie driving experience, even though Diana was used to it. The dark, nearly empty ribbon of road leaped across vast tracts of water, touching down briefly at a bright point of land before leaping into the darkness again.

"The whole year, I never missed my day at the institute," Diana said. "Even when I was really depressed, even when I was thinking I was going to kill myself, I always made it. Lots of weeks that was the only reason I didn't swallow a bunch of pills. I knew I had to go because there were these kids, and they were so much more screwed up than I was."

"More screwed up than you," Diver echoed, nodding thoughtfully and looking out the window.

"I guess I always figured helping them would help me. I mean, it was selfish, really. That's why I never told anyone else about it. I didn't want people thinking I was trying to be some kind of plaster saint, when I knew I was just doing it for myself."

"So why didn't you go today?"

"I don't know. I've been feeling . . . ever since Ross died. I don't know."

"Lost," Diver said.

Diana stared at him. She nodded slowly.

"Like you don't know who you are anymore," Diver said. He was still gazing off into the dark night. "You used to have a meaning. Hating Ross. Hating Adam."

"Hating myself is more like it," Diana said bitterly.

"Kind of the same thing," Diver said.

Diana turned off the highway, shooting down the off-ramp at twice the speed limit. The institute was dark but for a few muted lights behind shaded windows. The cars of the overnight staff were parked in a little knot to one side, clustered under a streetlight for safety.

The housemother led Diana and Diver straight to Lanessa. "She started about five hours ago, just sobbing," she said. "All she would say was that she had been bad. Then we figured out she was distraught because you hadn't come today. I think she feels she's being punished." It was not an accusation, but Diana didn't need any help to feel terrible.

They found Lanessa in her room, curled up with her thumb in her mouth. She was convulsing with dry sobs.

Diana rushed to her and lifted the little girl's head onto her lap. "I'm sorry, Lanessa, I'm so, so sorry."

But Lanessa didn't react.

"Come on, Lanessa, I'm sorry I didn't come today. I . . . I don't know what happened. I just wasn't feeling right, I guess. Come on, honey, come on." She stroked the little girl's hair. "Did you think I didn't like you anymore? Is that it?"

Lanessa shook her head.

"Did you think I was mad at you?" No response. "That's it, isn't it? You thought I was angry at you?"

Finally Lanessa nodded.

"Sweetheart, I wasn't angry at you. Not at all. I could never be angry at you." Diana remembered the details of Lanessa's case. For Lanessa, having someone angry at her had not just been a reason to pout. Anger had been followed by terror and pain. An adult's anger had nearly killed her.

"Lanessa, I was angry, but not at you," Diana said. "I was just mad at the world, and all these different things. But not at you."

"I don't think she understands the difference," Diver said. "The people who hurt her, they were just mad at the world, too. Just like the people who hurt you, Diana."

"And you?" Diana said to him.

"Yes," he said tersely.

"So what am I supposed to do?" Diana asked him. "What's *she* supposed to do?" she continued, stroking the child's head.

"I don't know," he admitted. He looked troubled, agitated, uncertain.

"And here I thought you were all-wise," Diana said sarcastically. She could feel Lanessa pulling away from her. "Lanessa, no, it's all right, this doesn't have anything to do with you."

"Of course it does," Diver nearly shouted.

Diana was stunned. She had never seen Diver upset. It didn't even seem possible that he could shout.

"Of course it has to do with her," Diver said more quietly. "It has to do with everyone. Everyone gets hurt. Everyone has bad things happen to them, and then everyone wants to hurt those who hurt them. Till pretty soon every single person on earth is either being hurt or hurting someone else. It's insane."

"So what's your brilliant solution?" Diana demanded. "You want us all to forgive and forget? You think Lanessa should maybe just forgive her parents for what they did? That's what you want?"

"No," Diver said. "I want the people who hurt

Lanessa to burn in hell, that's what I want. And the ones who hurt you, and the ones who hurt me. That's what I want." He clenched his fist in the air, as if choking a person visible only to him. "I want them to cry. I want to see them suffer."

Diana shrank away, shielding Lanessa with her arms. But Lanessa was not afraid. She was watching Diver with bright, glittering eyes.

He took several deep breaths. "But I figured out after a while that I couldn't spend my life punishing everyone who deserved to be punished."

"So you just forgive them?" Diana said.

He shrugged. "I guess so. Not because they deserve to be forgiven. They don't. It's just that when you go around hating people and wanting to hurt them . . . You just can't do that. That isn't life. You forgive so you can live." He sat down on the bed, rested his head in his hands, and stared at some remembered scene only he could see.

After a while Diana said, "I didn't know you could talk that much, Diver."

"I don't usually," he said, a little sheepish.

"You know what I've been feeling for the last couple of days?" Diana asked him. "I've been mad because Ross died. I was angry because he escaped, in a way, before I could hurt him."

Diver nodded. "Been there."

For a while none of them said anything. Even Lanessa was quiet, her sobbing stilled. "Can we go see Jerry?" she asked at last.

"Oh, sweetheart, Jerry is asleep now," Diana said. "We should let him sleep."

"No, he's up," Diver said wearily. "He'd like to see Lanessa. As a matter of fact, he's waiting in the tank for us to go see him. He thinks maybe Lanessa would like to see him catch his Frisbee."

Diana smiled at him. "Diver, you may be very smart about certain things—smarter than I am—but you *cannot* really communicate with animals."

Diver laughed. "Of course I know I can't communicate with animals, Diana. I'm not crazy."

Naturally, when they arrived at the tank, Jerry was up. He was waiting patiently by the side, amusing himself by tossing a Frisbee up in the air, as Diana was not really very surprised to see.

J.T. was not Jonathan. That single fact occupied Summer's entire mind. J.T. was not Jonathan.

The little boy in her dreams really was dead. The brother she had never met, but whose tragedy had shadowed her entire life, was not suddenly going to turn up in a big, happily-ever-after ending.

She had left J.T. at his parents' house, the three of them crying and laughing and retelling the story of how J.T. had come to be suspicious, and the story of why J.T. was not the biological child of his parents.

Summer had been crying too, but for different reasons. She left with a gaping feeling of loneliness, no longer anything like a part of their lives, and had walked back into town. She never had gotten any bar-becue. But the Bacchanal had opened its arms to greet her, drawing her into the crowds, squeezing her in, carrying her along in the shrill high spirits.

Someone handed her a paper cup, and she drank its contents without thinking. Some kind of punch. She winced at the sweetness.

J.T. was not her brother. She was surprised by how much it disturbed her. She hadn't ever really absorbed the possibility that he might be, until suddenly he wasn't. She told herself this was good, that she hadn't wanted to believe, because if J.T. had been Jonathan, then all the laws of probability had to be rewritten, and the impossible would have been possible, and miracles would have popped up in the fabric of ordinary life.

No, that wasn't true. She *had* wanted to believe. She'd wanted to believe in miraculous happy end-ings. She'd wanted to believe in improbable things . . . that long-lost brothers would be found, that true loves would not be lost at the end of the summer.

And yet J.T. was not her brother. And Seth was not even here. He was off working with his grandfather.

Just a taste of the endless stream of excuses she could expect in the future, after they each went to their separate homes. He would be in Eau Claire. She would be in Bloomington. How many times would they make dates and then break them because something had come up? Sorry, Summer, I know I said I would come, but the weather . . . this job I have to do . . . this exam I have to study for . . . I can't borrow the car. . . .

In the back of her mind, Summer knew she was being unfair. Seth wasn't like that. If Seth said he would do something, he could be relied on.

"Yeah," she muttered darkly, "like I could rely on him to be here tonight."

The crowd carried her toward music, two live bands pounding out competing covers of everything from salsa to punk, all at terrific volume. Everyone was dancing, and, without meaning to, so was Summer, rising and falling as dictated by the crush of bodies. A feeling of dizziness crept over her.

Then she saw Marquez atop a bench, dancing with someone Summer didn't know, someone Marquez probably didn't know, either. Her brown curls were flying. Her face was beaded with sweat.

Summer pushed her way through the crowd, ignoring various calls of "Hey, baby" and "Come on, dance with me." She grabbed Marquez's shorts by the pocket and yanked.

Marquez looked down, annoyed, then, recognizing Summer, gave her a rueful smile. She climbed down.

"You mad at me?" Marquez yelled in Summer's ear.

"What, for leaving me when you swore you wouldn't?" Summer said sarcastically. "Why would I be mad?"

"Don't be," Marquez pleaded. "Come on, it's the Bacch. Party and forget it."

"He's not Jonathan," Summer said.

This got Marquez's attention. She looked concerned. "He's okay, right?"

"Do you care?"

"Jeez, Summer, look, I never said I was good at this stuff. I don't deal with people's problems very well, all right? So I'm selfish. So I'm superficial. I don't care. I had to get out of there. I couldn't just sit there and watch. Either way it was going to be bad. If he *was* Jonathan, then probably J.T. would have lost the only family he's known. If he wasn't, then you . . . your brother was . . ."

Summer nodded. "Yeah, I know," she said, her eyes filling with tears again. "I guess I had started to buy into it. I mean, what if? What if Jonathan never died? Wouldn't it be the greatest thing on earth to be able to go to my parents and say, guess what? Your son didn't die in a gutter somewhere. He wasn't killed. Here he is! He's alive! No more sadness. Happy days are here again." There was more bitterness in her own voice than she had ever heard there before. "The world basically sucks, have I ever mentioned that?"

"No, and I can't believe you're saying it. Where's Seth?"

"He is working. He's working, and I'm here, and he's not, and I think that paints a pretty clear picture of my future with Seth," Summer said.

Marquez began to look uncomfortable. "Okay, well, then let's just dance and flirt with guys and forget all this stuff," she said. "Forget it all."

Summer grabbed her friend's arm. She knew Marquez wanted her to shut up and stop being so grim, but she didn't care. She felt desperate and sad. "I was going to go back to Bloomington in triumph. I mean, when I left I was just any other girl. But I was going to go back and say to my parents, hey, I found Jonathan. And at school I'd be one of those girls who's all sure of herself and above it all because I was in love with this great guy. And now you know what? It'll be like, yeah, I went to Crab Claw Key, and all I got was a tan. After a week that will fade, and I'll be right back to being the same old Summer Smith."

"Summer! There you are!"

Summer heard the voice but took a few seconds to recognize it. Sean. She managed to turn, elbowing a nearby reveler in the stomach.

Sean was right there. The crowd surged and threw her against him. He put his arms around her.

"Hey, I'm back," he announced.

"Yeah, I see."

"Back from Miami. Man, what a dump that place is. This is so cool! These people know how to party! Let's try to get something like this started back home."

Summer almost remarked sarcastically that it might be a little different throwing a street party in a place where everyone had to wear parkas instead of bathing suits. But she didn't. "Yeah, when we get home" was all she said.

"Here!" Sean handed her another cup of punch.

"Thanks," she said, taking a sip. In spite of the strange dizziness closing in on her, she didn't stop to think about what exactly was in the punch.

He kissed her, and she let him.

She felt sick and strange and irritated. Too many things to worry about. All of it stupid and pointless. It didn't matter, any of it. Marquez had the right idea— dance and party, and whenever anything serious threatened to rear up in your face, run away.

Summer looked around for Marquez, but she had been swallowed up in the crowd. So she danced with Sean and finished her second glass of punch, and let him kiss her and kissed him back, and stopped caring about everyone and everything. It was all going to come to an end, all of it: Seth, and J.T., and Marquez, and Diver. But mostly Seth.

She felt as if someone had stabbed a knife into her stomach and twisted it. Seth. He wasn't even there with her. And already the feeling of emptiness was so intense. She should never have let it happen. She should have kept him away, at arm's length. Then she would have been safe.

Sean drew her close. She felt strangely numb. Sean was holding her tight against him. She knew she should pull away, but she couldn't seem to summon up the energy. What was the point?

Then she saw him. Seth. He was staring at her.

"Seth," she whispered. He *had* come. Her heart leaped.

For a moment her view of him was blocked, and he was gone. As he would soon be gone from her life.

Sean grabbed her and kissed her again, pulling her against him. Seth reappeared, but now it was only a momentary glimpse as he turned away.

17

Terrible Truths: Sean Valletti's a Jerk and Maria Marquez Is a Sweetheart.

As a rule, Summer did not drink. Once or twice she'd had a single beer. Which was probably why she hadn't thought much about the sickly sweet taste of the punch. Which was probably why the weird dizziness hadn't clued her in about its alcohol content. Now that she'd spilled her third glass down the front of her shirt, she should have been worried, but instead she found it terribly funny.

In fact, everything was funny. The way she was walking. The way her words weren't coming out right. The way Sean was propelling her down the street away from the Bacchanal, half dragging and half carrying her.

"Is this the right way?" he demanded.

"What?"

"Is this the right way to your house?"

"My house? Why are we going there?" Summer asked. She tried to focus, but couldn't quite.

"Why do you think?" Sean said.

Summer didn't know the answer, but she had the feeling she should. "I want to go back to the party."

"We're moving the party to your place," Sean said. "Have a real party."

"I don't know." Suddenly she was very tired. She sat down on the curb too quickly, bruising her behind in the process.

Sean took her hand and tried to pull her to her feet. But Summer offered no help, and after a few tugs Sean gave up. He sagged to the ground beside her. A passing car honked and gave a jeer.

"I think I may be kind of drunk," Summer said.

"No kidding," he said. "That punch was spiked with grain alcohol."

"I'm sleepy."

"You can't sleep here," he said. "I'll take you home. You can sleep there. Or at least you can go to bed." He laughed uproariously.

Summer leaned close. He tried to kiss her, but she fended him off. She had something important to say. If only she could remember what it was. Oh, yeah. "You know, everyone thinks you're really cool. At school and all."

He grinned. "Yeah, I know."

She whispered into his ear. "Did you know I used to have dreams about you? You and me?"

"Tell me about them," he said. He kissed her and then trailed kisses down her neck.

"Now I dream about this little boy. The little ball boy."

"Yeah? Forget that. Tell me what you dream about me."

Summer realized that he had slipped his hand up under the back of her blouse. "What?" she said, squinting against a pair of headlights.

"Dreams. Tell me about them."

"Oh, anyway, like I said . . . um . . . everyone thinks you're really cool."

"Hey, and if you're with me, everyone will think you're cool too," he said.

"Who?"

"Everyone," he said.

"What?"

He became impatient. "I said, if you're with me, everyone will think you're cool too, all right? Come on, let's get back to your place." He dragged her upward with more determination this time, and she staggered against him. "Then I'll show you *why* all the girls think I'm the best."

Summer began to giggle. She pushed him away, laughing loudly. "You're such a jerk."

"What did you call me?"

"I don't care," Summer said. "Because, like . . . I mean, it doesn't matter. One way or the other, Seth and me . . . he goes boom, over that way, and I go the other way."

"Who is Seth?"

"Boy number three," Summer said, suddenly sad in a way that momentarily sobered her a little. "See, the tarot lady said guy one, he's dangerous, right? Well, that was Adam. And the mystery guy was number two, and that's Diver. And boy number three, the right one. That was Seth."

"Did you call me a jerk?"

"She didn't tell me that he was only temporary. Did I say that right? Tem-po-ra-ry. She didn't say, oh, by the way, you'll fall in love, but then it will be over. Like Jonathan, you know. Love someone, and then they go, and all you have is . . ." She started to cry, but at the same time she was laughing. "Then all you have is Sean Valletti."

Sean retreated in horror. "Wait a minute. You're only with me because this other guy dumped you?"

"He did *not* dump me," Summer said, offended.

"You, Summer Smith, are with me, Sean Valletti, because some other guy *might* dump you? Like I'm some kind of . . . of . . ." He was so outraged he couldn't speak. "Who is this guy? Are you telling me he's better-looking than *me*? Are you trying to tell me he kisses better than *me*? Who do you think you are?"

Summer leaned against a lamppost and considered going to sleep.

"Oh, man," Sean raved. "I told my sister I was going with you. She's probably told everyone by now. Okay, look, let me just make one thing clear here. I'm dumping *you*. All right? Listen to me! I am officially dumping you, so don't even think about telling anyone that you blew me off, because that would be a total lie."

"What?" Summer said.

"That does it. You are on your own," Sean said. He turned on his heel and disappeared back in the direction of town.

Summer used the lamppost to lever herself to her feet. Where was she? Not far from downtown. Maybe she could go and sleep in the restaurant. Home was way, way too far.

Then she saw a house she recognized. Just half a block down the street. She could make it that far.

Marquez paced a circle, staring all the while at the floor of her room, the area in front of the counter. Yes, it was time to start it. It would be a totally new challenge. She would have to paint it from the center out, otherwise she'd leave footprints, and that would ruin everything.

She could see the picture in her mind, the way it would grow over time, till it met up with the walls and everything came together as one vast mural.

She heard the pounding on her window, insistent, persistent. It had been going on for a while, she knew, maybe as long as half an hour, maybe more. But she wasn't going to react. She'd removed the extra key from its hiding place.

The floor would be an aerial scene. First the Bacchanal as if you were looking at it from above, all those dancing, gyrating, partying bodies. She'd paint that first, then over that paint a framework, and it would look as if you were walking on a glass floor, looking down through it at the town. Perspective, that would be the challenge.

The pounding at the window continued, varying in rhythm, each shift distracting her just a little.

"What?" she suddenly yelled. She stomped to the door and threw it open. "What? What? What?"

J.T. smiled, as if he had not been standing there pounding till his knuckles were raw. "Oh, hi,

Marquez," he said. "Can I come in?" He stepped past her without waiting for an answer. He noted the paints lined up ready on the counter, and noted the fact that she had cleared everything off a large part of the floor.

"What do you want?" Marquez demanded.

"I just came by to see you," he said.

"Well, I'm busy."

"Doing the floor, huh? Good. It's about time. I knew you'd be painting," he said smugly.

Marquez calmed herself enough to talk reasonably. "J.T., look, I'm sorry I ran out on you and Summer. Okay? Now can you just leave?"

"Yeah, I knew you'd be painting," he said. "You always do when you get upset. Or when you're hurt. Or even when someone you love is hurting."

"Don't psychoanalyze me, J.T. You're the one with the messed-up head."

"True, true," he said equably. "Although I'm feeling a lot clearer now. How about you?"

"I'm fine. Thanks for asking. I'll see you at work tomorrow. Afterward I'll do whatever you want. Just go away now."

"I love you, Marquez," he said.

This tack unsettled her a little. "I know. You said that the other night."

"And you love me," he said.

"Okay, so everything is happy happy, joy joy," Marquez said. "I love you. Now go away."

Instead he sat on the edge of her bed. "It wasn't what any of us thought," he began. "I was right about my parents not being my parents. About not having a birth certificate around anywhere, just a baptismal paper from when I was two."

Marquez fretted impatiently. She really wanted to be painting now. And J.T. was just distracting her.

"But all the reasons I'd worked out were wrong," he said. "I'm not Jonathan. I'm not some little kid who was kidnapped."

To Marquez's surprise, he started to leave.

"Where are you going?" she asked.

"Why do you care?" he said coyly.

"Look, just tell me the stupid story. You started it, now finish it."

"I don't know, Marquez," he said dryly. "It's got all these emotional parts, people getting hurt, people with problems. Like me. Complications. You wouldn't want to have to feel any of that, would you?"

"Fine, then go," she said. "No, wait. Listen to me, J.T., you think you have me all figured out, but you're wrong. I have a right to decide stuff for myself. I have a right to stay away from people who are going to drag me down, because I don't want to be dragged down.

Go talk to Diana—she gets off on being depressed. I
don't. I'm not an emotional person. What is that, a
crime?"

J.T. just laughed. "You're not an emotional person? Marquez, you are so pathetic. You're the most
emotional person I know. You feel everything, that's
your problem. You *feel* and then you can't stand it, so
you run away. You run away and put it all up there, on
the wall. You didn't run away from my parents' house
today because you're some coldhearted, unfeeling person. A person like that wouldn't have minded a little
family tragedy. That's why I wasn't mad at you. That's
why I knew you'd be here, trying to get it all out of
your head and your heart and putting it on the walls,
where it would be safe."

"Oh, yeah?" Marquez said, unable to think up any
better comeback.

"Yeah."

"That's a bunch of crap," Marquez said without
conviction. She sat down on the bed, and J.T. moved
beside her.

"You're right," J.T. said kindly. "Just a bunch of
crap. But don't worry, I won't tell anyone that underneath it all you're a warm, sweet, generous person who
really cares about her friends."

Marquez shuddered. "You're making me sick."

J.T. kissed her hand. "You want to hear the rest?"

Marquez sighed dramatically. "Like I have a choice?"

"It was my dad's sister. She was my mother."

"Excuse me?"

"She got pregnant—no one is exactly sure who the father was, or is. Anyway, my dad's sister got pregnant. But when I was being born, there were problems. She died in childbirth." J.T. shook his head in wonder. "She died *because* of childbirth. My folks didn't want me growing up with that kind of burden. I knew my dad had a sister who died, but I never knew she was my biological mother. That's why they never had a birth certificate around—it would have shown my real mother's name. Then I would have known, and I guess I would have grown up feeling as if I had been responsible for my mother's death." He gave her a rueful smile. "You think I'm messed up now? Just imagine how messed up I might have been."

"I don't know," Marquez said. "It might have been good. If you were even more messed up, I might have gotten the floor painted before now. So . . ." Her face grew sad. "So Summer's brother really is dead."

"Or at least he isn't me," J.T. said. "She tried to hide it, but I think she was kind of upset."

"She was," Marquez agreed. "I saw her at the Bacch. She was drinking punch."

"Summer? Drinking?"

"She was bummed. So naturally I took off," Marquez said unhappily.

J.T. squeezed her hand. "She'll be okay. Know how you're not as tough as you think you are? Well, she's tougher than everyone thinks she is."

18

Only a Miracle Can Cure a Hangover.

Summer woke very suddenly.

She opened her eyes. She was in the stilt house, in her own bed. Her head hurt. Her eyes hurt. Her mouth was dry and gluey. Everything around her was buzzing. Her stomach . . .

She jumped up, cried out in pain, and raced for the bathroom. She spent several minutes on her knees in overly close contact with her toilet.

When she got up at last, she was trembling, her knees were shaky, and she was feeling rotten and filthy and disgusting. The face in the mirror made her groan.

"How did I get here?" she wondered.

She remembered the lamppost. She remembered telling Sean Valletti something . . . she couldn't recall the exact word, but he hadn't liked it, she was sure of that.

Then she remembered Seth. The way he had seen her kissing Sean. The look in his eyes.

She threw up some more. Afterward she took a shower and brushed her teeth twice, gulping water as if she'd been in the desert for a week.

"Why do people drink?" she muttered. "This isn't fun. This isn't even anything like fun. This is the worst feeling in the world." What a total idiot she was for gulping down two glasses of that disgusting pink punch without even thinking about what was in it.

Her first thought was that she had to find Seth. And then the other memories began to trickle back into her mind. A dark jerky vision of herself staggering up a walkway, banging at a door, and collapsing.

Seth's house.

"Oh, no," she moaned.

He had brought her here. She vaguely recalled being in his truck. In the back. He had dumped her in the back of his truck. Like garbage or something.

He had carried her down here.

And someone . . . *someone* had gotten her out of the clothes she'd been wearing and into the boxers and baby-tee she wore to bed.

"Please, just let me die," she said. It would be a relief from the endless explosions going off inside her head.

There was an obscenely loud banging noise at her door.

She grabbed her head and went over to open the door. Sunlight hit her with physical force that sent her reeling back, shielding her eyes and crying aloud.

"That's the same reaction I had to your outfit, Marquez," Diana said.

"It was you she saw first," Marquez said. The two of them came in and, much to Summer's relief, closed the door behind them.

"Not hung over, are you?" Marquez asked Summer.

"Shut up," Summer growled.

"I think Summer may have been drinking," Marquez said, laughing.

"No kidding. I was the one who had to change her clothes last night," Diana said.

"You? Oh, man, thank you," Summer said.

"Me and Seth and Diver and these three guys we met," Diana said. Then, seeing Summer's look of horror, she relented. "Just me, it was just me. Your chastity and purity are intact. Seth came and got me to help."

"Seth brought me here? After . . . after what happened last night?"

Diana's eyes darkened. "Yes, because Seth is a truly

decent guy. You stab him through the heart, and he picks you up off the floor."

"He's upset?"

"No, why would he be?" Diana said sarcastically. "Just because he sees you swallowing half of that guy's face?"

Summer felt the urge to throw up again. She struggled to get it under control. "I was upset," she said.

"Did you trade Seth for that muscle-boy dweeb from Birdbrainburg?" Marquez said, making a disgusted face. "I guess you decided you really liked the hairy chest, huh?"

"You don't understand," Summer said. "I love Seth."

"Oh, *now* I understand," Marquez said. "That clears it up for me."

"You're the one who told me, Marquez—the end of summer. What about the end of summer? What am I supposed to do, just get closer and closer to Seth? Fall more and more in love, and then *wham* . . . Ohhh." She grabbed her head in pain. "Look, I don't live here. This isn't my real life. You two aren't even real. Reality is Bloomington. That's where I live. That's my life. And I don't want to be there and go to bed every night crying because . . ." A sob escaped from her, but she was too dehydrated for tears. She took several deep breaths.

"Summer, all that stuff I said about the end of August—why would you listen to me? You know I'm full of it," Marquez said.

"No, you're not," Summer said. "You were right. I'm sorry if I hurt Seth—"

"Just ripped his heart out, that's all," Diana said in a low voice.

"But it was never going to be for real. It was just a summer thing. And I'm not a person who can be in love for three months and then forget it and move on."

"Summer," Marquez protested, "you don't know for sure what's going to happen when the summer ends."

"I know you guys are trying to be nice," Summer said, "but I have to throw up."

"Okay. We'll, uh, get together later," Marquez said, sounding relieved to have an excuse to leave.

When she was done in the bathroom, Summer drank a lot more water. And thanks to the water, when she began to cry, she was able to shed tears.

She slept most of the day, her hangover gradually easing into a more general depression. She got up only once, to eat a dry sandwich, call in sick at work, and stare blankly at Letterman for a while, surprised that he was on so early, and then slowly realizing that it was almost midnight.

She turned off the TV and lay there in the dark, listening to the sound of the water lapping against the pilings, barely noticing the creaking boards and soft shushing of waves against the shore.

This was as bad as she had ever felt. She still felt sick. Worse by far, she felt heartsick. The thought of Seth hurting, in pain, feeling betrayed and abandoned by her . . . She couldn't stand the images that came into her mind, and yet she couldn't keep them from coming.

It doesn't matter, she told herself. *Now or later, it would have happened just the same. And later it would have hurt even more. Better that Seth just thinks I'm a worthless slut who would go with Sean Valletti. Better to make it quick and final, right now, than to let it drag out, let the dread build up day by day between now and three weeks from now.*

She'd been stupid to let it get started. She had wanted to fall in love this summer, thinking that love was just another form of entertaining fun, like scuba diving or sunbathing. Another cool thing to do at the beach. But it wasn't. It was dangerous. Without love you couldn't have pain. Without love you couldn't have loss. Grief. Emptiness. Love made it all possible.

If she had never loved Seth, she would be happy right now. Love. It was just like alcohol. A little fun followed by a long, painful hangover.

"Love is like alcohol," she said, liking the sound of it, as sleep crept over her again. It sounded very deep. It sounded wise. She would get it printed on a T-shirt. No one would understand what it meant.

She dreamed. She was on the plane again, just arriving on Crab Claw Key. The tarot lady was beside her, just the way it had really happened. Only now the lady had turned over a card with a picture of a cup full of punch.

"That's the love card, isn't it?" Summer asked the lady.

"Huh?" the lady said.

"You told me there would be three guys," Summer said. And then she was no longer on the plane, but back in the underwater cave, trapped in the dark with Seth. Seth was sleeping, and then the little boy appeared, dressed all in white. He was holding the red rubber ball.

"You again," Summer said.

"Still here," the little boy said.

"No. You're not," Summer said, feeling a terrible sadness. "You died. You're gone."

The little boy looked at her, his eyes uncertain.

"I'm sorry," Summer said. "You're just a dream."

"Oh, *that*," the boy said dismissively. "Everything is just a dream. So what?"

She closed her eyes, wishing him away, but when

she opened them again, they were standing in the grassy field.

"Jonathan, just leave me alone, okay?" Summer pleaded. "I don't like it here."

"I can't. I keep dreaming you," he said.

"No, I'm dreaming *you*," Summer insisted.

"I don't think so. You're sunny. You keep showing up here."

"I'm not sunny, I'm alcohol. No, no, I mean, I'm Summer," she said.

"Don't say that," the little boy said, suddenly frightened. "You're disturbing my *wa.*"

There were bright blue numbers. A five. A three. A two. Her clock.

She rubbed her eyes. It was 5:32. In the morning, she was pretty sure. Yes, it had to be morning. As for which day, who knew?

But she was awake. Awake and no longer sick. Groggy but alive. She would go watch the sunrise with Jonathan. No, with Diver. Go watch the sun come up with . . .

Every hair on Summer's neck stood on end. She stopped breathing. Her skin was tingling, electric. Oh, my God.

In a flash she was outside, out in the clinging predawn damp.

She looked up at him.

He was staring down at her with wide, awestruck eyes.

In his hand he held something. Without a word, he handed it to her.

Summer cradled it in her two hands. It looked as if it had been chewed by a dog. The rubber was dried and crumbly with age. In the faint, gray light it was impossible to tell its color, and yet Summer knew it had once been red.

"It's the only thing I've kept all these years," he said.

"I . . . I dreamed," Summer said.

"Yes," he said. "Sunny. I didn't know who you were. There are so many things I don't remember. Memories lost except in my dreams . . ."

"Yes. Me too," Summer said, her voice choked.

He bent over and helped draw her up onto the deck.

"Jonathan?" she asked in a whisper.

Diver smiled. "I guess so. I'd forgotten. They gave me another name, but I knew all the time it wasn't right."

"Jonathan," Summer said, definite now. "You're not dead."

"No," Diver agreed. He looked puzzled. "And what was that about you being alcohol? You said it in your sleep."

Summer laughed. She took his hand and held it tight. "That was some dumb idea I had. Back before I realized that there really can be miracles."

"Here she comes," Diver said as the fiery rim of the sun appeared on the horizon.

Summer watched with him for a while as the sun rose and the stars disappeared and the water turned from black to blue.

"I guess it's a good thing we never went out or anything, huh?" she said.

"Speaking of a very disturbed *wa*," he agreed. Then his expression grew troubled. "This means Diana's my cousin."

Summer shook her head. "Diana's mom is my dad's . . . *our* dad's sister." Every nerve in her body seemed to tingle at that thought. "But she was adopted. There's no actual blood relationship."

"Good thing," Diver said, smiling with relief. "That would have been sad."

Summer smiled. She laughed. "No way. Miracles are never sad."

19

Huh Huh, Huh Huh . . . Love Sucks

It was late morning when Summer at last parted from Diver. He would probably always be Diver to her, she decided.

A Federal Express package had arrived from the hospital in Minnesota. In it were the impossibly tiny footprints of Jonathan Alan Smith, born eighteen years earlier. But it no longer mattered to Summer. She knew the truth now. It was a true miracle, or else fate, or perhaps just a coincidence. That didn't matter either.

Four years earlier, at the age of fourteen, he had run away from the people who had taken him from his home, left behind the name they had given him, tried to leave behind the pain that had been inflicted on him. He had

followed the coast, always heading south, begging, steal-
ing, doing odd jobs, learning his way around boats and the
water so well that he'd earned the nickname Diver.

From New Brunswick, Canada, where he had
started, down to Weymouth, Maine, to Cape Cod, to
Ocean City, finally to Crab Claw Key. As if he'd been
drawn there, making a four-year trip to a rendezvous.

Or else, Summer thought, it was all just coincidence.

She borrowed Diana's car and drove to Seth's house.
She was bursting with excitement. Later she would tell
Diana and Marquez, and, soon, her parents. But first
she had to go to Seth. She had to tell him: Miracles *do*
happen. Maybe she was allowed more than one.

She knocked at the door and experienced a momentary flashback to the night before. No, it was the night
before that. She'd staggered here to this door, and Seth
had brought her inside, where she had . . .

. . . had thrown up on the kitchen floor.

"Oh, man, I could have lived without remembering *that*," she muttered. She knocked again, steeling
herself for his accusing, angry look.

The door opened.

"Oh, hi," she said, taken aback. It was Seth's grandfather. "I, um, I don't know if you remember me," she
said. "I'm Summer. I'm a good friend of Seth's."

He looked her up and down, a disparaging look.
"Some good friend you are."

"Is Seth home?"

"Not yet," Mr. Warner said. "He'll be home in about ten hours. Home in Eau Claire. Poor kid."

"What do you mean, Eau Claire?"

Mr. Warner shrugged. "He left. All of a sudden. He wouldn't even tell me why, but I haven't lived sixty years not to know that there was a female behind it."

Summer was staggered. No, this wasn't what was supposed to happen now. It couldn't be. She couldn't find Jonathan and then lose Seth. Not now. Not now.

"He can't have gone," Summer said in a whisper.

Mr. Warner looked at his watch. "Eleven-oh-five flight. He's gone, all right. And who's gonna help me with my business the rest of the season? That's what I want to know."

Summer looked at her watch. "It's only ten fifty-nine. Your watch is fast." She calculated quickly. Six minutes. No way. She'd get killed trying to make it to the airport in six minutes.

"Bye!" she yelled.

She raced for the car.

It was four minutes after eleven by the time she slammed to a screeching, rubber-burning halt in front of the tiny airport. She leaped out, leaving the door wide open. She had just reached the glass doors of the terminal when she heard the crash.

She spun and saw Diana's Jetta, half turned. The door

was off, lying in the road in front of a taxicab whose driver was shouting at the top of his lungs.

Summer ran inside. The gates, which way? Left! She ran.

The sign—Miami. That had to be it, there was always a plane change in Miami.

"I have to get on that plane!" she yelled to the frightened desk clerk.

"It's leaving," the desk clerk said.

"It can't," Summer cried. "I have to get on. It's a matter of . . . of . . . of true love!"

"You're kidding."

"No, please!"

"Well, you can buy a ticket if you're quick. How would you like to pay?"

Summer froze. "Excuse me?"

"The ticket. How would you like to pay? Cash? Credit card?"

"Credit card! My dad gave me a Visa card for emergencies. Good old Dad." She fumbled in her purse and produced the card. Good old Dad was going to kill her. Maybe she could just explain to him that it was a case of true love. Or maybe Diana would kill her first for having wrecked her car.

The metal detector! No, she couldn't just blow it off, they'd shoot her or something.

With excruciating slowness she was forced to walk

through the metal detector. Her purse took an eternity to pass through the X-ray machine.

She looked at her watch. Too late! No, no, it was too late. Still she ran. Out the door. Across the burning tarmac. They were beginning to roll back the steps.

"Wait!" She ran up the steps. The mechanics rolled it back into place and she hurtled through the door and stumbled against the flight attendant.

"Welcome aboard," the flight attendant said.

She caught a glimpse of Seth. The seat next to him was empty.

"Hi," she said, panting and gasping and grinning.

His look of amazement was almost worth the cost of the ticket. She hoped her father would agree.

"What are you doing here?" he demanded angrily. His eyes were red and swollen.

"What am *I* doing here? What are *you* doing here?"

"Going home," he said sullenly.

"Don't, okay?" she pleaded. "Don't go home. Not yet. It's still summer. It's not the end of August yet."

"That doesn't matter," he said grimly. "It's too late. You told me yourself. What's the point? It'll only come to an end, and then we'll both feel worse for having dragged it out."

"When did I say that?"

"The other night. Right before you blew chunks all over my kitchen floor."

Summer sighed. "Look, I know all that. I mean, it's still true. You can't have real pain without real love. You can't feel grief and loss and hurt without love. Love is the only way you can ever be really hurt, deep down. It's all still true."

"So?" he asked.

"So . . . it's also true that you can't ever really be happy without love, and you can't ever feel like . . . like I feel when I'm with you. I like that feeling." She took his hand and held it between both of hers. He did not pull it away. "It's basically just a messed-up situation."

He nodded reluctantly. "Yeah. Love sucks."

"It kind of does," Summer agreed.

"Pretty cool, though, too," he said in a low voice.

"I love you, Seth," she said.

"I love you," he said.

"Can we go now?"

"Um, Summer? We're in the air already," he said.

"Oh. Will you . . . will you kiss me when we get to Miami?" Summer asked.

"No," he said. "I'll kiss you right now."

He did. And she did. And when she opened her eyes she saw a woman sitting across the aisle. A very familiar woman.

The tarot lady winked at her and shuffled her deck of cards.

"Oh, no, you don't," Summer said. "Don't even think about it."

About the Author

After Katherine Applegate graduated from college, she spent time waiting tables, typing (badly), watering plants, wandering randomly from one place to the next with her boyfriend, and just generally wasting her time. When she grew sufficiently tired of performing brain-dead minimum-wage work, she decided it was time to become a famous writer. Anyway, a writer. Writing proved to be an ideal career choice, as it involved neither physical exertion nor uncomfortable clothing, and required no social skills.

Ms. Applegate has written more than one hundred books under her own name and a variety of pseudonyms. She has no children, is active in no organizations, and has never been invited to address a joint session of Congress. She does, however, have an evil, foot-biting cat named Dick, and she still enjoys wandering randomly from one place to the next with her boyfriend.

Love is in the air....

 the romantic comedies

♥ How NOT to Spend Your Senior Year ♥

Royally Jacked ♥ Ripped at the Seams ♥ Spin Control

♥ Cupidity ♥ South Beach Sizzle ♥ She's Got the Beat ♥

30 Guys in 30 Days ♥ Animal Attraction ♥ A Novel Idea

♥ Scary Beautiful ♥ Getting to Third Date ♥ Dancing Queen ♥

Major Crush ♥ Do-Over ♥ Love Undercover ♥ Prom Crashers

♥ Gettin' Lucky ♥ The Boys Next Door ♥ In the Stars ♥

Crush du Jour ♥ The Secret Life of a Teenage Siren

♥ Love, Hollywood Style ♥ Something Borrowed ♥

Party Games ♥ Puppy Love

From Simon Pulse
Published by Simon & Schuster